A
Natural
Woman

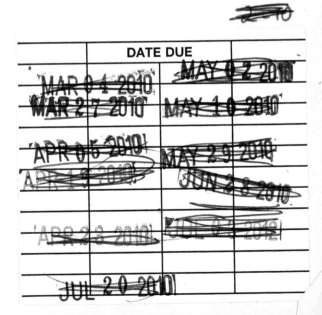

Also by Lori Johnson

After the Dance

Published by Dafina Books

01 - S

A
Natural
Woman

LORI JOHNSON

Dafina
BOOKS

KENSINGTON PUBLISHING CORP.
www.kensingtonbooks.com

2-10
15-

DAFINA BOOKS are published by

Kensington Publishing Corp.
119 West 40th Street
New York, NY 10018

All Kensington titles, imprints, and distributed lines are available at special quantity discounts for bulk purchases for sales promotion, premiums, fund-raising, educational, or institutional use.

Special book excerpts or customized printings can also be created to fit specific needs. For details, write or phone the office of the Kensington Special Sales Manager: Kensington Publishing Corp., 119 West 40th Street, New York, NY 10018. Attn. Special Sales Department. Phone: 1-800-221-2647.

Dafina and the Dafina logo Reg. U.S. Pat. & TM Off.

ISBN-13: 978-0-7582-2239-8
ISBN-10: 0-7582-2239-4

First Kensington Trade Paperback Printing: November 2009

10 9 8 7 6 5 4 3 2 1

Printed in the United States of America

For my nieces, Paula, Alexis, Roneisha, and Sherry,
all smart and extraordinarily beautiful children of God.
Always know and recognize your worth in the world.

By night on my bed I sought him whom my soul loveth:
I sought him, but I found him not.

The Song of Solomon
Chapter 3, Verse 1
The Holy Bible (King James Version)

Dear Reader,

I have no doubt that the more astute among you will recognize that many of the same elements that mark my debut novel, *After the Dance*, are very much evident in my second release. I'm sure, within the quick flip of a page or two of *A Natural Woman*, you will agree that my love of music; my embrace of African American folkways, symbols, and speech patterns; and my playful manipulation of both words and stereotypes are all readily apparent.

However, upon a more in-depth reading of *A Natural Woman* there may be those who will wonder why I stepped away from the type of humor that shapes and molds so much of my debut novel, *After the Dance*. My response may surprise you. But first, allow me to point out, for the benefit of those who might not know, I have long viewed the world through the eyes of a social critic. In a sense, humor is my mask and, whether tongue in cheek or all up in your face, typically, beneath it lurks a subtle, underlying message.

While the humor in *A Natural Woman* is admittedly a bit edgier than the humor in *After the Dance*, I want you to understand that truly the story is meant as an affirmation. Yes, an affirmation, not only of women, like myself, whose frequent adherence to a more natural hairstyle is often questioned, ridiculed, and frowned upon, but also for young women and girls like my niece Alexis, whose unexpected kitchen table confession, when she was barely a teen, *"You know the kids at school call me names.*

They're always laughing and making jokes about my dark skin," left me both enraged and brokenhearted.

The old adage *sometimes you have to laugh to keep from crying* is one I hope you'll keep in mind as you read *A Natural Woman.* And as far as the question of why I stepped away from the type of humor that marks *After the Dance,* well, I don't think I did. Not really. I simply adjusted my mask a bit before I stepped deeper into it.

Sincerely,

Lori Johnson

ACKNOWLEDGMENTS

A special thanks:

To all of my friends and colleagues whose paths, passions, and peculiarities led them to set up stakes in the ivory tower, Dr. Y. D. Newsome in particular, who so graciously responded to all of my inquiries, even the silly ones;

To my teacher and mentor, the late Dr. Juanita Williamson, of LeMoyne-Owen College, who apparently saw in me something worthy of nurturing;

To my grandmothers, Zenna Mae and Ethel V., and my great-aunts from "Johnson Sub" (Agnes, Mamie, Pearl, Viney, and Virginia, aka "Pig"), all of whom have long passed but whose spirits still guide me and whose smiles remain a constant in my life;

To my "church folks" and Sunday school classmates at East View United Church of Christ (Shaker Heights, Ohio) and at Parkway Gardens Presbyterian United (Memphis, Tennessee) who have been (and continue to be) instrumental in broadening my view of the "Peace of Christ" and deepening my experience of it;

To my editor, Selena James, and my agent, Janell Walden Agyeman, both of whom have shown themselves willing to take a chance on a new voice with a different style;

And, finally, to Al and Aaron, who fully embrace the "Natural Woman" in me.

PART I

CHAPTER 1

Aliesha sucked in a deep breath and pushed open the door. A bell tinkled over her head and seven pairs of male eyes swiveled in her direction. As if on cue, the rhythmic licks and beats of a guitar and a pair of sticks on a set of drums suddenly filled the air. Not more than a second or two later, Johnnie Taylor screamed and launched into the first verse of "Who's Makin' Love?" Aliesha exhaled, smiled, and strutted forward. Beneath the surface of her brave mask lurked the hope that she hadn't just made an incredibly egregious misstep. Today, rather than drive past Wally's Cool Cuts like she had for close to six months now, she'd decided to stop.

A white, nondescript concrete building housed the Jackson Avenue–based barbershop and two other tenants. Wedged between a beauty supply store on the left and a pawnshop on the right, indeed, Wally's Cool Cuts didn't appear to be particularly special from the outside. Yet for some reason Aliesha's gaze had routinely gravitated toward the business on her daily treks to and from work.

Once inside the shop, Aliesha quickly noted that the length, narrowness, and layout of the interior was not unlike that of a shotgun house. On one side, awaiting their turns on cushioned benches, sat less than a handful of customers. Positioned across from them were four separate barber stations, two of them empty and two of them occupied.

Most of the piercing, fixed stares that had accompanied her entry had fallen away. On having completed their assessment, most had found her unworthy of a linger, much less a leer. Most, but not all.

The barber closest to the door, a tall, light-skinned man who sported a thick but neatly trimmed mustache and goatee, shut off his clippers and nodded a greeting.

"Hi," she said. "Would you by any chance be Wally?"

"Yup, that would be me," said the man, who looked to be somewhere in the 45 to 50 age bracket.

When she reached him, she extended her hand. "I'm Aliesha. Aliesha Eaton."

She could tell by the sudden flickering of Wally's girlishly long lashes that he didn't know quite what to make of her overly formal introduction or her less-than-casual attire. A man of obviously good upbringing, he nonetheless pressed his palm against hers and returned her smile.

"Nice to meet you, Miz Aliesha. What can I help you with?"

She braced herself. "Well, I was wondering if I might be able to get my hair cut. You do take walk-ins, don't you?"

The barber's pleasant expression nose-dived into something more stoic. He turned to the barber next to him, a short, husky fellow who looked in dire need of a haircut himself. "Yo, Gerald, man," Wally shouted. "Turn down that music for a minute."

Gerald, who had been busy snipping scissors across the backside of a customer's head while carrying on a loud, animated telephone conversation, frowned at the sound of his name. He muttered an obscenity before reaching over and lowering the volume on the ancient-looking boom box that sat between his and Wally's workstations.

For a few uncomfortably long seconds, Wally eyed the thick, black, unchemically treated hair crowning Aliesha's head. Finally, with crinkled brows, he said, "Yeah, we take walk-ins. But to tell you the truth, I don't generally do women's hair. You might want to talk to my man Gerald here. Hey, Gerald, Miz Lady here is wanting a haircut. Think you could help her?"

Gerald rolled his eyes and shouted into the phone, "All right, man! All right! Come on down then. I gotta go."

After shoving the phone into the front pocket of his work smock, Gerald stared at Aliesha, but spoke to Wally. "Sure, I can take her. Might be a while though. I just got done talking to Sam Junior. Said he'd be over in 'bout ten minutes with them badass twin boys of his. Before them, though, I gotta finish this one here and take that one over there." He pointed toward the bench directly across from his barber's chair, where a slightly disheveled-looking man sat, nodding and fighting sleep.

Aliesha glanced at her watch. It was only 12:30 and her next class wasn't until 2:00. After the cut, she'd hoped to run by her house in order to wash her hair, change her clothes, and if possible fix something to eat. She sighed and, like Gerald, looked at Wally. "Maybe I'll come back another time. Do you take appointments by any chance?"

He shook his head. "Me and Gerald both are strictly first come, first served kinda guys. He gazed toward the rear of the shop. "You could check with *Dante*," he said, suddenly speaking in a much louder voice and with extra emphasis. *"He's on break right now, but I fully expect him to be back on the job by 1:00. Got that, D?"*

Aliesha followed Wally's gaze to the dark-skinned man stretched over the long bench at the back of the shop. An open-faced book rested atop his chest, his eyes appeared closed, and the wires of iPod earbuds trailed from either side of his head. Even though he raised a hand to his brow in mock salute and acknowledgment of Wally's spiel, he didn't bother to sit up, open his eyes, or remove his earplugs.

Wally turned back toward Aliesha. "Then I got a barber by the name of Yazz, who, as of late, has been clocking in around three or so. Both D. and Yazz generally stay till pretty late in the evening if you want to call and see about setting something up."

Before Aliesha could respond, the older-looking man seated on the bench across from Wally's chair said, "Appointments?" He laughed and widened his already-spread legs. "You not from 'round here, sugar, are you?"

"No," Aliesha said, trying her best to ignore the notes of condescension she'd readily detected in the man's voice and demeanor. "Not originally. I'm from Chicago."

"Chicago!" said the curly-headed man seated next to the old guy. "The windy city, huh? What on earth would bring a smart-looking girl like you all the way down here?"

"A job," Aliesha said. "I'm a professor at Wells."

"Is that right?" the curly-headed guy said, sounding impressed. "I guess that would make you one of them fine, educated, highfalutin Northern gals my poor Arkansas-raised daddy used to try to get me and the rest of my bone-headed brothers hitched up with back in the day."

Aliesha laughed and said, "Well, I don't know about all of that. The truth is—"

"*Psst,*" the older man spat with a dismissive wave of one hand. "The truth is, ain't nuthin all that special 'bout Chicago. What's it got besides a lot of racism, some poor, proper-talking Negroes, and a bunch of raggedy-ass streets? Hell, when you get right down to it, Chicago ain't too much more than Mississippi moved north."

Had it not been for his outright hateful tone, Aliesha might have voiced at least some partial agreement with her antagonist's harsh assessment. Instead, she said, "So, when was the last time you were there?"

The gray-haired man dropped his arms and leaned forward. "Beg your pardon?"

"Chicago? How is it you know so much about it? Tell the truth, I bet you haven't been so much as within a 100-mile radius of Chi-Town in, say, the last fifteen years or so—have you?"

A scowl narrowed his bloodshot eyes. "What difference do that make? I ain't never ate shit neither and don't rightly think I need to in order to say I don't think it's something I ever want to make a meal of."

Aliesha shouldered up her purse and took a step toward him. "You know what—"

But before she could tangle with him, a deep, barrel-toned voice rang out, "Say, yo! Miz Professor!"

Aliesha redirected her glare at the now-standing barber she'd seen lounging just a few seconds before. Momentarily captivated by her unobstructed view of his skin's rich ebony hue, she watched as he stopped shaking out a plastic cloak and draped it over one of his tight, muscular forearms.

He looked at her and said, "I've got an open chair back here if you want it."

She raised a hand to her hip. "I thought you were supposed to be on break."

"Yeah, I was, and now break time is officially over." He grinned and spun his chair around. "So, you gonna allow me the honor of taking care of you or what?"

The playful tease in his voice and the wide smile stretched across his dark face took some of the edge from her anger. Her nostrils still flared, she cast one last evil look at the gray-haired instigator before sashaying past him.

Rather than back off or at least turn his attention elsewhere, the old guy grunted and said, "And I'll tell you another something about Chicago . . ."

"All right now, Ray," the dark-skinned barber said, his smile replaced with a look of dead seriousness. "I'd really hate to see you slip up and get knocked down over some ole foolishness."

"Meaning what?" Ray said.

"Meaning, ain't gone be no more of that. You're either gonna respect my customer or else you're gonna step outside with me and take the ass-whupping you got coming like a man."

The old guy turned toward Wally. "You heard that, didn't you? I'll be damned if I ain't been coming up in here and giving y'all my money for close to 'leven years now. Since when do you 'llow your boys to speak to your regulars just any ole kind of way?"

Wally stopped lining his customer and looked up with a frown. "Ray, man, you started that mess. Don't even think about trying to drag me all up in it."

"Oh, oh so it's like that, huh?" Ray leaped from his seat. "Fine, then. Later for all y'all tired, backward-ass, pussy-whipped Negroes," he said, prior to stomping out.

Before she sat down in his chair, Aliesha looked directly into the eyes of the man who'd spoken up on her behalf, a man whose athletic build and dark magnetism reminded her of the singer-turned-actor, Tyrese; the pretty-boy model, Tyson Beckford; and the lyrical front man for the Roots, Black Thought, all rolled into one. "I could have taken him, you know," she told him in a quiet voice.

He nodded and without the slightest hint of amusement in his voice said, "Uh-huh, in a Chicago second, I'm sure. But is that really what you came in here for?"

CHAPTER 2

A decent haircut was all she really wanted . . . all she'd really come in there for. Rather than speak her mind, she stared at the dark-skinned barber's reflection in the mirror attached to the wall behind his workstation and said, "So is it D. or Dante?"

"Depends," he said, while standing behind her and tying the cloak around her neck. "Which do you prefer?"

She studied his face and said, "Personally, I like Dante."

He shrugged. "So, for you, Dante is who I'll be." He swiveled her around in the chair and smiled down at her. "Now, tell me how you want it cut."

Before she could respond, he reached out and buried the fingers of one hand into the hair above her left ear. Startled by the unexpected wave of pleasure that rolled off her scalp, ran down the length of her torso, and landed square in her lap, she jumped.

He withdrew his hand. "I didn't hurt you, did I? Don't tell me you're tender-headed."

"No," she said. "I'm not." She reached into her purse, dug out a comb, and started picking out her hair. "If you could just even it out for me, that would be great."

"It's pretty," he said, taking the comb from her and starting to fluff where she'd left off. "Healthy, too."

Was he flirting or simply affirming aloud what she already knew to be true? She couldn't tell. What she did know from thirty-three years of having lived in the world was that men like Dante didn't typically bother to look twice at women like her—dark-skinned Black women who avoided, elected not to, or simply outright refused to straighten or chemically alter their natural hair.

"So, Miz Professor, what is it you teach?" he asked.

"Anthropology," she said.

"Oh, yeah? Interesting," he said.

She waited for him to come back at her with some version of, *Come on, do you honestly think humans came from monkeys?* Or else the always popular in these parts, *An anthropologist, huh? Guess that mean you one of them atheist who don't believe in God?*

After several minutes passed without him asking either, she wondered if he truly lacked a sense of curiosity about what she did or was simply too clueless about her field of interest to even pose the most basic of questions.

At least he had yet to come at her with the line of inquiry Black men of all educational and socioeconomic backgrounds in the midsize Southern city she'd called home for the past couple of years appeared to enjoy assailing her with: *Why on earth would a nice-looking girl with such a decent head of hair choose to wear it . . . like this?*

Dante didn't seem to care one way or the other. After picking out her 'fro in silence, he handed back her comb and busied himself with the assortment of clippers, scissors, and hairstyling instruments on the counter behind his workstation.

"Do you have any other female customers?" Aliesha asked, attempting to make polite conversation.

"Nope. Not here," Dante said. "But I had several when I lived out in Cali."

His accent was unmistakably that of a Southerner, but Aliesha asked anyway. "Is that where you're from?"

"Nope, I was born and raised in Roads Cross; it's a little dusty town, not more than an hour and a half drive away from here. I moved out to Cali on account of a cousin whose got her own shop out there. All Styles is the name of it. They do both men and women's hair."

Her interest piqued, Aliesha said, "So how is it you ended up in Riverton?"

"Told you. I'm a Southern boy. That West Coast lifestyle just ain't for me. I like a slower pace and being around folks who are a little less fake and self-absorbed. Besides that, I missed hanging out with my Big Mama and 'nem."

Aliesha smiled. "I used to spend summers down here with my Big Mama when I was a little girl."

"Yeah?" Dante said. "For me, it doesn't really feel like summer unless I've spent a hot day or two sitting out on the front porch with my Big Mama, sweating, fanning, and shooing flies." Before he switched on the clippers, he pinched his thumb and index finger together and asked, "Is about this much good?"

Without giving it much thought, Aliesha reached out and gently guided his fingers closer together. "Right about there is fine," she said.

Their eyes met, and in that brief instance, Aliesha felt something unspoken transpire between them.

She settled against the barber's chair and spent a few minutes thinking about his hands. They were nice . . . large and midnight black without a trace of ash between the knuckles . . . and with skin that was smooth and pleasantly warm to the touch. His nails were clean, looked healthy, and bore tips that were short and well rounded.

Even though Dante had repositioned her with her back to the mirror and she couldn't see what he was doing to her head, Aliesha harbored none of the doubts and fears that usually accompanied her climb into a new barber or beautician's chair. She closed her eyes and gave herself permission to drift into that realm of semiconsciousness that exists somewhere between sleep and deep meditation.

After about thirty minutes, she heard him say, "All right, Miz Professor. What you think?"

On reaching for the long-handled mirror he offered, she swiveled from side to side, checking out her hair from every conceivable angle. The mirror attached to the wall behind her allowed for a nice view of both the back of her head and her neckline.

"Perfect," she said.

"I could wash it for you if you like," Dante said, while brushing hair clippings from the cape covering her shoulders. "I've got a nice-smelling shampoo with a built-in conditioner."

She glanced at her watch, then asked, "How much extra is it going to cost me?" Inwardly she cringed, realizing she'd failed to ask how much he'd charged in the first place and hoping he wouldn't attempt to gouge her.

"The total for everything?" he asked, as if reading her mind. "Cut, shampoo, and style? Oh, I'm thinking no more than twenty."

Aliesha nodded her okay and followed Dante to a dark room off the rear hallway. Even though he paused at the door and flipped a switch alongside the wall, it took her eyes a moment to adjust to the dramatic change in light. On focusing, she realized he'd led her into a utility room, one that housed not only a shampoo bowl but a washer, a dryer, and a couple of deep, wide sinks. She slowed her pace as they walked toward the shampoo bowl positioned in the dimly lit back corner of the windowless room.

When she finally eased onto the reclining chair in front of the bowl, Dante helped her properly position herself against the tub's curved neck rest.

"You comfortable?" he asked.

"Oh, sure, this is fine," she said.

Dante picked up the sprayer and turned on the water. "Let me know if it's too hot," he said.

The warm jet streams against her head soothed her in

much the same way a full body massage might. She smiled and an involuntary "Umm" slipped past her lips.

Dante smiled down at her. "Feels good, huh?"

Aliesha stared into the face hovering above her own. Ordinarily, she might have felt a twinge of embarrassment. However, in this instance, her smile only grew broader. She openly appraised his good looks, the large liquid brown eyes, the full lips, the dark and neatly groomed hairs nestled beneath the wide nostrils and shadowing the well-defined cheekbones, chin, and jawline.

I'll be damned if this ain't one hell of a pretty Black man, is what she caught herself thinking.

"If you enjoyed that, wait till I hit you with some of this," Dante said on removing the top from a bottle and squeezing a blob of the contents into his hand. He worked the shampoo into her hair. When his fingers commenced their repetitive rub against Aliesha's scalp, she found herself closing her eyes and biting her lip to keep the moan she felt stirring way down deep in her gut from bursting forth.

On composing herself, she braved a peek at him and said, "I don't know if it's the technique you're using, the shampoo, or a combination of the two, but just so you know, that feels absolutely wonderful."

Dante nodded. "I figured you'd like it." He squirted a bit more of the liquid mixture into his palm. "Just so you know—this isn't something you can just buy at any ole store. No, ma'am, this comes from my Big Mama's own private stash."

Aliesha's eyes widened. "Oh yeah?" she said. The upturned corners of her lips fell into a straight line and all her earlier confidence began to dissipate.

"Yeah," Dante said. "She makes and bottles it out on her little piece of land."

"So, what's in it?" Aliesha asked, trying to keep her mind from conjuring an all-too-vivid image of her hair as a clownish shade of orange and falling out in big clumps.

"Besides water from the creek and a healthy dose of lavender? Hell if I know," Dante said. "But don't worry," he added, as if sensing she were about to raise her fully lathered head off the bowl and make a fast break for the door. "I promise you, this is the milk and honey of shampoos. It's gonna have your 'do looking tighter than it's ever looked. And if it doesn't, come back and I'll give you double, naw, I'll give you triple what you paid me for it."

Aliesha didn't say anything, but the thought uppermost on her mind was, *Uh-huh, and if all my hair falls out, I'll be coming back up here with a summons and looking to sue you and your Big Mama's ass.*

After the wash and rinse, Dante toweled as much water as he could from her hair, prior to going over it with the forced heat of a handheld dryer. He used little more than her pick and his hands when it came time to style her.

She held her breath when he finally passed her the mirror again.

"Well?" he said.

She blinked at the stunningly regal image that greeted her. On exhaling, she looked up at him. "You were right. It's beautiful."

"Uh-huh, me and Big Mama had you worried there for a moment though, didn't we?" He handed her a card with the Wally's Cool Cuts address and phone number printed on it. "If you need me to hook you up again, give me a call. My hours are on the back."

"Thanks," Aliesha said. She paid Dante what she owed him, plus a generous tip. On rising from the chair, she noticed the paperback jutting from atop one of the wide, front waistline pockets of his work smock. She wondered if it was the same book she'd seen resting on his chest earlier.

"What are you reading?" she asked.

He pulled the book from his smock and passed it to her.

"Kafka's *Metamorphosis*?" she said.

"Not exactly what you were expecting, huh?" Rather

than give her an opportunity to respond, he added, "Give me a second and I'll walk you out."

After reinserting the earbuds connected to his iPod, Dante invited her to walk in front of him. He escorted her past the new group of customers who'd come in since her arrival, among them Sam Junior and his hollering-ass twin boys, as well as a small but rowdy group of young men who looked to be in their late teens or early twenties. He led her by Gerald, Wally, and the wailing boom box that had at some point wrapped up its Johnnie Taylor set and moved on to the likes of Bobby "Blue" Bland.

On stepping outside, Aliesha watched Dante bob his head to the music coming from his iPod. She motioned for him to remove the earpieces and on his compliance she said, "I thought you were a good ole Southern boy. What? You don't like J.T. and Bobby B.?"

Dante shook his head. "That's old man music. It's all right every now and then."

Aliesha reached for one of the iPod's earbuds and raised it to the side of her head. What she heard, Curtis Mayfield's "People Get Ready," shocked her. The song had been one of her father's favorites. She grinned and said, "If what they're listening to is old man music, what do you call this?"

"Who? Curtis Mayfield? Naw, see, Brother Mayfield is what you call retro. That's right, retro, progressive, and timeless. What? You didn't know? Come on now, Miz Professor. You'd better ask somebody."

He laughed with her, then said, "I hope you don't mind, but I'm going to need that back." He pointed at the book still in her hand. "I'm not exactly finished with it yet."

"Oh, I'm sorry," she said. After returning his book, she looked into his eyes and said, "Thanks . . . you know . . . for being such a gentleman."

He held her gaze and in a voice that was soft and serious said, "That's how my Big Mama raised me. I don't know any other way to be."

She walked to her car. The thought of him eyeballing her from behind sent a rush of warmth to her cheeks and gave rise to a hint of a smile on her lips. But when she reached her car and turned around, she found the sidewalk in front of the barbershop vacant. It almost felt as if Dante had never been there.

She slipped inside of the car and stuck her key in the ignition. The start of the engine coincided with the ringing of her cell phone. She fished the phone from her purse and glanced at the flashing number before flipping up the receiver.

"Hey, sweetie," she said. "What's up?"

"You tell me," Javiel said. "I thought you were gonna call and let me know what time to stop by. Are we still on for tonight or what?"

CHAPTER 3

Had the music pulsating against his eardrums not obscured the soft tinkle of the bell above the shop's door or if
the sleep tugging at his twitching eyelids hadn't already
sealed them shut, Dante might have witnessed Aliesha's
bold entry into the Black male dominated world known as
Wally's Cool Cuts. He might have very well missed Aliesha
altogether had it not been for her voice. Something in,
about, or having to do with the sound of Aliesha's voice
had circumvented the hypnotic hold of Ndegeocello's "The
Chosen," the song he'd been listening to on repeat, and
roused him to a more heightened state of awareness. Even
though he'd initially resisted the urge to rise up and peer in
the woman's direction, he had lowered the volume of the
music to increase his chances of being able to take in her
every word.

*Aliesha Eaton. A professor at Wells. Originally from
Chicago. In need, so she said, of a haircut.* Dante noted all
the pertinent details before he sat up and forced open his
eyes. What he'd seen had surprised him—a tall, slender,
dark-skinned woman with a regal bearing and a glorious
crown of hair; a woman whose beauty had become more
apparent the longer he'd gazed upon her; a woman whose
little Black girl innocence had quietly beckoned the soft,

hidden parts of the shy, little Black boy buried deep within him.

The guise she'd donned in the face of brother Ray's malicious and unwarranted attack—that of a sharp-tongued Pippi Longstocking capable of serving up an old-fashioned beat-down to any knucklehead who'd dare make the mistake of trying to run her out of the tree house—was one Dante had seen through in a glance. Here was an ebony-colored princess who, though well aware of her lineage, had yet to fully realize or appreciate her place in her Father's kingdom.

Before she could make the mistake of slipping completely off her throne in order to tussle and grovel about with one of the shop's most notorious, trash-talking jesters, Dante had called out to her. When she'd turned and their dark eyes had finally connected, he'd experienced a sharp piercing in his side. The pain had quickly migrated to his chest where it had synchronized its repetitive throb with the one-two beat of his heart.

Undaunted by the odd sensation, he'd invited her to a seat in his chair. Neither the untamed state of her hair nor the anger burning bright in her eyes had fooled or frightened him. The thought that he might not possess what it took to woo and soothe her never occurred to him.

He'd long been told he had a way with women. The smile. The good looks. The muscular physique. The impeccable old-school manners and the soft-pedaled charm. He knew how to use them all to his full advantage, and he harbored little shame about having done so with a number of attractive and willing women.

However, with Aliesha, Dante hadn't the slightest conscious clue that she was who or what he wanted until his fingers found their way into her hair. Certainly, he'd been instantly enthralled by the soft, thick, wiry strands. But he'd been struck even more by the intensity of her response to his touch. Beneath her obvious pleasure, he'd immediately detected a void—a void that he suspected he could more than fill if the right opportunity to do so ever presented itself.

Had he fancied himself some kind of line-spitting, woman-manipulating player, he just might have openly shared with her the most pervasive thought on his mind as he'd gently tended to her wild flock of curls: *More than any haircut, Ms. Professor, what you really want and need in you life right about now is an escape from the shackles and restraints that have your life on lockdown, someplace where you can feel safe and appreciated enough to not only let your hair down but let it go altogether. And by the same token, I'm thinking I just may know the perfect spot for you. . . . But the question remains, is this feeling something either of us really ought to pursue? And if so, to what extent and for how long?*

But since he lacked the sheer amount of vanity, arrogance, and verbosity necessary to play such a wild pimp card, he'd elected instead to heed the other voice in his head, the one that sounded an awful lot like his Big Mama: *How many times must I tell you, boy? Not every impulse or feeling need be acted on right away. If it's meant to be, granting it a little time and space ain't gonna make it go nowhere.*

So rather than step to Aliesha and risk fumbling all of his cards, he'd proceeded with caution and played to his strengths—pouring on all the laid-back, ain't trying to sweat it, Southern bad-boy savoir faire he could muster. And in no time at all, he'd had her alone in the utility room, smiling up at him from the shampoo bowl and openly searching his eyes for a glimpse into his soul.

He'd channeled all of his energy into extending his new customer the full royal treatment she deserved and coaxing her hair into looking its natural best. When he'd finished and passed her the mirror, she'd appeared genuinely pleased and impressed with his efforts. He knew, too, by the less formal and borderline flirtatious manner in which she'd engaged him afterward that she would have likely responded in a positive fashion had he shared his interest in getting to know her better. But on the advice of the disapproving voice in his head, he'd opted otherwise. Even when he'd walked her outside where the throbbing broke loose from his chest and descended into his belly, he'd managed to keep his more carnal desires in check.

While taking in the cars whizzing by on the busy thoroughfare just beyond Wally's Cool Cuts' parking lot, Dante had slipped back into his childhood for a moment. As kids, he and his cousin Reuben had been fond of a game that had no rules, except for the one which stipulated that when a player spotted a vehicle that really suited his fancy, one that really grabbed him by the balls and tugged, he was to stop whatever else he'd been doing in order to shout as loud as he could, "That's mine, man! That's my ride! See that bad, fire engine red Porsche over there? Yeah, buddy, that there is gonna be mine one day."

Dante had been seized by a similar thought at the end of his conversation with Aliesha, when she'd turned and headed toward her car. "Yo, Reuben!" he'd whispered. "You see that long-legged, fierce-haired, chocolate lovely who just walked away from here? That's mine, man. All mine."

CHAPTER 4

The old, round-faced clock hanging above the closed door of Aliesha's office read 1:22. Each passing second came and went with a resounding click. But Aliesha neither saw nor heard. Momentarily ignoring both the time and the piles of paper cluttering her desktop, she sat with her chair and face turned toward the soft, natural light peeking in through her office windows.

Unlike some of her more decor-obsessed colleagues, Aliesha's office contained few personal touches. No pictures. No plants. No knickknacks. No memorabilia or souvenirs from places she'd visited or lived. The only distinguishing feature of the fifteen-by-fifteen-foot area where Aliesha spent a sizeable portion of her waking hours were her bookshelves. Every inch of free wall space in her office supported an overstuffed bookcase of one kind or another, all hand-crafted and all she'd happily purchased with a significant amount of her own money.

The unadorned tops of three sets of bookcases stopped just below the office's single row of three rectangular-shaped windows. But the fact that the Anthropology Department resided in Sojourner Hall's basement meant the views, Professor Eaton's included, were anything but impressive. Not that it mattered much as Aliesha sat with her gaze fixed against the center window's recessed pane.

"*People get ready . . . there's a train a comin'.*" A full twenty-four hours had passed since Aliesha's visit to the barbershop, but she still couldn't get the song out of her head. The familiar lyrics and soft-spun melody conjured a flood of warm memories. Mixed in with her reoccurring thoughts of Dante flickered shadowy images of her long-dead father.

William "Will" Eaton had been Aliesha's rock. His presence in her life is what had kept her from believing that black and ugly were words that naturally complemented and enhanced one another in the manner of other well-known word combinations, like cake and ice cream or rhythm and blues. "You are a smart and extraordinarily beautiful child of God. Always know and recognize your worth in the world" is what he'd made a point of reminding her on a near daily basis and in direct defiance of the world's insistence on telling her just the opposite. It was because of her father's emphasis and influence that, unlike a lot of women who bore her same soft, ebony hue, Aliesha had never questioned her physical attractiveness, only the apparent blindness of others to it.

The unexpected, loud click and rattle of her office door jerked Aliesha upright in her chair. She knew of only one person brazen enough to ignore, so blatantly, the large, red-lettered DO NOT DISTURB sign she'd hung at eye level outside her door.

"Monica Wilbun!" she said without even bothering to turn her head. "How many times do I have to say this? Can't you at least knock before you come barging in like that? Hell, you nearly gave me a heart attack."

"And how many times must I remind you, my dearest Dr. Eaton? If you don't want visitors—get rid of the crappy-ass sign and lock your damn door! Mark my words, one of these days it's not gonna be me, it's gonna be Rufus the janitor and you're gonna be up in here changing your damn drawers."

Aliesha smiled as she swiveled toward her friend and colleague, the incredibly foul-mouthed but highly esteemed professor of history, Dr. Monica Wilbun. On first glance, the two women (one owning an obviously mixed racial heritage and the other whose African lineage visually dominated her DNA) appeared to be nothing alike, if not total opposites.

Nevertheless, beneath the surface of their respective veneers swam a multitude of similarities. They were both smart, self-motivated, highly driven women who had grown accustomed to being looked upon as "exceptional" by their peers in the world of academia but who refrained from buying into the notion themselves.

While Aliesha, the taller and darker of the two, owned her fair share of curves, voluptuous was a word that better suited her shorter and considerably lighter complexioned friend. And not voluptuous as a cloaked synonym for fat, either. Dr. Wilbun's womanly attributes came packaged in a way that made most of the men on campus, who didn't already know, stop, turn, and say to themselves, "Damn, who is that?"

Monica dumped her backpack and fell into the chair in front of Aliesha's desk. "Wow, I don't know what dude did, but my God, your hair is fucking gorgeous!"

Aliesha nodded. "Why, thank you for the overly generous, albeit incredibly vulgar compliment, Dr. Wilbun. I think the young man did an excellent job as well. So, what's your 'but' or should I say your beef? 'Cause I know you've got one. So, go on, spit it out already."

Monica crossed her shapely legs and leaned back in her chair. "Ooh, mighty defensive now, aren't we?" Her face split into a wide grin and for a few seconds her features became decidedly more Asian. "Uh-huh, just as I expected. Leave it to you to fall under the spell of some young slick who works in a damn barbershop. . . ."

Monica knew all about Aliesha's visit to Wally's. In the

hours prior to her Wednesday night rendezvous with Javiel, Aliesha had slipped in a call to her friend and dished her all the pertinent details.

"Hey, all I'm saying is, you might want to try shaking your head a couple of times, 'cause it sounds to me like a wee bit of granny's creek water has seeped into your ear canals and is pooling on the flat contours of your brain."

Aliesha laughed. "Come on, how many brothers do you know who listen to Curtis Mayfield, much less read Kafka? I'm telling you, there's something special about this guy."

"Oh, I'm sure there is," Monica said. "And in a good way, too. But why should you care? Last time I looked, you already had a man. So what's up? You and Javiel have a serious falling out or something?"

Aliesha sighed and thought back on Wednesday night. "We'll only stay an hour," he'd promised. But like always, one hour had stretched into two and leapfrogged into almost three. Wanting to be a good sport, Aliesha had refrained from grumbling, pouting, or protesting while Javiel and the loud group of regulars seated on either side of them had piddled away the bulk of the evening arguing stats, discussing strategy, bad-mouthing the officiating and cheering all of the phenomenal plays and fancy moves being broadcast on the bar's digitally enhanced wide-screen. She remembered picking over a plate of chicken tenders and fries and waving off Javiel's repeated suggestions for her to order a drink or two. He'd meant well. But rather than cause her to loosen up and relax, she'd feared the alcohol would only aggravate her boredom and agitation and lead to a public unleashing of her private discontent.

She tossed aside her pen and, with her eyes still averted from Monica, said, "A serious falling out? No, not really."

"Yeah, well, my womanly intuition tells me there's a whole bunch of *something* lurking all up in the 'not really' load of crap you're trying to sell." Monica propped her hands beneath her chin and rested her elbows on the desk.

"So, you wanna spill it now or would you really prefer that I drag it outta your ass later?"

"I don't know," Aliesha said before forcing herself to meet Monica's unyielding gaze. "It's just that . . . well, Javiel and I . . . we don't . . . talk as much as I'd like."

Monica shook her head. "See, that's your problem," she said in a much sterner tone. "Instead of being satisfied with the pretty-boy looks and A-1 stud services, like the rest of us, you want these fools to talk to your ass, too."

Aliesha's smile resurfaced. In the two years she'd known Monica, she had yet to stay mad at her for more than a solid five minutes. She reached for her pen. "Oh, and I suppose you and Jesus don't talk?"

Jesus and Monica had been dating, off and on, for the past couple of years. He was an affable guy with an outgoing personality who worked as a sports trainer and an instructor in the university's Athletic Department. He was also Javiel's cousin. Had Jesus and Monica not pressured Aliesha into a blind date with Javiel, she was almost certain their paths would have never crossed.

"Talk?!" Monica said. "Hell, no. Least ways, not if we can help it. All talking does is shine a big-ass spotlight on our differences and inevitably leads to discord. No, girl, with me and Jesus—it's just like Chris Rock said—we eat, we screw, we go to the movies, we screw some more, we go out to eat again . . . And hell, we look cute together while we're doing it. Why ruin a good thing by talking? For what? Believe me, I've got much better things to do than sit up and listen to Jesus cuss my ass out in Espanol."

As Monica rambled on, Aliesha couldn't help but agree with some of what her friend was saying. In fact, somewhere deep down, she knew the dissatisfaction she was experiencing in her relationship with Javiel had little to do with the way they communicated. She couldn't pinpoint it or give it a name, but she could feel it slowly eating away at her from the inside.

CHAPTER 5

Mr. Phillips reached for the showerhead Aliesha had purchased on her way home from work. Ordinarily, she handled simple tasks and improvements of that nature without any assistance. Not only had her father given her extensive hands-on training in the art of home maintenance, he'd left her an older brick-and-shingle, four-bedroom craftsman that in the brief time she'd lived in it had required only a couple of minor repairs. On arranging for her handyman, Mr. Phillips, to stop by and replace her leaky water heater, she'd decided to have him replace the outdated and partially clogged showerhead, too.

"All right, let me take a look at what you got," Mr. Phillips said. "Something fancy, newfangled, and overpriced, I imagine." Rather than break the package's seal, Mr. Phillips squinted at her. "There's something different about you. Did you lose weight since the last time I saw you or something?"

Aliesha chuckled. The last time they had seen each other had been a mere four days ago. Archie Phillips and his wife, Barbara, had sat in the pew directly across the aisle from hers at Garden View Presbyterian where they were all active members.

"Did Barbara tell you 'bout that boy of ours getting engaged?" Mr. Phillips asked. "The one that's up in Cleveland studying to be a doctor? Yeah, let me show you."

Mr. Phillips placed the unopened package on the toilet seat and fished his wallet from his back pocket. Sporting the quivering grin of a proud papa, he all but shoved the photo into Aliesha's face. "Nice-looking girl, huh? She smart, too, just like Duke."

Aliesha gazed at the smiling, petite blonde and the stern-faced young man, who looked like a younger, more athletic version of his father.

"You know that boy ain't dated nothing but White girls since he been up there," Mr. Phillips said.

Feigning interest while willing herself to ignore the boast and brag imbedded in his words, Aliesha said, "Is that right?"

"And you know what he told me one time when I asked him why?"

Ah, no! Aliesha thought to herself . . . *Nor do I really care.*

"He told me most of the young Black girls you see out here these days don't know how to appreciate a young man like him—you know, somebody smart and ambitious, who believes in living conservatively and saving his money so that later on in life he'll be free to travel, eat at fancy restaurants, buy nice things, and what have you."

Let it go, girlfriend. Just let it go, is what her wiser, calmer, internal censor advised. But the other voice, the reckless one who lived way down deep in her gut, egged her on with a defiant, *Oh, no he didn't!*

Aliesha massaged the back of her neck and between the clenched teeth of a forced smile managed a deceptively sweet, "And you mean to tell me in all the time your son has been away at school he has yet to encounter any smart, nice-looking, Black women who think like him?"

"Hey, I'm just trying to tell you what the boy told me. Now my other boy, Orlando, he's just the opposite. He don't date nothing but these ole loose tail hoochies that come straight out the projects and already got two and three babies by just as many different daddies."

She glanced at her watch. "You know what, Mr. Phillips? I've got go fix myself something to eat before I run back up the school. Can I get you something?"

"No, you go 'head on. Don't mind me. I'll be through in a minute."

Aliesha sucked in a head-clearing breath and hurried off to the kitchen. She felt as if someone had been holding her underwater and laughing at her efforts not to twist and flail.

If young Mr. Phillips and his fiancée were happy with one another, she was happy for them. To feel otherwise would have made her a hypocrite. After all, she'd dated outside her race before. Indeed, her current beau, Javiel, was a self-described, odd blend of Puerto Rican and Louisiana Creole. Moreover, Aliesha might have been able to stomach the twisted sense of pride and pleasure the elder Phillips seemed to derive from his son's interracial romance had he not seen fit to insult her and every other Black woman in the process. More and more, as of late, she wondered if what Monica had said to her once in jest wasn't in fact the honest-to-goodness truth: "You're looking at it all wrong, sweetie. Black men love themselves. It's your Black ass they can't stand."

Upon entering the kitchen, Aliesha grabbed a pair of protective mitts. She yanked open the oven and jerked out a sizzling pan of salmon and rice. She had a salad to fix, a dinner to eat, and a shower to take before she left for her department's latest meet and greet where she, the lone Black female in attendance, would be expected to maintain her assigned role of the poised, charming, articulate, exceptional Negro.

"See, I told you it wouldn't take me but a minute," Mr. Phillips called out from the hallway. "Mmm-mmm," he said on poking his head inside the kitchen door. "Something sure does smell good."

"Alaskan salmon," Aliesha said. "I seasoned it with some lemon juice, some butter and garlic, and a few other spices, then baked it over a bed of wild rice. I could fix you a take-home plate, if you'd like."

Mr. Phillips shook his head. "No, I prefer my salmon the old-fashioned way. You know, fried up in a cast-iron skillet with plenty of oil, a bit of onion, a little flour, and some cornmeal? And far as rice is concerned, if mine ain't white, it ain't right." Mr. Phillips squinted at her, like he'd done earlier. "Now I know what it is . . . you did something to your hair, didn't you?"

Even though Aliesha couldn't bring herself to grant Mr. Phillips a full pardon, she couldn't resist the urge to smile.

CHAPTER 6

Prior to walking into Wally's and lucking up on Dante, Aliesha's last decent haircut had been approximately eight months ago. The event itself wasn't one she would soon likely forget, even with it having taken place during those sad and uncertain days before Miss Margie's premature death.

Aliesha had been going to Miss Margie ever since she could remember. As a pigtailed youngster, whenever she'd made the trek down South and visited for any extended time, she'd always ended up sitting in Miss Margie's chair somewhere or else seated in front of her on Aliesha's Big Mama's porch. If she closed her eyes and squeezed them tight, she could see herself perched atop a couple of old telephone books and the back of her head bumping against Miss Margie's ashen and slightly swollen knees.

Miss Margie and Aliesha's Big Mama had been best friends who'd belonged to the same church. But unlike Big Mama, Miss Margie had been anything but the scripture-quoting, hymn-singing, motherboard type. Most folks could tell in a glance that the tall, leggy, natural redhead (before it all turned gray) had not only spent some time in the fast lane, but she had also skidded and slammed up against more than a curb or two.

Miss Margie had never tried to hide her past, nor had

she seemed particularly ashamed of it. "Britney, Whitney, Lil' Kim, and 'nem . . . Shoot, ain't none of them wild-ass heifers got nothin' on me. Yeah, chile, I been hooked on it all—dope, the bottle, and a whole bunch of no-good men. Done had all but one of my five children taken away from me. But I betcha one thang—you ain't gone never catch me sitting up somewhere crying 'bout none of it. You know why? 'Cause through it all, I know the Good Lord's been my comfort and my strength. Yeah, I might have forsook him a time or two. But He ain't never give up on me."

On the birth of Miss Margie's last child, Peaches, she'd cleaned up her life and turned it over to Jesus—or so she'd claimed. Given the perpetual slant of her half-closed eyes and her slightly slurred manner of speaking, there were those who occasionally wondered aloud if the ole sister wasn't still getting her snort and sip on every now and then.

Beyond dispute had been the fact that Miss Margie had known Aliesha's hair better than anyone, including Aliesha herself. The skilled beautician's long, tapered fingers had been the first to ease the sizzle of the curler and the hot comb through Aliesha's thick, black mane; the first to straighten the proud, stubborn kinks with a chemical relaxer; the first to wrap it, wave it, make it bounce, and lend it sheen. Likewise, Miss Margie had been the first one Aliesha had sought when, upon her return South and subsequent acceptance of the teaching position at Wells U, she'd decided to wear her hair natural.

When it came to Aliesha's hair and a whole host of other things, Miss Margie's death had left Aliesha alone to fend for herself. Before she'd passed, she'd made Aliesha promise not to let anyone at Sister Beulah's Beauty Boutique, besides Peaches, work on her hair. "Don't let none of these silly-ass heifers up in here fool with your hair. I know 'em, see. First thing they gonna do is overprocess it. Yup, and after they get it good and limp, they gonna make it they business to talk you into putting some God-awful color in it. You do that and your head gone end up looking just like theirs—ruint! Yup, all dried out, full of split ends, broke off, if not coming out in great big ole patches."

Honoring her promise to Miss Margie hadn't been a problem. But finding a new hairstylist had been a bigger headache than Aliesha could have ever imagined. Her search might not have been as difficult had she opted to go back to wearing twists or braided extensions. She wouldn't have had a problem at all had she only wanted her hair relaxed or had been willing to suffer through the singe, cringe, and stench of an old-fashioned press and curl. But incredibly enough, finding someone to properly cut and style her medium-length natural had proved darn near impossible.

After one particularly harrowing experience, Aliesha had shown up in Monica's office, hoping to find a sympathetic ear and shoulder upon which to unfurl her tightly woven grievances and sorrows, only to have her friend take one look at her and start laughing. "I'm sorry, girl, but you need to run right back up to whoever just did your hair and ask for a refund. I swear if they don't have you looking like some kinda wild-ass bush dog."

Thank goodness Dante had shown up in Aliesha's life and quite literally "saved the day." Beyond giving her drooping self-esteem a long-overdue boost of adrenaline, Dante's expert hands had helped ease away some of the apprehensions Aliesha had been harboring over her upcoming introduction to Javiel's parents.

Indeed, as her talkative church member, Mr. Phillips, has so perceptively put it, "there was something different" about her. That something was her hair. It had finally been restored to its full glory. Everyone from her friends and colleagues to her students and casual acquaintances had noticed it. Likewise, everyone seemed to have something to say about it, even if they couldn't exactly pinpoint what the "it" was. Everyone that is . . . except for Javiel.

CHAPTER 7

Javiel was one of the sweetest, gentlest men Aliesha had ever dated. That was part of the problem. Had he been a womanizer, a pathological liar, a kleptomaniac, a non-bather, an obsessive-compulsive hand-washing neat freak, anything other than the good-looking, soft-spoken, nice guy that he essentially was, she would have felt justified in having ended things between them months ago. How do you leave a man most women would consider a great catch? A man with a respectable career, his own car and house, and damn good credit. A man with no kids, ex-wives, or baby mamas and whose reverence and adoration makes you feel as if you are his very own wall-mounted Picasso. What kind of woman would seriously contemplate walking away from such a man, especially after having spent the sixteen months prior to meeting him unnoticed, unappreciated, unloved, and all by herself?

So what if they had almost nothing in common and even less to talk about. So what if their relationship lacked the passion, the plus/minus connection, the umpf factor of her last one. Who was she to be so damn choosy?

Not wanting to hurt Javiel or appear less than appreciative of his finer qualities, for weeks Aliesha had been stuffing back her feelings and swallowing her frustrations, hoping in time, perhaps, they'd all simply fade away. But in the days after her visit to Wally's Cool Cuts, Javiel's silence about her hair puzzled and annoyed her like nothing he'd previously done or neglected to do ever had. She might have broached the topic, as she sat beside him in the car that Saturday night, had they not been on their way out to the suburbs where dinner and her first meeting with his parents awaited.

Rather than address either subject, Aliesha squirmed in the passenger's seat and bitched about the latest gathering her department's chair had insisted his colleagues attend. "Hell, I'm not sure who benefits from those damn things, besides Shelton."

Javiel pulled into a long driveway and shifted the car into park. "So next time you oughta let me come and keep you company."

She clenched her teeth and stared out the window. "Javiel, in case you hadn't noticed, I'm a big girl. I don't need you or anyone else to hold my hand."

Javiel sighed. "No, what you are is *a mean girl*. You won't *let* anyone hold your hand."

They turned and glared at each other, but rather than trade heated barbs, they laughed. He leaned over and kissed her. "You're nervous. Don't be. It's just dinner, baby. Okay?"

She nodded and exited the car. On joining him in the middle of the driveway, she cupped a slightly moist palm against one of his cool, dry ones. He'd called it right, at least as far as her nerves were concerned. She'd been dreading the meeting ever since Javiel had first presented her with the idea a couple of Saturdays ago.

She didn't understand his excitement about the pending introduction, especially given the role he'd played in fueling her concerns about his parents' less-than-positive reaction to her involvement with their son. Time and time again, throughout the five or so months they'd been together, he'd spoken disparagingly of the joy his mother derived from bragging about her French heritage and Creole bloodline.

Aliesha would never forget how he'd nearly dissolved into tears while describing his mom's disdain for his dark-skinned Puerto Rican grandmother. And via words that had tumbled like stones from the hardened edges of his tightly drawn lips, he'd shared his feelings about the favor he claimed his folks had always shown his three lighter complexioned sisters.

Before Javiel could insert his key into the wrought iron front door of his parents' Tudor-style home, it opened. Aliesha seized his arm and braced herself for the shocked look or frowns of disappointment and disapproval. But nothing could have prepared her for the winning smile and friendly embrace of the stunningly gorgeous woman who ushered her and Javiel inside.

She had anticipated a woman much shorter, thinner, and Caucasian in appearance than the woman who'd introduced herself as Javiel's mother, Julia Malveau Perez. In truth, a stereotypical cafe au lait–colored Creole and one bearing all of the over-the-top haughtiness of Diahann Carroll's Dominique Deveraux from the old *Dynasty* TV series is what Aliesha had imagined. But within seconds of meeting the vivacious and youthful-looking 60-some-year-old, Aliesha's mind had filled with images from the 1950s movie classic *Carmen Jones*. While Julia's beauty and stylish form were reminiscent of Dorothy Dandridge's Carmen, her earthiness and searing wit were more on par with that of Pearl Bailey's Frankie. When Javiel's father, Juan, joined them in the foyer, Aliesha wasted little time in casting him as an older and grayer version of Harry Belafonte's Joe, the clean-cut, handsome soldier who'd been Carmen's love interest in the film.

It relieved Aliesha as well that the free-flowing conversation over their trout amandine, artichoke risotto, steamed carrots, and their glasses of Chablis had borne none of the strained awkwardness that she had suspected it might. Certainly, there had been a couple of those "almost" moments, those points at which things could have easily deteriorated into something unbelievably ugly, like when Juan said to Aliesha, "Dr. Eaton, Javiel tells me you're a Presbyterian, not unlike our illustrious former secretary of state Condoleezza Rice, who also, I might add, hails from the bright halls of academia. She's quite the brilliant stateswoman, don't you think?"

Before Aliesha could finish chewing her food and render a polite but honest response, Mrs. Perez laughed and spared her the effort. "Brilliant?! Oh, sure in some frighteningly awful, truly diabolical sense, I suppose. Aliesha is a bright, forward-thinking woman. I'm sure the last thing she wants is to be cast into the same ideological cesspool as that right-wing, fashion-challenged, conservative lackey."

At another point, Juan again looked at Aliesha and said, "Has our son told you that he was once on the path to priesthood?"

Javiel frowned and shook his head. "I was a monk, Dad, not a priest."

Aliesha didn't flinch. Though he had yet to give her a full account of the experience, Javiel had spoken to her about the three years he'd spent in a monastery and his participation in a dog obedience training program the monks ran in order to lead them to a deeper spiritual plane as well as help finance their monastic way of life.

Julia said, "Yes, dear, there is a difference. A huge one, actually. Were you a better Catholic, I'd suspect you'd know that."

Javiel's father said, "Ha! I'm afraid on some level, the same could very well be said of you, my dear."

"Oh really?" Julia said. "How so?"

Juan seized his wineglass. "Had you been a better Catholic, you most certainly would have never married me."

Without missing a beat, Julia raised her wineglass and bumped it against her husband's in a resounding *click*.

Aliesha smiled as she watched the couple complete their toast in a raucous round of laughter.

Having cleared the table, the two women were in the kitchen preparing coffee and gathering the bowls and utensils needed for the New Orleans–styled dessert—bread pudding with rum sauce—when Julia interrupted their light-hearted banter with, "So, what do you think? Could you possibly bear the thought of having someone like me for a mother-in-law?"

"If what I've witnessed tonight is any indication, I'm sure having you and Mr. Perez as in-laws is an absolute riot. I think you're both great. But need I remind you, Javiel and I haven't been dating long. Unless you know something I don't, marriage isn't even a blip on the radar just yet."

Julia let her slightly quizzical smile do the talking.

Aliesha said, "In any case, the better question might be, could you fathom someone like me as a daughter-in-law?"

Julia stopped moving and focused on Aliesha. "Fortunately for me, my son is attracted to women who are very much like his mother—smart, strong-willed, opinionated, and fiercely independent. You and I would get along splendidly. What's unfortunate for Javiel is that the combination I just mentioned isn't one I've known him to have much long-term success with in the past."

Aliesha searched Julia's eyes for a glint of hostility, and failing to find it she said, "I take it then that my relationship with Javiel gives you some reason for concern?"

Julia lowered her voice. "Aliesha, make no mistake, as far as I can tell you are a beautiful woman both inside and out. And it's obvious that my son adores you. My chief concern is whether you feel the same way about him. Javiel has always been the most emotionally vulnerable of all our children. I won't have him hurt again. The last time that happened he ended up in a monastery chanting, praying, and training dogs for three years. For the life of me, I still don't know how that ever came to pass. Javiel doesn't even like dogs. Anyway, who knows where he's liable to end up should it happen again."

"I'm sorry," Aliesha said. "But where's all this coming from? What did I say or do tonight that would give you the impression that I'm out to break his heart?"

Before Julia could respond, Juan poked his head into the kitchen. "Ladies, do you mind? I betcha the former Madam Secretary never kept her man waiting around for his hot coffee and pudding."

Julia shook her head and picked up the tray of dessert servings. "As much as I'm tempted, I'm not even gonna touch that."

CHAPTER 8

They'd exchanged warm good-byes with Javiel's parents and were almost out the door when Julia said, "Javiel, are you planning on sleeping in tomorrow or do I dare expect to see you at St. Peter's for morning Mass?"

Javiel said, "Well, actually, I was thinking about attending morning services with Aliesha tomorrow."

The heel of Aliesha's shoe got caught on the threshold and had she not been clinging to Javiel's arm she might have tripped and landed face-first on the brick porch landing. *Attend services with her?* It was the first she had heard tell of such.

Not unlike his father, Javiel was at best a lapsed Catholic, or what the good folks who worshiped at Aliesha's Big Mama's Missionary Baptist church commonly referred to as a backslider. His apparent lack of interest in matters of faith had never been a point of contention for Aliesha. Unlike a lot of "churched" folk, she wasn't inclined to question other people's relationship with God. She respected Javiel's spiritual journey and didn't feel it necessarily had to mirror her own. Even when he'd explained the three years he'd spent in a monastery during his early twenties by saying, "I needed some time away from all of the worldly distractions," she'd elected not to press him for details. If at some point he wanted to tell her more, she figured he would.

A few minutes into the long drive home, Aliesha glanced over at Javiel's smiling face, listened to the happy hum springing forth from it and thought, *Damn, why'd he have to go and pick this Sunday of all Sundays?* It wasn't like he'd never been a guest at her house of worship before. He, Jesus, and Monica had all sat in the pew next to her one Sunday morning after having spent an entire Saturday assisting with one of the Habitat for Humanity projects in which Garden View was involved.

She revisited her private conversation with his mother. If Julia's quip about in-laws was the unveiled hint Aliesha thought it might be, then perhaps Javiel's sudden interest in accompanying her to church was an indication of his deepening feelings. She frowned and closed her eyes as she contemplated Julia's stern warning about her son's delicate emotions. What did that mean? Was Javiel subject to nervous breakdowns? On medication? Did he possess an unstable, dark side that he'd somehow managed to keep from her? Aliesha shuddered and wondered what she'd inadvertently gotten herself into this time.

———— ⊰⊱ ————

She put off confronting him longer than she should have. She let him walk her to her front door. She invited him inside. She even agreed to help him finish off another serving of his mama's bread pudding.

They stood in the kitchen, Aliesha with her rear backed against a counter and Javiel positioned directly in front of her, cradling the porcelain bowl like a raised offering. While watching him lower his lids and savor a bit of the dessert she'd eased into his mouth, Aliesha decided to seize the moment. "Javiel, about church tomorrow—"

"Babe, you worry too much," he said with his deep brown eyes suddenly stretched wide open again. He took the spoon and set it and the bowl aside. "It'll be fine, just like dinner tonight. You'll see."

"I'm sure," she said. "It's just that—"

"Shhh," he said, before pressing his lips to her.

She felt the start of an involuntary tingle and stir. "Wait," she said, in hopes of keeping herself from being enticed any further.

"No, you wait," he said. "Before you say anything, I have something for you." He left the kitchen for a moment. On his return, he presented her with a small gift bag.

She reached inside the bag and pulled out a DVD. Earlier in the week, she'd joked about the dinner date with Javiel's parents turning into a disastrous Black/Latin/Creole 1967 version of *Guess Who's Coming to Dinner*. She chuckled and said, "Why, thank you. I've never actually seen the entire movie from beginning to end."

He moved his hands to her waist. "So, what do you say we climb into bed with what's left of our dessert, pop that baby into the DVD player, fool around a bit, and talk about all that other stuff in the morning?"

She said, "Yeah, right. You know once we get into bed we're going straight for the fooling around and all of that other stuff is gonna fall by the wayside."

"Mmm-hmm, I do," Javiel said. "So, what are we waiting for?"

The next morning, Aliesha awakened to a quiet room and an empty bed. She stretched to her right and rubbed her hand against the bare, fitted sheet. Atop the plush fullness of the mattress, coolness reigned even in the spot where only hours before they'd both lain, warm and wet and on the verge of sleep.

She rose and stumbled into the bathroom, praying all the

while that Javiel had really left, either earlier that morning or else at some point during the night. Maybe he'd never intended to accompany her in in the first place and had only been trying to either irk or appease his mother. On leaving the bathroom, she hurriedly slipped into her robe and headed for the kitchen, where upon entering, all of her optimism cracked and splattered like so many dropped eggs on a tile floor. He hadn't left after all. He was there, smelling freshly bathed and clad in what she knew weren't the same boxer-briefs she'd eased over his narrow hips the night before. In one hand, he clutched a tumbler of orange juice, and with the other he eased an iron over a shirt.

"I would have fixed coffee, but I figured the smell would wake you," he said. "You look so peaceful when you're asleep."

She shuffled over and stole a sip of his juice. After kissing him, she stood pondering the best way of softening the blow.

"What's wrong?" he said. "You look tired." He chuckled. "Papi didn't wear you out last night, did he?"

"Javiel, if you don't mind, I really would prefer that you didn't go with me this morning."

"Why not?" he said, the expression on his face teetering between stunned and hurt.

She placed the coffeepot in the sink and turned on the water. "This just isn't a good Sunday. Maybe some other time."

He reached over and shut off the water. "Not a good Sunday. What's that mean?"

She emptied the partially filled pot into the coffeemaker. "Look, I'm just saying. It would have been nice had you asked before you just up and invited yourself."

"Man, if this doesn't take the cake. What kind of a Christian tells somebody *not* to come to their church?" He walked over and yanked the iron's cord from the wall.

"Maybe I oughta clue you in on a little something. In case nobody's ever told you, this, my dear, is the Bible Belt. And down here, sweetie, every Sunday is a good Sunday."

They'd seldom argued in the brief time they'd been together. But when they had, the bitter sarcasm and biting vitriol of which he was capable always shocked her. She stared at him as if trying to determine what portion of him was Jekyll and how much was Hyde. "Be that what it may, that's just how I feel," she said. "And I don't need you to mock or patronize me about it. . . ."

He stared back at her through partially slanted eyes and with his chest rising and falling like a drunken polka player's accordion. "Yeah, well, I'm starting to wonder if you *need* me at all. Who's ever heard of making a got-damn appointment to show up at somebody's church? You embarrassed to be seen with me or something?"

"Of course not. And you're a fine one to question somebody's faith. I doubt they taught that you that in the monastery."

"What's my stay at the monastery got to do with anything?" He started gesturing with his hands—waving and thrusting them about in the tight, breath-filled space between them. "You know what, if you don't want me going to your church, fine. You wanna go to mine? I mean, really, that's not what this is all about, is it?"

She took a couple of steps away from him. "Look, Javiel, I'm not trying to insult you or offend you in any way. I'm just not ready to take our relationship to that level yet."

"I don't understand. What level? The 'going to church together' level?"

"Sure, if that's what you wanna call it."

He moved toward her. "Okay, so let me get this straight. You can sleep with me within the brief span of two weeks after having met me. But we can't go to church together after having spent five months as a couple?"

She tilted her head and pressed the fingers of one hand against the smooth countertop to her right. "So, now all of a sudden I'm a ho? Is that what you're trying to say?"

"Aliesha, you know damn well that's not what I meant. . . ." He reached for her, only to have her brush him off and move completely beyond his grasp.

"No," she said. "Really, Javiel, I think you ought to leave now." In the seconds prior to his response, she caught herself glancing at the knife set on the counter behind him and wondering if the hands that had caressed her so tenderly the night before were capable of doing her irreparable harm.

CHAPTER 9

She swerved her honey-colored Nissan Altima into the first available space she spotted in Garden View's modest parking lot. While grabbing her oversized leather attaché and other personal items off the seat beside her, she snuck a glance at her watch. 9:40. Only a deep and abiding respect for both the day and place kept her from uttering the curse souring the back of her tongue.

She'd intended to arrive at the church early enough to grab a doughnut and possibly wash it down with another cup of coffee. She'd intended to spend a few minutes reviewing the Sunday school lesson. But mainly she'd hoped to arrive before a certain someone beat her there.

The morning tiff with Javiel had scrambled her plans and dumped an additional set of burdens on her mind. On exiting her car and scurrying toward the church's entrance, she scanned the vehicles parked in the lot, looking for the large but otherwise indistinctive black SUV. Before she could ascertain its presence or absence, she caught sight of the grin of a familiar face.

"Well, now, look at you," Aliesha said. "Stepping up in here on time for once. Looks like Garden View is going to make a good Presbyterian woman out of you yet."

Tamara Howard, who for the past several months had been showing up at Garden View for Sunday school, was also one of Aliesha's students at Wells. On the surface, Tamara exuded a bright, confident, good-natured vibe. But underneath her ebony veneer hid a host of doubts and insecurities. She reminded Aliesha a lot of herself at that age.

"Nah, I wouldn't count on it," Tamara said. "I told you, the Baptist in me runs three to four generations deep. I'd dare say it would take an exorcism to get the bulk of it out. Anyway, what's your excuse for just now getting here? Hot date last night?"

Aliesha nodded. "Hmm, something like that."

"Ooh, Dr. Eaton! But I've gotta say, that's one of the things I like best about you Presbyterians. A prudish bunch, y'all ain't. Matter of fact, hanging with y'all is the next best thing to being an outright sinner."

Aliesha reeled in her grin. "Yes, well, to use one of your favorite phrases, don't go getting it twisted. Just because some of us aren't afraid to embrace a spirit of open-mindedness doesn't mean we espouse some sort of 'anything goes' philosophy or that our lives are any less Christ centered."

"Uh-huh, if you say so. Like I told you, I'm not trying to join anybody's church. I'm only here to hone my participant/observer skills and because I get a weird kick out of seeing you outside of your element. Oh, and the refreshments aren't too bad, either."

Aliesha took Tamara's teasing in stride. Not too many others would have gotten off as easy. It irritated her that so many both in and outside the world of academia found her involvement with church odd, if not outright contradictory. For some, along with her expertise in the field of anthropology came the assumption she was surely an agnostic if not an out-and-out atheist. Few seemed satisfied with her expressed desire to relegate God to the realm of mystery—that which exists outside the boundaries of logic and scientific reasoning. Or, as stated in the poetic language and worn pages of her mother's King James Bible,

Hebrews 11:1: *Now faith is the substance of things hoped for, the evidence of things not seen.*

As soon as the heavy metal door of Garden View's side entrance closed shut behind her, an indescribable sense of peace fell over Aliesha and all of her pressing concerns went on a temporary hiatus. In spite of Tamara's comments to the contrary, the church was one place where Aliesha felt very much at home.

Before her death, Aliesha's mother, Connie, had seen to it that her only child had been christened in the Presbyterian faith. Connie had made a point of taking Aliesha to the church she'd long attended with her own family every Sunday. After her mother's unexpected passing, when Aliesha was three, her father had seized the baton. Much to his credit, William Eaton had willingly overlooked his own disdain for his in-laws, as well as what he viewed as the unsavory dictates of organized religion, in order to keep alive the seed his wife had sought to implant in their much-beloved offspring.

With Tamara still chattering at her side, Aliesha walked into her Sunday school classroom with her shoulders back and her chin tilted forward. Quite naturally, the first person her eyes fell upon was the certain someone whose arrival she'd been desperately hoping to precede.

He smiled and said, "Ahh, my lovely successor will indeed be joining us today. I'd begun to wonder."

"Good morning, Kenneth," she said, in a voice that bore no hint of the sudden flutter in her stomach.

When he stood, all six foot four inches of him, Aliesha steadied herself, extended her hand, and said, "It's nice to see you. It's been a long time."

Kenneth took her hand and said, "It has, hasn't it?" before bending forward and pressing his lips to her cheek.

The kiss, the closeness, and the contact all stirred memories, not to mention a variety of hormonal responses that

Aliesha had been doing her best to keep at bay every since she'd received the voice mail message from Kenneth, her former lover, informing her of his pending visit to Garden View's 11:00 service and 9:45 Sunday school class.

—⟨❦⟩—

Aliesha opened her Sunday school text and her Bible prior to sitting at the head of the long conference table. Tamara, who parked herself in the chair to Aliesha's right, cleared her throat in a way that let Aliesha know she wanted her attention. Ordinarily, Aliesha would have granted the request. But in that place and on that particular morning, she was in no mood for silliness or those kinds of girlish games.

Nor did she feel the need to affirm what Tamara, no doubt, had already honed in on. Aliesha and Kenneth created an energy when they were together, a buzz, a hum, an irrepressible vibration that made all who felt it stop and stare, shake their heads or raise their eyebrows in acknowledgment. Indeed, even visually, they'd once made quite a striking pair. Both were tall, slender, and dark in color. While Kenneth's skin was a brown reminiscent of roasted nuts and late autumn leaves, Aliesha's was a deeper, darker, and richer hue, like the soft, black silt that washed up on the banks of the Mississippi.

Rather than turn in either direction, Aliesha fixed her gaze straight ahead and focused on the mesmerizing figure dominating the space at the other end of the table. She couldn't help but recall how they'd met. Oddly enough, had it not been for the insistence of one of Aliesha's colleagues in the Anthropology Department, Dr. Patricia Henson, her meeting and subsequent love affair with Kenneth might have never occurred.

Upon her arrival at Wells, Aliesha had taken an instant liking to Pat Henson, who with her sun-bleached hair, funky sandals, and beatnik ways reminded her of the down-to-earth, though somewhat sheltered and idealistic, White youths with whom she'd frequently studied and occasionally hung out while in grad school. On learning of Aliesha's interest in finding a Presbyterian church home, Pat had talked her into visiting First United, the church she'd belonged to as a youth. Even though Aliesha knew only a Presbyterian church with a predominately African American congregation, not unlike the one she'd grown up in while residing in Chicago, would ultimately suit her needs, she'd agreed to accompany her friend on a visit.

Meeting a man of any kind had been the furthest thing from Aliesha's mind when she'd shown up at church with Pat that Sunday morning. But at six foot four and with his scrumptious, toasted pecan coloring and shiny bald head, Kenneth had been hard to miss in the crowd of overwhelming White and predominately gray-haired congregants who'd participated in the church's coffee hour. The very sight of him in First United's small and densely packed fellowship hall had so mesmerized Aliesha, she'd stopped talking, stopped listening, and just gawked. The bright smile of acknowledgment he'd aimed her way had shaken her from her daze. She'd looked around, thinking surely his attention had been snagged by someone other than herself. Probably one of the few, young twenty-somethings, buzzing about the room. No doubt a blonde. And almost certainly White.

After having spoken with a couple of Pat's old friends, Aliesha had wandered over to the refreshment table with the intent of request a cup of punch. But the other offerings had looked so appetizing she'd lingered. She'd been trying to decide between a piece of cake and a slice of pie when a deep voice behind her said, "The pecan is what you want to go with. Don't get me wrong, the pound cake is excellent, but the pie with the fresh toasted nuts, the sweet filling, and the flakey, buttery crust, oh yeah, it wins hands down."

She'd laughed; thanked him; and, while reaching for the slice of pie he'd offered, hoped he wouldn't notice the array of goose bumps dotting the exposed flesh of her arm. After he'd introduced himself and treated her to his dazzling smile, which had proven even brighter up close, she'd said, "I take it you're a member here . . . I mean, given that you appear to be an expert when it comes to the desserts and all."

"No, ma'am," he'd told her. "What I am is a frequent visitor and a connoisseur of all things sweet."

Upon discovering that Aliesha taught at Wells, Kenneth had wasted no time in inviting her to visit his church, Garden View Presbyterian. "I teach a Sunday school class that's full of lawyers, professors, librarians, journalists, and a host of other studious types," he'd told her. "I think you'd fit right in."

"Well, if I didn't know any better, Mr. Baxter," she'd said, "I'd think you were calling me a nerd."

While scribbling Garden View's address and phone number on one of First United's programs, he'd said, "Please, call me Kenneth. And for the record, I was once married to a woman who, like you, was both smart and beautiful. I learned from experience that when it comes to gaining a woman's respect, much less winning her heart, it's best not to start off by insulting her intelligence."

She'd thanked him and watched him walk away. She'd been standing there wide-eyed and fanning herself with the program Kenneth had given her when her friend Pat had walked over and said, "Who was that? I mean, besides someone you'd obviously be a fool not to get to know better."

Once upon a time her and Kenneth's roles had been the exact opposite. He had been the class facilitator and she'd been one of the students seated at the table's end. The reversal hadn't been one she'd sought or had even been happy about. But he'd insisted, and given the circumstances, she'd been left with little choice other than to agree.

Kenneth leaned forward. His eyes searched her face, as if intent on reading her mind. Once upon a time, she'd almost believed he possessed that kind of power. She watched as he eased back in his chair and closed his eyes. Someone else might have taken offense at what was obviously a signal to her that it was time to start. But Aliesha knew he was so accustomed to being in charge, he couldn't help himself.

On bowing her head and shutting her eyes, she reached for Tamara's hand as well as the hand of the person seated to her left. She drew in a breath before opening her mouth and leading the class in prayer, just like Kenneth had taught her.

After the opening prayer, Aliesha asked the class to follow along as she read about the "beloved disciple" from the New Testament's Gospel of John. When she stopped, she asked, "In your assigned reading of the King James Version of the Gospel of John, did any of you happen to spot an actual mention of the beloved disciple's name?"

"I know I didn't," Tamara said. "And not only did I read it line by line, I even tried reading it backward a couple of times."

After the laughter died, Theodore Nelson, a stern-faced tax accountant and the one person Aliesha could always count to stoke the flames of debate, said, "And that proves what?" He stroked his scraggly beard, and the lines in his permanent frown deepened. "Isn't the Gospel in question named after John? Who in writing about oneself is in the habit of referring to oneself by name?"

Before Aliesha responded, she issued Tamara a quick look of admonishment when her young student muttered, "Probably the same kind of person who'd repeatedly use the word *oneself*."

"Actually, Theodore raises a very good point," Aliesha said. "But by the same token, what humble disciple of Christ would refer to himself as the 'beloved'? Furthermore, tradition holds that the apostle John was, by trade, a Galilean fisherman, while the Gospel appears to suggest that the 'beloved' disciple was someone more settled, someone capable of providing a stable home and seeing to the needs of Jesus's mother, Mary."

Aliesha paused before she asked, "Is it possible that the writer of the Gospel deliberately omitted the name of the beloved disciple? Wouldn't that to some extent, enable any of us to be that beloved disciple?"

While the class waged a lively and spirited debate over the matter, Aliesha again allowed her gaze to settle on her former beau. He sat in uncharacteristic silence and with his arms folded across his chest. But there was no missing the pride that beamed from every upturned line on his face.

Aliesha still recalled how simultaneously shocked, amused, and impressed she'd been upon her first visit to the Sunday school class Kenneth had once facilitated. At one point, he'd riled the class into a near frenzy by quoting passages from a book by Marcus Borg that purported to contain the parallel sayings of Buddha and Jesus. When his class had finally ended and they had been the only two left in the room, Aliesha had asked him point-blank to specify what he believed about the nature of God, the purpose of faith, and his own role as illuminator of all the aforementioned.

With a mischievous glint in his eyes, he'd told her, "Why, I believe the same thing you do, I imagine." Then in a smooth and nearly continuous breath he'd said, "*I believe in God, the Father Almighty; the Creator of heaven and earth; and in Jesus Christ, His only son, Our Lord: Who was conceived of the Holy Spirit; born of the Virgin Mary; suffered under Pontius Pilate; was crucified, died and was buried; He descended into hell; The third day He arose again from the dead; He ascended into heaven and sits at the right hand of God the Father Almighty; whence He shall come to judge the living and the dead; I believe in the Holy Spirit, the holy catholic church; the communion of saints; the forgiveness of sins; the resurrection of the body; and life everlasting."*

The Apostles' Creed was a prayer Aliesha had learned as a child and she, too, knew both the newer and traditional versions by heart. "Yes, and what else?" she'd insisted, determined not to let him off that easy.

"Well, beyond that," he said, "I think when people get too comfortable with what they think they already know, whether it be in a classroom, in the pews, or in life itself, they fall asleep. That's when you come to my class, my first goal is to keep you awake, even if I have to agitate you in the process. After I know that your eyes are wide open, my next goal is to goad you into stepping a bit beyond your normal thought processes. I guess what I believe, in a nutshell, is that once people are in the habit of thinking outside the box, they soon realize they aren't relegated to spending a life inside of one, either."

Aliesha remembered mulling his response for a moment before telling him, "Sounds a lot like some sort of liberation theology."

"Do you disapprove?" he'd asked in a serious voice, but with a bit of a smile riding his lips.

"Not necessarily," she'd said, still hesitant to let him in on her delight in having wandered upon what appeared to be such a like soul.

At the end of her own class's forty-five-minute discussion about the "beloved disciple," Kenneth waited until most of the room had cleared before approaching her. "Even though I've been hearing all of these glowing reports about the fine job you've been doing with my old class, nothing beats having seen it for myself. All I can say is, wow! When it comes to teaching, you, my dear, are a natural."

She smiled and gathered her material. "Yeah, as if the

mark hadn't already been set before me. I'm sure if I had fallen short of it, you would have heard about that, too. You thinking about coming back? I mean, if you're ever interested in resuming your old post here . . ."

"No, no, that's all in the past," he said. "It's all yours now. But I would like to speak with you after service if that's possible."

"Ah, sure, sure," she stuttered. "But I have a couple of administrative issues I need to go over with the new secretary. So I might be a few minutes."

Aliesha took her time in the secretary's office. She really didn't want to be alone with him. Just the thought of all they could have been still kept her awake some nights. But it was over. And even though she'd forgiven him for his one moment of insanity, she still couldn't see herself allowing him back into her life, let alone her bed.

On leaving the office, rather than take the side door that led to the parking lot and where she knew he would be waiting, Aliesha walked back toward the sanctuary. Oftentimes before leaving church on Sunday, she'd reenter the empty sanctuary. Sometimes she'd take a seat on one of the pews and, after focusing on the large, barren cross hanging on the wall behind the choir stand, she'd close her eyes and meditate. It was alone there, in those quiet moments, that she generally found "the peace of Christ" her Presbyterian brethren and sistern invoked on one another's behalf every Sabbath morning.

Other times she'd enter with the specific intention of finding said peace, only to instead find herself standing barely a few feet from the door and staring toward the image of her father she'd inevitably see in the back of the vacant room. Though William had never officially joined the church, he'd made it his business to have Aliesha there, bright and early every Sunday. After entrusting her to the care of the Sunday school teacher, he'd find a seat in the back of the empty sanctuary and sit with his eyes closed and his deceased wife's Bible resting on his lap until the sound of the organ alerted him that the call to worship would soon begin.

"Girl, why on earth are you still here? Church has been over. Don't you have someplace else you need to be?"

The shrill voice jerked Aliesha from her trance. She shifted her attention from the empty pew at the back of the church to the cherublike face of the petite woman who stood scowling at her from the still-opened doors that led out into the vestibule.

Aliesha's face brightened, as it nearly always did, at the sight of Barbara Phillips, the short, bossy, and always immaculately dressed woman who'd all but appointed herself Aliesha's advisor and surrogate mother from the day of her first visit. Barbara, who Aliesha always referred to as "Mrs. Phillips," wagged her finger and shook her head of tight salt-and-pepper curls in the manner of one who'd just walked upon a child in the middle of some mischief.

"Like I couldn't very well ask the same of you," Aliesha said. She'd started toward Mrs. Phillips when she felt the vibration from the phone in her purse. Thinking it might be Javiel, eager to make things right between them, she paused and dug around in her bag until she found the phone. To her surprise, the number on the display wasn't Javiel's, it was Kenneth's. Rather than answer, she resumed her meander down a long row of pews and toward Mrs. Phillips, who in the meantime had commenced a march of her own in Aliesha's direction.

The two women met in the center aisle. "What you doing in here?" Mrs. Phillips inquired again, in a softer voice. "You know that man is out there waiting on you."

"Oh, I just had a few things I needed to tend to first," Aliesha said.

"Uh-huh," Mrs. Phillips said, "Careful now. Church might be over, but you still standing up in one. And I ain't hardly trying to catch a lightning bolt that's got your name written on it."

The two women enjoyed a hearty laugh before Mrs. Phillips's face resumed its seriousness. "Far be it from me to try to get all up in your business, but I've got to say, chile, whatever it was that broke the two of y'all up must have been awfully bad."

Aliesha's own face turned somber. "Yes, ma'am, I'm afraid awfully bad is a fairly apt description." What she couldn't tell Mrs. Phillips, what she'd never discussed with anyone besides Monica, was that Kenneth's obsession with porn, an obsession that Aliesha had tolerated and indulged until one horror-filled night in Vegas, is what had led to their painful breakup.

Mrs. Phillips seized Aliesha's free hand. "Well, not that you asked my opinion, but I'm offering it anyway—it takes a smart woman to know that it's never good to love a man, or anyone else for that matter, more than she's willing to love herself."

"Now aren't you the wise one?" Aliesha said prior to enveloping her surrogate mother in a tight, loving embrace. She planted a peck on one of the older woman's perfectly rouged cheeks and whispered, "Thanks, Sister Phillips. I really needed that."

Looking as embarrassed as she was pleased, Mrs. Phillips said, "Aww, girl, you know you're quite welcome. But allow me to let you in on a lil' something about wisdom. It's kind of like hindsight. Most times, it's only good after the fact. See, had I been a smart woman, like you, I'da done a better job—as far as teaching my own two about loving themselves."

The two women turned toward the figure that suddenly materialized at the door. "All right, Barbara, come on, I'm ready to go," Archie Phillips said. On noticing Aliesha, he added, "Hey, Doc Eaton, I thought you were already gone. How long you planning on making that poor fella stand out there and wait? See, that's what's wrong with y'all Black women . . ."

CHAPTER 10

Before Aliesha could make it outside, her phone buzzed again. She looked at Kenneth's number and sighed. In the twenty or so months since their breakup, he'd always called her at work—never at home, never on her cell, and always during those hours when he knew she wouldn't be available to take his call. She knew why. He wanted to avoid making her feel pressed upon, uncomfortable, or obliged to talk to him. Nor did he want to risk the creation of an awkward situation, should she just so happen to be in the company, if not the arms, of another man. Kenneth was just like that—always on the lookout for her best interest. It was one of her favorite characteristics on the long list of things she adored about him.

Instead of ignoring his call, like she'd done while in the sanctuary, she answered it. "Hey, I'm sorry. I'm on my way out as we speak."

"No problem," Kenneth said. "I just wanted you to know I'm out here standing next to your car. Looks like it's been a while since it's had a real good washing."

Aliesha couldn't contain her amusement at what was, for them, a very private joke. The day they'd transitioned from being friends to lovers, he'd come to her house with the intent of helping her wash her car, only to have her invite him inside afterward for a shower, which had quickly turned into an encounter of a more intimate nature.

On regaining her composure, Aliesha said, "Need you any reminding, Mr. Baxter, looks can be awfully deceiving. So don't go getting any ideas. I'll see you in a bit."

Upon reaching the parking lot, the Phillipses waved at Kenneth before bidding Aliesha a wink and hug-filled good-bye. Kenneth, who'd moved his Lincoln Navigator next to her Nissan, stood between both vehicles with his cell phone pressed to his ear.

As she walked toward him, the expression on his handsome face told her exactly what he had on his mind. "Stop that," she said, upon spying the old familiar grin.

"You know I would, if I could," he said.

On reaching him, she stared at the thick, wide chest that still beckoned her fingers, that still called out for the soft press of her cheek, the moisture of her lips. In hopes of shaking the feeling, she shifted her gaze back to his face and said, "How come you aren't having lunch at the Piccadilly with Rihanna, KJ, and the kids?"

Aliesha remembered how on her first visit to Garden View she'd wrongly assumed that the young woman seated on the pew next to Kenneth was his lady-friend rather than his daughter, Rihanna. Even more shocking had been her discovery that not only was the youthful-looking Kenneth a widower and a father to several adult children, but he was also all of twenty years her senior. In the months since their breakup, the only time Kenneth had shown up at Garden View had been in conjunction with an activity in which either his kids or grandkids played a significant role.

"Because I can eat at the Piccadilly with Rihanna, KJ, and those little snot-nose grandkids of mine any ole time," Kenneth said. "But it's not every day that I get to see much less spend a few minutes alone with you." He reached out and caressed a spot behind her ear. "Your hair . . . it's nice. You must have finally broken down and gone to see Peaches."

She smiled and shook her head. She'd forgotten she'd confided in him about Peaches, Miss Margie, Big Mama, and all of the rest. She'd shared so much with Kenneth in the short time they'd been together—things that she'd yet to even think about revealing to Javiel, even though they'd been together longer.

"No, not Peaches. Someone new," she said. "A young guy who reads Kafka, actually." She wasn't sure why she'd felt compelled to include those particular details.

Kenneth acted as if he hadn't heard and asked, "So, you ever think about giving me another chance?"

"I'd be lying if I said it's never crossed my mind," she said, while staring at his suit and this time realizing it was the same Canali she'd helped him select at the men's clothier she'd accompanied him to in the weeks prior to their breakup.

"So what's the but?" he asked. "You still need more time?"

She gently brushed away a bit of lint she spotted on the front of his suit jacket. "Time isn't going to make what happened go away, Kenneth. I wish it would."

"Are you seeing someone? The young fellow who reads Kafka, perhaps?"

She bowed her head, shook it, but didn't say anything.

He placed three of his fingers beneath her chin and gently guided her head up again. "Tell the truth now, Miz Babygirl, you love him as much you loved me?"

"Miz Babygirl" was the pet name Aliesha's father had first tagged her with as a child, due to her stubborn ways, no-nonsense nature, and all too grown-up disposition. Most of the people who'd routinely called her that—her father, her Big Mama, and Miss Margie—had all passed. She remembered how much joy she'd initially felt at Kenneth's resurrection of the term. Over time her joy had all but dissipated and been replaced by a growing knot of sadness.

She smiled and looked away from him. "See, now you're just being mean."

"You did love me though, didn't you?"

She forced her gaze back onto his face. "That's the thing, I've never stopped loving you, Kenneth." She let him pull her into his arms. She nuzzled her face against his neck and bit her lip to hold back the hot flood of tears pressing against the corner of her eyes.

He held her and whispered into her ear, "I'm gonna keep on trying, you know."

"I suspect you wouldn't be *you* if you didn't," she said. "Just don't ever accuse me of giving you a sense of false hope. Because the truth is, Kenneth, as much as I still care about you and miss all that was good about what we had together, I'm not liable to change my mind. Not today. Not tomorrow. Not ever."

He looked as if he were about to speak, but a shake of her head silenced him.

"Good-bye, love." She granted him a soft peck on the lips, after which she turned and walked alone to her car's driver's side.

She got in, adjusted her seat belt, and stuck the key in the ignition. But before she drove away, she heard the rattling buzz of her cell phone again. Sure enough, when she peeked at her cell's blue display window, she again spotted his number. "Yes," she said, letting some of her exasperation with his antics seep into her voice.

"Forgive me," Kenneth said. "I had to say this one last thing. I know it's a Sunday and all, but I swear, girl, if you don't look just as good going as you do coming."

CHAPTER 11

Closing the book on the fairy tale, the one with the happily-ever-after ending, the one she'd once longed to live out with Kenneth, lent her an odd sense of relief. It still hurt. She still missed him. A part of her would always love him. But now that she knew for sure it was finally over, she felt a sense of freedom . . . at least in some respects.

The argument with Javiel still weighed heavily on one corner of her mind. Even though she'd played an active role in the nastiness that had transpired between them and even though she couldn't say with any certainty if reconciliation was what she really wanted, she'd fully expected him to make the first move toward such. But Sunday rolled into Monday without him either calling or showing up on her doorstep, looking contrite and seeking forgiveness. Was this her convenient out? Her no-fuss ticket to freedom? Did she dare jump at the opportunity and put herself at risk for being alone again?

She might have spend more time pondering those questions and others in earnest had it not been for her morning drive past Wally's Cool Cuts. A single glance toward the establishment was all it took to jump-start the craving she had yet to acknowledge. In an instant her mind was off and racing backward, like a fast-spinning, old-fashioned movie projector. Several dark and grainy images of Dante flashed before her in quick succession and the flood of pleasure she'd felt when his fingers first landed upon her scalp returned.

She tugged at the hair on the back of her neck and silently mouthed the word, *Damn!* Not even a week had passed since she'd last seen him. She hardly needed another haircut and calling him about one would only make her look like an idiot and a fool, if not a stalker. She banished the thought and chided herself for even going there.

But the longing wouldn't leave. She felt it again on her drive back home that Monday evening. As soon as her gaze fell upon the barbershop, she felt drawn toward it. She pictured a smiling Dante standing by the shampoo bowl in the back, cradling a huge bottle of his Big Mama's homemade shampoo in one hand and a big-ass magnet of some sort in the other.

Come Tuesday morning the itch . . . the pull . . . the distraction was such that she found herself slamming on the brakes to keep from rear-ending the car ahead of her. *Get a grip, girl,* she kept telling herself. *Whatever this feeling is, it's anything but normal.*

In an effort to lessen the chances of encountering the out-of-control sensation again, she chose a different route on her way home—one that took ten minutes longer and required her to drive several miles out of the way. Thinking she'd hit upon a workable solution, she took the longer route to work the following morning . . . only to find herself sitting in her parked car in front of the Wally's Cool Cuts parking lot by midafternoon.

She hadn't planned it. But as luck or fate would have it, she'd darted out of her house that morning without first grabbing the stack of important papers she'd deposited on the kitchen table the night before. While she'd managed to drive back home and collect the paperwork, without incident, on her return she'd slipped up and headed back down her old route instead of turning off on her new detour.

She contemplated mashing her foot against the accelerator and whizzing by the establishment without looking. But in the end, not only did she look, she slowed down, pulled over, and parked right outside the barbershop.

"Okay, I'm here. So what now?" she said aloud and feeling as crazy as she knew she probably looked sitting alone in her car, mumbling to herself.

Though it took everything in her, getting out of the vehicle and going into the shop was an urge she somehow suppressed. Instead, with trembling hands, she opened her purse, pulled out Dante's card, and dialed the number.

"Wally's Cool Cuts," a voice on the other end said.

"Yes, may I speak to Dante?" she said, hoping the person would tell her, "Sorry, but he's not here right now."

Instead, "A'ight. Hold on," is what she heard.

"Hey, this is Dante. How can I help you?"

"Hi, Dante, this is Aliesha. Aliesha Eaton. I stopped in last Wednesday and you gave me a haircut and a shampoo . . ."

"Oh yeah, sure, I remember. I tightened up your natural for you. Miz Professor, right? So, what's shaking? Don't tell me my Big Mama's shampoo didn't do proper by you and you're looking to collect on that get-triple-your-money-back guarantee?"

She laughed. "No, nothing like that. I was just calling to—"she squeezed her eyes shut as her mind raced to come up with something that didn't sound totally ridiculous "—umm, you know, to set up an appointment for next week."

"Yeah?" he said. "So whatcha thinking—next Wednesday, about this same time?"

"Yes, that would be perfect."

"Great, I'll make a note on my calendar. What else you need?"

"Well—" She paused and gave it a couple seconds' worth of thought. "You wouldn't happen to do eyebrows, would you?"

"Sure, I did a couple of my Cali clients on a fairly regular basis. But I'm strictly a tweezers guy kind of guy—no razors and no wax."

"Oh, that's fine," Aliesha said. "I prefer tweezers actually."

"Yeah?" he said. "You want me to do them now? I mean, seeing as you're already here and all."

Aliesha's closed eyes suddenly snapped open. She bent her head over the steering wheel and peered toward the barbershop's large, tinted storefront window. Behind the darkened glass, she spotted Dante gazing back at her. When he waved and smiled, she momentarily closed her eyes again to keep from turning the key in the ignition, yanking the car into reverse, and peeling out of the lot as fast as she could.

"I guess I look pretty silly, huh?" Instead of retreating, she'd made herself get out of the car and join him on the sidewalk in front of the shop.

Good Lord, could the man have possibly gotten better looking in the span of a week? Aliesha drank in the sight of him, pausing every few seconds to breathe and swallow, as if he were an extra rich, extra thick, extra chocolaty milk shake, handspun and with a cherry on top.

"Hey, everybody's got their own unique way of doing business," Dante said, managing somehow to keep the amusement in his voice to a mere smidgen.

Undaunted, Aliesha's wandering gaze tripped, fell, and rolled in the curly, soft-looking hairs she spotted peeking from the V-neck of his clean, white smock.

"You sure you don't want to come in?" he asked. "Right now, I'm prepping a guy for a shave. After I shave him and line him up, I'm free."

Aliesha peeled her roving eyes from the dark chest hairs

that sat atop the well-developed and even darker pecs. She glanced at her watch and said, "I really do have some things I need to take care of at school."

Dante raised a hand toward her face, then stopped and said, "May I?"

She nodded and managed not to tremble, moan, jump, or even blink as he eased a thumb across first her right eyebrow and then her left.

"They're not too bad," he said. "I'll be here until 9:00 if you want to swing by after you get off work this evening. Just give me a call."

"Okay," she said. "I may just do that."

Before she could summon enough spit to moisten her lips and tell him good-bye, he ran an appraising eye over her head and said, "Your hair still looks good."

"Thanks," she said, then added with a smile, "Or should that be thanks to you."

He grinned back at her and said, "Naw, if anything I'd say your genes and my Big Mama's shampoo deserve all of the credit and a fair share of the glory."

He'd smiled when he'd spotted Aliesha in her car outside the shop. Even though he'd silently hoped for her return, he hadn't expected to see her again so soon. Certainly he'd been flattered that she'd already begun making up excuses to stop by and see him. Most any man would have been pleased, even had he not been particularly interested in the woman who'd sought his company. It was one of those innate and peculiar features of his gender—the stuff that bound the male ego to the Y chromosome.

But when Dante had pocketed his phone and walked outside to join her on the sidewalk, he'd been taken aback by the hunger he'd seen in her eyes. He'd figured her much too smart and savvy and self-assured to venture there so soon. The intensity had stirred within him a wild flurry of long-winged second-guesses.

While he felt confident in his previous assessment of her needs, he realized he'd yet to determine what exactly, outside of a haircut, she thought she wanted. Something quick and casual? An exciting diversion from the norm? Someone she could keep tucked away in the shadows on permanent standby? If so, she'd have to look elsewhere, is what he told himself.

He'd had his fill of occupying those kinds of empty and less-than-satisfying roles in the lives of women who thought themselves too beautiful, worldly, educated, financially independent, ambitious, married, or otherwise attached to openly partner themselves with a man of his common upbringing and less-than-prestigious station in life. He longed for something deeper, something more substantive, and when it came to Aliesha, he knew he'd never be content to settle for less. No, if she were destined to be his, it would be on his terms, which, at the moment, were all or none.

His conclusion wasn't that of a man driven by arrogance or selfishness, but one who'd tired of being kicked where it already hurt. Even so, when he'd drawn his fingers across Aliesha's eyebrows, he'd experienced the gentle wrench and tearing in his side and the opening of his chest again. *Damn, what is that?* he'd wondered. He'd never known his body to respond in quite that manner with any other woman.

Beneath the poker face she'd quickly donned, he knew she'd felt something, too. She couldn't hide the hunger—at least not from him. Rather than gloat over the fact, the realization had troubled and saddened him.

Desperation didn't become her. Not that kind, anyway. Most women he knew wore it well—so well you couldn't tell it wasn't a natural part of them—like high-priced and professionally styled wigs or weaves, like fake nails and false asses, like silicone-plumped lips and tits.

Dante knew from experience that if he and Aliesha weren't careful, her hunger would consume them both and leave them with nothing but ashes and sand upon which to build. That wasn't what he wanted. Nor was that what he intended to let happen.

When he'd reentered the shop, the first thing he'd noticed had been the cloud of disapproval darkening his boss's face. "All right now," Wally said. "Don't forget that's a paying customer. One misstep and you done fooled around and messed up your money and mine. Besides, I thought you'd been burned enough times to know better than to play with fire."

What Dante knew was that his boss wasn't the type to put up with a lot of foolishness from any of his employees. Still, he'd been unable to resist uttering a cool-tongued, "What makes you think I'm playing?"

Wally laughed and shook his head. "Yeah, and when she leaves your ass broke, busted, and in a corner somewhere crying the blues, don't say I didn't try to warn you."

Gerald looked up from the neck he'd been lining and said, "You know you can't tell these young niggas nothin', man. And this moody, quiet-ass nigga here? Hell, he the main somebody, always trying to read shit into stuff that ain't there."

On his way back to his post at the rear of the shop, a grinning Dante bobbed his head in Gerald's direction and said, "Is that it, G? I'm saying man, you ever thought that maybe, just maybe, I'm privy to a few things you ain't?"

Her concentration broken, Aliesha looked up from the student essays she'd been attempting to read. She stared across her desk at Tamara, who'd been checking the multiple-choice answers of the tests they'd been grading for the past hour. But for the last several minutes, Tamara had been carrying on about some unforgivable slight she'd suffered in the university's cafeteria earlier in the day.

"See, those folks don't know who they're messing with. For real, I am not the one. I came this close to acting a fool up in there."

In many ways, looking at Tamara was for Aliesha like gazing into a mirror. With their large, expressive, oval-shaped eyes; their high sculpted cheekbones; their wide mouths and full lips; their long, willowy limbs; and with them both owning skin the same impenetrable shade of black, the two shared enough of the same physical features to be members of the same biological family, "if not from the same tribe," as Aliesha's father would have certainly declared with an appreciative chuckle had he still been alive.

Even beyond the many surface similarities, Aliesha saw in Tamara a shadow image of her former self. A sensitive, sharp-tongued, quick-witted, and deceptively intelligent Black/woman/child, who, while eager to ask all of the wrong questions, was way too impatient to hear any of the right answers. Aliesha hated to think she'd never been anywhere near as talkative or openly opinionated and contrary as Tamara. Still, she also understood all too well that most of the hardheaded defiance and feistiness her young charge exhibited to the world served chiefly as a protective cover.

The ringing phone interrupted Tamara's rant. On picking up, Aliesha said, "Hello, this is Dr. Eaton. Oh hey. Uh-huh. Give me another ten minutes or so. I'm grading papers with Tamara right now. Okay, sounds good. I'll be sure to do that. Thanks."

On replacing the receiver, Aliesha said, "That was Dr. Wilbun. She just received the official go-ahead for that project I was telling you about. From what I understand, the money is pretty good and you'd more than benefit from the experience. In the next couple of days, you need to set up a time to—" Aliesha paused, glared, and said, "I would appreciate you not rolling your eyes while I'm speaking."

Tamara scrunched her brows and twisted her lips. "I'm sorry, but you know how I feel about Dr. Wilbun. The thought of having to work and report to her on a regular basis doesn't exactly fill me with glee."

"That's why working with her might be just the thing you need. Once you get to know her, you're likely to discover the two of you have a lot more in common than you might have ever guessed."

"*Psst*, I doubt it," Tamara said. "You ever sat in on one of her classes? They're like 80 to 90% male. And it's not hard to see why, being that she doesn't seem to have anything in her wardrobe besides short skirts and skin-tight, low-cut tops. Matter of fact, Dr. Wilbun's class is one of the few you can find every Black male jock, nerd, player, slimeball, and 'brother man down for the cause' type vying for a front row seat."

Determined neither to lose the battle nor encourage Tamara's silliness, Aliesha checked her desire to laugh and said, "As much as you complain about not being able to find a decent guy, sounds to me like Dr. Wilbun's class is the place you'd want to be."

"Right," Tamara said. "As if any of those guys drooling over and gawking at Dr. Wilbun would ever bother to look twice at a skinny, dark-skinned Black girl like me."

Aliesha recognized the truth and hurt embedded in Tamara's words, and rather than blow them off, she honored and acknowledged them with a moment of silence. While the two largely maintained a normal teacher–student relationship, oftentimes the dynamic between them resembled more that of a big sister–little sister.

"And whose loss is that?" she said. "Certainly not yours. Hopefully one day, both you and the young men in question will come to recognize that fact. But in the meantime, you've got one of two choices—you can either deal with it or make a conscious decision and deliberate commitment to work toward changing those kinds of attitudes."

Tamara rolled her eyes again. "Yeah, that's easy for you to say. You've already established your career, and you've got your own house, a nice car, and as far as I can tell, at least two fine men jocking you."

Aliesha felt her jawline harden. "I beg your pardon?"

"Come on now, Dr. Eaton, don't play," Tamara said. "I knew about your light-skin Hispanic friend, but that big, tall hunk of Hershey's chocolate I saw eyeballing you at the church this past Sunday. . . . Uh-huh, you've been keeping that brother on the DL. And for good reason, I'm sure, 'cause—"

"Okay, enough of that," Aliesha said. "Nope," she said, when Tamara tried to protest. "If you really think I'm going there with you, well, you are sadly mistaken."

After enjoying a few seconds of hearty laughter at Aliesha's expense, Tamara refocused on the test papers piled on her side of the desk. She was still there twenty minutes later when Monica barged into Aliesha's office unannounced, dressed more like a contestant on *America's Next Top Model* than a serious professor of history. Her appearance sent Tamara's large eyes spinning into yet another roll.

"Oh, I'm sorry," Monica said. "I thought you two would be finished by now. I'll just wait out—"

"No, that's all right," Tamara said. She jumped up, grabbed her things, and rushed for the door.

Before she could complete her exit, Monica seized her by the arm. "Hey, you need to call me or stop by my office next week so we can discuss the project."

"Yeah, yeah, I'll do that," Tamara said, as she squirmed from Monica's grasp and bolted from the office.

Monica dropped into the chair Tamara had vacated. "I don't get it," she said. "How come she doesn't like me?"

Aliesha didn't look up from the grade book in which she'd been jotting notes. "Who, Tamara? Kind of obvious, isn't it? She's jealous."

After an extended pause, Monica crossed her arms and legs and said, "So how come you're not? Jealous, I mean."

Aliesha shut her book, lifted her downcast eyes, and leaned forward wearing a smile. "Because unlike young Tamara, it just so happens I know my worth in the world."

Monica laughed. "See, that's what I like about you. Quiet as it's kept, you're an even bigger bitch than me."

Still smiling, Aliesha said, "Oh, is that why you were in such a big damn hurry to get over here? So you could call me all out my name?"

"No, heifer," Monica said. "I'm here to get the real scoop on the little dinner party you attended Saturday night."

Aliesha's grin slipped and she lowered her eyes again. "Shockingly enough, everything was great. If you really want to know the truth, it far exceeded my wildest—or should I say—my lowest expectations."

"So how come you and Javiel aren't speaking?"

She sighed and leaned back in her chair until it creaked. "He tell you that?"

"Girl, please. You know I get most of my good dirt second-hand. Jesus told me. So, what gives?"

"Nothing. We had an argument."

"The kind of argument that would drive a girl back into the arms of an old love?"

Aliesha shook her head. "Not this girl and most certainly not that particular lover. I told you, seeing and talking to Kenneth face-to-face on Sunday was cathartic. That's all out of my system now and I'm ready to move on to other things."

"Mmm-hmm, I hear you talking," Monica said.

They both laughed.

"And what about Javiel? Does this mean things between

you and him are on their way to getting tighter? Or has, in fact, this thing between the two of you run its course?"

"Good question," Aliesha said. "In all honesty, I really don't know. What's he telling Jesus?"

Monica's face suddenly turned somber. "You mean besides that he's head over heels in love and not sure he could live without you?"

CHAPTER 12

Aliesha pulled up to Javiel's house. Rather than steer her car into the empty drive, she parked on the street. She sat for a moment and studied the large first- and second-floor windows that lined the home's brick exterior. All were dark except for one. She knew if she exited the car and walked up to the window bearing the light she'd hear the hard-driving notes of Coltrane's "Impressions" or "Giant Steps." She knew if she peered past the windows' sheer curtains, she'd more than likely find Javiel in front of a paint-splashed canvas, a brush in one hand and a glass of bourbon not far from the other.

Since she'd never bothered to tell, and he'd never bothered to ask, Javiel had no way of knowing he was her rebound lover, the first man to pay her any real attention after Kenneth's careless mangling of her heart. She often thought about all of those days and nights she'd spent alone after their breakup. All sixteen months' worth. She remembered how much she'd longed just to be touched, just to be held, just to be on the receiving end of a smile from a man whose love for her she didn't doubt. Javiel had yet to stir within her what Kenneth could in a mere glance in her direction, but she couldn't deny having found a considerable amount of solace in his welcoming embrace, particularly on those nights when what she'd needed most was to be held.

She sighed, took out her phone, and pressed in a series of digits.

"Wally's Cool Cuts," answered a voice.

"Dante?" she said.

"Speaking," he said.

"This is Aliesha."

"Hey, you 'bout ready to head this way or are you outside already?"

"No," she said. "Actually, something unexpected came up and I'm not going to make it tonight."

"You sure?" he said. "How much extra time you need? 'Cause I don't mind waiting."

"No, that won't be necessary. I appreciate it, though."

"No problem," he said. "If you change your mind between now and next week, just give me a call."

"Sure thing," she said. "Thanks."

After she finished speaking with Dante, she pressed one of the numbers on her speed dial and braced herself for the sound of 'Trane's maddening rush that she knew would precede Javiel's "Hello." Once upon a time, she'd hoped her and Javiel's mutual love of music would lead them to a tighter bond. But her well-intentioned attempt to surprise him with front row seats at a show featuring the smooth sounds of jazz saxophonist Boney James had proven disastrous when no less than twenty minutes into the performance Javiel had pleaded illness and asked if they might leave early. Later he'd confessed to being something of a jazz purist, the type who mainly prefers the music of dead greats like Miles, Dizzy, Bird, and 'Trane.

In response to the hollow-sounding "Hello" she heard over the music blaring in the background, Aliesha replied, "Hey, it's me. You feel like talking?"

"If you want," Javiel said, sounding none-too-enthused about the prospect.

"I'm parked outside," she said. "Can I come in?"

"That's fine," he said.

She left her car and walked up to the house. She muttered her irritation at having to find and use the keys Javiel had only recently given her. He hadn't bothered to assist her entry by turning on the porch light or unlocking the front door.

The moment she stepped inside, the spitting and hissing notes of Coltrane's tenor sax circled her. She followed their slithering lead down the hallway to Javiel's studio. Upon her entrance into the sparsely furnished room, the blistering notes snaked up her legs, winding and constricting themselves along the way, like a den of miniature and potentially deadly water moccasins.

The first thing Aliesha's eyes settled upon was Javiel's stiff, slender back. Rather than acknowledge her presence, he kept swinging his brush against the canvas on the easel in front of him. The artwork, which just so happened to be a painting of Aliesha's own long, slender, naked back, was the next thing she noticed.

Even though the torso had no head or any identifying marks beyond the coca brown skin, she knew it belonged to her. In the five months she'd known him, Javiel had amassed quite a collection of her drawn and painted body parts—her hands, her feet, her mouth, an ear, an elbow, her breasts, her behind, even the smooth curves of her stomach . . .

While standing there, thinking about the artwork and feeling the unrelenting squeeze and wind of 'Trane's tenor, Aliesha suddenly felt queasy and faint. She pressed a hand to her throat and quickly moved to turn down the music.

Javiel stopped painting and looked at her. "There's another man, isn't there?"

More shocking than the question was the dark, handsome face it summoned to the forefront of Aliesha's boggled mind. *Dante?*

"At the church, I mean," Javiel said. He brought the

tumbler of bourbon to his lips. After a sip, he said, "That's why you don't want me to go, isn't it?"

"Javiel, there is no other man," Aliesha said. "Okay, look, it's like this. . . . There *was* someone else, emphasis on the word, *was*, okay? My relationship with Kenneth ended long before I met you. But he showed up at church this past Sunday. And before you ask, no, I didn't invite him. He was there to hear one of his grandkids, who performs with the youth choir, sing a solo. And yes, I knew he was coming, not only to service but to the class I lead as well. I just figured it would be uncomfortable, for everyone, if you showed up, too."

"And this guy—Kenneth—he's someone you still obviously have feelings for?"

"Javiel, give me a break, all right? It's complicated."

"No, Aliesha, it isn't." He finished his drink and slapped the empty tumbler on the small table beside him. "Either you do or you don't."

"So, tell me, did you just stop having feelings for the woman who broke your heart and had you holed up in the monastery?"

"That was a long time ago," he said. "Anyway, it's not the same. But wait, 'holed up in the monastery'? That sounds like some shit my mother would say. Is that what you two were gabbing about in the kitchen the other night? All of my past, failed love affairs?" Javiel turned and started applying paint to the canvas again.

All his past love affairs? Aliesha wondered just how many there'd been. Rather than ask, she threw up her hands. "Okay, fine. I do. I do still have feelings for him."

Javiel spun around. The anger reddening, prickling, and contorting the area between his chin and forehead made it looked as though he'd been stomped in the face a couple of times by someone wearing a pair of cleats. "Are you fucking kidding me?!" he shouted. "You're telling me, you've been hooking up with this guy since we started seeing one another?"

"If you're asking if I've been sleeping with him, the answer is no. Of course not."

"I'm saying, 'cause if he's the guy you wanna be with, I don't even know why you wasted your time or mine by coming here tonight."

"I'm here, Javiel, because I want to try and fix this. But apparently, you don't." She turned and started toward the door.

"Aliesha, Aliesha, wait!" he called out. When she finally stopped a foot or so from the threshold, he said, "Look, baby, I'm sorry. I just wish you would have come clean about all of this before now."

She walked back and said, "Javiel, I promise you, Kenneth is not a threat to us." She moved closer and slid her hand along the contours of his slumped shoulders. "There's no reason for you to be jealous or concerned with the possibility of me ever going back to him."

"Okay," he said, while still looking and sounding anything but convinced.

"No, baby, it's not okay," she said. She dragged herself over to the drop-cloth-covered sofa and flopped down with a sigh. "So here's the deal—the thing with me and Kenneth ended on a really bad note. He hurt me, not just emotionally—physically, too, one night in Vegas."

"I don't understand," Javiel said. "Are you saying he hit you?"

"Worse," she said. "We were making love one night when he tried to cut off my supply of oxygen."

Javiel tossed his brush aside, stood up, and said, "My God, Aliesha, are you saying this man tried to kill you?!"

Aliesha settled back against the couch and closed her eyes before reliving the details of the tragic night that had taken place nearly two years ago and left her with wounds that still had yet to heal.

CHAPTER 13

She'd accompanied Kenneth to Vegas, where he'd participated in a work-related seminar for his job as a portfolio manager. It hadn't been the first time she'd traveled with him. In the days prior to their becoming lovers, they'd spent a weekend together in Atlanta where they'd visited some of the historic civil rights sites, dined at a number of nice restaurants, and relaxed by the luxurious five-star hotel's poolside, while still opting to retire to their separate suites at night. Aliesha still had fond memories of the brief stay that had drawn them closer as a couple.

Had they spent the majority of their free time in Vegas the way they had in Atlanta—with each other and engaged in activities that barely warranted so much as a PG-13 rating—things just might have turned out differently. But Vegas had been another story, one filled with bright lights, plenty of fast-paced action, and a surprise ending laced in horror.

In some ways, the series of events reminded Aliesha of a bad movie remake of either *Frankenstein* or *The Fly*. She'd watched for hours as Kenneth had drank, gambled, and traded off-color jokes with his business associates, while slowly turning into someone she didn't recognize or particularly care for. Rather than share any of her disgruntlement and risk being labeled a party pooper, at a little past midnight, she'd kissed him on the cheek and said, " 'Night, sweetie. I'm going back to the room."

He'd said, "Hey, I'm right in the middle of a hand, babe. Give me a minute or two and I'll go up with you."

"No, don't let me spoil your fun," she'd said. "I'll be fine."

Instead of leaving well enough alone, Kenneth had insisted that one of his young cohorts see Aliesha safely to back to their room. Her assigned escort, a young, dapper, proper-talking brother who went by the nickname "Skip" and who'd been eyeballing Aliesha on the sly all night, commented on the elevator ride up that he would have never guessed her to be "Kenneth's type."

"His type? And what might that be?" she'd asked, hoping things weren't going where she thought they might.

"Well, you know," Skip had said. "With him being a former athlete and all, I figured you'd be a young, blond, cheerleader type."

Aliesha had glared at him and said, "Sorry to disappoint you."

Skip had shrugged and said, "I mean, either that or one of those gorgeous Latina babes you see dropping it like it's hot in all of the rap videos."

Uncertain of just how much of the nonsense spewing from Skip was truly his own and how much of it stemmed from the countless rounds of drinks he and the other fellas in his and Kenneth's party had consumed, Aliesha had decided to cut him some slack. But on arriving at the door to her room, Skip had shown his ass again when, on leaning against the doorjamb and leering at her, he'd said, "So, exactly how much do you charge, if you don't mind me asking?"

For a moment, she'd been so stunned she'd just stared at him with her mouth ajar. "Okay, let me get this straight. Did you just proposition me? Seriously, you think I'm some kind of call girl? And after basically telling me that

I'm not young, attractive, or hot enough to be with some-one like Kenneth, you still want to have sex with me?"

Skip had grinned and said, "Well, yeah. I mean, it's not like Kenneth ever has to know. Plus, I'm perfectly willing to give you double whatever he's paying."

"Double?" Aliesha had said with a smile while reaching into her purse and pulling out both her key card and her phone. "Well, Skip, let me school you on a little something," she'd said on opening the door and stepping inside. "Not in a million years would you ever be able to afford my pussy or my time." She'd flipped open her phone, pressed a button and placed it against her ear. "Furthermore, I just dialed Kenneth. And if you're still here when he picks up, I'm gonna start screaming. So, if you want me to forget we ever had this conversation, I'd advise you to get the hell away from my door."

A suddenly sober Skip had backed away with his hands raised, like a perp who'd just been apprehended but who was still on the lookout for the first opportunity to flee.

Aliesha might have told Kenneth about the incident later that same evening had he not stumbled into their room a few hours after Skip's departure and seemingly even drunker. "I lost all of my money and I need consoling," is what he'd told her on falling down beside her and drawing her against him.

When she'd tried wriggling away from the moist grasp of his clammy hands and the sour stench circling from his clothing and his breath, he'd pulled her back. "What? You don't want to console me?" he said.

She'd rolled over, kissed him on the forehead, and said, "I'd love to, but why not wait until tomorrow when you're sober and can remember more of it?"

He'd pulled up her nightshirt and seized her breasts. "I don't need to remember it," he'd said, while fondling her in a way that was a lot rougher than she generally enjoyed.

She'd brushed off his hands only to have him peer back

at her with a hurt expression. "What's wrong, baby? You're not upset that I didn't come back to the room with you— are you?"

"Of course not," she said.

"So, console me, why dontcha?" he'd said, doing her the small favor of wiping his face clean of the excess sweat and slobber before leaning over and pressing his face against her chest.

"Okay, okay," she said, going against what she knew to be her better judgment.

Given her knowledge that Kenneth was in the habit of using either a massage oil or a water-based substance on himself when he watched his skin flicks and in hopes of adequately preparing for, if not putting off, an experience she knew had all the makings of a long and unenjoyable one, she said, "Okay, babe, but listen, did you by any chance bring any lubricant?"

"Yeah, give me a second," he said.

Please, take all the damn time you need, is what she felt like telling him. While she waited for him to finish undressing and listened to him root around in his bag, she prayed he'd lose his erection and decide it wasn't worth the effort of trying to get it up again. But when he'd returned to the bed without a tube or a vial, and with his proudly towering, naked member covered in enough lubricant to fry a whole package of chicken wings, she quietly resigned herself to the awfulness of her fate.

In hopes of slowing him down, she caressed his face, massaged his shoulders, and kissed him tenderly on the lips. For a minute or so he'd lain back and let her direct most of the action. But the moment she'd moved her lips to his chest and a hand between his thighs, he'd groaned then whispered, "Roll over. I want it from the back."

It wasn't like they'd never assumed such a position, but something about the way he'd said it had immediately caused her whole body to grow stiff and tense. She'd pulled away and said, "Only if you promise to take your time and remember to be gentle."

He'd laughed and said, "You act like I don't know what I'm doing. Just because I've had a few drinks doesn't mean I've forgotten how to make love to you."

"I'm just saying, Kenneth, if you fool around back there and end up someplace you shouldn't, neither one of us is liable to be very happy."

"Aliesha, have I ever hurt you before?" he'd said. He'd drawn himself up in the bed. "I've always made you feel good, haven't I?" He'd thrown back the sheets, risen up on his knees, and extended his hand to her. "Now stop talking and come over here and finish consoling me."

She'd reluctantly scooted toward him on the mattress. On reaching him, she'd taken his hand and pulled herself up on her knees. She'd stared into his handsome face and allowed her thighs to settle against his.

He'd smiled and rubbed the small of her back before drawing her into a tighter embrace. "Do you trust me?" he'd asked.

"Of course I do," she'd said, turning her head away from the overpowering stench of the liquor on his breath. Even though her enthusiasm for what lay ahead was probably about where Miss Celie's had been on all those nights in *The Color Purple* when she'd been forced to lay up under Mister and wait on him to hurry up and finish "doing his business," Aliesha had turned and maneuvered her legs between his, but rather than lean forward on all fours, a position she despised, she'd inched backward and pressed her behind against him.

He'd cupped her breasts, in a manner that was much gentler than before, and pressed his lips to her shoulder. For a few brief seconds she'd all but forgotten about his extreme state of intoxication and actually felt a twinge of pleasure. She'd been reveling in the moment and pondering what she could do to extend it, when she'd heard him say, "I love you, Aliesha. I've never loved any woman more. You know that, don't you?"

She didn't, actually. It was the first time he'd ever used the "L" word in conjunction with what he felt for her. Why then and why there of all places? He'd "never loved any woman more," is what he'd said. She'd wondered then and after if that included his wife. And had any of it really counted for jack given his condition and altered state of consciousness.

On settling into a semiseated position and with his bent knees on either side of her, Kenneth had moved his hands to her hips and drawn her toward him. She'd ridden against him, felt him arch his back, and listened to him groan. She might have secretly smiled and taken pride in her ability to work him into a frenzy had she not wanted the act to be over and done with.

After a few minutes of praying he'd come sooner rather than later, she realized that despite his drunkenness, he was deliberately holding off on his climax until she reached hers. Typically she appreciated his chivalry and consideration, but not on that particular night. In hopes of speeding things along, she decided to do something she'd never felt compelled to do before with Kenneth—fake it.

She quickened her pace and slipped into a breathy pant to which he immediately responded with a "Is that good, baby? Are you almost there?"

She'd answered him with her best-forced moan, but to her surprise rather than rev up the action, like he usually did at that point, he'd stopped and pulled out. On moving one hand to her shoulder and the other over the curve of her pelvis and down between her legs, he'd said, "You like that, don't you?"

Umm, that would be a no, is what she'd had half a mind to tell him. Instead, she'd squirmed and kicked up the volume on yet another contrived moan. And right about then is when it had happened. The hand on her shoulder suddenly fell away and the next thing she knew, her neck was caught in a viselike squeeze between Kenneth's muscular bicep and forearm.

"Relax, baby," he said as she struggled against him. "This is supposed to enhance your pleasure."

Enhance her pleasure?! Was he kidding? Had he lost his ever-loving mind, she thought as she'd felt the pressure against her windpipe increase.

"Kenneth, stop, you're hurting me," she'd managed to whimper as she'd grown lightheaded and the darkened room had swung into a slow spin.

Then it had struck her: *This drunken fool is gonna accidentally kill me trying to duplicate some sick and twisted shit he saw in one of his nasty-ass skin flicks.*

Driven by fear and the overwhelming will to survive, she'd stopping struggling, dropped her forehead, and let her body fall limp. But as soon as she'd felt his grasp loosen, she'd fastened her mouth against his arm and bitten down as hard as she could.

He'd released her with a deafening howl. "Dammit, Aliesha! What the hell is wrong with you?!"

She'd swiveled around and slapped him hard, twice, before leaping off the bed and out of his reach. "Me?!" she sputtered. "You damn near break my neck and I'm the one with the problem?!"

He looked stunned. "Baby, I wasn't trying to hurt you. I must have done something wrong. Come back to bed and let me make it up to you." He reached for her.

"No, it's done, Kenneth. It's done," she'd repeated as she grabbed up her discarded clothing, covered herself, and started backing away.

"No, wait," he'd said, sounding on the verge of tears. "I can make it right, Babygirl. I can."

When he'd looked as if he were about to climb out of

bed and come after her, she'd flung a couple of pillows at him. "No, Kenneth, it's done. It's over. And there's nothing you could ever do to make it right again."

With that, she'd fled into the bathroom, locked the door behind her, stepped into the shower, and on turning on the water, cried until she couldn't cry anymore. The last time she could remember having wept that long and that hard was at her father's funeral.

CHAPTER 14

Aliesha thrust her hands into the hot, sudsy water filling the kitchen sink. She could have easily placed all of the dirty plates, pans, cups, glasses, and utensils into Javiel's dishwasher and made short work of it all. But manually washing dishes had always been one of her favorite chores. The submersion, the cleansing, the rinse, the quiet roaming of her thoughts throughout the task, she typically found it all incredibly therapeutic.

She'd barely started on the first dish when Javiel tapped her on the butt with his rolled-up newspaper. He kissed her neck and said, "I'm glad we made up."

She turned and dabbed a finger covered with soapsuds onto his nose. "After your performance last night, I am, too. Maybe we ought to fight more often."

His lips sought hers. A kiss, reminiscent of those they'd exchanged between the darkened walls of his studio, followed—one full of hunger, surrender, and snatches of Coltrane's "Afro Blue." If only they could discover the secret to wrapping themselves in the silky cover of such moments and making them last, perhaps then her discontent for who and what Javiel wasn't would finally wither and fade away.

"You do know I'd never hurt you like that," Javiel said after she'd finished sharing the horrible details of her trip to Vegas, a tale that had ended with her leaving for the airport while a nude and inebriated Kenneth lay passed out across the bed. Once upon a time she would have sworn on her mother's Bible and daddy's grave to Kenneth's inability to hurt her in such a manner. But experience had taught her differently.

Near the end of their kiss by the kitchen sink, Javiel slid his hand beneath the shirt she'd borrowed from him and caressed the length of one of her bare, lean thighs. "You sure you don't have any problems with my plans for this weekend?" he whispered into her ear. "I could try to break away early or else stop by your place late sometime Saturday night, if you'd like."

His uncle Rafael, Jesus's father, was on his way into town and in his honor, an all-guy weekend had been planned. On Friday night they'd scheduled dinner and drinks at the same sports bar where Aliesha had spent more hours than she cared to remember, picking over cold fries while praying she wouldn't topple over from boredom. On Saturday, their plans included driving out to a lake and spending the day fishing.

"No, don't worry about me. Just enjoy yourself," Aliesha said.

He gave her a parting peck on the lips. "Okay, I'm gonna go take a shower."

As he started up the stairs that led out of the kitchen, the phone rang. "Would you get that for me, babe?" he called out.

Wondering who might possibly be calling Javiel's place so early in the morning, she picked up and said, "Hello?"

"Ah, yes . . . Aliesha?" a woman's voice said. "This is Julia, Javiel's mother."

"Oh, Mrs. Perez. I mean Julia. How are you?"

"Very well, thank you. I'm sorry to call so early. It never crossed my mind that Javiel might have company. I hope I didn't interrupt anything."

Even though Aliesha knew they were all adults well beyond the age of consent and Julia's voice had been steeped in tease, it didn't keep her from feeling a twinge of embarrassment. "No, Javiel just stepped into the shower. Shall I have him call you back or would you like to leave a message for him?"

"Actually, I just came from the bakery and I was hoping to drop off a little something for him. Would you mind terribly if I left it with you?"

"You mean now?" Aliesha said. She looked down in panic at her exposed legs and skimpy attire. "At this very moment?"

"Yes," Julia said. "I just pulled into the drive. Don't worry, I won't keep you long."

"Okay," Aliesha said, while *Argh!* is what she thought. After hanging up, she hurried to the front door and looked out in time to see a casually dressed, sneaker-wearing Julia emerge from her car. She walked up to the front porch while juggling her purse, a small white bag, and a carrier upon which sat two large, white containers of what Aliesha assumed was coffee.

Aliesha struggled to maintain a pleasant expression as she held open the door and helped Julia with the items.

Acting as though she didn't see Aliesha's semistate of nakedness, Julia said, "Have the two of you eaten yet?"

"Yes, ma'am," Aliesha said with a pained smile.

"Well, I'll just leave these in the kitchen," Julia said.

Aliesha followed, frowning and tugging at Javiel's shirt, which seemed to be growing shorter with every passing second.

"My, isn't this impressive," Julia said. She nodded at the pans, utensils, and dishware Aliesha had yet to remove from atop the stove. "You fixed breakfast." She walked over and picked up a pan. "And what looks to be crepes, no less. My son must have really poured on the charm last night."

"I'm not sure if charm is exactly what I'd call it," Aliesha said, allowing a bit of irritation to seep into her voice. "And I'd be remiss if I didn't tell you that your son was actually the one who prepared breakfast this morning."

Julia laughed. "Yes, you are definitely my kind of girl."

"I hope you didn't come all the way out here this early in the morning just to bring Javiel breakfast," Aliesha said, no longer caring if she sounded rude or what Julia thought about her one way or the other.

Julia's bright smile stayed intact. "Not just breakfast, my dear. Beignets." She removed one of the pastries from the bag and found a clean saucer upon which to place it. "I attend an early morning yoga class on this side of town. Across the street from my class there's a fabulous bakery that makes these and other equally fattening and decadent treats. Every once in a while, I drop some off for Javiel before I head for home."

"I see," Aliesha said, accepting the saucer Julia offered her, but only buying so much of the bull that was being ladled out with the sweetest of smiles.

Julia locked eyes with Aliesha. "I'm sensing you're a bit upset with me, perhaps about some of the things I shared with you in private the other night. Either that or Javiel has succeeded in painting for you a horribly unflattering portrait of me."

Aliesha hesitated, wondering if this was the best time and place to pursue such a conversation. "To be honest, it's a bit of both," she said. After offering up a weak smile of her own, she looked down at the beignet, an act of deference she hoped would assure Julia that she had no intentions of going on the attack. "I mean, since you brought it up, Javiel has mentioned a few things that have made me wonder."

"Like? And about what?" Julia said prior to inviting herself to a seat at the breakfast table.

Aliesha looked up and unleashed her concerns in one

continuous but steady breath. "Namely, your lack of support for his artistic aspirations, which, from what I understand, has been the case since he was a child. The preference he says you and Mr. Perez show your daughters. And your own intense dislike of his dark-skinned, Puerto Rican grandmother."

Julia nodded but didn't appear surprised. She reached for one of the containers of coffee and popped the lid from the cup. While staring off into space and between sips of the steaming brew she said, "I had a brother, a gifted jazz musician whom I loved dearly but whom I watched waste away at a young age. He was nineteen and I was twelve when I saw him get hooked on dope and resigned to living in a perpetual state of misery. As far as I could tell, he was always broke, running from creditors and begging my parents to bail him out of some sort of financial bind. They always seemed to be at war, my parents and him. It seemed their biggest ongoing fight was his resistance to their demands for him to at least get a teaching certificate. Poor, poor Ernest. The only time he wasn't sad when was when he was somewhere with the horn in his mouth or a needle in his arm. He was twenty-three and I was sixteen when I found him slumped over in my parents' bathroom, dead from what I'd like to believe was an accidental overdose."

She paused and looked at Aliesha. "I've always seen a lot of Ernest in Javiel. So, yes, it's true. His father and I encouraged him to use his skills in a manner we thought would help him stay self-sufficient. And yes, at times, we may have been overzealous in doing so, which he, I'm sure, views as us having been unnecessarily hard on him."

"I didn't know," Aliesha said, gazing down at her bare legs and suddenly feeling a mixture of embarrassment and empathy. "Javiel never told me any of that."

"No, I don't suppose he would," Julia said. "And as far as his dear old abuela, yes, it's true, I thought her a horrid woman, but trust me, the quantity of melanin in her skin had nothing to do with my ill regard of her. If anything, it was just the opposite."

"The opposite?" Aliesha said. "I'm not sure I understand."

Julia sighed and said, "The real irony of Javiel accusing his father and me of showing skin tone biases is that his beloved grandmother was guilty of exactly that. The fairer skinned children, like Javiel's cousin Jesus and my own daughters, she treated like royalty. Most of the brown-skinned ones, like Javiel, received decidedly second-rate treatment. And the poor dark-skinned ones, the ones who looked most like her, mind you, she barely wanted around. The only reason Javiel got better treatment was because his father had been her precious firstborn and only son. But she was constantly advising me to keep Javiel's hair cut short so the kink wouldn't show as much or else begging for us to send him to her during the summer months because she thought by keeping him out of the Southern heat, she could keep his skin from permanently darkening. And to think, to this day, he still worships that horrid woman!" Julia said, swinging her hand as if swatting away a fly and knocking over her coffee cup in the process.

Aliesha rushed to Julia's aid with a wet dishtowel. "I'm sorry," she said while wiping up the spilled coffee. "I didn't mean to upset you."

"I'm not angry with you, Aliesha," Julia said. She motioned for Aliesha to sit. "I'm simply trying to get you to see that Javiel has his own odd way of looking at things. Quite often, there's a whole lot more beyond his sometimes narrow view of the truth."

Still not certain how much credence to assign Julia's version of the truth, but not wanting to bypass an opportunity to dig further, Aliesha said, "Might that also include his stint in the monastery and the woman who you allege help put him there?"

Julia stopped wiping the table with the cloth she'd taken from Aliesha and said, "Has he talked to you about Evelyn?"

"Not really."

A glaze formed over Julia's eyes. "Oh, so you probably don't know that he very much wanted to marry this girl?"

Aliesha shook her head.

"Or how after she dumped him and gave him back his ring is when he decided that living out his days as a monk had a certain appeal."

Aliesha shook her head again.

"Well, you might want to ask him. And when you do, don't forget to have him tell you how shortly after he made his decision to enter the monastery, that same girl turned up missing and later was found in the woods . . . dead."

CHAPTER 15

Aliesha tried unsuccessfully to get Julia to stay and fill in some of the ominous holes in the story she'd shared. Julia insisted she'd already said too much. She advised Aliesha to take up the matter with Javiel.

After Julia's hurried departure, Aliesha immediately went upstairs and told Javiel of his mother's visit. But she kept the more disturbing details of their conversation to herself. She still wasn't sure what to make of the beautiful and charming Julia Malveau Perez. Had she been exaggerating? Outright lying? And if she had been telling the truth, whom exactly was she aiming to protect?

I need time to think is what Aliesha kept telling herself. Her rationale, though a weak one, allowed her to feel less guilt about her hesitancy to take up the subject with Javiel. Had she been brave enough to confront the truth, she would have confessed that the kernel of fear Julia had been out to sow had not only taken root but, like the leafy Southern vine known as kudzu, had already begun to sprawl in a number of different directions. In the five months they'd been together, why hadn't Javiel bothered to tell her about Evelyn? Wouldn't her having come clean about Kenneth the other night presented him with the perfect opportunity to have done likewise about his old flame and their obviously troubled relationship? Was he hiding some horrible secret? Had he anything at all to do with this woman's death?

As her anxiety grew, so too did her reasons for not asking Javiel about the matter. If Javiel had a sinister side, surely it would have shown itself by now. Besides, they'd just kissed and made up. She'd even made a point of inviting him to her church on Sunday. Interrogating him about some craziness his mama had dished out behind his back might lead to another round of hurtful words that, like the claws of a feline, neither would be able to fully retract. Perhaps waiting until he'd returned from his weekend outing with the boys would be a better time.

When they'd spoken by phone on Thursday and again that Friday evening, she'd been careful not to leak her growing concerns. But on retiring to her bed later that Friday night, she'd lain awake longer than usual, worrying about all of the things Julia had told her, along with all of those things Javiel still hadn't. Fortunately, after an hour or so, the weariness of the day, if not the entire week, came crashing down around her. With the shades momentarily drawn on her conscious concerns, she sank into the dark comfort of sleep and almost immediately began to dream about her mother.

Strangely enough, during those hours of the day when Aliesha was fully alert and wide awake, her memories of Connie, the woman she'd once called "Mama," were few. Only when she closed her eyes and drifted into the shadow-encased world of slumber did the sound of her mother's voice beckon her. Only then could she catch an extended glimpse of her mother's smile, feel her tight and loving embrace, breathe deeply of her intoxicating scent, and get a sense of the joy she'd contributed to the life of the woman whose stint in the land of the living had been all too brief.

But on that particular night, it wasn't long before the soothing, angelic visions of her mother were overrun by a more frightening sequence of images and scenes. Rather than one straight, cohesive narrative, the nightmare played itself out in a frame-by-frame series of near-blinding flash-backs.

In the first clip, she sees herself as a young child, one tossing and turning in her bed as she fights to block out the sounds of the adult strife she hears in the room at the opposite end of the hall. The woman's voice sounds muf-fled, pleading, and can only be detected in intermittent sound bytes while the man's voice is loud and accusing, and rushes forth in more frequent, rapid-fire intervals, like the repeated bursts from an automatic weapon. The voices spill out onto the second-floor landing and stop in front of Aliesha's bedroom where they increase in volume and are soon accompanied by slaps, thuds, thumps against the wall, and the unmistakable sound of a woman weeping.

Aliesha watches as the younger version of herself tosses off the covers, leaps from her bed, pushes open the door, and yells, "Stop it, Uncle Frank! You're hurting her."

Her uncle Frank, his eyes swimming in a murky sea of red and his face swollen like a pus-filled burn, turns and snarls, "Get your little, narrow, black behind back in that bed . . . unless you're aiming to get a taste of some of this, too!"

"Leave the child alone, Frank. Leave her be," her aunt Mildred pleas before making the mistake of grabbing her husband by the arm.

Frank snatches his arm away and, like a demented, hammer-toting John Henry, swings it back as hard as he can in the direction of Mildred's head.

Aliesha hears both screams and the sickening sound a woman's barely hundred-pound body makes when it tum-bles down a flight of stairs.

The scene fades to black, and in the next clip, the angry face of Aleisha's father fills the frame. "How come you didn't tell me this shit had been goin' on?!" he shouts.

"Don't you know your auntie is laying up in the hospital with a concussion, a broken wrist, and a dislocated jaw? And all of those bruises I saw on her shoulders and arms lets me know this is hardly the first time this shit has happened!"

A pigtailed Aliesha stops sniffing and wiping her eyes long enough to choke out, "I was afraid, Daddy. Uncle Frank told me what goes on in his house stays in his house. And you're always telling me to mind Uncle Frank. I didn't want to get in trouble."

Her father pulls her into his arms. "I'm sorry, baby. You don't ever have to be afraid. Hear me? You can always come to me, Aliesha. I'm always gonna be here to protect you, Miz Babygirl. Even after I'm dead and buried six feet under, I'm always gonna be here to protect you. Don't you ever doubt it. You don't ever have to be afraid."

The scene fades as a nodding and tearful Aliesha mouths the words, "Yes, sir," before snuggling deeper into her father's strong, tight embrace.

In the final clip, a number of men can be seen seated around a large dining room table. A sparkling chandelier dances and sways over their heads. A pajama-clad Aliesha stands beneath the arch of the room's curved entrance. She recognizes the men as her uncles—the blood brothers and brothers-in-law of her Aunt Mildred and her own deceased mother, Connie. Her father, William, isn't seated with the group, but his presence is evident in the heavy footsteps creaking against the second story's worn floorboards and echoing above the seated men's heads.

Josiah, Aliesha's favorite uncle and the youngest of the men present, says, "So, what we gonna do?"

"Whatcha mean, we? We ain't gone do a damn thing. It ain't our place," Aliesha's uncle Bruce growls. Her uncle Bruce is an uncle by marriage and one of Aliesha's least favorite relatives. He owns a butcher shop and often smells as rank as the meat he handles. He is also a big man, who likes to brag on how he has to use the scales at his shop to weigh himself. But more than anything, Aliesha hates the way the yellowish tint of his rubbery skin reminds her of boiled squash, cooked with chopped onions, the one vegetable dish that never fails to make her gag.

Her uncle Bruce removes the cigar jutting from the corner of his mouth before he finishes speaking his piece. "This here is between Frank and Mildred. And she said she didn't want to press no charges."

"Maybe we ought to see if we can't get them to agree to go see Pastor Lawrence for some counseling," Aliesha's uncle Alfred says. Alfred is a respected elder at the church they all attend. His role has long been to lead the family in prayer at weddings, christenings, funerals, and whenever they gather for the holidays. "After all," Alfred continues, "Frank didn't start all this drinking and carrying on until he lost his job."

Howard, the eldest brother, nods and says, "You're right. And that's probably best. But prior to that, I think we ought to sit them both down and give them a real good talking to."

Aliesha looks up as the footsteps above her uncles' heads suddenly fall silent and the chandelier stops shimmying.

Josiah, who's been twitching and squirming in his seat, finally says, "That's it, huh? That's the best y'all can come up with?"

"Why?" Scottie, another uncle by way of marriage, pipes up. "You got something better in mind?"

Aliesha cocks her head and listens as her father makes his way down the stairs.

"Yeah, I do," a red-faced Josiah sputters. "I say we find him, drag him back here, and whup his ass. Some low-life piece of shit damn near kills one of the women in our family and all y'all niggas wanna do is sit around and talk? To hell with that."

William enters the room. Swinging from each of his closed fists are fat, fully stuffed, dark green plastic bags. He calmly walks over to the dining room table and tosses the bags onto the center of it. "Aliesha," he says. "Go and get me another bag."

Not wanting to miss anything, Aliesha hurries to do what she's been told.

"Man, what the hell you call yourself doing?" she hears her uncle Scottie ask.

"What the hell it look like?" her father says. "I'm packing up all of Frank's shit. Y'all can sit here and analyze the situation until the wee hours of the morning if you want to. But after all is said and done, brother man can't stay here no more."

"See, there you go!" Josiah shouts. Aliesha reenters the room just in time to see her favorite uncle jump up with a big boyish grin and slap his hands against the table. "That's what I'm talking about!"

"Who the hell are y'all to try and run a man out his own house?" Uncle Bruce says with his boiled squash and chopped onion face all twisted up every which-a-way.

"Settle down," Uncle Howard says. "I think we're all capable of discussing this civilly and without any of us getting all bent out of shape."

William takes the bag Aliesha hands him and laughs. "Yeah, you right. 'Cause the only somebody who's really bent out of shape behind any of this is poor Mildred. But I don't guess she counts for all that much, huh?"

Howard pushes back his seat and stands up. "What? You accusing me of not caring? That's my little sister you're talking about, man. What gives you the right—"

"What gives me the right?!" William bellows. "You see this child?! Her presence here gives me the right. Long as she's here, Frank can't be."

"I don't mean no harm," Bruce says, squinting in Aliesha's

direction. "But who's to say little Miz Babygirl gotta be here anyway? It ain't always good for a man to have children in his house that ain't his own blood."

"First of all," Alfred says in a voice that is louder than usual, but still calmer than the others. "This isn't Frank's house. It's Mildred's, legally passed down to her and in full accordance with the dying wishes of both our parents. Secondly, Aliesha stays. That's what Connie, her mother and our sister, would have wanted. Connie always hated the fact that Mildred couldn't have children of her own. Besides, at this point, taking Aliesha away from Mildred would not only be cruel to the both of them, it would probably put Mildred that much closer to an early grave."

"Exactly," Josiah says. "So, it's settled. Frank's ass has got to go, whether peacefully or by force. Those are his only two choices."

"That's not how we do things in this family," Howard says. He resumes his seat and shoves aside a pair of men's underwear that has spilled from the contents of the garbage bag in front of him. "I suggest we take a vote. Okay, so, by a show of hands—"

"Damn all that, man," William says. "Haven't you been listening? All right, I tell you what, y'all let Frank come on back. But the next time he lays his hands on Mildred, I'm gonna have to kill him, plain and simple. And God forbid if he should lay a hand on this child . . . 'Cause if that should happen, Lord knows." William extends his arm and sweeps his hand in a wide circle around the room. "Lord knows, excluding Josiah, I'm gonna have to come and gut every last one of y'all."

"Why you got to go and take it there?" Scottie says. "Ain't no call for all of that. Frank'll be all right and everything will be back to normal soon as he finds himself another job. Ain't like none of us ain't never been there before."

"Been where?" William says. "So low you had you raise yourself up by knocking some woman down? Naw, not me.

I ain't never been that low. 'Sides, I offered Frank a job. But just like all the rest of y'all siddity Negroes he thinks he's too good to stand out in the sun all day, stanking and sweating and getting paint and dirt on his hands and beneath his pretty little nails. Ain't that right?"

"See, there you go again. Ain't nobody said all of that," Scottie says, sounding genuinely offended.

Bruce laughs and says, "Don't pay Midnight here no mind."

Aliesha gasps at her uncle Bruce's daring to make an open reference to the nickname she knows he, Scottie, and a few of the others in her family called her father behind his back.

"You know how them country boys are. Always wanna make shit personal, that ain't. Well, take it from somebody who knows, boy, it's a world of difference between slaughtering a farm-raised hog and a grown-ass man who's been reared up on the South Side of Chicago, much less four of them bloods, like you standing up here threatening to do. You sure you got them kinda balls?"

William grins and shoves his right hand into his pants pocket. "You think I don't? Well, try me then. And see if your big, fat, greasy, yella throat ain't the first one I slit."

That's when all hell breaks loose. Uncle Bruce bolts from his seat, turning over the dining room table in the process. Aliesha's father pushes her out of the way before snatching up a dining room chair and raising it over his head. In the bloody, knock-down, drag-out that ensues, the chandelier breaks away from the ceiling, crashes to the floor, and shatters into a million little pieces.

Rather than flicker and begin to fade, the scene's lighting and the sounds of violence grew harsher and increased in intensity. Feeling herself on the brink of being rendered completely deaf and blind, Aliesha woke herself up screaming.

CHAPTER 16

After a few sips of coffee that next morning, Aliesha reached for the phone and punched in a number. The phone rang seven or eight times before it fell silent and a groggy voice said, "Hello?"

"Hey," Aliesha said. "Sorry to wake you, but I need you to go somewhere with me this morning."

"Damn, girl!" Monica said. "It's barely six AM and on a Saturday, no less. Is something wrong?"

"I don't know. Possibly. Can you be ready in a couple of hours?"

"Yeah, I'm sure I can. But what—"

"I'll fill you in later," Aliesha said. "I'll be there to pick you up around eight."

Two hours later, Monica answered the door of her cute little bungalow dressed in a conservative pair of sandals, a dark pair of jeans, and a screen print T-shirt, which while clingy didn't reveal any of her cleavage or midriff. "Is this okay?" she said, in reference to her outfit as she collected her purse and her keys.

"Sure, you look fine," Aliesha said.

"Well, I wasn't sure about the occasion. So what gives? You need me to help you bail somebody out of jail? Help you dig a ditch and get rid of a body or what?"

Aliesha nodded and said, "Umm, definitely more the latter than the former."

Monica stopped in midstep. "Please tell me this is not another one of those church things. For real, Aliesha, I am in no mood this morning to be spreading manure or pulling weeds out of sister so-and-so's garden or helping build brother 'down-and-out' and his thirteen badass kids a place to call home."

Already off the porch and halfway up the walk, Aliesha turned and grinned. "You're going straight to hell. You know that, don't you?"

"Oh yeah, and with bells on!" Monica said before breaking into a laugh and resuming her trek toward Aliesha's car.

Aliesha waited until she had the vehicle in drive before she said, "I had the dream again. The one I told you about before."

"Oh, you mean the one with your dad and all of your uncles fighting over how to handle the situation with your auntie?"

Aliesha nodded. Monica was the only person she'd ever confided in about the nightmare or the depths of her feelings for Kenneth. The couple's three-month relationship had spiraled to an end before Aliesha had been afforded the opportunity to introduce the two. However, over the course of time, she'd shared with her girlfriend all of the pertinent and ugly details, including the awful encounter in Vegas. Monica knew that the last time Aliesha had experienced the nightmare had been that first night after her tearful return home without Kenneth.

"So, you think maybe the dream is somehow tied to your most recent interaction with Kenneth? Come on, girl, 'fess up now. You sure you and dude didn't get together after church for a little boot-knocking for old times' sake?"

She shook her head. "Sorry to burst your nasty little

bubble, but nope, nothing like that ever even came close to happening. To tell you the truth, I think this particular dream has more to do with my current relationship with Javiel."

"What?!" Monica said. "Girl, stop. Javiel is crazy about you."

"Yeah," Aliesha said. "And for all it's worth, so was Kenneth."

"Okay, besides a messed-up dream about something that happened more than twenty years ago and that in no way, shape, or form involved Javiel, what could possibly make you believe he'd ever want to do you any *physical* harm? And do note that I deliberately left off mental and emotional damage because I'm starting to believe that your ass really is the one who's got a few screws loose."

"Remember all of that crap I told you Javiel's mom unloaded on me the other day? About how some woman named Evelyn was responsible for Javiel's three-year stay in the monastery? And how he'd intended to marry this woman, but she'd dumped him. And how shortly thereafter, she'd turned up dead?"

"Yeah, yeah, yeah," Monica said. She took a moment to process the information and then frowned. "So what are you suggesting exactly? That Javiel had something to do with this woman's death?"

Aliesha looked at her friend and in a flat voice said, "That's what I need you to help me figure out."

Monica swallowed hard and said, "Okay, okay, and we're supposed to do that how?"

Aliesha turned her eyes back onto the road. "Just wait. I'll show you."

Obviously none-too-thrilled about the Saturday morning mission for which she'd been recruited, Monica remained uncharacteristically quiet for the remainder of the drive.

But she kept her reservations to herself until Aliesha pulled up to Javiel's house and parked in front of his garage. Before Aliesha could get out, Monica grabbed her and said, "Wait, you've got a key, right? 'Cause if breaking and entering is what you've got in mind, you're on your own."

"Yes, I have a key," Aliesha said. She jiggled the full key ring she kept in her purse, then turned and opened the car door, only to have Monica grab her again.

"Okay, good. But hold up. Listen, if what you're about to show me involves skulls, bones, bloodstained clothing, a body in the freezer, or any combination of the aforementioned, I suggest you call the Riverton Police Department and let them handle it. Barring that, why not call Pat? Isn't that kind of crap sort of like her area of expertise?"

"Would you just come on," Aliesha said. "All I want is your take on something that strikes me as peculiar."

After leading her muttering friend to the house, Aliesha unlocked both the security and the wooden doors, before stepping over to the keypad and typing in the numbers that disarmed the alarm. Monica said, "Damn, a key and a code? This boy must really be feeling you. Mine, on the other hand, just barely lets me spend the night."

"As much lip as you give him, I'm not surprised," Aliesha said.

"*Umph*, I don't know what you're talking about. My lips are what won him over in the first place."

When Aliesha cut her eyes and shook her head, Monica said, "Oh, I know—to hell with bells on, right?"

They laughed, entered the house, and turned down the hall that led to Javiel's studio. "Have you seen the room where Javiel does his work?" Aliesha asked.

Monica shook her head. "Nope. Can't say that I have."

Aliesha pushed open the door. Her eyes widened at the sight of the artwork she'd thought she'd have to pull from the various stacks of unhung canvases that rested on the floor and leaned against the studio's walls. Instead, as if anticipating her arrival, each individual painting had been neatly arranged, according to size, around and atop the drop cloth–covered sofa.

"What do you make of that?" she asked.

Monica pulled her glasses from her bag and walked over for a closer inspection. "What should I make of it? Aren't artists known for painting women's bodies?"

"That's not just any woman," Aliesha said. "Or even a series of different women. It's me, me, and only me." She walked over, folded her arms across her chest, and peered down at the work.

"Huh, I guess it is," Monica said. "Being as I've never seen you butt-ass naked, it's kind of hard to tell." She picked up the portrait of Aliesha's backside, brought it closer to her face, and said, "Damn, girl, is that a birthmark or what?"

Aliesha dropped her arms and said, "Would you stop kidding around. Doesn't any of this strike you as strange?"

"What? That your man likes painting you?" Monica smirked. "I would think you'd be flattered."

"Maybe I would if I didn't feel like I was being dissected. Why does he insist on painting me like this?" Aliesha paced in front of the odd display, like an annoyed art teacher or critic. "A little piece here and a little piece there? And if you'll notice, there's not a single painting of my head in this entire collection."

Monica scrunched her brow and gazed over the array of canvases resting on and against the sofa. "Maybe he just hasn't gotten around to that yet. Maybe this is part of some special series he's working on. . . ."

"Yeah, maybe," Aliesha said, seizing the painting of her backside from Monica and returning it to the empty spot from which it had been removed. "And maybe . . . just maybe I need to find out if this woman, Evelyn, was missing any essential body parts when she turned up dead in the woods."

In a more serious and measured tone, Monica said, "Okay, seeing that you've pretty much concluded that Javiel is some kind of mild-mannered, paint-brush-wielding ax murderer, before you alert the FBI, why not let me see what I can pull from Jesus? Having three separate accounts can't hurt and might get us that much closer to the truth."

Aliesha pondered the suggestion before she sighed and said, "Okay. You're probably right. But when you bring up the subject with Jesus, try to do it without disclosing too much about what we already know."

Monica laughed and, while stuffing her glasses into her bag, said, "I can't believe I'm standing here letting you talk me into taking part in some ole *Nancy Drew, Murder, She Wrote* type of bullshit. I knew I shouldn't have answered the phone this morning."

She hadn't intended to call him. She'd ventured into the second bedroom she primarily used for storage in search of a misplaced reference book. Her "junk room," as she labeled it, was full of cast-off furniture, a few suitcases, partially taped-up boxes of books, knickknacks, old clothes, and other seldom used and similarly discarded items.

After a careful zigzag across the room, she'd located the book on one of the two large and cluttered bookshelves. Instead of leaving the room the way she'd come in, she'd set out on a different path, one that led her to bump against a midsized, gray suitcase. On pausing to rub the sore spot just below her knee, she immediately recognized the offending suitcase as one of a pair she'd taken on her trip to Vegas with Kenneth. Upon her return, she'd been so distraught, she'd tossed the bag into the room without ever bothering to unpack it. Since that time, the luggage and all of its contents had sat where Aliesha had left it, deliberately abandoned and forgotten.

She clutched the book to her chest and stared down at the bag. A part of her felt inclined to kick it as hard as she could. Another part of her wanted to hug it as tightly as she was hugging the book. Finally, she knelt, placed the book on the floor, and reached out for the bag's zipper.

The first thing she spotted when she raised the flap was one of Kenneth's white T-shirts. She'd been in the habit of lounging and sleeping in them when they'd been together. Thinking it might still contain a whiff of him, she picked up the cotton jersey and brought it to her face. Instead of Kenneth, what greeted her nostrils was a soft, subtle blend of the scent the two of them had created together.

The discovery forced her eyes shut. She shook her head to keep the tears at bay. When she felt composed enough to look again, she noticed the book . . . not the academic text she'd set aside . . . but rather the novel Kenneth had given her as a gift, *Their Eyes Were Watching God*. Aliesha pulled the accompanying card from between the pages of the book, opened it, and reread Kenneth's scribbling. *"If you'll be my Janie, I promise to be your Tea Cake."*

A sad smile tugged upward on the corners of her lips. The book was one she'd never read, but she'd heard so much about it and its author, Zora Neale Hurston, a Black, female anthropologist, like herself, she almost felt as if she had.

She remembered telling Kenneth, "Thanks," after he'd first presented her with the book and she'd finished reading the card's inscription. "But just so we're clear, at some point, doesn't Tea Cake get bitten by a rabid dog and try to kill Janie?"

She flipped through the pages of the book, only to find herself muttering, "Damn you, Kenneth." If only she could summon something akin to outright hate for him, maybe then the thought of having to live without him wouldn't hurt so much. By the same token, she knew she'd feel so much more at ease if only she could piece together a small portion of what she'd felt for Kenneth and deposit it in the gaps, crevices, and flat empty spaces that loomed between her and Javiel. In spite of his shortcomings, his mother's persistent warnings, and even her own nagging doubts and suspicions, she still desperately wanted to love him.

Maybe Monica was right. Maybe she was getting worked up over nothing. Maybe after she talked to Javiel and got him to open up about "Evelyn," like she'd finally done about Kenneth, maybe then they could clear away some of the stagnant air between them and move forward. But before she could draw any real comfort from the thought, another one occurred to her, one so disturbing she jumped up and knocked over the contents of a nearby box as she scrambled about the messy room in search of the phone.

"My, this is quite the surprise," Kenneth said on answering.

Aliesha eased herself back onto the floor and next to the still-opened suitcase. Somewhere in the background, she heard the sweet sound of Kem's voice. The song, "I Can't Stop Loving You," was one that she had introduced to Kenneth. Hearing it brought back a flood of warm memories and made her smile.

"I hope it isn't inconvenient," she said. "Do you have a minute?"

"For you?" he said. "Always."

She reached into the bag and stroked his old T-shirt. "I need a favor," she said.

"Sure, Miz Babygirl. What can I help you with?"

"You weren't by any chance planning on attending services at Garden View tomorrow, were you?"

"No, I wasn't. But I certainly can if—"

"No! No!" Aliesha said. "Just the opposite. I'd really appreciate it if tomorrow, you'd stay as far away from Garden View as possible."

He laughed. "Okay, any particular reason?"

She hesitated, then said, "Remember the guy I told you I was dating? He's planning on visiting tomorrow and I'm not so sure bumping into you is liable to go over too well."

"I see. You obviously told him about Vegas."

"Yeah, just a few days ago. He really hasn't had a chance to process it all yet."

"Okay, if it helps ease your mind, I can assure you, tomorrow I will make a point of being somewhere other than Garden View."

She picked up the Hurston novel and ran her fingers over the title. "Thanks, Kenneth. I know it probably sounds strange and I really hate having to ask it of you at all. But the last thing I need is any additional drama in my life right about now."

"Hey, whatever it takes to make you happy, you know I'm more than willing to do. But I've gotta ask, and I know with our relationship ending the way it did, this is most certainly none of my business, but are things between you and this guy okay?"

"Sure, they're fine," she said.

"I mean, he hasn't done anything that would cause you to be afraid of him, has he?"

She grabbed the card Kenneth had given her and shoved it back between the pages of the book. "Oh, you mean like try to choke the shit out of me?" she said. "Nope, he's yet to pull a stunt like that, if that's what you're asking."

"Aliesha," Kenneth said after a strained and extended pause. "You know if I could take back that night, I would. I know I was wrong and I know you're still entitled to be hurt about it . . . But dammit, woman, what else do you want me to do? Sit here and pretend like I don't hear the fear in your voice?"

She tossed the book aside and said, "Everything is fine, Kenneth, really."

"Yeah, okay. If you say so. But as a friend and someone who truly cares about your well-being, in spite of my one moment of gross and inexcusable idiocy, if you ever need me, baby, I'm here, okay? Just call me, Aliesha, and I'll be there—no strings attached, no questions asked."

"All right," she said, struggling against the urge to break down and unleash the words knotting her throat in their search for a way out. *So why don't you come now. I need you. And I've missed you more than you'll ever know.* She shook her head and finally summoned forth a whispered and less revealing, "Thank you . . . and good night."

On hanging up the phone, she stared at the opened gray suitcase, the crumpled T-shirt, and the book she knew she'd probably never read. *You really do need to clean up in here,* she told herself. *And getting rid of these things would be the perfect place to start.*

She carefully repacked the items she'd removed from the bag and zipped its flap closed again. But rather than lug the suitcase from the room, like she'd originally intended, upon rising she walked away and left the bag sitting where she'd found it. Her textbook once again clutched to her chest, she turned off the room's light with her free hand and, without looking back, closed the door behind her.

PART II

CHAPTER 17

After parking in front of the barbershop, Aliesha sat in her car and chuckled at the trio she saw stumble from the establishment's entrance. Sam Junior and his rambunctious twins deserved their own half-hour comedy special. The little boys sported the same fresh, new haircuts, the same dirty blue shorts and stained SpongeBob T-shirt ensemble. Suckers jutted from the corners of their downturned lips as they snarled, kicked, and swung what appeared to be rolled-up comic books at each other. In his valiant efforts to keep them from maiming one another, their father, Sam Junior, appeared to be absorbing the bulk of the hard blows in the already bruised and banged-up space between his ashy knees and ankles.

So much had transpired in the two weeks since Aliesha had last stepped inside Wally's Cool Cuts, it felt like two months or more had passed. But a twinge of déjà vu hit her the moment she walked up to the door and placed her fingers against the handle.

She entered, not unlike the time before, to the tinkle of the bell above her head. Likewise, the same blues, though a different singer and a different song, asserted its presence with a wail and a holler from the oversized speakers of the shop's '80s-style boom box.

Wally looked up from the customer seated in his barber's chair and smiled. "Hey, Miz Ahh . . . Wait, I mean . . ." He snapped his fingers. "Eaton. Doctor Eaton, right?"

She paused, smiled, and said, "Really, plain ole Aliesha is fine."

She glanced at Gerald, who, once again, was working a pair of scissors over the head of the man seated in his chair while yapping nonstop into the phone mashed against his ear. But as Aliesha strolled past, he made eye contact and extended her the courtesy of a "What up?" head bob.

While her pace slowed, her heart rate rose with every step she took toward Dante's station. Unlike her first visit, this time she found him already on his feet and working on the customer in his chair. Also, swiveling from side to side in the barber's chair nearest Dante's station was a long-legged, baby-faced young man who greeted Aliesha's curious gaze with a wide, goofy-looking grin.

"Miz Professor. Nice to see you again," Dante said without gazing up from his clippers. "A little early, aren't you?"

Aliesha pulled a textbook and a highlighter from her bag. "Take your time," she said. "I'm in no big hurry."

Not long after she sat on the empty bench directly across from Dante's workstation, the young man seated in the adjoining station stopped swiveling and openly gawked in her direction. Finally he said, "Yo, D., man, you were right. She does kinda look like a nice cross between Max from *Living Single* and the singer India.Arie."

Dante shut off his clippers and rose from his crouch wearing a glare. "Man, you ain't even suppose to be here. But since you are, why don't you make yourself useful and go see if those towels are ready to go into the dryer."

The young man shook his head, leaned forward, and broke into his wide toothy grin again. "Man, like you said, I ain't even suppose to be here. And since I'm not officially on the clock, I ain't studyin' 'bout you or those towels. Now why don't you stop tripping and introduce me to this nice lady?"

"Because she didn't come in here to listen to any of your nonsense," Dante said before he switched his clippers on again.

"Yeah, like you the only somebody up in here with enough going on to talk to a female that's got book smarts and a degree." The grin the young man aimed at Aliesha struck her as more mischievous and playful than low-down and lecherous.

When she smiled back, he leaped from his chair and thrust his hand in her face. "Pleasure to meet you, Miz Professor. They call me Yazz. I'm the baby boy of this here ragtag, hair-cutting operation, but I'm by far the smartest and most uniquely talented."

The man in Dante's chair, who had looked asleep, suddenly blinked open his eyes and chuckled. "You mean the biggest smart ass with the most mouth, don't you?"

"All right, Willie, man," Yazz said. "Don't start none, won't be none, hear?"

Dante looked at Aliesha, his eyes apologetic and baring a hint of embarrassment. He nodded toward Yazz. "Don't mind him, Miz Professor. He's young and mainly a threat to himself."

"Oh, see!" Yazz shouted. "See the disrespect I've got to put up with around here? Mark my words, though, y'all gone miss y'all some Yazz when I'm gone."

"Is that right?" the customer named Willie said. "Well, where you going, son? And 'bout how long you 'spect it's gonna take you to get there?"

All three of the men, including Yazz, laughed.

Aliesha watched as Dante removed the cape from around Willie's neck and flung it at Yazz. "Here, take care of this for me. I've got to prep him for a shave. And while you're at it, go 'head and see about those towels."

Yazz balled the cape under his arm and said, "I swear if y'all don't treat me like I've got flunky or something stamped on my forehead."

Rather than reply, Dante picked up a thick strap and started drawing a long, old-fashioned straightedge razor up and down it. As a still-muttering Yazz trudged off in the direction of the laundry room, Dante smiled and winked at Aliesha before launching into a conversation with Willie about some local sporting event.

Aliesha turned her attention to the textbook she'd brought along. A couple of minutes passed and she'd become somewhat engrossed in her reading when she heard Wally say, "Yo, Gerald, man. Ain't that Roz just pulled up out there?"

Gerald, whose last customer had left just as Dante had begun preparing Willie for his shave, walked over to the window, stooped, and peered out. "Oh hell!" he said. He spun around and, while hightailing it back to his workstation, he shoved a hand into his pocket and jerked out his cell phone. By the time the visibly angry woman barged into the shop, Gerald had positioned himself in his barber's chair with his back facing the door and his phone locked against the side of his head.

The up-and-down heave of the woman's ample chest reminded Aliesha of the in-and-out swell of a bullfrog's throat, while the crooked blond wig on her head looked like a worn and tattered reject from Tina Turner's old collection. The woman adjusted her hair and wiped the sweat from her brow before she shouted to no one in particular, "How long has it been since Sam Junior was in here? And where he'd say he was headed?"

Wally shook his head and began sweeping away the loose hair from the neck and shoulders of the man still in his chair. "I'm sorry, ma'am, Sam Junior isn't one of my customers. Might want to ask my man Gerald, here."

The woman marched over and slipped behind Wally and Gerald's workstations. After lowering the volume on the boom box, she jabbed Gerald in the shoulder. "Uh-uh, don't act like you don't see me standing up here. Where Sam Junior go?"

Gerald swung around, wearing an ugly scowl. "Look here, woman, can't you see I'm on the phone?!"

The woman threw up her hands. "Hell, man, when is yo' talking ass not on the phone?!"

When Gerald mumbled something, turned his back, and resumed his previous conversation, Yazz, who by then had returned from his banishment to the laundry room, clapped and unleashed a loud, mocking hoot.

The noise drew the enraged woman's attention. However, when she ventured a few steps to the rear of the shop, Yazz hollered, "Hold up there, Miz Lady. Ain't no need of you even wasting your time. Everybody back here's name is Bennett and ain't none of us trying to be up in it."

The woman flipped Yazz her middle finger and said, "To hell with you and all the rest of y'all's trifling asses. You can play deaf, dumb, blind, and crazy if you want to, but I know damn well that fool was up in here. Tell you what, if you see him again before I do, be sure to let him know I wants my damn child support. Them big-headed twin bastards ain't his only responsibility. He got a eight-year-old daughter been needing new shoes and a chipped tooth fixed for months now. You'd best be glad I didn't catch his lying ass up in here, 'cause it sho' wouldn't have been nothing nice."

The woman glared into the barber's mirrors behind Wally's station and adjusted her wig one last time before storming out.

"Don't you think that was kind of mean?" Aliesha said. "Somebody could have at least told her he'd been in here. I came pretty close to doing so myself."

"See, that's the problem," Yazz said. "Y'all women know everything, but the rules. Brother Man Rule #1 reads as follows, 'When at all possible, as it pertains to matters of the heart, particularly those not involving you, mind your own.' Hate to be the one to break it to you, Miz Professor, but if Sam Junior hada wanted ole girl to know where he was, he'da told her."

Aliesha looked at Dante. "You agree with that?"

Dante stroked the hairs on his chin and said, "All I know is the last time Roz got hot behind some of Sam Junior's mess, dude ended up with a sliced tendon in his calf and a huge chunk missing out of his thigh."

Yazz snickered. "And you'd best believe neither of them places was hardly what she was aiming for. Had she not been drunk, them twin boys of Sam Junior's just mighta never made it here, if you catch my drift."

"Humpf," Willie said. "I always wondered how he got that jackrabbit gait of his. Fool had the nerve to tell me it was some old war injury."

The men's loud laughter deepened the frown lines cutting trenches in Aliesha's face. Deciding she'd had her fill of their Brother Man rules and childish chatter, she reset her sights on the pages of her textbook. Still, every so often, bits and pieces of their conversation drifted past her filter and forced her to look up.

Yazz: "You know what that was all about, don't you? Sam Junior got himself a new woman."

Willie: "What? You means besides Roz and that girl he had them twins with?"

Yazz: "Yup. Dude got him some little ole Mexican chick who stay over in Midtown somewhere."

Willie: "How he gone juggle three women when he can't hardly halfway take care of one?"

Yazz: "According to what I heard, that ain't much of an issue when it comes to the senorita."

Willie: "Yeah? She got a good job or something?"

Yazz: "Man, this slim done went from being a newbie, slinging fries and apple pies, to being manager over at one of them McDonald's on Union."

Dante: "Why you say it like that? You one of those insecure types who can't stand seeing a woman in charge?"

Yazz: "No man, I'm just saying, seem like everywhere

you look these days some Juan Carlos, Maria Gonzales type is getting cut a break."

Willie: "Hate to say, it but the boy got a point. Just about anywhere you go 'round here now, all of the maids, the janitors, the groundskeepers, and the folks working on these here housing construction sites are all Hispanic."

Yazz: "Yeah and how they end up with all the damn jobs when most of them are here illegally and can barely speak English? Hell, I made the mistake of going through the drive-thru at Popeyes the other day and dude's accent was so thick, I couldn't understand a freaking word he said. I swear, man, you'da thought I was talking to Pepe Le Pew or Ricky Ricardo or somebody."

At that point, Aliesha slammed her book shut and cleared her throat, but Yazz ignored her. "And a lot of those jokers are nasty, too, man. You ever watch any of those old episodes of *Sanford and Son*? Remember how Fred was always warning Lamont about hanging out with his Puerto Rican neighbor, Julio? And how he was always having to chase dude's goat outta his yard?"

Dante said, "Come on, man, even you gotta know television and reality are two different things. Besides, wasn't like Fred was ever gonna be up for a housekeeping or best yard of the month award his damn self."

Yazz said, "Naw, man, I'm saying though. My cousin Trey live right next door to some of these Puerto Ricans, Dominicans, or what have you. And man, you look over there and all you see is goats, chickens, dogs, and cats all up on the porch, in the yard, and probably in the house, too."

When Yazz noticed Aliesha squinting in his direction, he said, "What? I guess you think I'm wrong for saying that too, huh?"

"Maybe if you could hear yourself, you'd realize just how ignor . . . insensitive you sound," she said. "How much you wanna bet that not more than 30 to 40 years ago, a bunch of White guys were sitting up in a barbershop somewhere saying the exact same things about folks who look like you and me?"

"Hell," Willie said. "I'll do you one even better. No doubt as we speak, somewhere in Riverton a bunch of good old boys and rednecks are having this same conversation about the Mexicans, the Niggas, the Asians, and damn near anybody else they feel is a threat to they little patch of dirt and so-called privileged way of life."

Dante put down his razor in order to slide his palm against Willie's. "That's right, man. Talk about it."

Aliesha looked at Yazz, who was smirking and shaking his head. Without even being conscious of it, she slipped into her lecture voice. "Just try not to use one or two case scenarios to make such wide-sweeping, blanket judgments, is all I'm asking. They're not all here illegally. They're not all ignorant, dirty, and nasty. It may surprise you to know that quite a few of them come from families that've lived here for generations. By the same token, many of them have a wonderful command of a language that a lot of our own people routinely butcher. I'd dare say, all most of them want is to be afforded an opportunity to make an honest living, just like you and me."

"Yeah, nice speech," Yazz said. "But I'm saying, this ain't the classroom. How you know what they're really like? You ever lived around any?"

"For what it's worth," Aliesha said, "the man I'm currently dating just so happens to be of Latin descent."

Yazz slapped his knees and grinned. "Oh! Oh, my bad. I didn't realize my comments were hitting so close to home. You hear that, Dante, man? I guess jobs, houses, and business loans aren't the only places where our Hispanic hombres are getting cut in on a piece of the action."

"What's that supposed to mean?" Aliesha said. "Aren't

I as free to date whom I please, in much the same way your friend, Sam Junior, is?"

Yazz stopped grinning and said, "Well, if you really wanna know what I think—"

"We don't!" Dante said. He reached into this pocket and yanked out a twenty-dollar bill. "Why don't you do us all a favor and run on over to your next favorite spot to hang out, Popeyes, and get yourself something to eat?"

"Yeah," Willie said as he stood up and pulled out his wallet in order to pay Dante. "Go on over to the chicken shack and worry them folks over there for a while. Matter of fact, I think I just might stop in there for a minute myself. You need a ride?"

Yazz bolted from his seat and snatched the bill from Dante's hand. "Hey, if Willie's driving and you're paying, it's all good by me. You want me to bring you something back?"

Dante shook his head. "Nothing other than my change." He looked at Aliesha. "What about you, Miz Professor? You want anything?"

"No, thanks, I'm good," she muttered, still silently seething.

"Cool then," Yazz said. He cut his eyes at Aliesha before stretching an arm over Willie's shoulders. "Come on, Willie, man. Let's roll on down here and see about getting us some chicken, a goat, and maybe even a little hard-working Mexican gal or two."

Aliesha watched in silence as Dante finished tidying his workstation. A couple of minutes had passed since Yazz and Willie's departure. But rather than dissipate, the irritation that had seized and twisted her guts with Yazz's every word had only worsened. By the time Dante finally beckoned her to his chair, her insides were spinning and twirling like an open stream of white-water rapids.

She wasn't sure why she was still so upset. She'd certainly heard worse, and it wasn't like Dante had cosigned any of Yazz's ignorance. Still, she clung to her anger as if it were a buoy, the one thing that might keep her from drowning in the churn and swirl of an uncertain sea.

Without uttering a word, Dante combed out her hair and began cutting it. A solid five minutes passed before he shut off his clippers and, while standing behind her, asked, "So, what's your boyfriend's name?"

She stiffened, narrowed her eyes, and said, "Why?"

He restarted the clippers and said, "No particular reason. I'm just trying to make conversation, is all."

Aliesha lapsed back into her moody silence. But when Dante moved in front of her and began trimming the hair around her face, she found herself blurting, "For what it's worth, his name is Javiel."

Dante's gaze bumped against hers. He nodded and said, "Javiel. Hmm, I bet he's in a line of work that requires him to make use of his hands a lot, isn't he? And before you bite my head off, no, my name is not Yazz, and no, that wasn't some sly segue to an incredibly stupid and politically incorrect joke about migrant workers."

The tight corners of Aliesha's lips relaxed, and something she saw in Dante's eyes soothed her warring spirit. "Actually, you're right. He does work with his hands. He's a draftsman. But he's also a very talented artist and painter. How'd you guess?"

Dante stepped away from her and examined her head. "I don't know. You just look like the kind of woman who'd be with a man who works with his hands."

Inwardly it horrified Aliesha that Dante had not only honed in on her attraction toward him but felt comfortable enough to tease her about it. Still, she managed an awkward laugh. "In spite of your protests to the contrary,

I'm starting to believe you're about as full of it as your friend, Yazz."

Dante smiled. "Yazz is all right. He doesn't mean any real harm. He's just got a lot of growing up to do and he hasn't quite learned yet how or when to shut up."

Aliesha wasn't sure she concurred, but rather than challenge Dante's assessment, she decided to drop the topic altogether. "So what about your girlfriend?" she asked in an attempt to toss back the ball Dante had originally bounced her way.

"My girlfriend?" Dante said, his voice rising an octave.

"Yeah, what does she do?" Aliesha pressed, even though she wasn't really sure she wanted to hear the answer.

Dante cleared his throat. "Well, at the present time, she doesn't exist. It's been a while since I had a steady girl."

Torn between relief and disbelief, Aliesha spent a few seconds processing the information before she offered him a softly worded, "No disrespect, mind you, but I've gotta say, that's really kind of hard for me to believe."

"Yeah? Why is that?"

While staring at his reflection in the mirror behind his station, Aliesha decided to take a chance on truth. "You just don't strike me as the type of guy who'd be alone for any length of time."

"Well, it's not like I don't have a couple of female friends who'll come over and keep me company when the nights get too long and lonely, if you know what I mean."

Aliesha found herself rolling her tongue to remove the bad taste that had risen in her mouth. "I see. So you're into that whole 'friends with benefits' type of thing?"

He laughed. "What? You don't approve?"

She shrugged. "Hey, you're grown. It's not like you need my or anyone else's approval."

Neither one of them spoke again until he'd finished with her cut. On passing her the mirror, he said, "We doing a wash today?"

"Sure," she said. "And what about my eyebrows?"

He looked away from her and said, "Yeah, well, I know that's what we agreed on. But if you don't mind, I'd really prefer to do them another time."

"Okay," she said. On failing to decipher his body language, she asked, "Is there a reason why?"

"Well, if you must know," he said, still avoiding her gaze and sounding right sheepish, "right before you came in this afternoon, I caught Yazz using my tweezers to pluck his nose hairs."

Aliesha shook her head, laughed, and followed Dante to the dark room in the back. This time when he opened the door and flipped the switch alongside the wall, it didn't take her eyes long to adjust to the change in light. She noticed, almost immediately, how the corner containing the shampoo bowl and the reclining chair appeared encased in an odd sort of shimmer and glow. The phenomenon, though strange, only increased her eagerness to sit down, lean back, and submit herself to the process. She couldn't help but succumb to a sigh of relief upon doing so. The rush of the hot water, the repetitive stroke of Dante's thick fingers over her scalp, and the gentle massage of his Big Mama's shampoo into her hair felt even better than before. This time, however, she kept her eyes shut and succeeded in squelching her desire to moan.

She didn't permit herself to look at Dante until he'd finished the wash, shut off the sprayer, and was dabbing at the stray drops and rivulets of water dancing across her forehead and sliding down her temples. Upon easing open her lids, she took note of both the seriousness in his face and the tenderness in his eyes. When he finally stopped moving the towel and rested his gaze against hers, she nearly stopped breathing. For a moment, she could have sworn he had every intention of leaning over and kissing her.

Instead, he asked, "Your man like your hair this way?"

She moistened her lips and wondered why all of a sudden they felt so incredibly parched. "To tell you the truth, I don't know. He has yet to say anything about it and I have yet to ask him."

After Dante helped her sit up, he finished toweling dry her hair. While he worked, Aliesha noticed the slim paperback peeking from his smock pocket. "New book? Or the same one?"

"Same," he said without bothering to glance down.

"Surely you've finished it by now," she said. "You're not having problems with it, are you?"

He paused and smiled. "What? Now you think I can't read?"

She cringed. "I'm sorry. I guess that did sound rather condescending."

He assisted her to her feet. "You ever read it?"

"*The Metamorphosis*? Yeah, it's been years, though," she said as she followed him from the room. "If I remember correctly, it's about a man who upon awakening discovers he's turned into a roach."

"Yeah, I guess that pretty much sums it up, huh?" Dante said as they reentered the main room of the barbershop.

She longed to ask more questions, specifically about the book, but had a feeling he wasn't exactly raring to give too many answers. Disappointed, but figuring there'd be yet another opportunity on some other occasion perhaps, she allowed him to finish her blow-dry and style without any additional interrogation.

After she paid him, he donned his iPod and walked her out, like he'd done at the end of her first visit. On stepping outside, rather than thank him again and bid him a friendly and prompt good-bye, she asked, "So, what's the tune this week?"

He pulled out his earbuds, gave them a quick wipe, and passed them to her. On inserting them, she closed her eyes and listened for a good thirty seconds to the sad, poignant lyrics of Curtis Mayfield's "We the People Who Are Darker Than Blue."

"Is it always Curtis Mayfield?" she asked.

He shook his head. "Now what did you caution Yazz about earlier? Don't go putting me in a box just yet, Miz Professor. There's a lot more to me than what you see."

The way he'd said it made it sound like both a challenge and an invitation. She relished the thought. A smile lit up her face and, rather than leave, she lingered. "So you really think I look like a cross between Erika Alexander, the actress who played Max on *Living Single,* and India. Arie?"

Dante shrugged. "Depends."

"On?" Aliesha said.

He laughed. "Primarily on whether or not you think that's a good thing or a bad thing."

The twinge of embarrassment she saw in his face and heard in his laughter made her smile grow brighter. But rather than submit to the allure of seeing just how far he'd be willing to indulge the flirtation, she shook her head and turned to walk away.

"Say, Miz Professor," Dante said.

She stopped, her heart pounding against her chest as she wondered what he'd say next. He waited until she'd turned and faced him again before he continued. "Be sure you ask your man what he thinks."

"About what?" she asked.

"You know," he said, tapping an index figure against his temple. "Your hair."

A wave of somberness overtook her joy, and without the barest hint of the smile that had been there only seconds before, she said, "Sure, I'll do that."

———— ⌘ ————

A boyfriend? Well, at least it wasn't a husband. Not that either was something Dante had a mind to or a stomach for dealing with or navigating around, especially after having already wasted half a lifetime doing so.

"You just look like the kind of woman who'd be with a man who works with his hands" had been the partial truth he'd shared with her as apposed to the fully stripped one . . . *you look like the kind of woman who needs to be held and stroked and caressed on a regular basis* . . . the one that had actually been streaking through the dark corridors of his mind. Try as he might, Dante couldn't keep himself from wondering if this boyfriend, this draftsman, this Latin lover, artist wannabe, was falling short in some essential area, if he owned neither the hands nor the heart for holding this woman like she needed to be held . . . for touching her where she needed to be touched. What else, Dante wondered, would account for the interest in him Aliesha appeared so unwilling if not unable to hide.

Nope, I can't. Not with her. Not this time around, he silently vowed even though the role of "odd man out" appeared to be one to which he'd been permanently assigned. A number of experiences, but one in particular, had Dante all but convinced that he'd landed in his own private Hades where, for reasons unknown, he'd been sentenced to reach for all of eternity, apparently, toward a woman who'd forever remain just beyond his grasp. Perfect wasn't something he'd ever been, but damn, what kind of sin could he have committed in this life or the last to warrant such a horrible plight?

If it mattered any, he felt a considerable amount of remorse at having been less than honest with Aliesha—not only about the whole "a man who works with his hands" bit, but the eyebrow thing as well. Yes, he had caught Yazz using his tweezers on his nose hairs, but that had been little more than a convenient excuse, particularly in light of the well-stocked beauty supply store right next door. The uncomfortable and unadulterated truth was, Dante didn't trust himself to peer into Aliesha's eyes for any length of time. He wasn't ready for her to know, just yet, that the current between them ran both ways and at the same, if not an even greater, level of intensity.

So he'd done his best to keep the conversation and his interaction with her light and easy. And being that he enjoyed making her smile and hearing her laugh, it had been anything but a difficult or thankless task. Besides, his being able to work his fingers through her hair had already become something of a pleasure-filled bonus and one that helped ease the pain he felt at once again being denied a woman he didn't know how to keep himself from wanting.

Even though Aliesha was making it excruciatingly difficult for him to stay strong and true to the all-or-none promise he'd made to himself, Dante couldn't stand the thought of her becoming the next notch on his belt, much less the newest Laylah in his life. She didn't deserve that. Nor did he. So, he understood that a full and steady application of the brakes was in order, even if it meant turning the speeding cart upside down as it barreled through the turn with him still securely buckled up and strapped down on the inside.

CHAPTER 18

The two occupied opposite corners of her king-sized bed. Aliesha sat on the left side, near the foot of the bed and with her legs folded beneath her yoga style. Spread open in front of her was the same textbook she'd been leafing through at the barbershop earlier in the day. Next to the book sat a note-riddled legal pad. On the right, at the head of the bed, Javiel reclined with a mountain of pillows propped behind his back. Next to him sat the sketchpad and the charcoal pencil he'd abandoned for the television's remote.

For a moment, the dense fog, which constantly loomed between them and often totally obscured their view of one another, had appeared on the verge of lifting. A surprised Aliesha had found herself greeting a refreshed and considerably less uptight Javiel upon his return from his weekend outing with the fellas. To her relief, even their Sunday morning church date at Garden View had come and gone without a single troubling incident.

After service, instead of driving her to the nearest fast-food joint for a take-out meal of burger and fries (a convenience that would keep him from missing too much of whatever televised ball game he was raring to see) Javiel had suggested they dine downtown at Wilhelm's, a new German restaurant she'd once casually mentioned wanting to visit. Over lunch, a smiling and laughing Aliesha had happily indulged Javiel's playful teasing about her doting surrogate parents, the Phillipses, and Garden View's sincerely spirited but awful-sounding men's choir. When he'd started telling her the details of his Saturday fishing expedition, rather than zone out, like she might have in the past, she'd listened with interest and had been genuinely touched by the desire he'd expressed to treat her to a picnic down by the lake as soon as the weather turned warmer.

They'd had such a uncharacteristically pleasant time all that day and even later that night, Aliesha had, yet again, talked herself into putting off her plans to bring up the whole dead fiancée issue. But in the days thereafter, the air between them had again slowly thickened and ever since driving off the parking lot in front of Wally's Cool Cuts, Aliesha had felt her buoyant mood tumbling steadily downward. As she sat in the corner of her bed with anxiety riding her neck and shoulders, like a backpack full of broken bricks, she couldn't help but feel like an inexperienced skier trying desperately to outrun the avalanche on her heels.

"Would you mind turning down the volume if you're going to do that," she asked as Javiel aimed the remote at the television and flipped from one channel to the next.

He frowned. "Can't you finish that later?" he mumbled in reference to the lecture notes she'd been working on for the last half hour.

She cut her eyes at him. "I'd kinda prefer to finish it now."

He lowered the television volume a notch and said, "What's got you so grumpy this evening?"

"I'm not grumpy," she said.

"Yeah, you are," he said. "You've been snapping at me ever since I got here."

Unable to deny the small amount of truth in his assertion, Aliesha shoved her legal pad inside her book and tossed them both aside before crawling toward Javiel's side of the bed. On reaching him, she snuggled against him, fingered the buttons on his shirt, and said, "I'm sorry."

He planted a kiss on her lips and said, "That's my girl."

She drew her fingers over his chest, but before he got the wrong idea about her intentions, she said, "You know, Javiel, ever since the last time your mother and I spoke, there's been something on my mind."

"Yeah? And what might that be?" he said.

"Is there a particular reason you've never mentioned anything to me about your fiancée, Evelyn?"

Javiel sat silent and still for a moment. "Probably for the same reason it took you so long to tell me about Kenneth," he said, when he finally answered. "It wasn't exactly the most pleasant episode in my life."

She could tell by his chilly tone that he wanted her to drop the subject. But she'd grown tired of giving in to his wants. "Why'd the two of you break up in the first place?" she persisted.

When he turned toward her, she saw an ugliness in his eyes she'd never seen before. "Why do any two people break up, Aliesha? Things just don't work out sometimes."

She nodded and bit her bottom lip before she said, "You want to know what I think? I think you're being deliberately evasive."

His eyes grew colder and all of the color disappeared from his face. "Is that a polite way of calling me a liar? What in the hell did my mother say to you anyway?"

"It's not what she said, Javiel, as much as what she didn't say that disturbs me. And I just thought I'd bring it up rather than keep jumping to my own conclusions, which, by the way, don't exactly paint you in the most favorable light."

"Well, the thing you might want to keep in mind about my mother, Aliesha, is that she has a flair for being overly dramatic. Now as far as Evelyn is concerned, what happened between us was painful and tragic. And for now, that's all I care to say about it."

When he shifted his gaze back to the television, Aliesha

had to talk herself out of snatching the remote from his hands and hurling it across the room. "Wow, just like that?" she said. "End of story and on to the next topic?"

"Please, Aliesha, it's been a long day. Can't we discuss that another time? Isn't there something else we could talk about?"

"Actually, there is," she said. "In case you haven't noticed, I got my hair cut today."

"Umm, it looks nice," he said with his gaze still riveted to the flickering TV screen.

"Yeah, right," she muttered. She picked up the drawing he had made of one of her bent knees and tossed it at him before she crawled back to the spot she'd vacated at the end of the bed.

"What?! What'd I do now?!" he said.

She grabbed her book and stretched out on her side with her back to him. "Nothing. Forget about it," she said.

After a few minutes more of channel surfing, Javiel paused on what to Aliesha sounded like a commercial. "You ever thought about that?" he asked.

"Thought about what?" she replied without looking up from her book.

"Coloring your hair?"

She rolled over and stared at him. "Why would I think about that?"

"I don't know. I see women doing it all the time. I just wondered if you'd ever considered it."

"So you think I'd look better with a different hair color?"

"You're putting words in my mouth. That's not what I said."

"Well, what are you saying exactly?"

His frown deepened. "Look, Aliesha, stop tripping. I think you're beautiful. I told you as much the first time I laid eyes on you. I just wondered what you'd look like with your hair colored is all."

She sat up and laughed. "Oh, so *you've wondered* that, have you?"

He resumed his channel surfing and mumbled, "Yeah, a time or two."

"Wow!" she said. "Okay, so what color? What color would you like to see on me?"

He sighed and looked at her. "If you must know, I've always thought a nice honey-blond might look great on you."

"Honey-blond?!" she said. "You can't be serious. This is a joke, right?"

"Why not?" he said. "A lot of stylish African American women wear their hair blond. Take Beyoncé, for instance. I think her hair looks gorgeous. It's just a look."

"Yeah, frankly a look that would translate into a right hot mess on me. In case you hadn't noticed, dear, I'm like twenty shades darker than Beyoncé."

"What difference does that make?" he asked. "Look at the tennis star, Serena Williams. She's a beautiful, dark-skinned woman and she colors her hair blond all the time."

"Great," Aliesha said. She leaped off the bed and started putting her work away. "I guess while I'm at it I might as well get it straightened, so it can hang down my back and blow in the wind, too, huh?"

"Why are you getting so damn bent out of shape about this?" he shouted.

"Because a couple of weeks ago I starting seeing a new hairstylist," she shouted back at him. "And since then, everyone has been complimenting me on my hair—everyone that is, except you. I don't think you've even noticed, have you?"

He got off the bed and reached for her. "Look, baby, had I realized it meant that much to you—"

She held up her hand, like a traffic cop. "Stop! Just save it, all right?"

"Good idea," he said, before moving away from her and

launching into a pace. "What do you say we just save all of this empty drama and hysterics for something that matters? Because for the past couple of weeks you've been picking fights with me over nothing and I've had just about enough of it."

She followed him with her eyes. "Fighting with you over nothing? Oh, okay, so the things that matter to me aren't even worthy of your time or consideration?"

"See, there you go putting words in my mouth again. I didn't say that. I just think there are a lot more important issues we could be dealing with."

"Like what? Go ahead, name one."

He stopped in front of her and said in a fierce whisper, "I'm so not having this argument with you, Aliesha, not tonight."

"Fine!" she spat back at him. "And maybe you're right. Maybe we need to take a break . . . a real one this time. Spending a bit more time away from one another just might do us both some good."

"What?! You know that's not at all what I meant. When in the hell did I ever say that?"

"You didn't. But I am." She spun away from him, flopped down on her bed, and buried her face in her hands. "Really, Javiel, I need a break from this . . . from you . . . from us."

"I see. Just so I'm clear, you wanna break up with me because what? I failed to notice your new hairdo? Or because I suggested you try a new hair color?"

She looked up at him, her face contorted but her eyes clear. "If you honestly think this is about my hair, I feel sorry for you."

"Okay, so what?" he said, raising his arms and gesturing with his hands. "Is this about me not wanting to discuss the morbid details of a decades-old, failed relationship, a relationship that truly has little bearing on what's currently going on between you and me?"

"No bearing? None whatsoever?" She jumped off the

bed and locked her gaze with his. "Well, why don't you let me be the judge of that? After you first explain to me how she wound up dead."

She couldn't decipher the expression on his face. He appeared trapped somewhere between shocked, scared, and totally dumbfounded. Finally, he blinked and reached for her. "Look, babe, why don't we just call it an early night and talk about all of this in the morning?"

She shook her head and in a soft, quiet, but unwavering voice said, "No, Javiel . . . enough already. I'm through."

He'd made a relatively quiet exit. No yelling or screaming in protest. No ranting, raving, or calling her out her name. On receipt of his walking papers, he'd simply and silently slid into his shoes, straightened his clothing, and with her trailing a couple of paces behind him made his way to the front door. But before stepping out into the dark, still night he'd turned to her and said, "For the record, Evelyn and I broke up because she wasn't happy. Not just with me, but with life in general. So, one beautiful Sunday afternoon, she went out into the woods, put a revolver to her head, and pulled the trigger."

Suicide. The story Monica managed to siphon from Jesus was pretty much the same. Apparently, Javiel's fiancée had a bipolar disorder. A couple of weeks prior to their nuptials, she'd told him she didn't love him and had insisted they call off the wedding. Though she had vehemently denied it, Javiel suspected Evelyn had stopped taking her meds. For months he'd tried but ultimately failed to convince her to reconsider. The day after he informed her of his decision to enter the monastery, she'd disappeared. A week later her decomposing body had been found in the woods, slumped against a tree. The gun she'd used to fire a bullet through her skull had been discovered on the ground beside her.

"So why would Julia go out of her way to make me believe that her son may have played an active role in this woman's death?" Aliesha wondered aloud.

"Who knows," Monica said. "Didn't Javiel say his mom was a bit of a drama queen? On the other hand, has it ever occurred to you that Javiel's mom just might be the real nut-job in this whole scenario?"

Aliesha laughed. "Why is it you're so quick to assign someone other than yourself the label of 'crazy'?"

"Anyway, now that you know the score, don't you think you owe the man another chance? Javiel is, by no means, a bad guy. You can't deny he's been good to you."

"Good to me?" Aliesha said. "So is candy. But it's not filling and very seldom is it really what I need."

It was Monica's turn to laugh. "Uh-huh, keep on over-intellectualizing it. You and I both know you giving Javiel the boot didn't have damn thing to do with your *needs*. No, that slick little move was all about your wants, more specifically your *wanting* a taste of that Kafka-reading Mandingo who cuts hair over there on Jackson Avenue. As if that's liable to last longer than the time required for him to jump in and out of your bed."

"What makes you think that's even where I'm trying to take it? Okay, sure, I'm not denying a rather strong physical attraction to the man. And yes, I do get a kick out of the flirtation and the magic he's able to work on my head, but—"

"But nothing," Monica said. "You know, it's only a matter of time before he's working those magic fingers over something other than the knots and kinks in your natural. Hey, I'm not hating. If you're bored and you've got a hankering for something new, go for it. Guys do it all the time. Just understand what you're giving up and what you're getting into."

"As much as I appreciate your concern, Ms. Ann Landers, I think I can handle this."

"All right, Nancy 'Smarty-Pants' Drew. Whatever! But wouldn't it be something if, instead of Javiel or Kenneth, that dream about your daddy kicking ass turned out to be a warning about your favorite new barber? And say, while we're on the subject of ass-whuppings, for the record, whatever happened with your aunt Mildred and her Mike Tyson wannabe of a hubby? Did they ever end up getting back together?"

Aliesha went on to tell Monica how after her aunt Mildred had seen her off to college, she'd quit her job, sold her house, moved to Cleveland, and reunited with her uncle Frank.

"Damn!" Monica said. "You mean to tell me that after all those years they still got back together and ended up living happily ever after?"

"They got back together, all right," Aliesha said. "But happily ever after? I think not. A couple of years after she left, my aunt Mildred ended up perishing one cold winter night in a house fire that was later ruled to be arson. My uncle disappeared and far as I know was never heard from again."

"Dag, girl, that's messed up," Monica said before changing gears in the conversation and charging off in a different direction.

But over and beyond the buried memories of her aunt Mildred's sad and untimely end, the point Monica had raised about Dante stayed with Aliesha for the next couple of days. Was Dante someone she needed to keep at arm's length, if not avoid altogether? The possibility was one that had never even occurred to her.

She'd been so sure of her interpretation of the nightmare. What else could it have been besides her father's way of warning her—that there'd be hell to pay if she chose to stay in a particular relationship? She'd readily marked the relationship in question as her troubled one with Javiel. But what if she'd been wrong? What if the trouble she feared wasn't right next to her or even behind her, but instead loomed straight ahead?

She knew of only one living person capable of providing meaningful insight to those kinds of questions. And by Friday evening Aliesha had become resigned to the fact that she'd have to do what, shamefully, she'd been putting off for weeks now—make arrangements to see Peaches.

CHAPTER 19

Peaches was Aliesha's old hairstylist's only child, at least, the only child of the five Miss Margie had given birth to that the local DHS had seen fit to let her keep. Rather than handicapped or disabled, Peaches was what most who knew her politely referred to as "special."

Hairless, blind, and said by some to be blessed with the gift of discernment, all from birth, Peaches was only a couple of years older than Aliesha. But it might as well have been a hundred as far as the latter was concerned. Everything about her bald contemporary—from the pinched-shut eyelids with the dark, sunken sockets to the clicking sounds she employed when navigating around objects and the unexpected truths she was in the habit of whispering—had long spooked the hell out of Aliesha. While Miss Margie knew Aliesha's hair, Peaches seemed to know Aliesha better than any mere mortal should have.

The blind woman's gift was no secret and appeared tied somehow to her handling of an individual's hair. Some actually sought her out for that very reason, but Aliesha had never been one of them. When Miss Margie finally confessed to Aliesha that she lacked the energy required to continue doing her hair on a regular basis, a reluctant Aliesha had asked Peaches to pick up where her mother had left off.

All had gone well, until near the end when Peaches had leaned over and whispered, "Aliesha, I don't mean no harm, but I've gotta say this. That man you seeing, the one at the church? He's a good man . . . a good man hell bent on doing a bad thing."

To Aliesha's shock and horror, within days Peaches's prediction about Kenneth had proven true. Much too rattled to seek her out for a return visit, Aliesha had slunk back to Miss Margie and practically begged her to cut her hair.

Even though Miss Margie, as was her habit, had laughed off Aliesha's unspoken desire to keep plenty of space between herself and Peaches, Aliesha couldn't help but feel a considerable amount of embarrassment and shame. Eager to redeem herself, when a gravely ill Miss Margie had finally become bedridden, not only had Aliesha readily assisted in the dying woman's care, she'd made her a promise to do even more.

"You and Peaches is all the love I got left in this world," is what Miss Margie had told her. "I need to know y'all gonna at least try to watch out for one another."

"Yes, ma'am. We will," Aliesha had assured her, even as she'd wondered where she'd ever find the courage and resolve to do so on any type of consistent basis.

In the days following Miss Margie's funeral, Aliesha had thrown herself into the task of making good on her vow. She'd called Peaches at least once a week and visited her either at the beauty shop or at home. But having so little in common, and with Aliesha being at a complete loss for how to gracefully hide or erase her feelings of discomfort, the conversations had been strained and the visits awkward.

Before long, Aliesha began to resent the toll on her psyche, even more so than her time. While she didn't completely renege on her promise, the number of days and weeks between her calls and visits increased. Feeling guilty about having fallen short of her own expectations, one day shortly after she'd started dating Javiel, Aliesha had stopped by

Miss Margie's old house to say hello to Peaches. During the course of their visit, Peaches had touched Aliesha's hair and asked, "Are you all right?"

Aliesha's neck had stiffen, as her blood had slipped into a deep freeze. "Far as I know, yeah," she'd said, unable to keep anxiety and fear from tumbling out with her words. "So, if you're getting ready to tell me something different, I really don't want to know, particularly if it has anything to do with me and Javiel."

Peaches had tilted her face upward and twisted her head from side to side, a mannerism that Aliesha had long associated with blind musical geniuses like Stevie Wonder and Ray Charles. "Javiel?" Peaches said. "Is he your new boyfriend?"

"Yeah," Aliesha had responded in a flat voice.

"What's that like?" Peaches had asked with an innocence so pure it had cut through some of Aliesha's angst. "Having a boyfriend, I mean."

Though the question had caught her off guard, Aliesha had always known Miss Margie to keep her daughter on a short leash. On more than one occasion Aliesha had heard her say, "Peaches being bald, blind, and ugly as all get out ain't hardly a deterrent to a lot of these rogues. But I tell her all the time, fooling around with one of these old knuckleheads is only bound to make her life that much more difficult."

Had Aliesha not been so tightly tethered by her own apprehensions, she might have used Peaches's inquiry as a genuine first step toward a more meaningful bond. Instead, her primary thought had been getting away from Peaches as fast as possible, but not before giving voice to a sentiment that Miss Margie, no doubt, would have approved. "A boyfriend? Trust me, in the long run you're probably better off not knowing."

Unlike Wally's Cool Cuts, no more than a couple of the ten to twelve heads at Sister Beulah's Beauty Boutique bothered to cast a glance in her direction when Aliesha walked in that Saturday with several large bags containing cartons of Chinese food. The beauty shop's owner, Jill, had been among the few. Jill had taken over the business from her mother, Beulah, whose name still appeared prominently on the business's marquee, even though she'd long since retired her curling irons and hot combs to spend her days tending to her roses, keeping up with her favorite TV judge shows, and spoiling her grandchildren and great-grandchildren.

"Hey girl! Where the hell you been keeping yourself?" Jill said on recognizing Aliesha as one of Miss Margie's longtime regulars.

Aliesha readjusted her purse and bags of food in order to give a friendly hug to Jill, a short, solidly built woman who probably weighed a good 300 pounds or more. "Oh, I've been around," Aliesha said. "Just tied up with work, church, and life in general."

"*Humpf,*" Jill said. "That must mean you got yourself a new man." She laughed at her own joke while conducting a thorough visual assessment of Aliesha's head. "You know I ain't never been too partial to them afros, but whoever hooked that up for you did a really nice job. 'Cause, honey, let me tell you, the last time you come stepping up in here, your head looked a right hot mess."

"Yeah, yeah, yeah," Aliesha said, pretending to take the teasing in stride as she stepped around the stout woman, who'd launched into another round of raucous laughter.

Aliesha knew her less-than-positive feelings about Jill had been shaped by all of the negative things she'd heard from Miss Margie over the years. "Lord knows I'll never understand Sister Beulah's decision to turn her shop over to the likes of this big, lazy heifer. Jill ain't never been of the proper mindset to do no hair, much less run a damn business. This used to be a classy joint. Now folks ain't trying to clean up in here like they used to, ain't showing no respect for other folks' space, equipment, or customers. We got a couple of sinks damn near 'bout to fall off the wall and three to four dryers don't halfway work. And hell, most times, it be more riffraff up in here trying to sell shit than customers. But you think Jill care? Shit, 'bout all that fat heifer know how to do is collect booth rent, run her mouth, and eat. Had me and Sister Beulah not worked out a deal years ago that allows me and Peaches to work up in here for the half the price they charging these other trifling heifers, shoot, we'da been gone."

Aliesha found Peaches seated in the stylist's chair at her workstation. A pair of sunglasses and a colorful scarf adorned her bald head, while a contented smile brightened her face. "Hey there, Miz Babygirl," she said in her soft, shy voice.

"Hey there yourself, Miz Peaches," Aliesha said. "I think this is the first time I've ever come in here and seen you without a customer."

"Since I knew you were coming, I picked up the pace a bit and didn't let nobody waste a whole lot of my time yakking. You being so nice to treat me to dinner and all, I didn't want to keep you waiting." She leaned forward and inhaled. "Sure smells good."

"Well, come on and let's get our grub on," Aliesha said.

Peaches led the way. Had it not been for her unveiled and sunken eyes, few onlookers would have been able to tell she couldn't see a thing. She walked with confidence, employing a series of soft clicks with her tongue to navigate the room and steer around obstacles that might have caused her to trip, fall, or injure herself.

Upon entering the shop's break room, Peaches kept walking straight toward the refrigerator, while Aliesha detoured toward the banquet table in the center of the room, where she began removing the warm cartons of food from the bags she'd brought in.

"Can I get you something to drink?" Peaches asked.

"A bottle of water would be great," Aliesha said.

In addition to Aliesha's water, Peaches brought a soft drink for herself, a couple of paper plates, some plasticware, and a handful of napkins to the table. Aliesha watched, marveling at the blind woman's keen sense of balance and spatial orientation as she first arranged the items on the table and then helped herself to the egg rolls, bourbon chicken, and shrimp fried rice and all without knocking over anything, accidentally dipping a stray finger anywhere, or spilling so much as a single grain.

Peaches had never been known to be much of a talker, so as usual the burden of keeping the conversation flowing fell on Aliesha. But in anticipation of their meeting that evening, she'd vowed not to let that fact fluster her, like it had on so many other occasions in the past. Truth be told, in the last few months she had grown more tolerant of lulls and dead space, if only because her relationship with Javiel had provided her with plenty of them. She and Peaches chatted about a number of mundane things: the food; the weather; how business had been lately at the shop; how Peaches had been doing as far as managing the affairs of the house by herself; and even "King," the last stray mutt Miss Margie had insisted on making her pet before her passing.

Most of Peaches's replies had been of the basic "yes, no, maybe, I don't know" variety and without much elaboration. But when the topic of church arose, she'd surprised Aliesha when she asked, "So, how are things with you over at Garden View?"

"Great," Aliesha said. She went on to mention a few of the outreach projects in which she'd recently become involved. But somewhere in mid-ramble, she'd suddenly recalled Peaches's dead-on prediction about Kenneth. She wondered if the church inquiry had, in fact, been a subtle dig for clues on the status of her and Kenneth's relationship.

"Remember that time me and Mama surprised you by showing up there for your birthday?" Peaches said. "We had a good ole time. The sanging wasn't all that great, but I really enjoyed the sermon and the fellowship."

The memory swept through Aliesha like a soothing balm and eased some of the tension in her neck and shoulders. Outside of a great uncle and few cousins, none of whom she spoke to or visited regularly, her only real family since she'd moved back to Riverton had been Miss Margie and Peaches. She smiled. "I'll have to make arrangements for you to visit with us again sometime. If you want, I'll swing by and pick you up tomorrow."

Peaches nodded. "I would, but I don't want to be no bother. Mama told me before she passed, 'Aliesha's got a tough job up at that school, so don't be pestering her with a whole lot of nonsense after I'm gone.' So, if another Sunday's better for you—"

"No, no," Aliesha said. "Tomorrow's good. It's no bother at all." She told Peaches what time to expect her and went on to mention the chapter and verses they'd be discussing in her Sunday school class. The almost girlish delight Peaches expressed about the prospective church outing both tickled and humbled Aliesha. Even though their conversation became much more relaxed and effortless from that point on, Aliesha waited until they'd both eaten their fill before she mentioned that she'd started seeing a new hairstylist.

"Yeah," Peaches said. "I heard you talking to Jill about it. I started to ask you to let me see, but then I remembered how that sort of thing always seems to weird you out."

"It's still natural," Aliesha said. "All he does is cut, wash, and style it. But given that everyone's been complimenting me on it, I was kinda hoping to get your professional opinion."

"Really?" Peaches said.

"Sure," Aliesha said, hoping she wouldn't live to regret the decision.

Peaches wiped her fingers clean before she stood and walked around to Aliesha's side of the table. When she stretched out her hands, Aliesha braced herself and resisted the urge to close her eyes. Peaches patted the contours of Aliesha's natural. Around the temples, at the base of her neck, and at the very top of Aliesha's head, Peaches eased her fingers into the soft tangles and curls until she touched scalp.

"Well," Aliesha said, unable to keep from breaking into a squirm.

A huge grin formed on the blind woman's face. Aliesha couldn't recall having ever seen her stretch her lips that wide or show that many teeth.

"He's good," Peaches said with a slow twist of her head that cast her smile toward the heavens. "Real good."

The garage door's grind ended with a resounding click against the cement floor. Aliesha glanced at her reflection in the car's rearview mirror, patted her hair, and smiled. After having spoken with Peaches, she felt a sense of relief and reassurance, not only about Dante but also about her own ability to keep her word.

She reached for her bag and was about to open her car door when she heard the phone. She pulled it out and frowned at the scroll of Javiel's number in the brightly lit display window. For a few seconds she contemplated whether to answer.

She hadn't spoken with Javiel since accompanying him to her front door after their spat on Wednesday night. A break from one another is what she thought had been their mutual agreement. So after the passage of barely two and a half days, what would ever possess him to call and take a chance on further stoking her discontent?

She bit her lip and muttered a curse prior to mashing the phone against her ear and offering up a louder than usual "Hello" as she exited the vehicle.

"It's over," he said. "I'm coming by to get my things."

"What?" she said, simultaneously confused and irritated. She stopped jiggling the keys in the door that led from the garage into the house and said, "What are you talking about?"

"I'm talking about you and me!" Javiel said in a raised and excited voice. "We're done. I'm on my way over to get my things and to bring you yours."

Aliesha gave the key stuck in the knob a hard twist and pushed open the door. "You mind telling me what brought all of this on?"

"Like you care," Javiel said. "I guess you didn't think I'd find out about you snooping around my house and telling people you suspect I'm some kind of mad serial killer."

Aliesha walked across the kitchen and pressed her forehead against a cabinet. "Would you calm down. If you'd give me a chance, I can explain."

"No more explanations! No more chances!" Javiel shouted. "It's over between us. Why would you want to be with someone you think is capable of murder, anyway?"

He hung up before she could respond. A few minutes later when her phone rang again, she snatched it up and said, "Look, Javiel—"

"It's not Javiel," Monica said. "But he's on his way over. And he's mad as all get-out."

"Yeah, I know," Aliesha said. "He just called. So what did you do? Start running your mouth and accidentally spill all the beans?"

"No, I did not," Monica said, sounding sincerely insulted. "Obviously, he and Jesus started trading notes about some of the questions you and I have been asking of late and they put two and two together. When Jesus called me a few minutes ago, I could barely hear him over all of Javiel's ranting and raving in the background."

Aliesha groaned. "I'm sorry I got you guys mixed up in this. Hopefully he will have calmed down by the time he makes it over here."

"I don't know, girl. I've always know Javi to be such a mild-mannered guy. To be honest, listening to just how irate and out-of-control he sounded kind of frightened me. Just to be on the safe side, I made Jesus follow him in his car. Matter of fact, I should be there myself in about ten minutes or so."

"Yeah, that's the ticket. We'll just have us one big, im-promptu farewell bash. Are you planning on stopping along the way and picking up a few refreshments, too?"

"Shut up," Monica said. "Like I said, I'll be there in a few. But if things get out of hand before then, give me a call. Okay?"

Aliesha agreed, and after hanging up she nearly followed through on her sudden urge to pop the cork on the leftover bottle of white wine in her refrigerator, turn up the bottle by the neck, and have herself a good, long guzzle. But she knew the liquor wasn't likely to do much beyond loosen her tongue, which in turn would only end up making even funkier the foul attitude Javiel had let her know he was bringing with him.

Deciding she'd make it easier on everyone, she trudged upstairs and started collecting Javiel's belongings from her closet and out of her drawers. There really wasn't a whole lot—a few shirts, a couple sets of underwear, some socks, and a spare pair of jeans. She laid each item neatly across her bed. While going about the task, it struck her that even though she and Javiel were on the verge of splitting up, she didn't feel even the tiniest bit of sadness, anger, or remorse. Instead, she felt oddly resigned to the fact, the exact opposite of what she'd felt on the onset of her breakup with Kenneth.

She'd ventured into the bathroom and had begun arranging Javiel's toiletries in a central spot on the vanity when she heard the doorbell. By the time she reached the living room, the insistent chime had been replaced by a repetitive thump and pound.

"Hold on! I'm coming!" she yelled. When she finally opened the door, Javiel barged in swinging a small overnight bag at the end of one arm and cradling a wadded pile of her clothing in the other. A sheepish-looking Jesus trailed behind him.

"Is this really necessary?" Aliesha asked.

"Oh, you expect me to be civil?!" Javiel shouted. "Me, the man you've accused of being a got-damn murderer?"

"I never accused you of—" Aliesha stopped and threw up her hands when instead of even pretending to listen, Javiel marched past her and proceeded upstairs.

Jesus raised his own hands prior to falling into a chair. "Hey, don't look at me. I tried reasoning with him. But the more I talked, the angrier he got. I wouldn't be here now if Monica hadn't insisted I come along just to make sure he didn't make an even bigger ass of himself."

When she started upstairs, Jesus said, "Aliesha, forgive me for getting any deeper into your business, but you sure you just don't want to leave him be? Sometimes when he gets like this, it's just best to leave him alone."

She shook her head. "No, I'd rather we'd both say whatever's left to be said and be done with it. Don't worry. It'll be fine."

Even though she'd reassured Jesus and blown off Monica's concerns, she wasn't one hundred percent sure how Javiel would react once alone with her. She paused at the top of the stairs and spent a moment doing her breathing exercises until she felt centered and calm. When she walked in, she found him double-checking the drawers she'd already emptied of his clothing and personal items. She circled past him and sat down on the side of the bed where he'd deposited her belongings.

For a couple of minutes, neither uttered a word as he packed the small bag he'd brought in with him. Finally, he paused and looked at her with eyes that were simultaneously inflamed and water-filled. "If you didn't want to be with me anymore, Aliesha, you should have just said so. Instead, for the past couple of weeks you've been picking fights with me over dumb shit like meeting my parents, going to church, your got-damn hair. Now I find out you've been telling people you think I'm a murderer?"

Had she consumed some of the wine, like she'd wanted to earlier, she just might have voiced her initial thought, which was, *Well, you really do have your meddling-ass mama to blame for that last item.* Instead, she dropped her head and said, "I'm sorry. I didn't mean to hurt you."

He shoved an item into the bag. "In the five months we've been together, I've been nothing but faithful and loving and attentive. For most women that would have been more than enough."

She looked up and, in a voice minus any rancor or maliciousness, said, "I'm not most women."

"Yeah, well, maybe that's your problem," Javiel said, raising his own voice a bit.

"No doubt it is," she said, turning her focus to a flaw she'd noticed in her bed's comforter.

"I loved you," he said in angry whisper. "What more could I have possibly done?"

Moved by the depth of his hurt and helplessness, and the role she'd played in their creation, she placed a hand against the knot growing in her throat. "Javiel, all I ever wanted was for you to see me. I thought you did. But I was wrong."

"See you? I built a holy fucking shrine to your image. But according to you, I'm blind?!" He zipped up his bag and snatched it from her bed. "Whatever, babe. I'm through trying to please you. This is some bullshit I could just as well live without."

He skipped the formality of a good-bye, bolted from the room, and practically ran down the flight of stairs. By the time she made it down to the living room, he had already jumped into his car and started the engine. Monica, who'd arrived at some point, whispered a few parting words to Jesus before sending him off with a kiss.

"You okay?" Monica asked, after the front door closed.

"Yeah, I'm good," Aliesha said. She wrapped her arms around herself and put on a fake happy face.

Monica studied Aliesha for a couple of seconds, then tossed her purse into a chair. "Why don't I make us some tea?"

Aliesha shook her head. "Be my guest. I'm in the mood for a bit of wine myself."

Monica walked over and gently pried apart Aliesha's self-embrace. She then circled one of her own arms protectively around one of her friend's. "Well, you know I'm not much of a drinker," she said as they ambled toward the kitchen. "But watching you get sloshed might be kinda fun."

Aliesha chuckled. "Sorry to disappoint you, girlfriend, but all I want is a little something to take the edge off. I've got a Sunday school class to teach in the morning and I'm not about to step up in there with a hangover."

"Oh hell," Monica said. "Like it would devastate any of those Holy Rollers you hang with to see you let your hair down just this once. From what I understand, even Jesus himself got his sip on every now and then."

CHAPTER 20

Similar to the meeting at the beauty shop, the Sunday church outing with Peaches turned out a lot better than Aliesha had anticipated. Her jaw dropped considerably on noting that rather than settle into a quiet corner and be content with listening, Peaches wasted nary a second in jumping tongue first into the fray—asking questions, sharing her own opinions, and at times adamantly voicing her dissent—when the highly opinionated regulars of Aliesha's class launched into their usual lively discussion and debate of the Sunday school lesson. Aliesha realized she was witnessing a side of the bald, blind clairvoyant she never even knew existed. She wondered if that particular feature of Peaches's personality was something new or if perhaps it had always been there and she had just been too silly and skittish to look for the length of time required to see it.

She'd found equally pleasing the way Tamara had immediately taken to Peaches. Had anyone asked prior to her arrival at Garden View that morning, Aliesha would have been forced to confess she had prayed that her mouthy student would either stay at home or select some other church to visit. But during the course of the occasionally heated discourse, Tamara had not only shown an early inclination to side with Peaches's point of view, but before the class ended she'd all but designated herself the woman's cheerleader. "I know that's right, girl. Uh-huh, talk about it. Amen! Amen!"

After Sunday school rather than head out after a quick good-bye, Tamara stayed through the end of service and pestered Aliesha into letting her join the twosome for lunch. Unable to contain her fascination and intrigue, while walking with them to the church's parking lot, Tamara had peppered Aliesha with a barrage of questions and comments. "So how long have you known her? Is she a professor or a seminary student somewhere? And that beautiful singing voice! I can't decide if she sounds more like a Mavis Staples or a Cassandra Wilson. She kind of reminds you of that African model, Alek Wek, don't you think?"

When Tamara had finally paused for a breath, Aliesha had quickly seized the opening and said, "We've known each other since we were kids. And no, she's not a professor or a student, she's a hairstylist. I'd definitely say her sound is more Cassandra than Mavis. And now that you've mentioned it, I guess she does resemble Alek Wek a bit." When Aliesha noticed Tamara raring up for another round, she'd quickly added, "But for the record, you might want to keep in mind that Peaches is blind, not deaf."

With that, Peaches, who'd been holding on to Aliesha's arm, had giggled, while a shame-faced Tamara had stuttered her way through an apology.

Though she'd pretended otherwise, Aliesha had been anything but oblivious to all of the stares, double takes, and sideway glances the happy trio had garnered over the course of their hour-long lunch at the crowded, family-style restaurant in which they'd chosen to dine. Given their obvious similarities as far as body type and skin coloring, Aliesha wondered if most onlookers assumed they were related. Later, after having given the matter some thought, she marveled at how collectively they could all be so visible and yet on an individual, everyday, one-on-one basis remain so ignored, if not virtually unseen.

Aliesha's grief over what had transpired between her and Javiel lasted all of one night. By the following Sunday morning, the one she'd spent in the company of Peaches and Tamara, the thick clouds over her head had already begun to dissipate. By that Sunday evening, the clouds had scattered and turned into feathery streaks. Come Wednesday, they'd faded into memory altogether and she'd felt a sense of freedom that bordered on giddiness.

But when she strutted into Wally's Cool Cuts that Wednesday afternoon and didn't spy her new hairstylist in his usual spot, her high sank a little. *Damn, I knew I should have called and reminded him,* she chided herself as she walked toward the back where Yazz sat, swiveling from side to side and sporting the same goofy grin she'd seen plastered across his mug at the onset of their first meeting.

"What up, Miz Professor?!" he said. "Your boy just called. He told me to let you know that he had to run a quick errand. Said he'd be along in fifteen minutes or so. You can go 'head and sit in his chair if you want."

With Yazz still grinning, spinning, and charting her every move, she walked over and eased herself into Dante's chair. Determined not to let the young barber rattle her, on removing her day planner from her bag, Aliesha turned the chair so that she faced the shop's entrance. She opened the planner and prayed he'd get the hint.

"Aww, now, it's not like that, is it?" he asked.

Rather than swerve back around or even glance sideways over her shoulder, Aliesha stared at his reflection in the mirror against the wall. "Not like what?" she asked.

Yazz stopped grinning, slowed the motion of his chair, and stared back at her. "Look here, Miz Professor, last week I was just being silly. I really didn't mean no harm. That's just how I do. You not fixing to hold it against me, are you?"

"No," Aliesha said, grateful for what she gathered was his way of apologizing. "We're cool."

"Good," he said. "'Cause I don't think D. would ever let me live it down if we weren't."

Before either of them could say another word, Gerald called out, "Yo, Yazz! Man, where them clean towels you was supposed to be bringing us, like half a damn hour ago?"

Yazz threw back his head and in a loud voice said, "See, that's why it don't pay for me to come through here early. These fools act like I'm they errand boy or something."

He stood and stretched his long limbs until the joints popped and cracked. "Excuse me while I go tend to my unpaid and unappreciated servant duties, Miz P. Can I get you anything while I'm back there? Soda? Some chips?"

"No, thanks," Aliesha said, rewarding the courtesy he'd shown her by actually turning and addressing him directly. "I'm good."

He flashed his goofy grin and yelled, "Clean towels coming up!" before spinning around like one of the Temptations or else J.J. from the old *Good Times* sitcom.

Aliesha sat back and reflected on Yazz's statement about Dante never letting him live it down. It suggested they, or specifically Dante, had been talking about her. To her annoyance, she still couldn't tell if the vibe she was picking up from him was one of true interest or simply playful cordiality.

Also, this being the second time in a row he'd shown himself unprepared to work on her eyebrows, she'd begun to suspect that doing them was something he either didn't want or else didn't really know how to do. She glanced at her watch. While debating on whether to leave or just calm down, relax, and wait, she noticed Dante's work smock hanging from the coatrack tucked in the corner of his barber's station. Her gaze almost immediately fell upon the now-familiar paperback that peeked out from one of the smock's pockets. *What is it with him and this book,* she wondered? Without thinking twice about it, she rose and removed the paperback from the garment.

On returning to her seat and peeling open the pages, she discovered a photo wedged inside. Based on the strong resemblance, she initially assumed the two little boys she saw in the picture were Dante's offspring. But within seconds, she realized the larger and darker of the two, smiling youths was actually Dante. Her gaze then turned to the petite, middle-aged woman seated between the two boys. On noting the proud tilt of the woman's head, her naturally styled hair, and the undeniable twinkle in her eyes, Aliesha took an instant liking to her. She smiled and tucked the photo back into the book. But her face soon wore a puzzled expression on her discovery of the words scribbled on the paperback's inside front cover: "Property of Reuben Reese."

Who was Reuben Reese? A friend? An acquaintance? Or simply the book's previous owner? If so, how did Dante come to possess his book? Then again, maybe Dante had picked up the book secondhand—possibly at a used bookstore or a yard sale.

She'd taken leave of her seat again when Yazz reappeared with a tall stack of folded towels. "Curiosity got the best of me," she said, feeling the need to confess before shoving the book back into the pocket of Dante's smock.

"D. won't mind. There's plenty more where those came from." Yazz sat down the towels and opened the tall, free-standing locker in the corner opposite the coat rack. On every shelf sat a tight row of both softback and hardback books. Yazz opened up a cabinet beneath the counter and showed Aliesha more of the same. "Here's where he keeps most the kids' books."

"Kids' books?" Aliesha said.

"Yeah, you know, for all the lil' shorties who come in here, like Sam Junior's two. Sometimes to keep 'em quiet while they're waiting for their turn in the chair, D. will give 'em a handful of comics or a book." Yazz pulled out an oversized children's picture book and handed it to Aliesha. "Sometimes when it's slow and the kid's young enough and cutting up tough enough, D. will even sit down and read to 'em. And this here is just a drop in the bucket. Dude's got loads more back in the laundry room."

Aliesha nodded and passed the book back to Yazz and watched as he returned it and refastened the cabinet doors. But before she could properly absorb and make sense of it all, the bell over the shop door clattered and Dante strode in with a backpack slung over his shoulder. He nodded a greeting at Wally and Gerald.

"You got a customer waiting on you," Wally said, sounding none-too-pleased. He looked back and gestured with his head toward Aliesha.

"Yeah, I know," Dante said, picking up his pace. "My apologies, Ms. Professor. I had every intention of being here. But I've been waiting for the past couple of weeks for this guy to call me about a headstone." He tossed his backpack aside and reached for his smock. "How about, in addition to taking care of your eyebrows, I make it up to you by throwing in a free shampoo, condition, and style?"

"Oh, I don't really think that's necessary. You didn't keep me waiting *that* long."

"What?!" Dante said, feigning shock. "You turning down one of my shampoos? I could have sworn the main thing bringing you back was my Big Mama's lavender-scented creek water."

Yazz laughed, grabbed up the towels, and said, "Man, you a trip!" He bumped fists with Dante before heading up front.

Forgetting all about the books and feeling like the butt of some private joke, Aliesha fell silent. They had been talking about her.

After Dante washed his hands at the small sink on the

counter of his workstation, he removed a pair of tweezers from a drawer and moved toward her. He made a few adjustments to the chair and its headrest before instructing her to lean back. When he ran his fingers over her brows, rather than close her eyes or even give in to the urge to bat her lashes, she stared blankly ahead.

"You just want them cleaned up, right?" he asked.

"Yes," she said.

He lowered his hands and stared at her until she finally steered her gaze his way.

"I'm sorry I was late and I'm sorry if my teasing offended you," he said.

"It's fine. I'm not upset," she said.

"No, it's not. And yeah, you are," he said as he brought the tweezers to her face and began plucking at the stray hairs. "And because of that, I'm going to let you in on a secret. My Big Mama wears her hair like you do—in a natural. And whenever I go see her and stay for an extended period of time, guess what ends up happening?"

"She begs you to wash her hair?"

Dante stopped plucking and shook his head. "Nope. Believe it or not, I'm the one who ends up doing all of the begging. I don't know what it is, but I've always enjoyed washing her hair."

Aliesha smiled. "And I thought I was strange."

He smiled back. "No, you and I are fine. But my boy, Yazz, on the other hand—"

They both laughed.

When Dante finished a few minutes later, he said, "All done!" and passed her the mirror.

She held it up, turned her head from side to side, nodded her approval, and said, "Excellent."

"Good," he said. "So, do I get the additional pleasure of washing your hair?"

"If you insist," she said. She followed him to the back and positioned herself on the bench in front of the bowl. Before he draped and fastened a cloak around her, he positioned a towel around her neck to keep the water from running into her clothes. While he worked, she stole a glance at the cabinets fixed against the wall above the washer and dryer and the ones between and above the two large sinks.

"Something wrong?" Dante asked when he moved in front of her. With his help, she stretched out on the bench and eased her neck against the curve of the bowl.

Unable to keep her mind off the book in his smock, she said, "I was just wondering. That woman, the one I saw in the picture you keep in your book, that's your Big Mama, isn't it?"

"Wait a minute," Dante said, while reaching for the sprayer. "A brother can't be a few minutes late without folks using it as an opportunity to snoop through his stuff?"

The film reel in Aliesha's head spun backward until it found and flashed a few minutes worth of an angry Javiel's similar accusations. "I'm sorry," she said. "Really and truly, I didn't mean any harm. It's just—"

"Miz Professor," Dante said with a grin. "It's okay. Why are you so sensitive?" He turned on the sprayer and worked the jet streams over her head. He used one hand to guide the water and the other to part, stroke, and manipulate her hair.

By the time he finished and turned off the water, she'd relaxed and her alarm had been replaced by embarrassment. "I'm not usually—hypersensitive, that is," she said, picking up where they'd left off.

He nodded. "Well, your fascination with this book is starting to remind me of Reuben's." He slapped his hand against the pocket that contained the paperback. "And before you ask, he was the little light-skinned kid with the glasses you saw in the picture with me and my Big Mama."

"Is he your brother?" Aliesha asked as Dante worked the shampoo into her hair.

"For all practical purposes," Dante said. "Our Big Mama raised us both, but we're actually cousins, and technically she's our aunt."

Aliesha fell silent again. Several minutes passed before she allowed her natural curiosity to resurface. "So, why is it you have his book, if you don't mind me asking?"

Dante shrugged. "I don't know. I guess in a way I'm looking for clues. *The Metamorphosis* is something I first noticed him reading right before he took off for college. For years, every time I saw him after that—when I went to visit him or he came home—he'd have the book with him or else somewhere nearby. Just recently, I found out he owns at least seven identical copies. I'm saying, what's up with that?"

Perplexity seized her freshly shaped eyebrows. "Why don't you just ask him?"

Dante frowned. "I could, but even if he told me, I probably wouldn't understand him."

Aliesha chuckled. "He's that deep, is he?"

Dante paused for a moment and, on resuming the motion of his hands, looked away from her and laughed. "In a manner of speaking, Miz Professor, I guess he is. But it would probably be equally accurate to say—he's dead."

Dante turned on the sprayer again, forcing Aliesha to spend a few minutes pondering his last statement. She waited until he'd finished rinsing her and had begun toweling her dry before she said, "You do realize the whole time you were talking about your cousin, not once did you ever speak of him in past tense?"

Dante sighed. "I thought you said you'd spent a lot of summers down here with your Big Mama? Didn't she ever teach you that just because a body has died, that doesn't necessarily make them gone?"

Before they vacated the utility room, Aliesha had meant to ask Dante about the other books, the ones Yazz had shown her and ones he hadn't. But after Dante's peculiar reference to the dead, she'd become distracted and wrapped up in trying to figure out if she'd stumbled upon a fully sighted and hair-having, male version of Peaches.

She slipped so deep in thought, she didn't think to make any additional inquiries until after Dante had finished with her hair and walked her outside. "So, how long ago did your cousin pass?" she asked as they stood out in front of Wally's Cool Cuts.

"'Bout a month ago," Dante said.

"You have my belated condolences," she said. "I suppose all those books Yazz showed me behind your barber's chair were his, Reuben's?"

A glaze descended over Dante's dark eyes. "Yeah, I don't guess a big, black strapping buck like me would look much like the type who'd get caught spending money on books, much less reading them, huh?"

Taken aback by the bitterness and unwarranted hostility she'd heard in his voice, especially after the pleasantries they'd just shared and the door he'd voluntarily opened into his world, Aliesha said, "I don't think I said or implied anything of the sort. Who's being overly sensitive now?" Rather than wait for an answer, she walked away and had stepped off the curb when she heard him call to her, "Say, Miz Professor?"

A part of her wanted to keep on walking and pretend as if she hadn't heard him. Given all of the traffic noise, she probably could have gotten away with it. But she stopped and turned.

Wearing a hint of a smile, he said, "You forgot to ask me what I was listening to."

Fighting against the urge to tell him she didn't rightly

give a damn, she strolled back toward him. She took the buds he'd wiped clean for her and inserted them into her ears. She'd been fully prepared for yet another selection from what had been her mother and father's extensive R & B collection. But what she heard instead was a song by a more contemporary musician, Eric Benét, singing "Pretty Baby," a stunningly beautiful song that Aliesha had always assumed Mr. Benét had penned in honor of his former wife, the actress Halle Berry. On recognizing the tune, Aliesha closed her eyes and listened longer than she had on either of her previous two occasions.

On her return of the earbuds, Dante said, "You like?"

"Yeah, I do," she said. "*Hurricane,* the CD that particular song is from, is actually one of my favorites." What she didn't tell him but wished she could have was that the CD was one she'd listened and cried to for days on end in the aftermath of her breakup with Kenneth. "'Pretty Baby' is nice," she said, trying to will back the melancholy she felt coming on. "But to be honest, I like the thirteenth cut, 'I Wanna Be Loved,' even better."

In a quiet voice and wearing an expression she wasn't able to read, Dante said, "So, should I pencil you in on my calendar for the same time next week?"

"Yeah, I guess you could do that," she said.

He hadn't meant to snap so hard when she'd mistaken his books for Reuben's. She had no way of knowing about his sore spots, the wounds he constantly nursed, though they never seemed to fully heal. She'd unintentionally stumbled upon two. Hard, fast assumptions, whether about his intellect or his aspirations, had never ceased to annoy him, and those that granted Reuben a claim to what was rightfully his incensed Dante the most. Even from his grave, it seemed his cousin owned the uncanny ability to outshine his light and cast shadows of discord and doubt where none ought be.

With that sole exception, Dante hadn't minded Aliesha's inquiries. He'd readily taken them as a sign that she'd found him worthy of further exploration. A certain part of him longed for her to know that he, too, possessed a curiosity about life and the world, a curiosity that went beyond sports, sex, food, politics, and the concrete terrain outside of his dirt-streaked windows. But given the circumstances, he couldn't be sure how or if such revelations would benefit either of them.

Why put yourself in the position of courting temptation? Hasn't the girl already told you she's spoken for? So what if you feel an odd twinge, ache, or pain here or there whenever she comes around. What evidence suggests it's anything other than a weakness of the flesh—one you know is subject to lead you both astray if you let it?

Unable to argue affectively to the contrary, Dante resigned himself to staying in brake mode. While he'd spoken openly with Aliesha about his deceased cousin and Reuben's odd fascination with Kafka's *Metamorphosis*, he'd stopped short of revealing his own theory about the matter or how a certain woman fit snugly into the picture—if not between the two cousins and in much the same manner as their Big Mama in the picture Aliesha had found inside of the book.

He'd spent the past several weeks mulling the mystery and had finally concluded that not unlike Gregor, the main character in Kafka's puzzling literary masterpiece, at some unknown point in time, his cousin Reuben must have awakened one day and found himself changed into something horrible and completely unrecognizable—a monster of some form or fashion. He doubted such a revelation would have made sense to Aliesha. No, it probably would have made her suspect he was a bit touched or possibly a mite unstable, even more so than his quip about the dead not being gone no doubt already had.

So, again, like the voice in his head advised, he'd held back, except in that one area where neither his will nor the voice's warnings seemed to have any sway—the music. It wasn't like he planned any of it. His iPod stayed fixed, as it normally did, on random play. The songs, the ones most befitting of the mood and the moment just sort of happened, as if spun in some alternate universe on an old-fashioned turntable and during the late-night shift of a nameless deejay whose quiet storm tastes mirrored Dante's own.

Had she noticed? Or was she too caught up in her own desires to pay the struggle he'd been waging with his the least bit of attention?

While watching her listen to Benét's "Pretty Baby," Dante reflected on the similarities between her and his Big Mama. The blackberry-colored skin, which celebrated their descent from the cradle of civilization and marked them as the original descendants of Eve. The hair, owning the dense and alternating blend of elasticity and resistance his fingers so loved to roam. The royal bearing and stern veneers, which deterred all but the most aggressive and determined detractors and even kept them from scoring direct hits against the soft, tender parts hidden inside.

But on finding his gaze hungry for more, even as it savored the quiver of Aliesha's lowered lashes and the twitch of pleasure riding the span of her full lips, he knew the time had come to embrace the truth. The unsettling mix of boyish longing and mannish desire the professor stirred within him was much more aligned with how he'd once felt about another woman. A woman who like his Big Mama had long been a fixture in the center of his world. A woman whose ability to render murky both his past and his present easily surpassed that of Reuben's. A smart, beautiful, cunning enchantress whose warm body and bewitching ways had, in fact, once come between him and his cousin. A woman named Laylah whose spell Dante was yet uncertain he knew how to break without severing his own heart.

CHAPTER 21

Late Thursday afternoon found Aliesha seated behind the desk in her office and discussing by phone a draft of an article Monica had written and asked Aliesha to proof before she submitted it to one of the prestigious academic journals in which her work routinely appeared.

"Thanks, girl," Monica said. "Good thing you called when you did because I was fully prepared to send it out 'as is' within the next hour or so."

"No problem," Aliesha said. "I would have gotten back with you about it sooner, but I really didn't get around to reading it until last night."

"Wednesday night, huh? Isn't that the night you and Javiel generally got together?"

"Yep," Aliesha said.

"You heard from him at all?"

"Nope."

"And I can tell you're not terribly bothered by that fact, either—are you?"

"Not really."

Monica laughed. "Girl, what are we gonna do with you? Okay, so what's been cooking up between you and the hot stuff barber you dumped Javiel for?"

"Nothing," Aliesha said. "Besides, that's not why Javiel

and I broke up, and I really wish you'd stop suggesting otherwise."

"Okay, back up," Monica said. "Didn't you stop by
dude's shop the other day?"

"Yes, I did."

"And? Why are you going coy on me all of a sudden?"

"I'm not," Aliesha said. "It's just . . . I don't know. I'm
not sure how to read him. As of late, the signals he's been
sending my way have been mixed, at best."

"Hell," Monica said. "He's probably gay."

"He's not gay," Aliesha said.

"How do you know? Have you asked him? Has he ever
said anything about having a wife or a girlfriend?"

"Monica, I'm sure if he were gay I would have picked
up on the fact by now. Don't you think?"

"Not if he's perfected the art of being on the down-low.
A lot of brothers out here have, you know."

"Sheesh, would you stop with that already?"

"Okay, fine," Monica said. "So maybe he's got a thing
for White girls. . . ."

Aliesha laughed. "I swear if you're not as bullheaded
and stubborn as Tamara."

Beaming as hard as any proud parent, Aliesha passed
Tamara's clipboard full of neatly transcribed notes across
the table. "Well done!" she said. "When we get back to
campus, remind me to give you a list of journals to start
researching. By the end of the semester, you should be more
than ready to draft and submit an article or two."

A grinning Tamara put away her material and dived
into the taco salad on the table in front of her. Their food
court lunch date at a mall not far from Wells had been her
idea. Besides her ongoing boycott of the university's cafe-

teria, she'd been determined to have Aliesha's undivided attention, something not always possible in the professor's campus office—where interruptions by students, faculty members, and a ringing phone were common. Beyond Tamara's expressed desire to give Aliesha a detailed update on the ethnographic research she'd been conducting at a local strip club was her unspoken one to simply hang out with her favorite professor.

While the smile on Aliesha's face faded enough for her to take a proper bite out of her turkey sub, the smile she kept housed on the inside stretched even wider. Outside of her tendency to lead by the lip and talk when she should be listening, Tamara had proved the ideal student. From day one she'd shown up in Aliesha's class on time, always sat near the front, never failed to ask provocative questions, aced most of her tests, and consistently turned in all of her assignments when, if not before, they were due.

After a bit of digging, prying, and asking around, Aliesha had ascertained that the then senior behaved similarly and performed just as well in all of her classes. Tamara, in fact, had a long history of academic excellence. After having quickly exhausted the limits of her public school's advanced placement courses and gifted programs, she'd been moved up a couple of grades. She'd ended up graduating from high school at age fifteen and entering college when she'd barely turned sixteen, which helped explain, at least in part, some of the immaturity she so frequently exhibited. In light of her high test scores and her exceptional academic record, she could have gone to school most anywhere. But not wanting to be too far from her mother, who'd been in failing health for years, Tamara had elected to stay in Riverton and attend Wells University. At age nineteen and on the verge of completing her undergraduate course work, but unsure of what she wanted to pursue after graduation, she'd landed in Professor Eaton's class and shortly thereafter realized she'd found both the calling and the role model she'd long sought.

Aliesha took seriously the task of steering Tamara in the right direction. She understood that the attention the young girl seemed to crave so desperately, she genuinely needed, if only to keep herself from succumbing to the legions of doubt—both internal and external—primed to take her down.

"You know what Peaches told me the other night?" Tamara asked. "She said even though the two of you have known each other practically all of your lives, she thinks she still makes you highly uncomfortable. Is that true?"

Aliesha lowered her sandwich. "When did you see Peaches?"

"I didn't. I talked to her on the phone the other night. Remember when we exchanged numbers after lunch last Sunday?

After wiping her mouth, Aliesha said, "Listen, Tamara, if making a pet project out of Peaches is what you have in mind, I really don't think that's such a good idea."

"Now why on earth would I want to do that? I happen to like Peaches. We have a lot in common, actually."

"Yeah, be that what it may—"

"Besides," Tamara said, before Aliesha could finish, "she needs a friend. And if anyone knows what it's like to want and need a real friend and not have one, it's me."

Rather than argue the point, Aliesha let it go. She wasn't totally unfamiliar with the social isolation Tamara had no doubt experienced as an academically gifted Black girl in a predominately White environment.

"Lord have mercy, would you get a load of this?" Tamara said while rising halfway out of her seat and glaring over the railing that roped off the mall's elevated food court. "Isn't that Professor Bastard's wife over there?"

"Who?" Aliesha said, shocked that Tamara would actually feel comfortable enough to utter the Anthropology Department chair's nickname aloud.

"You know—'Shithead'—ooh, my bad, I meant Dr. Beale. Well, his wife, Mrs. Beale, anyway. Yeah, that's her. Remember when I told you I'd seen her walking around in Macy's with those poor babies hooked up on leashes and you acted like you didn't want to believe me? Well, have a look for yourself."

Aliesha peered over the railing and quickly spotted the trio traipsing along the mall's lower level. She shook her head at the sight of the two cute, biracial little girls who were straining against the harnesses strapped around their tiny torsos.

Tamara tossed her napkin onto the table. "I still say somebody needs to say something to her about parading around here with those babies on choke chains and leashes, like they're rabid dogs or something. And where in the world is she taking them to get their hair done? Over to Don King's? If she's not careful, she's liable to walk into the wrong place at the wrong time and one of these street corner militant types is gonna give her a not-so-nice piece of his mind."

"Don't forget, she didn't grow up here," Aliesha said, hoping to defuse some of the outrage she heard gaining strength in her young student's voice. "Where she's from, it may not be all that unusual for children to be harnessed when they're taken out."

"Yeah, well, ole girl is in Riverton now." Tamara seized her napkin and began twisting and wringing it as if it were full of water. "And if she doesn't know any better, that sorry excuse for a brother she's married to dang well oughta."

"Careful. Bring it down a notch," Aliesha warned, deciding the time had arrived for her to take advantage of both her seniority and position of authority.

"Come on, Dr. Eaton! We can't just sit here!" Tamara said, her voice caught between a whine and a shout. She stood and shouldered her backpack. "Let's go say something to her."

"I'm sorry," Aliesha said with a slow shake of the head. "It's not our place."

"Since when?" Tamara asked. When Aliesha didn't budge and went back to eating her sandwich, Tamara dropped back into her seat, leaned forward, and said, "Who was it who said, 'If we accept and acquiesce in the face of discrimination . . .'"

Aliesha readily recognized the quote as one by Mary McLeod Bethune and, at the end of it, couldn't help but laugh. However inappropriate, the girl was attempting to take the words of one of her own personal sheroes, and use them against her.

"Okay, we'll go," she said. "But please, let me do most of the talking."

Aliesha had hoped in time her issues with Dr. Shelton Beale, the only other African American professor in the Anthropology Department, would pass. Instead they had only intensified. Shelton's assumption of the department's chairperson position had occurred after Aliesha's hiring but shortly before her arrival at Wells. She suspected that had he already been at the helm he would have done everything within his power to prevent her from ever having come on board in the first place.

Shelton had no real reason to be jealous of her. After all, as he was so keen on proclaiming to all those willing to listen, he was the one who held the highly esteemed Ivy League degrees and the much-coveted tenure. And try as she might, Aliesha had yet to pinpoint what, if anything, she'd ever said or done that might have warranted the intense animosity he so routinely hurled in her direction.

According to her friend and colleague, Pat, who'd known

and worked with Shelton for a number of years, "Shelton's always been something of a jerk and all-around rat bastard. He hates and looks down on just about everybody, and in turn most everybody hates and looks down on him. Don't waste your time trying to take it personally."

However, increasingly, Aliesha had become more inclined to align herself with Monica's way of thinking. "The problem with a fool like Shelton is, not only does he want to be viewed as the bright, shining example of the exceptional Negro, he wants to be the sole representative of such. You showing up on the scene messed up his whole program, not to mention his warped image of himself."

Aliesha didn't know a lot about Shelton's wife, Kristen, other than she hailed from Norway and wasn't too much older than Tamara. Rumor had it the couple had met overseas one summer and during the course of some research project in which Shelton had been involved. Shortly after meeting, they had embarked on a very much frowned-upon May–December, student–teacher type of romance. In the two years she'd taught at Wells, Aliesha could only remember having seen Kristen a couple of times, and on both occasions she'd been struggling to keep up with the adorable wild-haired children with the creamy peanut-colored faces and the shockingly sky blue eyes.

Unlike so many other children of mixed heritage, whose locks leaned decidedly toward the straight and wavy, the gene pendulum for Shelton and Kristen's two had evidently swung in another direction and landed in some yet-unnamed territory. Wiry, willful, defiant, and bypassing the uniformity of most afros, their jet black hair stood up every which-a-way on their heads, giving them the appearance of frightened porcupines.

Aliesha knew most Black women, mothers in particular, couldn't help but wince when they caught a glimpse of the pair, if not get hit by visions of either dancing hot combs, stiff brushes, jars of smelly hair oil, or cheap no-lye relaxer kits.

Hoping not to startle the ruddy-cheeked blonde, who appeared to be losing the battle to keep her toddlers from charging off like a couple of ill-trained Eskimo sleigh pups and dragging her, their ill-equipped driver, through the mall, Aliesha approached them cautiously and with a smile, "Hi, Kristen. How are you?"

When the young, harried mother looked up with a frown, Aliesha said, "You may not remember meeting me, but I'm Aliesha Eaton. I work in the same department as your husband."

"Oh yes, Dr. Eaton," Kristen said. Her expression softened. "Of course I remember you. How could I ever forget? Shelton talks about you all the time."

Aliesha wasn't sure how or if she even cared to interpret that last odd kernel of information. "And this is Tamara Howard," she said. "She's a graduate student and research assistant in our program."

Even though Aliesha could tell that Tamara was raring for a chance to charge off on a verbal rampage, the youth managed to contain herself long enough to step forward and exchange pleasantries with Kristen.

"Looks like you've got your hands pretty full," Aliesha said as she watched the harnessed children circle in opposite directions around their mother and, as a result, bind the poor woman's legs together. "I don't know if you've ever noticed, but near the main entrance of the mall they have these double-seated strollers with nice-sized compartments attached, which allow you to store your bags and keep your hands relatively free."

"Yeah," Tamara said. "'Cause unless you all are headed to or from a Snoop Dogg video shoot, those leashes you've got on your little girls are SO NOT cool. And pardon me for saying it, but what's up with their hair?"

The smile on Aliesha's face held steady, in spite of her desire to treat Tamara to a royal chewing out.

"Oh, I'm sorry," Kristen said. Her eyes skittered between the two Black women standing before her, as if afraid to settle for too long on either the natural-haired Aliesha or the perm-sporting Tamara. "It never even occurred to me that keeping them in tow like this might strike anyone as offensive. And their hair, again, you'll have to forgive me. I really didn't feel like hassling with it this morning. I'm afraid I haven't exactly figured out a way of dealing with it that doesn't leave them in tears and me at my wit's end."

Before Aliesha could interject, Tamara said, "You ever thought about taking them to somebody's hair salon?"

"You don't think they're too young?" Kristen said, sounding thoroughly embarrassed and confused.

"Well, you might not want to subject them to anything harsh or chemically based just yet," Aliesha said, grateful that Tamara allowed her to get that much in.

"So what would you recommend?" Kristen asked. "I've thought about taking them somewhere to have their hair braided. You know, like that gorgeous singer, Alicia Keys? From what I understand, she's a child of mixed heritage, too."

"Ooh! Ooh! And I know just the perfect person for the job," Tamara said.

Aliesha shook her head and prayed, *Oh, please God, no. Don't let this child open her mouth and say what I think she's about to.*

"Yep, our good friend Peaches. I'm sure she could do wonders with their hair," Tamara said, sounding right proud of herself.

Aliesha nodded politely but didn't say a word. Of course, on the inside she was letting loose with her best Florida Evans imitation: Damn! Damn! Damn!

CHAPTER 22

On her subsequent visit to Wally's, Aliesha got lucky and wound up having Dante all to herself. No other customers ahead of her or behind. No grinning, big-mouthed Yazz with whom to contend. Just pure, unadulterated Dante. Of course, she hadn't thought of it in those exact terms when she'd walked in and spotted him seated alone at his barber's station with a stylish cap pulled down over this brow and the ever-present book clutched tight in the dark, smooth capable hands she still longed to know better.

Intellectually, she fully accepted the attraction for what she thought it was, a physical response to a good-looking man who possessed a special knack for making her feel and look wonderful. However, emotionally, she couldn't stop herself from wanting, craving, and needing so much more.

On first glance, she'd thought him asleep. But as she'd drawn nearer, she'd realized she'd actually stumbled upon him deep in thought. When his eyes finally flickered open, they seemed to take her in fully and completely without veering off course to look past her, through her, or zone in or any particular feature of her anatomy.

When she smiled, he sat up and removed his cap. "How are you?" she said.

"Very good," he said, returning her smile. He stood, pocketed both the book and the headgear, then waved his hand over his chair. "And at the moment, all yours."

"That you are," she said on climbing into his chair. "So, where's Yazz?"

He whipped out a cloak and draped it around her. "What? Don't tell me you're actually trying to miss him?"

Aliesha laughed. "Yazz and I have arrived at what I would call a proper understanding."

"Good, I'm glad to hear it. Underneath it all, Yazz is a pretty decent guy. He's always trying to get me involved with some morally uplifting activity at his church or community center. Just this past weekend, he had me helping him give free haircuts and shaves to some of the guys down at the homeless shelter."

She nodded. "It's nice to know his actions speak better of him than do his words."

Dante laughed. "Yeah, I figured that would score us at least a few brownie points in your eyes."

"Am I that bad?" Aliesha asked. "I'd hate to think I make you feel like I'm grading you."

"Hey, I don't take it personally. I'm sure it's nothing more than the matronly schoolmarm in you who can't help but stay hard at work, 24/7."

"The matronly schoolmarm?!" Aliesha said. "Thanks a lot. If I didn't know any better, I'd think I was talking to Yazz."

"See, there you go getting all sensitive on me again," Dante said. "I've got nothing but mad respect for school-teachers, be they matronly, hot-to-trot, or something in-between."

She turned and issued him a look that prompted them both into a round of laughter. She noted their more re-laxed give-and-take and hoped it would last.

He picked out her hair and while working his way from

back to front he said, "I'm sorry if I came off as somewhat defensive about the whole book thing the last time you were here. That's been sort of an ongoing sore point for me."

"Why is that?" she asked, realizing he finally felt like talking about it.

Speaking slowly and hesitantly, he said, "I guess growing up, there was always this sort of division between me and my cousin Reuben, not one necessarily of our making, mind you, but one nonetheless. He had the rep for bringing home good grades, the smart one who always had his nose in a book. Me, I was the big, quiet kid who hung out in the gym and on the ball field and who nobody expected much from as far as academics were concerned. Back in the day, people were constantly trying to shove us into these neat, little, confining boxes, ignoring the fact that they didn't always fit."

Unsure if she truly grasped the gist of the tale he'd shared, she asked, "Should I take that to mean *he* wanted to be the jock and *you* wanted to be the scholar?"

Dante paused, tossed aside the hair pick, and snatched up the clippers. "To tell you the truth, Miz Professor, all I ever wanted was the same chance, the same type of encouragement and attention he got. Who knows where I might be today had that happened."

Sensing her inquiry had scraped against a sensitive nerve, she waited until their eyes connected in the wall-mounted mirror at his station before she said, "Is where you are today so bad?"

"No, I suppose I could have done worse," he said. "And don't get me wrong, I'm not blaming my Big Mama or my uncle Mack. Neither one of them made it past the ninth grade. They were only taking their cues from everybody else around them."

Dante turned off the clippers and moved in front of her.

She stared into the deep pools of his dark brown eyes and saw sadness where she'd expected to see anger. Before he could lean forward and switch back on the clippers, she reached out with her words as gently as she knew how. "There's nothing wrong with being athletically gifted. You could very well have taken that path to college and then gone on to to do other things. It's not unheard of."

He responded in kind. "Yeah, see, but that's just the thing—sports was never really in my blood, at least not like it is for some guys. I had to work hard to stay competitive. But the more I played and practiced, the less time I had to devote to anything academic. I was in my junior year when I went up for a pass, got hit, came down wrong, and shattered my leg in six different places."

He turned the clippers back on and glided them over her head. "After that, I didn't even have the heart to try anymore. About all I could do was sit on the sidelines and watch while all of the world, including my cousin Reuben, passed me by."

She winced. "I can see where an event like that might cause some additional strife and tension, particularly in a relationship that's already marked by jealousy."

"You got that right. I went through a real hateful and destructive period. It's a wonder I didn't land in jail or kill somebody. I guess it's like my Big Mama always says—it was only by the Grace of God that I didn't."

"But there obviously came a turning point," Aliesha said. "What was it?"

A pained expression gripped Dante's face. He traded the clippers for a small pair of scissors. "My uncle Mack's stroke. It knocked him off his feet, both literally and financially. When it got to point where he started talking about selling some, if not all, of the little piece of land his daddy had passed down to him, I knew I didn't have but two choices—either man up or let everybody down. So I got myself together. Got a job on a roofing crew with the father of one of my old teammates, started doing what I could as far as seeing after both the old man and my Big Mama's personal needs, and during the course of it, discovered I had something of a talent for cutting hair."

———∞———

A phone call cut into Dante's spiel. He stepped away from her to speak with the caller in private. At the call's end he resumed his work on her hair in silence.

She fought back her urge to drill him with additional questions and instead used the quiet time to reflect on the peek inside his world he'd granted her. The quiet but volatile mix of bitterness and disappointment she'd heard raging beneath his words reminded her of that expressed by her father on those rare occasions when he'd slip and say, "It wasn't that I lacked ambition, like your mama's people want to believe. Painting houses all my days isn't what I originally set out to do. But sometimes things happen. You get off track and then you find out, there ain't no easy way of getting back on."

Aliesha waited until Dante had finished cutting her hair and they'd moved to the now-familiar darkness of the utility room before she attempted to tug on one of the loose threads from their previous conversation. While seated on the bench in front of the shampoo bowl after her wash, waiting for him to finish wiping the area down, she'd started thinking about the cabinets full of books Yazz had told her about. "So what do you like to read?" she asked, carefully and cautiously extending her words through the silence and hoping he'd view them as a bridge.

Dante's bright smile acknowledged her inquiry and on completing his clean-up tasks, he motioned for her to follow him. He led her to the row of cabinets hanging over the washer and dryer. After he eased open the doors, one by one, she reached up, ran her fingers across some of the spines, and took in some of subjects and the titles: *The Autobiography of Malcolm X* with Alex Haley, *Miles: The Autobiography* with Quincy Troupe, bios on Tupac, Biggie, Michael Jordan, and Muhammad Ali, none of which really surprised her. But the ones she spotted on Arthur Ashe, Barbara Jordan, Winnie Mandela, Thurgood Marshall, and Nina Simone all gave her a moment of pause. "You've quite an impressive collection," she said.

"It's a habit I picked up as a kid, thanks to my Big Mama. Back in the day, she use to clean up at the library and just about every week she was bringing me and Reuben books they'd discarded. I've been hooked on biographies and autobiographies ever since. Besides providing me with an escape of sorts, a way of stepping out of my world and into someone else's, I've always been intrigued by the things people do to change their lives."

Beneath his obvious pleasure, she picked up on a note or two of melancholy. But rather then pry, she said, "Wally doesn't mind you taking up so much cabinet space?"

"Nah, Wallace is cool. There was a big storm a couple years ago that flooded the basement apartment I was subletting at the time and forced me to move in here temporarily and sleep on a cot. The books that didn't get ruined came with me. I'd fully intended to take them with me when I moved out, but by then Wally and Gerald had started using them as backup in the disputes that are always going on around here. You know, somebody says one thing about Hank Aaron or Ali's record and somebody else wants to challenge it. Sometimes when I know a customer's interested in a particular person or topic, I'll see if I can't find a book to give him to thumb through while he's waiting, and if he's regular, I'll even let him borrow or take one home for keeps."

She smiled. "From what I understand, on occasion you even read to some of the kids. Now that," she said with her voice full of tease, "I'd love to see."

"Yeah, I guess in the eyes of some, that would make me look kinda soft, huh?"

His embarrassment surprised her. She turned toward him. "Nothing wrong with a man being soft every now and then. Matter of fact, I'm kind of partial to certain amount of softness in a man myself."

What she'd handed him was an opening, one big enough for him to step through if he were so inclined. Before she'd turned to face him, they'd been standing shoulder to shoulder and barely an inch apart. As she stood staring at him and waiting for his response, she could feel the heat radiating from his body and she knew he could feel hers.

But rather than seize the opportunity or even acknowledge it, Dante rubbed the stubble on his cheek and while still staring straight ahead, said, "You know, I think I've got a couple things here you'd probably like." He reached up and brought down two texts.

"Nice try," she said on scanning the pictures on the book covers—Mary McLeod Bethune on one and Marva Collins on the other. "It just so happens this particular schoolmarm has already read both of those." She reached in front of him and on removing from the shelves a book about Harriet Tubman and another on Sister Thea Bowman she said, "But here are a couple I'd love to borrow, if you don't mind."

He'd finished with her hair, she'd paid him, and they were standing outside of the shop. While his candor had taken her by surprise, she'd appreciated the fuller view of him it had granted her. She felt like they'd moved into a different space, even though his refusal to acknowledge her shameless flirtation with the barest hint of a smile she viewed as further proof of his lack of interest in anything beyond friendship.

While standing next to him on the cracked sidewalk in front of the barbershop, she knew the time had come for them to say their "see ya laters," though, like usual, she wasn't ready for the conversation to end. Hoping to extend the length of her visit, she slipped into her schoolmarm voice and said, "So you became the book-loving barber and your cousin, the dedicated attorney. At least you both ended up working in fields you enjoyed and that have potential benefits for both society and our community. Where did your cousin end up practicing law?"

Dante stared at the traffic beyond the parking lot. "He didn't."

"But I could have sworn you said something about him being pre-law."

"I did and he was. He even got admitted to Ole Miss, he just never finished."

"Because of your uncle's health issues?"

Dante shook his head. "No, not that. I can't really say why, for sure. It wasn't something he ever talked about. After he dropped out of law school, he sorta just disappeared and we didn't hear from him for years. When he finally resurfaced, we found he'd changed fields and was working in a university library."

"That book-loving gene you two share must be a pretty strong one."

"It would seem that way, wouldn't it?" He sounded amused, but strangely enough, the smile she saw on his face looked absent of any joy. "After his death we discovered he had a will. In it, he'd made a point of leaving me, of all things, his books. But you know, when I went to clean out his place, the only books I found amongst all of

his things were multiple, dog-eared copies of this one—"
Dante slapped a hand against the book in his smock before jamming his fists into his pockets "—a perplexing tale
about a man who turns into a roach."

"You're still angry with him, aren't you?" Aliesha said
softly.

He looked at her briefly before turning away again. "To
be frank, Miz Professor, yeah, I am. Now even more than
ever."

Why? Because he became a librarian instead of a lawyer?"

"No, because he took what could have been my shot,
my opportunity, and just pissed it away." Dante pulled the
paperback from his pocket and dropped his gaze to the
cover. "He hated being a librarian. From what I can tell, he'd
even grown to hate books, except for this one. At some
point, he even took to hating his own damn fool self—
enough, in fact, to walk out into the river one night . . . as
if for a split second he thought he was the disciple in the
boat, you know, the one Christ told to come to him? If
not, perhaps, the Savior himself."

"Your cousin took his own life?"

"Yeah, his and from the looks of things Big Mama's,
too. She hasn't been the same since."

On noticing the mist rising in Dante's eyes, Aliesha
longed to touch his face, pull him into her arms, and tell
him it was going to be all right. But they weren't those kind
of friends . . . not yet, anyway. She settled for taking one of
his hands and giving it a squeeze. "I'm sorry. In recent years,
I've lost a number of people near and dear to my heart, so
I do have some idea of how you must feel. If you trust and
believe, in time, it'll get better. Some of the hurt may even
go away."

When she went to let go of his hand, his fingers caught
and folded around hers. She looked into his handsome face
and watched as the jagged lines faded and the mist cleared.

"I'm not so sure I believe that. But I appreciate you saying it, just the same."

She nodded. Her eyes conducted a brief survey of his chest before drifting upward again to his neck and around his ears, searching for evidence of the iPod that was generally there. "What? No music today?" she finally asked.

His face marked by a look of surprise, he searched his pockets, but the only thing he turned up was the book. "Well," he said. "I guess I owe you a song then, huh?"

She grinned. "Yeah, I guess you do."

A phone call, one from Laylah, had interrupted the conversation he'd been having with Aliesha. Rather than inquire about his or his Big Mama's well-being or even ask if he might possibly have been busy, the first thing out of Laylah's mouth had been a bitter, "So, what happened to you last night?"

"I'm in the middle of something right now," is what he'd told her. "I'll call you back later."

But being blown off that easily wasn't something Laylah could very well allow. "The least you could have done is let me know you weren't coming. I don't know what's gotten into you lately, Dante. You never used to behave this way."

Rather than answer, he'd sighed and listened as, predictably, Laylah's voice lost its sharp edge and slipped into a dull whine. "Baby, come on now, I understand you're probably still in shock and mourning over Reuben's death. We all are. But still, we should be trying to comfort one another and—"

"You're right, we should," he said, no longer bothering to disguise his impatience. "But I can't talk now. I'll call you later." Knowing she'd deny him the proper good-bye he so rightfully deserved and understanding the lengths to which she'd go to keep him from offering up one either, he'd simply hung up without giving her a chance to utter another word.

He hadn't lied when he'd told Aliesha he didn't have a girlfriend. He'd stopped thinking of Laylah as such years ago. Indeed, they had a relationship, an understanding and one that in recent years had grown primarily sexual in nature, and almost obscenely, if not grotesquely, one-sided.

He was her man, but she wasn't his woman. Typically, when she called, he went to her and gave her what she wanted, no questions asked and without so much as a moment's worth of hesitation. But it never worked the other way around, mainly because Laylah didn't belong to anyone—never had and probably never would—not to him, not Reuben, not even Stewart, her husband of the past seven years.

But lately, Dante had begun to pull back even as Laylah persisted in assuring him that their day would soon come. "Be patient," she scolded. "Grant me just a little more time, why don't you?" as if he hadn't already granted her the bulk, if not the prime, of his thirty-plus years.

It was true, he'd deliberately ignored her request to meet her at the Hilton in Harvestville. And the reason? The one he could barely admit to himself—he'd begun to look forward in earnest to Aliesha's visits and he hadn't wanted this latest one tainted by any remnant of Laylah's bittersweet presence.

When Aliesha had strolled into the shop that day, Dante had been daydreaming about the possibility, however minute and improbable, of aligning his life with hers. But as always, the golf-ball-sized doubts broke through the blue-tinged skies of his fantasy and began covering the ground beneath his feet with a frightening amount of hail. In the familiar and accompanying thunder, he'd heard the mocking voice of his cousin Reuben. *A barber and a professor? Yeah, right, that's a likely pair. About as likely as a barber and an attorney, don't you think? Face it, boy, you peaked in high school and all of your best years are behind you. It happens sometimes. Get over it and move on.* Dante wondered if Aliesha owned the wherewithal required to help him separate the truth from the lies.

Already he'd shared more with her than he had with any number of others, men and women alike, whom he'd known longer. He'd even gone as far as to tell her about the football injury that had ripped his dreams out from under him and marked his descent into an extended period of chaos. But what he'd stopped short of revealing, what he still couldn't summon the words or the courage to say aloud, was the role a conspiracy, the traitorous one forged by Reuben and Laylah, had played in the deepening of his despair.

He thought it significant that Aliesha had asked about his books and had appeared impressed when he'd shown her his utility-room-housed collection. He couldn't remember the last time Laylah had made the most basic of inquires about his literary pursuits. Her interest in such had waned years ago. Even his recent preoccupation with Kafka's *Metamorphosis* had yet to draw her attention.

Hours later, long after Aliesha had driven away, a smile would creep across Dante's face whenever his thoughts drifted back to their conversation and the wonderfully odd way his body responded to her presence before settling on her bold attempt to lure him from the safe confines of his silence. . . . "I'm kind of partial to a certain amount of softness in a man myself."

He'd heard the claim before and had learned the hard way that rare was the woman or man who viewed softness as anything beyond a character flaw, a deficit of some sort. And then there were those, like Laylah, who viewed softness as little more than an invitation to manipulate, to squeeze, knead, mold, and pinch from like so much Play-Doh or putty. A part of Dante wanted to believe that Aliesha was different. Like him, she was one of the rare ones. He yearned to fully embrace and openly reciprocate her interest in what they might be together. But another part of him, the part of him that still belonged to Laylah, wouldn't allow it just yet.

PART III

CHAPTER 23

Shelton Beale reminded Aliesha of a boy named Kevin Piedmont who'd come up through the grades with her in middle school. There had only been a handful of African American students in the private school in which her aunt Mildred had seen fit to enroll her. But somehow, every year, Aliesha and Kevin always landed in the same class. As the two lone dark specks set adrift in the churn and swirl of an overwhelming white sea, surely at some point their paths should have intersected. But they never did. They were both smart, articulate, capable students, who in all their years together never found an occasion or compelling reason to work on a classroom assignment together or even sit on the same side of the room. The two barely exchanged ten words in the entire time they knew one another, despite Aliesha's occasional effort to reach across the divide between them.

"Don't worry, it doesn't rub off," she'd assured him one day during eighth-grade P.E. class, when he appeared to recoil at the mere prospect of having to mesh the fingers of his sweaty, coconut-husk-colored hands with the blackberry glaze of her own.

It was almost as if Kevin had concluded that an association with her could only lessen his lot in life, if not taint him further. The same appeared to be true for Shelton, whose modus operandi, like Kevin's, generally involved either ignoring or outright avoiding her. On the rare occasion they did speak, it was only because they'd both failed in their attempt to maneuver around it. So Aliesha wasn't too surprised when, upon his return to Wells on Monday, Shelton didn't immediately approach her about the change in the children's hair or the club outing she'd only recently learned about herself.

Tamara had overseen all of the schedule juggling and coordination associated with the children's hair-braiding appointment. She'd also been present when Peaches spun her magic on the defiant quills adoring the two little girls' heads. Surprisingly, they'd all hit it off fabulously. While Peaches had politely passed, Kristen had eagerly accepted Tamara's invitation to hang out with her one night at her favorite Neo-Soul dance club.

Upon her discovery of the additional details, Aliesha had asked Pat if she'd heard word of any negative fallout. Pat, who lived only a few houses down from the couple and who surpassed Monica when it came to keeping up with the latest campus-linked gossip, said, "According to Kristen, he's surprisingly okay with the braids. So much so, he wants to visit the shop where Peaches works and personally extend his thanks."

Even though Aliesha would have paid good money to see the expression on Shelton's face when he finally got a good look at Peaches, she knew his visit to the shop wouldn't likely result in a happy outcome. She'd been doing her best not to stoke the tension between them. But rather than continue trading the fake smiles and curt nods whenever they encountered one another while trekking down the winding corridor where their offices and classrooms were located, a part of her wanted to confront him and just get it over with once and for all. On the other hand, she secretly enjoyed the thought of him stewing over that which he had so little control.

Shelton and Aliesha managed to keep up the pretense until the Friday night in the same week of his return, when, at Shelton's insistence, members of the Anthropology, Sociology, and Social Work departments convened for food, drinks, and small talk at a nearby bar and grill.

Aliesha had hoped not to be the lone Black woman at the event. But when she'd dropped by the Social Work Department and asked the only other African American female among the invited guests if she'd, in fact, made plans to attend, Dr. Francine Cummings, a heavyset, older woman, had snorted and leaned back in her chair until it begged for relief. "You're trying to be funny, aren't you? Wanna know what I'm doing Friday night? Same thing I do most every Friday night. I'm staying home, turning on the Lifetime Channel, ordering a pizza, fixing myself a nice, hot bubble bath, and painting my toenails. That's what I'm doing. You might be wise to follow suit."

Unlike Francine, Aliesha hadn't earned herself enough clout or formed enough of the right alliances to pull a flat-out no-show without having to pay for it later in some form or fashion. But she couldn't help but ponder Francine's advice as she grabbed herself a large apple martini and smoothed out the low-cut, sunburst-colored dress Monica had insisted she purchase on one of their rare shopping excursions. Though more Monica's style than her own, the dress flattered and showcased Aliesha's toned physique and lean curves, a fact she doubted few at the gathering would notice. She downed a couple sips of her drink before slapping on her game face and marching off to make the required rounds.

Exhausted and ready to call it a night after forty-five minutes of grinning and greeting, gabbing and glad-handing, she'd worked her way back over to where Pat and her husband, Michael, stood, the latter of whom looked as spent as and even more agitated than Aliesha. She smiled at her friend's handsome silver fox of a mate, who at the moment resembled a sad-faced teddy bear.

"Tsk-tsk-tsk," Pat said, waving a finger between her husband and Aliesha. "You both know it is far too early to speak of leaving. How would that look?"

"Like we've got better things to do," Michael grumbled before turning to Aliesha. "Hey, how come you didn't bring your guy, Javiel? And why does he get a regular pass on the torment, but I don't?"

A frowning Pat spared Aliesha the effort when she addressed her husband. "I could have sworn I'd told you. Don't you remember? It seems as if poor Javiel went and got himself issued a permanent get-out-of-jail-free card."

"Oh," Michael said. "I'm sorry to hear it. Well, who's to say you won't get lucky and land yourself one of the fine specimens here tonight?"

Aliesha held up an arm, as if trying to block a physical assault, and said, "Stop right this moment or I'm leaving now!"

Before her smile could fade, Shelton stepped into the happy circle of three and brought the dark clouds hovering over his larger-than-average head with him. "Aliesha, did I hear you say something about leaving? You were only kidding, right?"

"Well," Aliesha hedged.

"Because there are a couple of issues I'd hoped to discuss with you before the night's end."

"Sure," Aliesha said. But before she could utter another word, Shelton stroked her back and said, "Lovely. I'll catch up with you again shortly." He then seized Michael's hand. "Mike, Patricia, good seeing you both. Glad you could come."

Aliesha muttered under her breath and threw imaginary daggers at his back as she watched him waltz to the other side of the room.

"What the heck was that all about?" Michael asked.

Pat squeezed her husband's arm and whispered, "Trust me, dear, you don't want to know, nor would you even remember if I told you."

In the hour that she awaited what felt like her pending trial, already-formed decision, and prearranged execution, Aliesha treated herself to a couple more apple martinis. Instead of taking the few minutes required to verbally sever her head, Shelton appeared intent on letting her sweat it out for as long as possible.

Aliesha watched as he drifted from one group to another, looking for someone who might yet be impressed with the pompous B.S. he so freely served up and distributed in huge chunks, as if it were in fact diamonds or nuggets of gold. "If only we could get the kids at Wells to share the kind of zest for learning I witnessed among the students at Harvard, my alma mater . . . Now that Obama is in office, I sincerely hope the message to African Americans and other minorities will be one of no more lame excuses. . . . The problem, you see, with most of the Black youths who grow up in communities like Riverton is their lack of drive coupled with a maddening inability to see the big picture."

For the first time, she noted with some alarm how much larger his head swelled whenever he landed a female audience. His philandering was no secret in or outside of the department. To hear Pat tell it, before his marriage to Kristen, he'd earned quite the rep for bedding a host of young, impressionable grad students and the gullibly ambitious first-year professors. Such information only fed Aliesha's long-held suspicion that the periodic faculty get-togethers Shelton insisted they all attend, but to which he never saw fit to bring his own wife, were just his way of sniffing out new prey.

When she tired of eyeballing and eavesdropping on Shelton, Aliesha turned her attention to some of the other *fine specimens* populating the room, focusing in particular on the three other African American males in attendance. The bearded and bespectacled Dr. Clifford Myers of the Sociology Department shared her interest in Tamara, as well as the other half a dozen or more African American students who drifted back and forth between their separate but somewhat similar fields of academia. They got along well and often traded notes about the progress and peculiarities of individual students. Although he was not the best-looking guy in the world, Aliesha viewed him as an earnest and likeable sort, though one totally off-limits in any romantic sort of sense, given his legal and emotional ties to the lovely and equally likeable native of Hong Kong he'd met and married while attending grad school at the University of North Dakota.

While Aliesha had spoken on occasion to the other two Black men present, she didn't know either very well. Neither had been in their respective positions in the Sociology and Social Work departments for more than a year. Nor had either seemed particularly interested in getting to know her better on either a professional or a personal level. But based on what she observed, they'd already become chummy with quite a number of the other single women present at the gathering, several from her own department.

As she studied the four men of color, she thought about the question she'd once admonished Tamara for posing: *Why is it they get to choose, but we have to settle for whatever?* but now found herself pondering, only with a slightly different spin, *Why is it when you get to choose, you seldom if ever choose someone who looks like me?* She reached for another drink to offset the melancholy she felt trying to take root only to find herself being scolded.

"Exactly how many of those have you had?" Pat asked, her voice infused with motherly sternness and concern. "You do want to have all of your wits about you when ole shithead finally finds time to read you the riot act, don't you?"

Aliesha lifted her glass and said, "Not necessarily."

Pat shot a glance at her husband. "Maybe we ought to hang around just a little while longer."

Michael threw up his hands, stamped his feet, and let out a yelp that sounded like that of a tired, frustrated puppy. Aliesha went over and planted a kiss on his cheek. "Don't worry, I wouldn't dare let her do that to you. You two go on home. I'll be fine."

"Okay," Pat said, sounding doubtful. She hugged Aliesha. "But call me first thing in the morning." She pointed at Aliesha's glass. "And take it easy on those."

Not long after Pat and Michael disappeared and Aliesha settled on a seat at the bar, Shelton's deceptively friendly mug materialized in her slightly affected line of vision. *Good Lord, the pickings must have been pretty damn slim in Kristen's neck of the woods if she thought this fool was a catch* is what she caught herself thinking before Shelton opened his mouth. While he was far from outwardly unattractive, aside from his pumpkin-sized head, Shelton's devouring T Rex of an ego made his the worst kind of ugly.

"Aliesha, I'm sorry if I've kept you waiting. I hope you haven't been too terribly inconvenienced. Did you by chance get an opportunity to speak with Rosa before she left?"

Personable, laidback, unlike Shelton, Dr. Rosa Rodriguez of the Sociology Department was extremely popular among the students on campus. The fact that she, like Monica, owned a body more becoming of a member of the Dallas Cowboys cheerleading squad only enhanced her appeal for some students and faculty alike.

As she often did with Shelton, Aliesha started having an inner monologue that coincided with her actual one. *No, I didn't get a chance to chat with Rosa, but I noticed you did. At one point, you were scoping her cleavage so hard, I thought you just might lose your contacts, your partial, and your drink in there* is what she thought. "Rosa? No, why?" is what she said.

"Well, from what I understand, she and her partner, Joan, recently went their separate ways."

Aliesha's eyelids twitched. *And this would concern me, why?* "Really?" she said. "Gosh, that's too bad."

"You know, a nice-looking girl like Rosa is probably not going to be on the market for too long."

Aliesha swirled the contents of her glass. *Do you just sit at home and work at being an asshole, or is this something you come by naturally?* She swallowed a sip before she said, "I don't mean to be rude, Shelton, but what would make you think I would be at all interested in that particular aspect of Rosa's personal life?"

"Well, I just thought—"

"Ah, no, actually, it doesn't sound as if you thought through that little quip at all."

"Aliesha, come on. It's not like I've ever actually seen you in the company of a man. And there is the curious matter of the way you choose to wear your hair."

Is that what you plan on telling those wild-haired daughters of yours, you f-ing moron?! She stopped biting her tongue and said, "My hair? Oh, so the way I choose to wear my hair is supposed to be an opened window into my sexuality?"

"You're right. I'm sorry. Do forgive me for being so presumptuous. To be frank, I'm glad we cleared that up. It certainly eases my mind, to some extent, about your relationship with Tamara."

She shook her head. "I didn't think it was possible, but this conversation has truly gone from bad to worse."

"You must admit, you do spend an awful lot of time with her. Do you really think it's appropriate for the two of you to be attending church together?"

Aliesha felt a surge of warmth flood her face. "Look, we don't go to church, okay? On her own and purely out of curiosity one day Tamara dropped in on the Sunday school class I teach and discovered she enjoyed it. Most times, she doesn't even stay for service. Why am I attempting to explain this to you? Obviously, you've already made up your mind that I'm some sort of nappy-headed, proselytizing jezebel who sleeps with her students, right? When everyone knows that last little item is more your cup of gruel!"

Shelton crossed his arms. "I don't know why you're getting so upset. I'm just trying to gain a bit of clarity on a situation that's long puzzled me."

Maybe if you tried pulling that big hog head out your ass sometimes . . . "Seriously, Shelton, is this what you had me hanging around here all night for? Or is this just your own messed-up way of getting back at me?"

He moved his hog-sized noggin closer to hers and, wearing a grin that made him resemble the Joker from the Batman series, said, "See, you are a smart woman, aren't you? Which is why I still can't fathom why you'd ever think it proper to invite that freak of nature you call a friend into my house and around my kids while I was away."

Aliesha sat down her empty glass. "Okay, first off that wasn't my idea. Second, the name-calling isn't necessary. Peaches is one of the gentlest, kindest, most soft-spoken souls you're ever likely to meet. She doesn't have it in her to hurt a fly, much less somebody's kids. Furthermore, if you don't want her around your precious little ones, I suggest you speak with your wife, instead of—"

"And that's another thing," he said. "In case you haven't figured it out already, one of the many reasons I discourage Kristen from spending too much time on campus or at university functions is because I don't want her falling under the influence of women like you and Monica."

Aliesha laughed. "And what kind of women would those be? The type your own two, willful, high-spirited daughters are likely to grow up resembling?"

"God forbid," Shelton spat.

"I bet that's your nightly prayer, too, isn't it? I suppose only time will tell how and if that works out for you. Of course, you could always save yourself a wait and ask Peaches. . . ."

CHAPTER 24

She should have driven straight home. Or, better yet, called Monica or Pat to come and pick her up. Push come to shove, she could have even asked Cliff and his wife if they wouldn't mind dropping her off. But she hadn't been thinking straight enough to weigh all of her options or even realize the necessity to do so. Had Nelson's Barbecue not already been on her route, she probably wouldn't have thought about the coleslaw until that next morning.

"Even though Nelson's is known for their barbecue, their coleslaw isn't half bad either," is what Mrs. Phillips had told her. "If you don't feel like making any, I suggest you go by Nelson's and pick up enough to feed twenty for the women's meeting on Saturday."

As soon as Aliesha spotted the sign, Mrs. Phillips's words flooded her ears and she responded with, "Okay, let me save some time and do this now," before cutting in front of a car and making a hurried right turn into Nelson's brightly lit parking lot.

The thick aroma of hickory-smoked barbecue that greeted her walk across the parking lot in the cool night air only intensified on her entrance into the establishment. The smell made her mouth water. But she knew given all of the liquor she'd consumed she probably wouldn't be able to enjoy it or keep it down.

Still, while waiting for the person in front of her to finish placing his take-out order, she began debating the merits of purchasing a sandwich and saving it for later. She was weighing the pros and cons when an unexpected voice startled her.

"That's quite a dress. No doubt, tonight, all eyes will be on you."

Mrs. Phillips it wasn't, thank goodness. Wearing a big smile, and smoothing out her dress, Aliesha turned toward Dante. "Actually, this was in honor of an excruciatingly boring work-related event, which thankfully just ended. But I'll gladly take the compliment and any others you feel like doling out tonight. "

Dante chuckled and said, "In that case, you look absolutely fetching, Madame."

She cut her eyes at him. "Uh-huh, for a matronly schoolmarm, I'm sure."

They both laughed and he said, "You dining alone this evening?"

"I'm here to pick up some coleslaw for a women's group meeting at my church tomorrow. What about you?" She peered around him. "Here with one of the lucky ladies from your friends with benefits list?"

"You don't plan on letting me live that down, do you? I'm just grabbing a bite before I take on some of the fellas in the back for a round or two of pool."

A moment of awkward silence passed between them as they stood staring into each other's eyes. Before Aliesha could decide where to take the conversation next, Dante said, "Well, I'll leave you to your coleslaw. It was nice seeing you."

When he turned, both his natural scent and that of his cologne cut through the barbecue's hickory-thick fog and grabbed Aliesha like a pheromone elixir. "I take that to mean you're not in the mood for any female company," she heard herself say aloud.

He stopped and looked back at her. "Oh, I'm sorry. No, by all means, you're welcome to come join me if you're not in a hurry. I'm in one of the booths near the poolroom."

When he turned again and began walking away, Aliesha got so caught up in the view of his wide, muscular back; thick, tight thighs; and perfectly sculpted ass, she almost didn't hear the attendant behind the counter call out, "Ma'am? Excuse me, ma'am, are you ready to place your order?"

She carried a large tub of Nelson's coleslaw and a wine cooler with her to the booth where Dante sat alone with a half-eaten meal on the table in front of him. When she reached him, he stood and helped her with her items.

Before she sat down on the cushioned, semicircular bench, she spied *Dreams from My Father* lying cover-side up on the table. "No Kafka tonight?" she teased.

He shook his head. "No, I do give it a break every now and then."

She looked around. "Is this where you generally come to unwind?"

"Yeah, Nelson's is cool. Not too crowded. Not too trendy. And the food, hey, you can't beat it. The barbecue is good, no lie. But the pound cake, the pound cake is what I really come here for. You ever tried it?" He wiped his fingers on a napkin, then broke off a piece of his cake. When he raised the morsel, she scooted closer and let him guide it to her lips.

She nodded and said, "It's good. But mine is better."

He grinned. "Oh yeah? You cook?"

"Now why'd you have to say it like that? Yes, I cook. And if you're nice, maybe I'll bring you a sample by the shop one day."

While Dante picked over what remained of his dinner

and appeared slightly uncomfortable, Aliesha turned up her wine cooler and took several long swallows. On quenching her thirst, she said, "Can I ask you something? Why is it you've never hit on me?"

Dante jerked up, like a driver who'd just slammed on the brakes in order to keep from hitting an object in the road. "Woah! Awfully forward tonight, aren't we?"

She reached over and pinched off another piece of his cake. "Where I'm from, if there's something you wanna know bad enough, you ask."

He relaxed a bit and pushed the cake closer to her. "I've got this rule about mixing business and pleasure. Typically, it's something I just don't do. The risk of losing a customer is just too great. Say, for instance, in the event that things didn't work out between us, then what? I lose both your friendship and your business, right?"

Aliesha paused and gave his explanation some serious thought before she said, "Yeah, sure. . . . You only date White girls, right?"

He leaned over and peered into her face. "Oh, you're on a roll tonight. Where on earth did that come from?"

She laughed. "I'm just asking is all."

"Well, to be honest, I don't encounter a whole lot of White girls in the circles I run in. Man, those folks at the university must really be doing a job on your head."

"Umm," she said before finishing what remained of the cooler. "In more ways than you could probably ever imagine." She set down the empty bottle. "Listen, it's been real, but I'd better be going."

When she made a move to rise, he said, "Wait, did you drive here?"

She looked at him. "Yes, why?"

He slid toward her. "Maybe you'd be better off sitting here awhile longer. Let me order you some pound cake and some coffee or something."

She shook her head. "Nah, I'd better call it a night."

He reached across her lap. "Wow, that's a really nice bag. May I see it?" He plucked it from her grasp. "It's got a pocket for your phone, too, doesn't it?" On locating her cell phone, he took it out and flipped it open.

"What are you doing?" she asked.

Dante started pressing buttons. "I'm looking for your man's number. What's his name again, Juan?"

"Give me that!" She snatched the phone back. "His name is Javiel. And why do you need to know?"

"So I can call him and have him pick you up. You really shouldn't be driving."

Aliesha shoved her phone back into her purse. "Oh, so now I'm drunk?"

He nodded. "You look and sound pretty damn lit to me. Why don't you call him? I'm sure, given the circumstances, it's what he'd prefer."

"No, see, that's where you're wrong. Calling Javiel is out of the question for a lot of reasons, the primary one being that we're no longer together."

"How about a cab?" Dante fished out his own phone. "'Cause as much as I hate to, if you walk out of here and try to get behind the wheel, I'm calling the cops."

Her face contorted and her voice rose a notch. "A cab? I don't need a damn cab. So what, you're supposed to be like my daddy or something all of a sudden?"

He leaned toward her and in a calm and steady whisper said, "Where is it written that I've gotta be your daddy to be concerned about your well-being?" He took her hand and peeled her keys from them. "Look, Aliesha, I don't want to see you get hurt, all right? Now, tell me your address so I can see that you get home safely."

It was the first time she could recall him ever using her given name, *Aliesha*. The sound of it tumbling from his lips tore deep into the hurt she'd been trying to bury beneath the alcohol. She stopped resisting and after a moment quietly told him what he wanted to know.

When Dante handed over his own keys to one of his buddies from the poolroom and assigned him the task of trailing behind Aliesha's car, an alarm sounded in her head. "Isn't this the way a lot of bad B movies start?" she said. "Some chick who's had one too many puts her trust in a couple of seemingly kind strangers only to have them take advantage of her?"

She saw the anger her comment evoked beneath Dante's mask of cool, but rather than explode, he said, "What's that supposed to mean? You actually think I'd try to hurt you or stand by while someone else did? Tell you what, why don't I just call you that cab?"

Rather than respond, she climbed into the passenger side of her car and fastened her seat belt. Without another word, he did the same on the driver's side and started the engine. For several minutes, they rode in a tense silence. She closed her eyes and leaned into the headrest.

"You okay?" He reached over and pressed the back of his hand to her cheek, as if checking her body temperature. "If you start to feel sick, let me know and I'll pull over."

Stifling the sudden urge to cry, she pushed his hand away and turned her face toward the passenger side window.

"You wanna talk about it?" he said softly

"Talk about what?"

"Whatever it is that's got you so upset. I'm saying, if you wanna talk about it, I'm more than willing to listen."

"No thanks."

After a few more minutes, she gazed over at him and said, "I'm sorry, you know, about what I said earlier. It was mean and totally uncalled for."

"We'll attribute it to the liquor and leave it at that," he said without taking his eyes from the road. "You mind if I listen to some music? You got any CDs?"

She reached into the glove compartment and pulled out a handful. He plucked *Phrenology* by the Roots from the batch and slid it into her car's player. He skipped over the songs he didn't want to hear and listened to the ones he did, which she noted included the ones she too most preferred: "The Seed," "Break You Off," "Water," and "Complexity."

After they arrived at her house, he parked in the drive and accompanied her to the front door. When he offered her his arm to steady herself, she took it without a word of protest. On reaching the porch, she thanked him and waved at the guy seated behind the wheel of Dante's idling Jeep. But rather than enter the front door that Dante had taken the liberty of unlocking, she turned to him and said, "So what are the chances of me convincing you to come in for a while?"

He shook his head as if to clear it. "Wow! Well, see, I can't, not tonight." He shoved his hands into his pockets and looked down at his feet. "Maybe, maybe some other time."

She stared at him. "Yeah, right, right, some other time. You know what? I don't get you."

He peered up at her with a smile. "Maybe that's because I'm not trying to get got."

Rather than see any humor in his words, she suddenly saw red. "Tell the truth," she said, hurling her words at him, one after the other, as if they were sharp-edged stones. "Even if I was totally sober, you wouldn't come in, would you."

His face grew somber. "And what makes you say that?"

"Because," she said. "You're scared, aren't you? Tell the truth. That's what's wrong with brothers like you. You wanna blame everybody and everything for your sorry lot in life, for all of your shortcomings as well as your permanent state of unhappiness. But the real deal is, you're just scared. Scared of life. Scared of women like me. Hell, scared of your own damn reflection . . . Am I right?"

"Yeah, Miz Professor," Dante said. He withdrew his hands

from his pockets, ran one across the dark stubble on his cheeks, and nodded. "Maybe you've got a point. Maybe that is my real problem. I mean, it's either that or White women, right?"

The first thing Aliesha did after she stormed inside of her house and slammed the door shut behind her was race to the bathroom and throw up. As she clutched the toilet seat and emptied the contents of her stomach into the commode, she still owned the presence of mind to hope that come Saturday morning, she wouldn't remember any of it. Unfortunately, it must not have been a prayer the Lord felt particularly inclined to answer.

Try as she might, she couldn't shake the awful memory of the mean, angry, hypersexual monster the liquor had coaxed out of her. She remembered verbatim every nasty word she'd hurled at Dante and, even worse, the look of hurt and disbelief on his face. Not a day went by that she didn't contemplate calling the shop and apologizing.

But in the end, she'd listened to Monica. "Don't you think it's best to just leave it be? You know he's probably told all of the fellas down there. If not to your face, they'll certainly be laughing about it behind your back. And the next time you decide to get your drink on, just call me, okay? Instead of allowing not but one but two men you barely know escort your drunk ass home."

Aliesha decided her friend was probably right. The schoolgirl crush she had on Dante wasn't liable to lead her anyplace she really wanted to be. So why bother? She prayed for the strength to just let it and him go and marveled at how difficult it proved. She'd had a far easier time detaching herself from Javiel, a man whom she'd dated for all of five months.

Her outburst had blindsided him in much the same manner as the career-ending hit he'd taken in high school. While he'd donned the brave face, it would have been a lie to say it hadn't rattled him. In fact, as he'd stood on her porch, he'd been gripped by a pain in his leg so sudden and severe, for a few split seconds he'd feared it would again crumple and collapse beneath him.

But as agonizing an experience as witnessing her coming apart had been, he understood enough about women to know better than to take it personally. He sensed something was eating away at her in much the manner of an aggressive cancer that was rapidly spreading and metastasizing at will. She wasn't the first woman to assume he owned the cure for what ailed her. But like so many of the others who'd pinned their hopes on such, she'd been wrong about where to find it. There wasn't any black magic in his wand. It was his heart that held the key to her recovery, the same heart he'd vowed never again to fully unveil for any woman, deserving or not.

He knew the pain she felt. The gnawing ache of rejection. The intense longing to be wanted, to feel worthy of another's desire. He recognized and sympathized if only because he'd felt it, too. He could have slept with her that night and granted her the temporary comfort and refuge she sought and his body longed to offer. It wasn't for any lack of desire that he'd declined. Nor had it been out of any overt sense of respect or allegiance to Laylah.

With Laylah's full knowledge and silent consent, Dante routinely bedded other women. On several occasions, he'd even fallen in deep enough to maintain a steady girlfriend. Not that any of those relationships had ever, in the end, mattered much or lasted very long. Laylah's unrelenting presence in his life had a way of trumping all, and over the years she'd had become so confident of her grasp, she'd stopped caring with whom he slept, as long as he found his way back to her bed whenever she beckoned.

So, in part, Aliesha had been right. Fear had kept him from stepping across her threshold that night—a fear tied and bound to the very real possibility of losing her, Laylah, and himself in a sobering wave of regret the morning after.

CHAPTER 25

On the Sunday morning following his painful and perplexing Friday night exchange of words with Aliesha, Dante rose, showered, and dressed earlier than usual. After a few bites of toast and a quick cup of coffee, he flung both his sports jacket and a tie over his shoulder and headed out the front door of his South Riverton condo. He was on his way to Roads Cross and eager to see the look of surprise and delight on his Big Mama's face when he showed up unannounced at her church that morning.

Typically, he spoke with his Big Mama by phone every evening and drove out to see her every other weekend. Over the past several weeks, he'd become even more diligent about checking up on her. She hadn't been the same since Reuben's foolish and ultimately fatal walk across the river. Gone was most of the feistiness Dante had come to associate with the big-hearted woman who'd raised him and his cousin Reuben as if they'd spun from the loins of her husband Mack and spent a full nine months in her own womb.

Often times, those who didn't know Vivian Lee very well were shocked to discover that for all of her bragging, doting and spoiling, she wasn't even blood kin to the two young men who knew her as "Big Mama." Reuben and Dante were, in fact, the children of her husband's two troubled sisters, Helen and Miriam. Reuben, the elder of the two boys, had come to live with Mack and Vivian Lee as an abused preschooler. Dante, on the other hand, had drifted back and forth between his Big Mama and uncle's stable home and his mother's chaotic one, until age nine—the age he was when, for a brief spell, his mother became sober and lucid enough to commit the merciful act of leaving him in the couple's care for good.

While Dante had always made a point of showing his aunt and uncle his appreciation for the lengths to which they'd stretched and sacrificed on his behalf, his cousin Reuben had spent most of his relatively short lifetime doing just the opposite. The last interaction between Reuben, Dante, and their Big Mama had been one full of unfounded accusations and unnecessary strife. Dante could still see the look of bewilderment and devastation on his Big Mama's face as Reuben, pacing and snarling like a rabid dog, had launched into a hateful rant about what he perceived as his gross mistreatment and all the things in life that he felt he'd been unjustly denied.

Dante glanced at the copy of *The Metamorphosis* on the car seat beside him. When had it had happened? At one point, had Reuben awakened and discovered himself transformed into something that on the outside appeared so hideous and nonhuman? Had it been shortly after he'd entered the ninth grade—when circumstances beyond every-one's control had denied him an opportunity to further his education at the East Coast prep school he'd wanted so badly to attend? During that stretch of time after he'd dropped out of law school and broken off all contact with the family? Or had it occurred somewhere in-between? Say, at the tail end of his senior year of high school, around the time he'd commenced to flaunting his relationship with Laylah in Dante's face.

Determined to free his mind of both Laylah and Reuben's haunting grasp, Dante turned up the Marvin Gaye drifting from his Jeep's speakers and took in the budding trees, rolling hills, and outstretched farmland filling his peripheral vision. He loved the freedom of the great outdoors and took pride in describing himself as a country boy with small-town ways. Even so, that was hardly the whole story. Unbeknown to most, he'd always quietly hungered for a life larger in scope and grander in scale than the one available to him in Roads Cross. The same quiet hunger fueled his love of biographies and autobiographies, and quite possibly his attraction to a certain kind of woman.

His type? Smart. Proud. Beautiful. Inquisitive. Complex. A natural woman with few pretensions and one owning a raw fragility beneath her noble air. He rubbed the dull ache in his side as Aliesha's face bumped Laylah's from the forefront of his mind. ,

---

Dante arrived in Roads Cross approximately an hour and thirty minutes after leaving Riverton. After securing a place for his Jeep on Blessed Rock's dirt and gravel parking lot, Dante spent an additional ten minutes greeting, grinning, hugging, and glad-handing his way across the church grounds and into the sanctuary. He still remembered how taken aback he'd been during his brief stay in Cali upon learning that people there didn't normally bother to acknowledge one another unless they were engaged in a beef or a business transaction. The folks in Riverton were at least cordial enough to nod a greeting and speak in passing. But in Roads Cross, not only would folks look you square in the eye as they delivered a bright and boisterous, "Morning!" "Afternoon," "What up, man?!" or "Hey now!" more often than not, they'd stop to inquire about your well-being, your past whereabouts, and if they didn't already know, those of your mama 'nem, too.

Given that the eleven o'clock service hadn't yet officially begun, worshippers were still milling about, fellow-shipping, gossiping, and finding seats. Dante stood at the rear of the church and scanned the pews until he spotted the familiar gray halo. Even with the added lift of her modest pumps and the three-inch-deep natural crown that graced her head, Dante's Big Mama topped out at all of four feet and five inches. Had she not been standing and embracing the parishioner in the row in front of her, he might have had a more difficult time locating her.

Politely waving off old friends and acquaintances and with an index finger pressed to his pursed lips, like a stuffy librarian of old, Dante walked down the right-side aisle and positioned himself in the pew directly behind Vivian Lee. But unable to contain his joy at successfully pulling off his feat, he burst into laughter as he leaned over and kissed his Big Mama on the cheek.

Wearing a big grin of her own, Vivian Lee turned and seized him. After releasing her hold on his face and neck, she rose and said, "Boy! You could have at least warned me that you were coming this way. Had I known, I would have taken something out to cook for you. . . ."

"Why you always worried about cooking for somebody?" he said. "That's why they have restaurants, cafeterias, and takeout available every day, Sundays included, in case you didn't know."

"Tell her, Dante," chimed in Irma Bell, the gray-haired friend of the family who tended to Vivian Lee's needs in Dante's absence and who wasted little time in rising from her seat on the pew next to his Big Mama in order to get a kiss and hug from Dante, too.

"Ain't like I hadn't already told Vivian Lee that I've got a whole mess of pork chops, okra, gravy, and rice, plus a big ole coconut cake she's welcome to come by and help me get shed of." Miz Irma squeezed one of Dante's thick biceps. "If your appetite is anything like it was when you was playing ball, I don't suspect I'll be having to ask you twice."

"No, ma'am!" Dante said. "The way you got my stomach growling, we can leave now if you want."

After service and a laugh, lie, and story-filled dinner at Miz Irma's, Dante drove his Big Mama back to the small but sturdy wood frame house his uncle Mack had built for his new bride on the little piece of timber-rich land he owned. It was Dante's understanding that his uncle had intended on adding to the house, if not build a bigger one, when all of the children he and Vivian Lee planned on having started arriving. But the Good Lord, in all of His wisdom, had only seen fit to bless them with two, Reuben and Dante, and both of them the abandoned offspring of others.

Given that his Big Mama had napped and nodded through the bulk of the fifteen-minute drive, upon their arrival at the house Dante tried to coax her into lying down and resting in earnest. But on climbing out of the Jeep, she scoffed, "It's too pretty of a day to be sleeping it away. 'Less you in a big hurry to get back, why don't you come on out on the porch and sit with me for a while?"

Dante, who still kept several changes of clothing in the bedroom he and Reuben had shared as youths, assured his Big Mama that he didn't plan to depart until the following morning, unless she'd already invited some other man over to spend the night.

She swatted at him. "Boy, hush your mouth. Your uncle Mack hear you say that and he'll be stumbling and bumbling around here all night long."

Dante laughed and kissed the chuckling Vivian Lee on the forehead. His uncle Mack had been dead going on five years. But the joke, which was more like an understanding, particularly in light of how the house creaked, rattled, and moaned at the oddest times, was that the old dude's spirit still kept a close watch over the house and all of his loved ones who still opened and closed their eyes within it.

After an obligatory tour of the raised flower beds gracing the front and back yards, Dante joined her on the front porch where she already sat, clad in her favorite duster, with the ads from the Sunday paper in her lap, a tall glass of ice water on a little stool beside her, and rocking in one of the four big, white rocking chairs her dearly departed husband had made for his family's use in the years prior to his debilitating stroke.

"There's some Cokes and a pitcher of ice tea in the refrigerator," she said.

"Naw, I'm good right now," he said, while examining an orange-colored flower he'd plucked from the yard. "I'll probably have a glass of that ice tea later on this evening when I get another slice of Miz Irma's cake."

The pair rocked in silence for several minutes. Vivian thumbed through the sales ads, while Dante pulled one petal after another from the flower in his lap until all that remained was the naked bulb and stem. After collecting the orange-colored bits and pieces and tossing them into the yard, he fell back into his rocking chair and heaved a sigh, one that inadvertently led to a slip of the jovial front he'd been wearing on his Big Mama's behalf.

She stopped rocking and said, "Something on you mind, son?"

He closed his eyes and folded his hands behind his head before deciding to tell her the truth. "Uh-huh . . . a woman."

They rocked in silence for several more minutes before his Big Mama said, "If it's worth anything to you, I talked with her the last time she was in town. I think she's serious about moving back here to help Mr. Jessie and 'nem with the funeral home."

The woman who'd been on Dante's mind for the past couple of days and the one in the center of the tale his Big Mama was piecing together were not one and the same.

But rather than address the difference, Dante stopped rocking and opened his eyes in order to let his Big Mama know she had his full attention.

"She come by the house," his Big Mama went on with her gaze buried somewhere among the papers in her lap. "I asked her to so that I could give her that piece of money Reuben left me. I told her I wanted the boy to have it. Why Reuben could never see fit to do right by that child, I'll never know."

In the brief silence that followed, Dante shut his eyes again and pushed the rocker back as far as it would go without toppling over. He hated how much it pained his Big Mama that Reuben hadn't done better by the son he and Laylah had conceived. The boy, now a big, strapping thirteen-year-old named Ozzie, had been blessed with a blended version of both his mama and his daddy's good looks and intelligence. But rarely had Reuben ever even made an effort to see the child, and as far as Dante knew, his cousin had never offered up so much as a single dime toward his care. Still, he lacked the heart to tell his Big Mama that Ozzie wasn't Reuben's only child. He personally knew of at least two others, by two different women.

His Big Mama puffed a sigh of her own and wrung her hands. "I thought, if nothing else, surely he'd leave the baby a little something in his will."

Dante grunted and resumed his rocking. In keeping with his spiteful and contemptuous nature, Reuben had used his last will and testament as a vehicle for one final, reckless act of vengeance. A cheap bastard all of his life, his frugal ways had enabled him to amass a small fortunate in both his savings account and his stock portfolio. He'd also had the foresight to secure a lucrative life insurance policy for himself. But at the reading of his will, Dante had been among those left aghast by his cousin's decision to leave no provisions for Ozzie or, for that matter, any of his other unclaimed heirs.

A miserly $2,000 is all he'd seen fit to leave their Big Mama, while to Dante he'd bequeathed his books—all seven dog-eared, paperback copies of Kafka's *Metamorphosis*. After covering his funeral expenses, the remaining portion of his estate had been earmarked for the coffers of the East Coast prep school he felt he'd been wrongly denied an opportunity to attend as a youth.

"Anyway, she wouldn't take the money," his Big Mama said. "She assured me that all of Ozzie's financial needs were being met. Then she had the nerve to turn around and try to write me a check for even more than what Reuben give me. She said I ought to put it all together and go somewhere nice. You know, somewhere in the Caribbean or else way overseas in Italy, Egypt, France, or Greece somewhere."

The kindness of Laylah's gesture brightened Dante's disposition and put a hint of a smile on his face. Oddly enough, she'd always been Reuben's exact opposite when it came to money, and Dante had long viewed her financial generosity as one of her redeeming qualities. But then again, she'd always had more of it to give. "That's not a bad idea," he said. "Taking a trip somewhere just might do you a world of good."

His Big Mama snorted and started fanning herself with a handkerchief she pulled from a pocket of her duster. "Chile, what am I gonna look like trying to get on a plane and go somewhere as old as I am? And who am I gonna go with?"

Dante reached over, grabbed one of her hands, and gave it a slight squeeze. "You can go with me," he said. "I've got a little change squirreled away. Just tell me when."

She pulled away. "No, what I'ma tell you is the same thing I told that girl—you keep your money. Enjoy it, put it to good use, save it or whatever. Ain't no use of wasting it on some old bird whose days on God's green earth are just about done for."

"I wish you'd stop talking like that," Dante said. He

folded his arms across his chest and closed his eyes again. "Anyway, for the record, Laylah Louise Thomas-Bryant was the furthest somebody from my mind."

"Oh? Now that's a shock sho' nuff. I don't suspect I've ever known you to have any woman but Lil Miz Laylah Louise on your mind," his Big Mama said in a voice rising and falling with amusement.

His own voice hard and flat, Dante responded with, "Things change. People, too."

"I see," his Big Mama said, readjusting her tone. "This new woman—she got a name? Could be I know some of her people."

Dante's face softened. "Eaton. Aliesha Eaton. I think she's got some people in Riverton, but she moved down her from Chicago. She's a professor at Wells."

"A professor, you say? That's nice . . . real nice. She ain't married, is she?"

Dante's eyes snapped open and he glared into the yard. "No, Big Mama, she ain't married. What? You think those are the only kind of women I know how to get involved with?"

"Well, don't go biting my head off, chile. I'm just asking is all. Must be awfully serious, the way you carrying on."

Dante grunted and lowered his lids again. "She's on my mind is all."

"She know how you feel?"

"No . . . not yet."

"What about Laylah? She know about your feelings for this here other woman?"

Dante laughed. "Wait a minute, whose side are you on? Don't tell me you're rooting for Laylah all of a sudden. How much money did you say she gave you?"

"Hush now!" his Big Mama said. "You know good and well I ain't take that girl's money. Just like you know I ain't never been one to choose no sides. Even if I don't approve—what goes on between you and your lady friends is y'all's business." Her face somber, she reached over and placed a hand on Dante's knee. "All I've ever wanted is the best for you, Dante. Always have. Your uncle Mack felt that way, too. We always wanted the best for you and Reuben both."

He nodded. "I know, Big Mama. I know."

She tightened her grip on his leg. "Then know this. If you're serious about this Eaton woman, you need to be honest with her. You need to be a man and do right by her. Tell her how you feel. If you don't know what to say, open up your Bible. There's always an answer or two in there somewhere."

Dante laughed again. "Is that how Uncle Mack got you? Yeah, I can just imagine that Ole Devil coming by to court with the Bible tucked under one arm and a mack daddy rap straight out the New Testament rolling off his ole forked tongue."

His Big Mama laughed with him before she said, "I ain't studyin' you, boy! Make fun all you want to, but me and your uncle Mack had a love that was built on something solid, something that stood the tests of time."

CHAPTER 26

After her second missed hair appointment, Aliesha slipped into a noticeable funk that Monica appeared determined to extricate her from late one Saturday afternoon.

"Hey, if you're not doing anything, and I know you're not, I need you to come by here and watch something with me."

"Something like what?"

"Just something I TiVoed earlier this week and I've been saving for the right time."

"Can't you call Jesus? I'm working on my Sunday school lesson right now."

"Like that's really going to take all damn night. Bump that, girl, and just bring your sanctified ass on."

"Well, since you asked so nicely, the answer is NO! Me and my sanctified ass are going to stay right here with our Bible and pray for you and your heathenish one."

"Okay, I'm sorry. Seriously, Aliesha, this is something I'd really prefer not to watch alone or with Jesus. I need your company."

The earnestness Aliesha heard in Monica's voice broke her resolve. She knew over the past several months Monica had been working at reconciling the strained and difficult relationship she'd had for years with her Amer-Asian mother, Mina. Monica still held Mina accountable for a lot of the pain she'd endured in her life, including her molestation at age nine by one of Mina's sorry-ass boyfriends and having to flee, at age fourteen, to Riverton in order to protect herself from some other fiend Mina had married. Aliesha put away her Sunday school material and without bothering to change out of the T-shirt and sweats she'd been bumming around in, she drove over to the east side of town where Monica lived.

On her arrival, she found her usually bubbly friend subdued and her always tidy abode cluttered with what looked like the discards and remains from the previous week. Piles of clothing, randomly tossed books, stacks of unopened mail, and a variety of empty fast-food bags and containers were strewn everywhere. Aliesha stepped over and around the mess on her trek with Monica to the kitchen.

"You want something to drink?" Monica asked. "A soda or something stronger?" She reached into a cabinet and pulled down a bottle of cognac.

Aliesha shook her head and watched Monica pulled a tumbler from the cabinet and go into the freezer for some ice. She frowned at the sight and the sound of the liquor's splash and crackle into the glass. "You feeling all right?" she asked as she watched her friend, who owned a rep for being a teetotaler, raise the drink to her lips.

Monica made a face and sputtered, "Good Lord, I don't know how you lushes do it." After a cough-filled laugh, she said, "Don't mind me, girl, come on." She led Aliesha to the room housing her wide screen television and other entertainment equipment. After plopping down on the sofa, she reached for the remote and started clicking buttons.

Aliesha sat beside to her. "So what is this? Something for one of your classes?"

Monica shook her head. "Not hardly. Just wait and see."

But as soon as Aliesha heard the intro of the Maury Povich show, she unfurled the legs she'd folded beneath herself, swiveled toward Monica, and said, "Oh, hell no! Tell me you did not have me drive all the way over here to watch some ole 'mama's baby, daddy's maybe' type of madness."

Rather than keel over with laughter, like Aliesha fully expected, Monica picked up her drink and with a straight face said, "I'll have you know, this isn't just any ole 'mama's baby, daddy's maybe' type of drama."

"Yeah?" Aliesha said. "What's so special about this one?"

Monica nodded at the screen. "See that guy right there? The Ike Turner–looking son of a bitch who is so vehemently denying he fathered any of those women's children? Well, guess whose daddy I'm 99.9% sure he is?"

Like Aliesha, Monica's people on her father's side hailed from Riverton. While Monica's father and grandmother were still both very much alive and well, unlike Aliesha, Monica seldom expressed anything remotely resembling fondness for either. Aliesha remembered how taken aback she'd been when on asking Monica an innocent question about her grandmother she'd received an icy "Who, Bertha Wilbun? Girl, I ain't studying that heifer or most of those other fools in South Riverton who call themselves kin to me. Except for my cousin Gabe and my aunt Gert, the only time I hear from any of them is when they need something—car note money, rent, bail, just a little something extra till they get their check or their food stamps. . . ."

Aliesha had gleaned additional details about the source of Monica's hostility toward her Riverton relatives one night when the two of them had been out dining with Gabe, the always dapper, smooth-talking attorney who'd provided Monica a home when at age fourteen, she'd run away from St. Louis and her abusive stepfather.

"Oh, Monica knows she's always been Bertha's favorite,"

Gabe said with a discernable twinkle in his eye. "Bertha was always brushing little Monica's hair, dressing her up, and showing her off to all of her friends. I can still hear her now." Gabe waved his fork from side to side and, with a mock feminine inflection in his voice, said, "Would you look at that hair and those eyes?! My word, isn't she just the prettiest little thing you ever did see? My very own little China doll is what she is."

While he laughed, Monica said, "Yeah, and even back then I had half a mind to tell her, 'Bitch, don't you know I'm part Korean, not Chinese?' But a doll is what I felt like, all right. One of those damn White 'chosen' dolls from Dr. Clark's experiment in the '40s with all those poor, psychologically scarred little Black boys and girls."

But Monica appeared to save the bulk of her fury for her father, Ulysses. "Not once do I ever remember him sending me so much as a crappy-ass card on my birthday. Not once did he ever call just to say, 'Hi' or to see how I was doing. But every year, just like clockwork, he'd turn up on my mama's doorstep, either right before Easter or Christmas, and whisk me off to spend the holidays with him and his folks in Riverton."

According to Monica, after parading her around and soaking up all the praise bestowed upon him by his kinfolks for having sired such a beautiful daughter, Ulysses would disappear to drink and carouse until the time arrived for him to drive her back to St. Louis and deposit her with her mother until the next Christian holiday.

"He treated me like I was a damn toy, a gift that he brought home on a yearly basis for his mother's pleasure and warped amusement. And would you believe till this day, old as his ass is, he's still pulling that same ole trifling shit? Yeah, girl, I made the mistake of going by Bertha's house last Christmas, and who was there but him and not one but two little curly-headed, snot-nosed boys, who looked just as lost and bewildered as I know I used to be."

Monica turned off the program well before it ended and picked up the drink she'd barely touched. "I wouldn't be surprised if all three of those babies were his. Hell, including me, he's got eleven that I know of. None of them by the same women. And not a single Black baby mama in the bunch. I think that's all part of the appeal for him. Being able to drag home to his mama all of these half-Asian, half-Latino, half-Caucasian babies with their light skin and quote, unquote, good hair that he could really give less than a shit about. Dumb, sorry-ass bastard."

She wiped her eyes on her sleeves and stood up, spilling some of her drink in the process. "I'll be back. I need to replenish this."

Aliesha leaped to her feet. "Oh, no, you don't. Trust someone who's recently been there and done it, that's not the remedy for what's ailing you."

"Yeah, well, what would you suggest?"

"I don't know. Umm, let's see, how about shopping?!" she finally said.

"Please, you hate shopping," Monica said.

"Uh-huh, with a passion," Aliesha said. "But you don't. And I think it might do us both some good to spend some time outside of our own miserable little worlds. So I'm willing to let you drag me from one overpriced boutique and shoe store to the next if you'll let me choose the movie we see afterward."

Since Aliesha wanted to change and freshen up and Monica needed to run a quick errand, they decided to leave for the mall around six PM. Monica, who insisted on designating herself chauffeur, drove over and picked Aliesha up. They'd been walking, talking, laughing, and trying on shoes and outfits for a couple of hours when Aliesha finally convinced Monica they needed a break, if only to grab a bite to eat.

They were in the food court, waiting to place orders for cheese-steak sandwiches, when Monica nudged Aliesha and whispered, "Uh-oh, girl. Would you get a load of this hunk of well-done beefcake that's got my mouth watering and my heart trying to skip a beat? Think you could muster up an appetite big enough to handle all of that?"

Aliesha turned in the direction Monica was grinning only to have her eyes descend upon familiar territory. She turned away. "Not only do I think so, the truth is, I already have. That's Kenneth."

"What!" Monica screeched. "I thought you said he was in his fifties?"

"He is."

"Please, all this time I've been imaging dude as some Grady geezer from *Sanford and Son*. He doesn't look a day over forty. And how come you didn't tell me he could pass for Michael Jordan's twin? Oops, hold on, 'cause he's headed this way and he's bringing some long, tall Sally of a sister with him."

"Hell, like I really need this," Aliesha grumbled. But she turned and smiled ever so graciously when she heard Kenneth call her name. "Aliesha?"

"Kenneth," she said before nodding a greeting at the tall, attractive, well-dressed woman on his arm.

"Aliesha, this is Donna," Kenneth said. "Donna, this is Dr. Aliesha Eaton, a professor at Wells and one of my old church members."

Wow! One of his old church members? She felt a rush of anger, but then thought, *I don't guess it would be entirely appropriate from him to introduce me as his former lover . . . or the woman he nearly accidentally killed one night . . . or the woman whose heart and dreams he'd left crushed.*

After Aliesha introduced Monica, they all exchanged a few benign pleasantries before uttering their smile-filled good-byes.

"You okay?" Monica asked on their rejoining of the sandwich line after the hand-holding pair disappeared.

"Of course. How many times do I have to tell you? I'm over Kenneth."

"I guess until one of us actually believes it," Monica said. "If it's any consolation, you're a whole lot better looking than his new Ms. Thang."

Aliesha laughed. "Right. She's freaking gorgeous and you know it."

"Okay, fine then. So you're a whole lot smarter and no doubt ten times the Christian soldier."

"Shut up," Aliesha said with a Tamara-like roll of the eyes.

"What?!" Monica laughed. "I'm just trying to help you feel better."

At the end of their meal, Aliesha and Monica set out for the movie theatre. The film Aliesha had selected was some quirky, independent feature that ordinarily she would have thoroughly enjoyed. But after the encounter with Kenneth she'd found herself barely able to concentrate.

Far from jealousy or even anger, what rose up in Aliesha whenever her thoughts settled on Kenneth was something more akin to remorse and sadness for what they'd lost, for what they might have been, if only . . .

———————⬤⬤⬤———————

It was close to midnight when they arrived back at Aliesha's house on their return from the movie theatre. Needing to make use of the facilities before her drive back home, Monica accompanied Aliesha inside. On depositing her shopping bags on the sofa in the den, Aliesha noticed the red message light blinking on her landline. She picked up the receiver, dialed her voice mail, and listened as Kenneth's voice said, "Seeing you tonight really messed me up. I know it's not what you want to hear, baby, but nothing's changed. I

still love you and I'm still not ready to stop trying. My seeing another woman or even your seeing another man isn't
likely to change that."

By the time Monica entered the room, Aliesha had listened to the message twice and still had the receiver against
her ear.

"Something wrong?" Monica asked on noting the look
on her friend's face.

Aliesha mashed the button that allowed the message to
be heard via the phone's loudspeaker. After listening, Monica
narrowed her eyes and she said, "Maybe you oughta call
the police."

Aliesha made a face. "The police? It's not like he threat-
ened me."

"No?" Monica said. "Well, if a brother tried to choke
the living daylights out of me, the last thing I'd want to
hear is a message like that on my phone late one night."

"It didn't sound like he'd been drinking," Aliesha said.
"Besides, I'm not afraid of him."

Monica walked over and peeked out the window. "Yeah,
I know, Ms. Fearless, your ass ain't afraid of anything. That's
half your damn problem. But remember what you told me
Kenneth did to that fool who asked you how much your
boy was paying to hit it?"

Aliesha thought about poor Skip, the man Kenneth had
assigned as her escort back to her room on that disastrous
evening in Vegas. After Kenneth's return from Riverton,
he'd insisted he and Aliesha meet for dinner so she could
tell him everything that had happened that night. Most of
it, he claimed, he couldn't remember. So she'd recounted
the events for him, including her unpleasant exchange with
Skip, after which Kenneth had calmly driven her over to
Skip's house. Without a word, he'd exited the car, banged
on Skip's door, and when the man, clad in nothing but his
undies, had answered, there had been a brief and heated
verbal confrontation. Sensing what might come next, Aliesha

had opened her car door, but before she could exit the vehicle, Kenneth had already pummeled the half-naked Skip, broken his jaw, and was headed back to the car.

"And your point is?" she asked Monica.

Monica said, "As hella fine and sexy as your friend Kenneth is, he's also both unpredictable and capable of violence. So, anyway, do you happen to keep a gun around?"

A chill swept over Aliesha. "A gun?! Are you outta your mind?"

Her face bearing the same mix of seriousness and outrage Aliesha had seen on it earier when she'd been talking about her father, Ulysses, Monica said, "Well, I've got one at home and I'd be more than happy to let you borrow it."

CHAPTER 27

A gun? She'd dismissed Monica's fears and told her it would be a cold day in hell before she ever considered keeping a gun in her house or on her person. Before she left, a smug Monica had advised her to keep her overcoat on standby.

A shudder snatched Aliesha from her trance and she looked up at the clock above her office door. Twenty minutes past six. Another long day had slowly wound to an end. She rose and started collecting the items she intended to take home with her. She'd nearly finished stuffing everything into her bag when the phone on her desk rang.

Ignore it. If it's important enough they'll leave a message, she told herself. But before the phone could roll over to voice mail, she thought about Kenneth's old habit of calling and leaving messages for her when he knew she wasn't likely to be in her office.

She picked up the phone and uttered a tentative "Hello?"

"Yes," a male voice said. "May I speak to Professor Eaton?"

"Speaking."

A pause followed before the voice said, "I bet your head's starting to look awfully doggone raggedy."

Aliesha frowned. "I beg your pardon? Who is this?"

There was another pause before the caller said, "I'm sorry. Did I reach you at a bad time?"

Aliesha circled her desk and fell into her chair. "Dante?"

"Yeah, it's me. Can you talk?"

Her heart began to race. "Umm, sure ... What can I help you with?"

"Well, why don't you start by telling me why you stopped coming by the shop?"

She winced at her unsettling memories of the evening at Nelson's and later on her porch. "As if that weren't rather obvious. I made such a fool of myself the last time I saw you. ... Frankly, I've been too embarrassed to show my face around there again."

"Well, as much as I appreciate your honesty, there's really no need for you to be embarrassed. As far as I'm concerned, what happened that night stays between us."

She closed her eyes and leaned back in her chair. "Uh-huh, like you and Yazz don't talk."

"No, Yazz talks," Dante said in a voice that sounded deeper and sexier with each passing second. "That's why I don't tell him anything anymore, particularly where it concerns you."

She smiled. "That's awfully considerate of you, I think."

"So—when are you coming back?"

Her eyes snapped open and she sat up straight. "I don't know. I mean, I guess this coming Wednesday," she said, hoping she didn't sound as eager as she suddenly felt.

He said, "Is that a promise or are you just saying that to get me off the phone?"

She laughed. "No, I'll be there, same time as usual, if that's okay."

"Perfect," he said. "I'll see you then."

———◦∞◦———

She didn't bother to bring up Dante's call or the appointment she'd made to see him in her next conversation with Monica. She had a fairly good idea of how her friend might respond. Not that she cared. She'd decided that barring death, weather catastrophe, or some other unforeseen act of God, nothing and no one would keep her from going back to the shop and seeing that man.

In anticipation of her next visit and her need to make amends, she contemplated stopping by Nelson's and buying Dante a couple slices of the pound cake he'd raved so much about. Then she got an even better idea. Why not just make him one?

Cake in hand, she arrived at Wally's Cool Cuts at the appointed time and determined not to allow anything or anyone, including Yazz, faze her. Yazz being Yazz, as soon as he spied her, he leaped from his barber's chair and launched into a series of silly and provocative dance moves. After exchanging nods with Wally and Gerald, Aliesha continued on to the rear of the shop.

"Do you ever actually cut anyone's hair?" she asked Yazz, who brought his dance routine dangerously close to the lemon-flavored pound cake she'd cut into individual slices and arranged on one of the cake plates she'd inherited from her Big Mama's collection.

"You brought us dessert?" Yazz asked, before attempting to pry open the plate's plastic lid and sneak a peek.

"Careful," Dante said on coming over and pushing Yazz aside in his attempt to assist Aliesha with the item. He smiled. "You made this? I mean, from scratch? Not out of a box with the instructions on the back?"

She gave him a look. "Yes, I made it. Why is that so hard to believe? You think girls with book smarts can't cook?"

Yazz said, "Oh snap, D., man. Babygirl can cook, teach, talk smack, and she's got a PhD? Man, you'd best jump on that for real, dog!"

As Yazz clapped and howled over his own joke, Dante leaned toward Aliesha and whispered. "Thanks. And don't worry. I won't let him have any."

"Be nice," Aliesha scolded with a smile.

"See, I knew in time you'd grow sweet on him," Dante said as he placed the cake in a clean, safe spot on a shelf high above his work area.

Umm, there's only one man up here I've grown sweet on, Aliesha caught herself thinking while seating herself in Dante's barber's chair. *And it damn sure ain't Yazz.*

Dante started picking out her hair. On moving in front of her, he tilted her face toward him and said, "I'm glad you decided to come back."

She felt the onset of a blush, but managed a quiet, "I'm glad you thought enough to call me and ask."

"Hey, hey, hey! Cut out all that whispering," Yazz said. "Y'all keep that up and you'll have folks 'round here thinking something's going on between the two of you."

Dante winked at Aliesha before he moved behind her.

With Yazz spouting off every few minutes, Dante and Aliesha weren't able to engage in much by way of conversation. Even the pair's trip to the utility room to wash her hair coincided with a contractor's visit and a demonstrative exchange between Wally and the work crew about the room's planned renovation.

But Aliesha didn't really need to hear anything from Dante. His body language told her everything she needed to know. *You can relax. All is forgiven.*

On their way out, Dante grabbed a piece of her cake and brought it outside with them. "You were right. It's good," he told her as they stood in their usual spot in front of the shop. "Almost as good as Nelson's."

"Almost, my foot!" she said, and reached for his dangling earbuds. He grinned and helped her insert the buds.

She looked away from him while immersing herself in the smooth, sensuous blend of Luther and Martha Walsh's voices on the classic "I (Who Have Nothing)." When she returned the earbuds, she saw something in Dante's eyes she'd never seen before, something she couldn't quite name. But it didn't deter her. "So how come you're willing to let me off so easy? If memory serves me right, I was pretty rude that night."

"Correction," he said softly. "What you were that night was drunk and upset. It happens sometimes, even to the best of us."

"Still, even more than a cake, Dante, I owe you a formal apology . . ."

"No, if you owe me anything it's dinner to go along with that cake. I mean, being how you keep bragging so tough about being able to throw down in the kitchen and all."

She smiled. "Hey, my Big Mama showed me a thing or two. I don't think it's bragging to say, I think I'm capable of holding my own."

She'd intended to let that be her parting shot before she offered her, *see you next time,* and she was all but poised to take a step forward when she heard him say, "Yeah? So when are you gonna invite me over?"

Stunned, she turned and studied his face. Was he serious? Or teasing again? "I thought you said you had a rule about mixing business and pleasure," she said, deciding to play it safe.

He nodded. "I do—one, for you, I'm fully prepared to amend. Just tell me what time and after I leave the shop, it'll be strictly pleasure—yours and mine."

She blinked and thought, *Damn! Where'd all that come from?!* She waited for him to laugh or break into a wide grin, but the expression on his face couldn't have been more earnest and hopeful. "Okay, let me think about it and get back with you," she said, suddenly feeling a need to move before the tingling, which had begun in her feet, became any more intense.

"Sure, you do that," Dante said. "You know where to find me."

She thought about it, all right. In truth, it was all she thought about on her way back to Wells. She carefully weighed all of the pros and cons, and by the time she reached the faculty parking, she'd made up her mind. She called him, and when he came on the line, she said, "I don't do pork or lamb. So what's it going to be—fish, chicken, or beef?"

"Tell me you are not letting that man come to your house" was the first thing out of Monica's mouth when she learned of the Friday night plans Aliesha had made with Dante.

"And why shouldn't I?"

"Because the only thing you really know about him is that he works up at that damn barbershop, that's why."

"I know more than that about him."

"Oh yeah, like what?" Monica said. "Ooh, no, wait, let me guess. That's right, you know he's finally summoned enough balls to come over and hit it. You do know that's the only reason he's coming over, don't you?"

"Has it ever occurred to you that maybe I don't have a problem with that?"

"Yeah, and then what? You know, you are undoubtedly the most whorish churchgoing girl I've met in all my life."

"Look, Monica, I've been out here long enough to know better than to have any grand expectations. Whatever happens, happens. If it's good, wonderful. If it's bad, I start looking for a new barber. . . ."

"Or take your fast behind back to Peaches."

"Shut up!" Aliesha said with a laugh.

CHAPTER 28

She spent Wednesday night planning her menu and giving
her house a thorough cleaning. Since her classes on Thursday
were all in the late afternoon and evening, she did her gro-
cery shopping in the early part of the day. By Friday she'd
decided that Vera Wang would be her fragrance of choice
for the evening. And on a last-minute impulse during her
free period on Friday, she'd even run out and purchased a
couple sets of fluffy towels and a gift for Dante. But it had
taken her forever to pick out the right outfit. Definitely
nothing too revealing, on one hand, or schoolmarm-like,
on the other, is what she decided. When she'd approached
Monica for advice, without skipping a beat, her good friend
had told her, "Why not dispense with the formalities altogether and just meet him at the door butt-ass naked?"

She finally settled on a casual pair of black slacks and a
simple red blouse with a block neckline that stopped right
above her cleavage and tapered ever so slightly at the waist.
She kept her jewelry and makeup simple, too. After all, she
reminded herself, what they had planned—a friendly home-
cooked dinner at her place—was barely even a date. No
need to go rushing into it with any romantic notions only
to wind up disappointed later. Still, she couldn't help but
feel like a jittery teen on prom night. She ran to the mirror

any number of times to check her hair, adjust her clothing, and touch up her makeup.

Thankfully, Dante didn't keep her waiting. At 7:30 sharp he showed up at her door smelling freshly bathed and wearing dark-colored slacks with a matching vest, which he wore buttoned atop a nicely starched and perfectly creased dress shirt. For a moment, Aliesha was so taken by his scent, how nice he looked, and the bright smile beaming at her beneath the rakish angle of his cap, she didn't even notice the gift-wrapped box tucked beneath his arm.

"For you," he said, handing her the present and whipping off his headgear on entering her home. "I know it's traditional to bring wine, but given our last, wild adventure with the bottled spirits—"

When she flashed him a look, he laughed and followed her to the sofa. "Anyway, I thought about flowers. But since I didn't know the kind you might prefer—"

"Petunias and lilies," she said as she unwrapped the gift. "I'm a simple girl with simple tastes."

"You like it?" he asked, sounding a bit worried as she pulled the dark chocolate-dipped colored doll from the box.

Aliesha stared into the large, expressive coca-coca brown eyes. She raised her fingers to the doll's curly, jet-black crown of hair and startled a bit when Dante's fingers joined hers in caressing the full, soft strands and locks.

"I was out one day, back during those couple of weeks when you disappeared on me, and I noticed her in a shop window," he said. "She actually made me stop, back up, and go inside."

"Thank you. She's wonderful," Aliesha said. She nearly acted on her desire to reward him with a kiss on the cheek, but chickened out at the last moment.

"Yeah, I think Miz Babygirl is pretty special, too," Dante said as his fingers brushed the back of Aliesha's hand. "So much so, I almost didn't want to give her up."

Aliesha looked at him. "What did you call her?"

He withdrew his hand from the doll's hair. "What? Miz Babygirl? Oh, I didn't mean any disrespect. It's sort of like a spin on Miz Professor. Don't you think she looks a lot like a miniature version of you?"

Aliesha nodded. "Miz Babygirl. That was the childhood nickname my daddy pinned on me."

Dante smiled. "You're a daddy's girl, huh? You think your daddy would approve of me?"

She smiled back at him. "Oh, I know he would. And before I forget . . . " She retrieved a gift bag from the floor beside the sofa. "I got something for you, too."

She watched as his eyes lit up when he reached into the sturdy bag and rescued the thick book from the sheets of decorative tissue paper. "Now, I know this doesn't fit the profile of the books you normally read," she said. "Chief Big Foot isn't exactly an African American icon."

"No, but this will make a nice addition," Dante said as he opened up the book and began thumbing through the pages. "Wasn't Big Foot the Lakota Indian chief who wiped out Custer and his crew at the Little Big Horn?"

"Well, actually that was Sitting Bull, who was a shaman, or what we typically call a medicine man. But both Big Foot and Sitting Bull were involved in the Ghost Dance movement." She reached over, flipped to the book's picture section, and pointed out the two different men.

"The Ghost Dance movement?" Dante said. "Wait, I think I saw something about that in a movie once. Wasn't that sort of a like a religious belief among some Native Americans? Didn't it have to do with them being reunited with their dead ancestors and their return to the life they led before the Europeans' arrival?"

"Very good!" Aliesha said. "You know, sometimes when you read about other cultures and people who on the surface seem nothing like you, it can, if you let it, lend a fair amount of clarity and insight into your own world."

Dante eyes twinkled with amusement. "You just can't help channeling that inner schoolmarm, can you?"

She winced. "I'm sorry. I didn't mean to go all stuffy and academic on you."

He laughed. "No, don't apologize. I don't mind being one of your students, as long as I get a turn at playing teacher sometimes."

She smiled as the lyrics to Al Jarreau's "Teach Me Tonight" started playing in her head.

What Aliesha had secretly feared, that her infatuation with Dante was one born of simple lust and nothing more, as Monica kept implying, and that the evening would be filled with awkward moments and uncomfortable stretches of silence, never came to pass.

She found herself pleasantly surprised by the ease at which Dante held up his end of the conversation even as he wolfed down several large helpings of the meal she'd prepared at his request—fried chicken, macaroni and cheese, green beans, and hot water cornbread, slathered with lots of butter and chased down with one glass after another of her raspberry-flavored ice tea. She could tell he was comfortable when, on seeing her kick off her shoes, he not only followed suit but dispensed with his vest, too.

After dinner and on consuming an embarrassing portion of the peach cobbler dessert Aliesha had thrown in as a bonus, they'd remained at the table, talking, laughing, and growing closer, even with all of the empty plates, glasses, saucers, and bowls scattered between them.

"You know, when I called you, I was afraid I might have waited too long," he said at one point. "I thought maybe you and your old boyfriend might have already patched things up and gotten back together."

The loose, happy lines in Aliesha's face suddenly tightened. "Well, I assure you, there's little chance of that happening."

Dante leaned back in his chair and studied her. "Was he one of the reasons you were so upset when I saw you that night at Nelson's?"

She shook her head. "No, what you were unfortunate enough to witness that night was just some silly, work-related drama that got mixed and stirred with one too many martinis and ended up getting blown way out of proportion."

He nodded and said, "So why did you and your guy break up? You catch him cheating on you with a White girl or something?"

After a nervous bit of laughter, Aliesha said, "Given some of what spilled out in my drunken tirade, I can certainly see how you might arrive at that conclusion. But no, he wasn't cheating on me with any woman—at least, not that I know of. Javiel is a sweet guy. We just weren't right for one another. I tried to make it work and stayed with him longer than I probably should have, in part because I was tired of being alone and in part because I was hoping he'd help me forget the man I was in love with before he showed up in my life."

Dante stared off into space. "I guess now you know it doesn't work—trying to forget an old love, I mean. You either keep chasing them or else find the strength to relegate them to memory and move on."

After several hours at the dining room table, their shared interest in books and music and their mutual reluctance to bringing their evening to a close led them into Aliesha's den. She found herself biting her lip to keep from laughing out loud at the way Dante's eyes lit up when he saw the rows and rows of books in the handcrafted cases that lined the walls of the room. The joy and excitement she saw written all over his face was not unlike that of a little fat kid with a sweet tooth who'd just learned that his family had inherited a candy store.

During a lull that occurred while they browsed the shelves and bobbed their heads to the smooth jazz playing softly in the background, Dante drifted over to the den's iPod listening dock and sound system. "You mind if I play something for you?" he asked.

"Sure, what do you have in mind?"

"The song I owe you." While replacing her iPod with the one he pulled from his back pocket, he responded to her puzzled expression with, "You remember that time when I got caught outside without my tunes?"

"Oh, okay," she said on having her memory jogged.

"But you have to do something for me," he said. "First, I want you to sit down here," he said, pointing to the pillowed spot on the carpeted floor where Aliesha sometimes stretched out and listened to music and/or read when she was alone. "And then, I just want you to close your eyes and listen. You can't say anything until the song is over. All right?"

Though still not certain what he was up to, Aliesha agreed. She joined him on the floor, closed her eyes, and listened. The slow and teasing piano and guitar intro eased over her like a warm blanket and helped settled her nervousness about being in such close proximity to Dante. It took her a moment to recognize the soulful, sultry voice as that belonging to jazz vocalist Cassandra Wilson. But she immediately identified the lyrics as bits and pieces culled from the Old Testament's Song of Solomon and reassembled in a manner that was both haunting and mesmerizing. Within seconds Aliesha felt herself being drawn into the tune's beauty and captivated by its haunting refrain, "Come bare your soul to me."

When she opened her eyes at the song's end, Dante was staring at her. "It's called 'The Chosen.' So, what do you think?" he asked.

She nodded. "It's pretty."

He stretched out on the floor next to her, wedged a pillow beneath his head, and stared up at the ceiling. "Yes. And?"

She smiled and stretched her body out beside him. "I'm not sure I know exactly what you're asking."

He drew his focus away from the ceiling and looked at her. "What is it you want from me, Miz Professor?"

She sighed and picked at the carpet. "You know, the usual, a friend, a confidant. Someone who's easy to be with, easy to talk to, someone considerate, patient, gentle, and kind. And preferably someone open to seeing and accepting me for the fiercely independent and natural woman that I am." She grinned and tugged at her hair.

His face remained serious. "Is that all? Is that all you really want?"

Her smiled faded and she gazed into his eyes for a few seconds before she said, "Well, right now . . . all I want right now, Dante, is for you to stop asking all of these confusing questions, so you can kiss me."

She didn't have to tell him twice. He rolled toward her, cupped her face, and kissed her with a tender urgency that suggested he'd been longing all night to do so. She felt her heart rate increase, but more from a sense of titillation and excitement than fear. Within seconds she'd abandoned all sense of caution and found herself returning his kisses with the kind of passion she generally reserved for men with whom she'd already shared both her body and her bed. Other than when he moved closer and eased her knee between his thighs, Dante made no attempt to touch or grope or fondle. But there was no mistaking the intensity of his desire.

Several minutes later, when he finally pulled his lips away from hers, he closed his eyes and rested his head against a pillow. Unable to resist the temptation and still hungry for more, she reached over and touched him, first his lips, then the hairs peeking from the open neck of his shirt, and finally the raised nipples pushing against the fabric stretched across his slightly heaving chest.

He opened his eyes and stared into hers. "Should we wait?"

"Probably. But there's certainly nothing written in stone that says we have to, unless of course that's what you'd prefer."

He looked down at the conspicuous rise in his pants and back at her. "I think, at this point, my preference is pretty obvious."

She laughed, then said, "So, did you bring any, you know, protection?"

He sat up. "Actually, I have an overnight bag out in the car. I wasn't sure you'd want me to stay, but I figured I'd come prepared, just in case."

They both stood up. The sight of him moving away from her as he started toward the door gave rise to a bubble of tension in her chest. "Look, Dante," she said softly. "If this is only going to be one night, I'm fine with that. Really, I am. And if it works out and evolves into something more, that's even better. But that whole friends with benefits thing and being a part of some rotating harem of women, that's really not for me. Okay?"

He walked back toward her and reached for her hands. "Now why you wanna go and take it there? Huh? Didn't I just say I came ready to take care of you? What? You think I'm gonna want to stop after tonight?"

"I don't know. Men say a lot of things, most of which they typically don't mean."

"Okay, fair enough. So watch and see what I do. All right?" He kissed her before going outside and retrieving his things.

Before she went into the bathroom, he asked her not to put on anything beneath her kimono. So, she didn't and on emerging from the bathroom, she found him naked on the side of her bed. When he stood and turned toward her, even from a distance and in the room's dim lighting, she realized she'd never been with a man as dark or with a physique as cut and chiseled as Dante's.

He smiled and said, "So what you think, Miz Professor? Do I get an A?"

She allowed her gaze to linger on the growing erection angling toward her before she smiled back and said. "Uh, not only do you get an A+, you just earned a semester's worth of triple extra-credit points, too."

When he held out his hands, she moved toward him and placed the flat of her palms against his. When his mouth descended upon hers, she caressed him and marveled at the firmness she felt beneath the warm, smooth cover of his skin. Aroused and eager to feel the full press of his body against hers, she unfastened the sash of her robe. But before she could unveil her nakedness, he moved his mouth to her ear and whispered, "Not so fast. Turn around for me."

For a moment she had a flashback of being with Kenneth in Vegas. But when she peered into Dante's eyes and saw a clear reflection of herself staring back, she let go of her fears and clung to her faith.

When she turned, he eased the robe off her shoulders and down one side of her body. He planted his lips on her exposed shoulder and on her collarbone before moving to a spot behind her ear. After the robe's fall into a puddle on the floor, he placed his hands against her waist, glided them over the curve of her hips, and muttered, "You're beautiful."

A rush of air escaped her lips when he pulled her against him. In addition to the searing hard-on, she felt first his breath and then the swirl of his tongue on the back of her neck. As he kissed her hairline and eased his tongue in and out of the indented area on the back of her neck that Ms. Margie used to call "the kitchen," Aliesha felt the tension slowly leave her body and pleasure take its place.

When Dante moved his fingers to her breasts, she was struck by the near-perfect blend of his skin against her own. She cupped her hands atop his and guided his gentle squeeze and pull.

"That's right, Miz Professor," he said. "Show me how to keep getting those As. Wait and see if I'm not your best student ever."

She thought to herself, *Well, I'd dare say you're doing a damn excellent job of it thus far.*

He eased a hand into the moistened area between her thighs and said, "Why you so quiet, Miz Professor? You trying to hold back on me? Am I doing something wrong?"

"Of course not," she whispered while fighting against her desire to break into a whimper. "You passed the first lesson with flying colors. But if you keep calling me Ms. Professor, I'm going to start taking off points."

He chuckled. "So how's Aliesha? Is that better?"

She turned and looked at him. "Much better, thank you."

He touched her face. "What about baby? Can I call you baby? Can I call you my woman?"

"Yes," she told him, prior to kissing him and pulling him onto the bed with her. "But only if you really mean it."

Dante's uninhibited bedroom banter amused her. He whispered, panted, and moaned about how beautiful she was, how wonderful she felt, and how good she tasted—"one part honey, two parts heaven" according to him. She found him a dangerously unselfish lover. While he declined to enter the pulsating warmth of her body or the soft pucker of her lips without the benefit of a condom, he insisted on foregoing the placement of any kind of barrier between his tongue and her clitoris.

But she had no complaints and had been only too happy

to oblige when in urging her to straddle him, he'd said, "I want to see your face when you come." She'd opened her body and bid him entry, like a queen intent on determining if he was fit to reign in her dark world as king. And he hadn't disappointed. He'd made her hear and feel both the beat of the drums and the call to prayer. In his sweat she'd tasted the waters their souls had crossed together—not the Atlantic or the Mississippi—but the ancient ones Langston had immortalized in verse, the Niger and the Nile. He'd made her behold and cross backward through the point of no return.

On her arched back slip into ecstasy, he'd lifted his own back from the mattress and kissed her neck and her face before gently seizing a fistful of her hair and saying, "Whose world is it, baby? Whose world is it?"

"Whose world is it?" she teased the next morning when he awakened next to her.

He smiled, snuggled against her, and with his face pressed to her breast, he muttered, "The correct response to which is, 'It's our world, baby. Yours and mine.'"

She laughed. "You, sir, are something else." She caressed his head and ran her fingers over the stubble on his cheeks. "Dante . . . is there really any chance of this lasting?"

"Yes, if you want it to."

"So, why's the burden on me?"

"Because you're the highly educated and much-respected professor who teaches at Wells. And I'm just that brother who cuts hair down at Wally's."

She pulled away from him to get a better look at his face. "For what it's worth, right here and right now, you're the only man this highly educated and much-respected professor wants in her bed and in her life. Doesn't that count for something?"

He raised up on an elbow. "Is that what you live for— the here and now?"

"Yes, don't you? If nothing else, I think we can both agree that tomorrow isn't exactly promised."

———— ∞∞∞ ————

When he finally made his groan-filled and reluctant rise from her bed, he apologized for having to leave her and run off to work. She told him she'd fully expected as much and asked if he wanted or had time for any breakfast. His only request was a cup of coffee, black, no sugar, no cream. Upon his exit from the shower, she had a steaming cup waiting for him, along with a tray of sliced fruit and some warm cinnamon rolls.

While he drank his coffee at her kitchen table and thumbed through the morning paper, she ran a sink full of hot, sudsy water for the dishes she'd left there the night before. She couldn't remember the last time she'd felt so much happiness and satisfaction churning through her every cell. She lifted her head toward the heavens and silently prayed, *Oh, dear God, please let it last.*

When Dante rose from the table and brought his empty cup to the sink, she raised her wet, bubble-covered fingers to his face and rubbed her nose against his. "If you could spare a minute, I'd like a chance to play something for you."

After drying off her hands, she placed a CD into the player next to her microwave. On returning to the sink where he still stood, she said, "Now, close your eyes and don't say anything until the song is over."

Wearing a grin, spawned by her mimicking of his instructions to her the night before, he folded his arms over his chest before lowering his eyelids and bowing his head.

The lines and muscles in his face fell smooth and slack as Aretha Franklin's "A Natural Woman" filled and energized the space between them. Sister Ree's soulful litany and testament about a man whose kiss helps a woman place a name on what's been ailing her had long been one of Aliesha's favorites and lent voice to some of what she herself didn't yet own the words to say.

At the song's end, Dante drew her against him and buried his hands in her hair. "You really feel that way?"

She pressed her lips to his shoulder and said, "Yes, I'm afraid so," she said.

"I'm glad. But I think you should know that what you said before about me being a scared little boy still holds true."

She knew he was referring to something she'd said the night they'd run into each other at Nelson's. It pained her to know that in spite of all his reassurances to the contrary, he might never forget or truly forgive the awful way she'd treated him. She pulled back from his embrace and peered up at him. "You know I didn't mean any of that, Dante. It was just the liquor talking."

"No, to some extent you were right. I have been running scared from a lot of things and for a long time. It's time I faced some of those fears."

She stroked his chest. "Okay, but if last night is what scared looks like on you, then I hate to tell you, babe, but you wear it well and I'm not so sure I want you to change."

He moved her hand from his chest to his face, and in a lighter tone he said, "Well, far be it from me to brag, but when it comes to what we did last night, I can assure you that's one place where I ain't never been scared."

She laughed. "That's good to know because the next time I see you I'll definitely be expecting an encore performance."

"Oh yeah?" he said while backing her against the counter. "Well, how's this for a sample?" He kissed her deeply and with a raw and unabashed passion similar to the kind he'd displayed with in her bed the night before.

When he finally stopped, and her racing heart slowed a bit, she whispered, "Now that was truly worthy of its own standing ovation."

He grinned, then glanced at his watch and said, "Good, because it's gonna have to hold you until I get back." He put on his cap. "As much as I'd love to stay and finish what we've started here, I'd better go before Wally sends either the bloodhounds or Yazz out looking for me." He planted a parting peck on her lips and said, "I'll call you."

PART IV

CHAPTER 29

He didn't call. At first she thought little of it. She knew from personal experience how chaotic any given Saturday at the hair salon could be and suspected the barbershop wouldn't be much different. She also knew from personal experience that an "I'll call you" coming from a man was typically more of a sweet exit line than a genuine promise to do so. She figured Dante had probably gotten busy with the Saturday crowd and by the end of the day had been exhausted and simply put off placing the call. If nothing else, the rationale proved plausible enough to get her through Saturday night and into Sunday.

She blew a cooling breath over the steam circling from her coffee mug. She'd awakened on the Sabbath with a strong sense that she was about to embark upon a journey to a place she'd never ventured before. Unable to shake the feeling, and unsure if she ought be rightfully concerned, she'd arrived at Garden View early and spent a few minutes mediating in the quiet of the empty sanctuary. Upon centering herself and reclaiming a bit of peace, she'd made her way into the church's kitchen and prepared enough of the morning brew for the other members of her class, many of whom, like her, needed that extra jolt to properly launch them into the day.

She stole a few quick sips of the still hot beverage before entering the conference room and pulling out her notes for the morning's lesson. With her mother's worn Bible opened to the Song of Solomon, Aliesha had assumed her position at the head of the table. But her backside had barely graced the seat of her chair when in walked Tamara.

"Hey, Dr. Eaton, what are you doing here so early? We were hoping to surprise you."

Her eyes widen at the sight of the other half of the "we" who came strolling in behind Tamara. Even had she been granted twenty guesses, Aliesha never could have predicted Kristen's presence at Garden View.

"Good morning, Dr. Eaton," Kristen said with a pronounced twitch in her smile. "I hope you don't mind my showing up unannounced like this. Tamara insisted it would be all right."

Tamara giggled and fell into the seat next to Aliesha's. "Yeah, Doc, try not to look so shocked."

"No, it's fine," Aliesha said, glancing at the door and wondering if Shelton and the two wild-hair girls would come trooping through it next. "I am, quite naturally, somewhat surprised. Pardon me for asking, but did Shelton know you were coming here this morning?"

Kristen took a seat directly across from Tamara's, which put her on the other side of Aliesha. "Dr. Eaton, I know you and Patricia believe I'm somehow obligated to have Shelton approve my every move. But I assure you, that is not at all the case. He knows exactly where I am. That's not to say he necessarily likes it—"

Tamara laughed. "I'm gonna go grab some coffee and see if anyone's arrived yet with the doughnuts. Can I bring either of you anything?"

Both women declined. After Tamara's exit, Aliesha turned

to the young, ruddy-cheeked woman, who appeared engaged in a quiet, visual assessment of the room. Aliesha cleared her throat and said, "Do you mind me asking what brings you here today?"

"Several things, actually," Kristen said. "First, Tamara has only had wonderful things to say about your command as a teacher—here and at the university. She's also shared with me some of the fascinating research in which she's engaged with your guidance and assistance. From what I understand, you've published quite a bit of research in the area of sexual commerce."

"Yes," Aliesha said. "Up until this point, my specific area of interest has been on what many refer to as the world's oldest profession. I spent a couple of years studying a group of prostitutes who work some of the meaner streets of Chicago's South Side."

"Well, I've been dying for an opportunity to speak with you in-depth about some of your and Tamara's research and how I might get involved."

Had Aliesha been drinking her coffee, she might have choked or spewed it everywhere. "Excuse me?" she said.

"After I return to school, of course, which I'm aiming to do sometime in the next year or so. And I certainly hope you won't let Shelton's bombastic nature stop you from serving as one of my advisors."

Kristen went on to shock Aliesha even further when she brought up the research in which she herself had been involved with a group of prostitutes in Paris and prior to her marriage and subsequent move to the States with Shelton. As sincere and enthused as Kristen sounded, Aliesha couldn't help but wonder how Shelton felt about his wife's plans, specifically as they pertained to her, a woman he viewed as a nappy-headed, proselytizing, same-sex-inclined seductress. But her concerns didn't prevent her from expressing her full support of Kristen's desire to resume her education and academic pursuits.

It wasn't until Sunday rolled into Monday without her having heard a single word from Dante that Aliesha started feeling slighted. *Okay, I can understand and fully accept the passage of one day. But two?* That, in her book, was pushing it—especially given the time and energy she'd put into the dinner preparations and the truly wonderful night they'd spent together afterward. Why hadn't he called, if only to say, "Hey, babe, I'm too busy or tired to talk or come and see you. But I'll get back with you soon."

She knew she didn't dare raise the subject with Monica, unless she wanted to hear some version of the "What I tell your ass?" lecture. So she hid her growing anxiety and only let Monica in on those things that cast Dante in the most favorable light—his promptness; the darling brown-skinned baby doll he'd given her; the healthy appetite and appreciation he'd shown for her food, her conversation, and her body. She even went as far as to share some of the tender and provocative things he'd whispered while in her bed.

"Well, I'm glad to hear it and I hope it continues to work out for you," Monica told her. "'Cause you know, I still have my doubts. . . ." *Yes, I know. That's why I'm dishing you the gravy and keeping the bullshit portion to myself,* Aliesha thought.

By Tuesday she'd reached her breaking point. *Okay, fine. So I'll call him and see what's up.* But when she reached for the phone, she realized the only number he'd ever given her was for Wally's Cool Cuts. She found the shop's business card and examined the days and hours Dante had scribbled on the back. According to the information, on Tuesdays he worked until nine PM. Her watch read seven, so she picked up the phone and dialed the number.

"Hello? May I speak to Dante?"

"He's not here," the voice replied.

"Wally?" she asked.

"Yeah," he said.

"This is Aliesha Eaton. Would you mind leaving Dante a message? Would you please tell him that I called."

After a pause, Wally said, "Ah, sure, Dr. Eaton. I'll leave him the message."

She waited, figuring surely at any moment Dante would call, anxious to beg her forgiveness for having behaved so rudely. She sat next to the phone for a full hour before acknowledging that she was only making herself crazy. What was going on? Later that night while tossing and turning in bed, she asked herself a dozen different versions of that question. Had Wally given him the message? If so, why hadn't Dante called? Was she missing something? Had she said or done something that might have upset him?

She racked her brain and reviewed the details of their night together and the morning after. The last words she could recall him saying were, "I'll call you." So why hadn't he? Unless of course, that had been the whole point all along . . . Oh hell, was this some kind of freaking game to him?! Or worst yet, part of some elaborate scheme to get back at her for insulting him the night he'd escorted her home?

She woke up the next morning tired from mulling all of those things he'd said in the hours before his disappearance and angry because she couldn't understand how a man could go from, "Can I call you my baby?" to pulling something so insensitive. Her regularly scheduled appointment wasn't until the following week. But she knew she wasn't about to wait that long before breaking him off a piece of her mind. She double-checked the days and times on the back of the card before driving to Wally's.

She tried to steel herself as she sat in her car outside of

the shop, feeling as if at any moment a hot blast of steam would burst forth from her ears. *I'm not going to curse. I'm not going to get loud and ignorant. I'm not going to cause any kind of a scene. I'm just going to ask him one question: "Why?"*

But on entering the establishment, the first thing she noticed was that the spot in the rear where Dante should have been was vacant. She turned to Gerald, the only barber in the immediate vicinity, and said, "Where's Dante?"

Gerald, who barely looked up from the customer in his chair, said, "I don't know. He ain't here."

"So what time do you expect him back?"

"I don't. Only somebody's hours I keep up with around here are my own."

"Thanks!" Aliesha snapped. "You've been so incredibly helpful." When a laugh behind her caught her attention, she spun around only to see the gray-haired antagonist from her very first visit to Wally's.

Like the time before, Ray sat with this razor-creased khakis gapped wide open and his hands folded behind his head. "Hey there, Miz Chicago, how you be? I reckon by now you've discovered that the nights around here can get just as chilly as they do where you from, huh?"

She shot him a heated glare and before she could catch herself spat a terse, "Kiss . . . my . . . ass!"

The man seated next to Ray and the one in Gerald's chair roared with laughter.

"What?! What, I say?!" Ray said, dropping his arms, closing his legs, and looking both shocked and confused.

"Man, leave that woman alone," Gerald said with a wide grin before he whipped out his cell phone. "Look here, Miz Professor, if you wanna talk to Wally, he's 'round back with the contractors. Want me to call him up here for you?"

The man seated next to Ray broke in with, "Hell no,

she don't wanna talk to Wally's ass! Didn't you hear the woman? She say she wanna speak to Dante."

The two customers, the who'd just spoken and the one seated in Gerald's chair, slapped palms and fell out laughing again.

As a flustered Aliesha spun around and charged toward the door, she heard Ray say, "What the hell she bite my head off for? Shit, all I was trying to do was be polite and make small talk. Told you them women outta Chicago wasn't nuthin nice."

⊷⊷⊷

She leaned against the check-out desk at the university library. She'd just finished filling out the slip required to reserve the stack of books she'd assigned her Race, Class & Gender class to read before the end of the semester. When she passed the form to the librarian, she caught a glimpse of a Black male figure out the corner of her eye.

She turned and appraised the dark-skinned youth, whose athletic build, Stagolee strut, and tilted Kangol reminded her so much of Dante that a smile wriggled up from the tight grasp of her hurt and brushed against her lips. In spite of her resolve to forget about him and the feelings he'd aroused in her, everywhere she'd turned, over the past couple of days, she'd found herself being pulled back into the twisted fabric of her memories.

Even the library itself, with its endless rows and shelves of books, its tables, chairs, and lounging areas full of readers, made her think of Dante and the passions they shared, both in and beyond the bedroom. But the pleasure she found in the recollections were fleeting and, inevitably, led back to the pit she felt growing deeper on the inside. On collecting her receipt from the librarian, she headed for the exit.

The fresh air and sunshine lent a nice shot of adrenaline to her drooping spirits. On her meandering stroll toward her basement office in Sojourner Hall, she made special note of the students she saw walking hand in hand, playing Hacky Sack, and acting like the goofy kids most of them were. Their antics made her think about the short-lived innocence of her own youth and all of the carefree summer days she'd spent in Riverton. She'd nearly reached her building and was contemplating a quick detour to a cozy spot she noticed beneath a pair of giant oaks on the front lawn when she heard, "Nice day to play hooky, huh?"

She grimaced before she turned and smiled at Monica. Thus far, Aliesha had succeeded in avoiding coming into close proximity to people, like Monica and Pat, who were more likely than some others to notice the change in her demeanor and would insist she let them in on the reason why.

"Maybe for a minute," she said as she strolled with Monica toward the spot beneath the trees. "Gotta maintain our role-model status, you know."

"Where have you been hiding the past couple of days?" Monica asked. "Did you get that e-mail I sent you this morning?"

Aliesha shook her head. "Haven't had a chance to look at it. Too much work, not enough time."

"You've probably read it already, anyway. It's an article about macaque monkeys and how, according to a group of scientists who've been studying them, the males of the species use grooming to barter for sexual favors from the females. Kind of sounds familiar, doesn't it?"

Aliesha narrowed her eyes and said, "Ha-ha!"

"Ooh, kind of testy today, aren't we?" Monica laughed. "So what do you and barber boy have on tap for this weekend, besides more hot monkey sex?"

On reaching the stone bench beneath the trees, Aliesha

deposited the bag hanging from her shoulder before she said, "Not a damn thing, if you really must know."

Monica studied Aliesha's face. "What is your problem? Wait, don't tell me there's already trouble in paradise. Yeah, I knew his ass was too good to be true. What did he do?"

Aliesha sighed. "It's what he hasn't done, like call. He said he'd call and I haven't heard from him."

"Girl, now you know they all do that. No biggie, so he missed a call. Chew him out and keep on keeping on."

"No, Monica. He hasn't called *at all*. I haven't heard from him since last Saturday morning when he left my house."

Monica grabbed her arm. "You're shitting me! Well, hell, have you tried calling him?"

She shrugged and started gesturing with her hands. "I don't have his number. I left word for him at the shop and even stopped by there the other day. Still, no Dante. He's obviously laying low and the fellas at the shop are covering for him."

"So roll by his place and set his ass straight."

Aliesha heaved a sigh of exasperation. "Monica, are you even halfway listening? I don't have the man's private telephone number—cell, home, or otherwise. I don't know where he lives. Hell, I don't even know his last name."

Monica stared at Aliesha for a few seconds, then laughed. "I'm sorry, girl, I just never imagined you as the type who'd give it up without first getting a social security number and running a thorough background check."

"Well, I'm glad to be able to brighten your day."

"Oh, come on, it's not the end of the world. You're not the first woman out here to be duped, nor I suspect will you be the last."

"I guess it's still hard for me to believe he'd actually do something like this."

Monica stared out over the lawn. "Well, maybe he didn't.

Maybe something happened to him. Could be Kenneth was lurking in the bushes in front of your porch and when he saw barber boy come tripping out your house Saturday morning, he snatched his ass and carted him off somewhere."

Aliesha felt her heart skip a couple of beats. "You don't think that could be a real possibility, do you? That Kenneth actually did something to hurt Dante?"

A frown took hold of Monica's face and her voice turned hard and flat. "Aliesha, you really need to get a grip. I was only joking. Wanna know what I really think? That fool did something that got his ass locked up. That's right, he probably got hauled downtown on some outstanding warrant shit and he's laying up on a cot behind bars somewhere now."

A thin layer of ice formed over Aliesha's eyes and the words tumbled off her lips like frozen sickles. "What is it with you? You don't even know this man. What leads you to automatically assume he's got a criminal background, much less has done something that would land him in jail?"

Monica widened her stance and crossed her arms. "You asked for my opinion. Forgive me for not coughing up one more to your liking."

Aliesha lowered her voice. "Go ahead, blow it off if you want. But don't think I haven't noticed how you consistently jump to the same negative conclusion when it comes to brothers like Dante and Kenneth, the latter of whom, if memory serves correct, you were ready to all but gun down a weekend or so ago. But Javiel could have had my ass dismembered and chilling on ice and you, no doubt, would still be sitting up somewhere defending his holy name."

Monica nodded and looked as if she were about to turn and walk away. Instead she took a step toward Aliesha and in a fierce whisper said, "You know, that must have been some hellafied, spellbinding dick ole boy laid on you.

'Cause from the looks of things, it's got your ass speaking in tongues, ready to fight the devil and some of everything, and Sunday is still two days away yet."

"I guess I should have known not to expect any better coming from you." Aliesha snatched her bag from the bench and slung it back across her shoulder. "But can I let you in on a little something? Not every Black man in the world is like your trifling-ass, deadbeat daddy."

For a moment, Monica looked as if she'd just been slapped. She emerged from the stupor in a burst of laughter, followed by, "Yeah, well, by the same token, not all of us were fortunate enough to get blessed like you and end up with our very own 'Black prince in shining armor, can't do no wrong, Jesus on the cross' type for a daddy, and one who from the looks of things is still never more than a fucking nightmare away."

Having leveled her parting shot, a red-faced Monica spun around and stormed off in one direction while Aliesha did likewise in the other.

CHAPTER 30

Aliesha hung around campus for as long as she could that Friday. It wasn't as if she had anyplace special to go or anything to do—much less anyone special with whom to go and do anything. She felt awful about the argument she'd had with Monica and wished she'd kept some of the uglier sentiments, particularly those about Monica's father, to herself. Even so, she couldn't help but stew over some of the nasty and insensitive comments Monica had hurled her way. Did she actually believe all that crap she'd spewed about Dante? Did she honestly think the view Aliesha held of her own father was some goody-two-shoes, grossly distorted, larger-than-life one?

When a tired and desponded Aliesha finally slid behind the wheel of her car and sped off, her plan to drive home quickly turned into a hunt for signs of Dante. The first stop on her unplanned tour wound up being none other than Nelson's Barbecue. She circled the small, congested parking lot, and even got out for a minute to search for a vehicle that might resemble Dante's. On finding none, she left Nelson's and burned rubber in the direction of Wally's Cool Cuts.

Again, upon arriving, she found the parking lot packed. As in most Southern urban communities with a sizeable Black population, in Riverton, Friday and Saturday nights were traditionally busy ones for barbers and salons, barbecue joints and chicken shacks, clubs and liquor stores, ER rooms and the morgue. Aliesha sat in her car and watched as one man after another left or entered the shop. Rather than call or enter the establishment herself, when she saw an older gentleman amble out of the building and into the parking lot, she cruised toward him and rolled down her window.

"Excuse me, sir? Would you happen to know Dante? A barber who works in the back of the shop here?"

"Ah, yeah, I know Dante. Friendly dark-skinned fella? Looks like he mighta once played ball?"

"Yes, sir, that's him. Did you happen to notice if he was working tonight?"

"No, sweetheart, I can't say that he was. Only barbers in there this evening are Wally, Gerald, and some new fella."

"Okay, thank you." *Some new fella?* Aliesha shook her head and started for home.

But on pulling up to her house, she thought about the snide remark Monica had made about Kenneth jumping out of the bushes in front of her porch. While he didn't own Dante's youth or athletic build, Kenneth was large and fit enough to overpower Dante, especially if the element of surprise was on his side.

But was he truly capable of such? Her thoughts wandered back to the brutal beating he'd given Skip before fast-forwarding to the message he'd left on her phone:

"I know it's not what you want to hear, baby, but nothing's changed. I still love you and I'm still not ready to stop trying. My seeing another woman or even your seeing another man isn't likely to change that."

Had that been some sort of veiled threat? Aliesha shifted her car into reverse and set back out across town, headed for the wealthier still yet unincorporated part of the county, where Kenneth lived. Due to the absence of streetlights and sidewalks, Aliesha had never cared much for driving there alone after dark. But she didn't feel as if she could wait until the next morning for answers. She'd arrived in Kenneth's neighborhood still unsure as to how she'd even go about broaching such a topic with him. *Umm, did you do something to make Dante disappear?* didn't strike her as the best conversation opener.

As fate would have it, no sooner had she pulled within sight of his house did his black Navigator appear. She slowed her own car to a halt across the street and a couple of houses down. She watched as Kenneth and his new lady-friend, Donna, climbed out and spent several seconds smooching underneath the porch light before entering the house. Several minutes after the couple's disappearance, Aliesha still sat, staring toward the home and with her mind stuck on the smoldering image of Kenneth showering his affection on someone other than her. The sight saddened her more than she thought it would.

When she finally restarted her engine and drove off into the night, she did so with no real destination in mind. If asked, she would have sworn her only thought had been to clear her head. But somehow, no less than thirty minutes after leaving Kenneth's neighborhood, she found herself pulling up in front of Javiel's house. On noticing the light in his studio, she couldn't resist the urge to call.

"Hi," she said.

"Hey," he replied.

"I was in your neighborhood tonight and I saw the light. You working on something?"

"Yes," he said. "Something I think you'd like. Would you like to see it sometime?"

"Sure . . . how's now?" she asked.

"Now?" He paused then said, "Okay. Where are you?"

"On the street outside your house."

He fell silent again. A few minutes later, his porch light blinked on and he appeared at the door.

She pulled her car into his drive and walked up to the

house. On approaching the door, she heard a distinctive and repetitive yap, followed by what sounded like a gentle scold and reprimand from Javiel. She peered through the door's glass inset and saw a wiggling, barking puppy skittering in-between and around Javiel's bare feet.

"Forgive me," she said on entering. "I didn't know you had company." She bent down and reached for the frisky pup, whose bright eyes sparkled and pretty black coat glistened.

Javiel joined Aliesha on the floor. "Her name's Sheba. I think she likes you."

Aliesha studied his face. He seemed different and definitely a lot calmer than when she'd seen him last. "She looks like a sweet pup," she said. "Dogs generally take after their owners, you know."

He smiled and helped Aliesha to her feet. "She's a Lab. They're a nice breed. I trained quite a few of them while I was in the monastery." When she grinned, he said, "And what, may I ask, is so funny?"

"Oh, I just thought about something your mother told me. According to her, you don't even like dogs."

Javiel's eyes narrowed. "My mother, as we both well know, says a lot of things."

The coldness Aliesha heard in his voice gave her chills. But rather than let him see her tremble, she stared into the dark slits that had become his eyes. "So who are you still more angry with—her or me?"

He reached down and picked up the pup. "I'm not angry, Aliesha, I'm hurt, or at least I was." He bent his head so the dog could lick his face. "Having Sheba around has done a lot to lessen the pain. You're always gonna love me, aren't you, girl?" he said while nuzzling the quivering black bundle. When he turned his face toward Aliesha again, she noticed that all signs of the tension she'd seen there just seconds ago were gone.

She reached out and rubbed Sheba's ears. "You want to show me the painting?"

Puppy in tow, Javiel led Aliesha to the studio. On entering the room, the first and only thing she saw for several minutes on end was the nearly complete image on the oversized canvas. She moved toward the painting and stood in front of it as if in a trance. Her eyes teared at the stunning, full-length reflection of herself that stared back at her. He'd painted her partially nude, her breasts and pelvis just barely covered by a long, white sheet, but all of her limbs, thankfully, appeared intact. And there was no denying that the proud, dark face and the head with the crown full of black, unruly curls belonged to anyone but her.

"You like it?" Javiel asked, in a voice quavering with a note or two of anxiety.

She nodded. "Oh, Javiel . . . It's beautiful."

"I got rid of the other ones," he said. "I'm sorry they disturbed you. It never even occurred to me that they might. I wish you'd said something sooner."

"It's okay," she said. "I was just being overly paranoid."

"You can have this one when I'm finished, if you'd like."

"No, I couldn't. I wouldn't feel right," she said.

He sat on the stool in front of the easel. "It would certainly make me feel better if you did. I can't stand the thought of you thinking I'd ever do anything to hurt you, Aliesha."

"Finish it first and then maybe we'll talk. Who knows, you just might want to keep it." She laughed. "It might even be worth something one day."

When she turned to him, still wearing a smile, he reached for her hand. "I want you back, Aliesha. Tell me what I need to do."

She looked away and shook her head. "Nothing's changed between us, Javiel."

He stood, held her hand tighter, and on moving closer to her whispered, "I beg to differ. You wouldn't have come here tonight if it hadn't. What? You still don't think I see you?"

She gazed at the painting, then back at him. "Javiel—"

He pressed his forehead against hers. "Tell me what to do, baby. What is it you need? You came here for a reason tonight, didn't you?"

Rather than move away or attempt to tell him the whole sordid, selfish truth behind her sudden appearance on his doorstep, she stammered, "I-I don't know. I guess I was a little lonely and—"

When he tried to kiss her, she said, "No, Javi, don't. Just hold me. Okay? Right now, I really just need to be held."

He folded his arms around her and squeezed her tight. As soon as his body touched hers, she knew she'd made a horrible mistake. She had no business being there. Javiel wasn't who she wanted, much less who she needed. No matter how earnest his attempt, he'd never adequately fill the void she felt. But driven by desperation and need, she let him try anyway. When he moved to kiss her, she didn't resist or tell him no. She followed him to his guest bedroom around the corner. She let him help her disrobe and willingly climbed atop the mattress and against the sheets with him.

Afterward, she tried to sleep through her guilt. But later in the night she experienced a nightmare. She dreamed of Dante and death. She reached out for his ghostly image, only to have him frown and shake his head in much the manner of the pup, Sheba, before floating beyond Aliesha's reach. In the dream she ran after the image only to see it float backward and descend into what looked like a river. She awakened in the throes of a violent shudder, on the verge of a scream and drenched in sweat.

The next morning, after feeding the dog and preparing their coffee, a quiet and pensive Javiel joined her at the small table in his breakfast nook. They studied their separate sections of the newspaper and drank their coffee in silence. When he finally lifted his gaze to hers, she noticed that his eyes were larger and sadder than she'd ever seen them before.

"You've been seeing someone, haven't you?" he asked.

She nodded and sighed. "Yes."

"Must be serious. You called his name a couple of times in your sleep. Dante, right?"

"Yes," she said again.

Javiel clenched his hands and closed his eyes. "So why in the hell weren't you out driving around in his neighborhood last night? Why'd you stop by here?"

She looked Javiel, longing to tell him something other than the truth. "Because . . . I didn't know where else to go. I don't know where Dante is. And I needed . . . I needed to be held."

Javiel's eyes snapped open and he leaned toward her with his face fixed into a snarl. "So, in other words, last night with you and me—that was just about convenience? I was, what? The fucking substitute? I'm be damned if my mother wasn't right about you." He rose up abruptly, knocking over his chair in the process. Before he left the room, he looked down at her with his eyes aglow and his chest heaving. In a coarse, raspy whisper, he said, "You really ought to count your blessings. Because for the record, if I were a murderer, you wouldn't have woke up this morning."

She sat at the table alone and finished her coffee. She even thought about washing up the dishes before leaving, but ultimately decided that would be pushing it and possibly him too close to the brink. Next to his unfinished cup of coffee, she placed the house key he had yet to request she return. She paused long enough to kneel, give Sheba a parting pet, and whisper, "Take care of him, okay?" into the pup's ear before she grabbed her purse and went out to her car.

While driving home, she checked her phone for messages. To her surprise there'd been several, one from Tamara, one from the department's secretary, one from Mrs. Phillips, and a bunch from Monica demanding that she answer "the damn phone." When Aliesha arrived home and checked her landline, she found more of the same, some of every darn body had called except the one person from whom she really wanted to hear.

Since she didn't feel up to speaking with any of the others, she took a long, hot shower before downing a couple of sleeping pills, crawling into her king-sized bed, and drawing the covers up over her head. Her actions didn't stop the phone from ringing, though. Monica called several times and on the answering machine left messages imploring as to why Aliesha hadn't bothered returning any of her previous calls, asking why she insisted on acting so damn silly, and telling Aliesha how she'd stopped by her house on Friday night with the intent of offering an apology, only to discover her gone.

Finally, around midday, when she heard Pat's voice on the answering machine asking, "Aliesha, are you all right? Monica just called and said something about us needing to come by your place and do some sort of intervention?" Aliesha rolled over and snatched up the phone.

"Hey, Pat, do me a favor? Call Monica and tell her I'm fine. I'm just tired and I need some rest. Tell her I'll call her later. Okay?"

Aliesha hoped to put off speaking with Monica for as long as possible, if only because she knew she'd have to address the embarrassing subject of just how it was she'd ended up in Javiel's bed again. Given Monica's undeniable affection for her boyfriend's cousin, the matter might even spark another round of angry words between them.

After silencing her answering machine, unplugging her landline, and placing her cell phone on mute, Aliesha hunkered back beneath the covers and drifted in and out of sleep for the better part of the day. At one point, she thought she heard a car drive up outside the house. If anyone, she figured, it would be Monica arriving to chew her out some more about her behavior over the last couple of days. So she didn't even bother to get up and peek out the window, like she would have at any other time. She waited until after dark before rising to take care of all the necessary bodily functions, including the appeasement of the persistent gnawing in her belly.

She dumped a can of soup into a pot and placed it on the stove to simmer before plugging back in and switching back on all of the phone equipment she'd shut down prior to her siesta. The light indicator on both phones immediately lit up, letting her know she'd received even more calls. Instead of checking any of them, she fixed herself cheese and crackers and a tall glass of Coke with several handfuls of crushed ice to accompany her chunky beef and veggie soup. She plopped down with her meal in front of the television. For hours on end, she sat and channel surfed while picking over the food, sipping the Coke, and trying to will herself into a state of not giving a damn about anything, which she considered highly preferable to incessantly dwelling on Dante's whereabouts or the additional damage she'd no doubt done to Javiel's ego.

When the phone rang at 9:30 PM or so, rather than expend the energy required to pick it up, she again let the answering machine do the honors and listened while Monica launched into a tirade. "Okay, I've had about as much of this shit as I'm gonna take. Aliesha Eaton, if you don't answer this phone or call me back within the next five minutes, the next number I dial will be the police."

Knowing Monica might make good on the threat and not wanting the unnecessary hassle of having to reassure the men in blue or any of her nosy neighbors, Aliesha groaned and scrambled for the phone. "Why is your solution to every problem calling the damn police?"

"Well, it certainly gets your attention every time, now,

doesn't it?" Monica snapped back. "Oh, apology accepted, by the way."

Aliesha sighed. "I am sorry about going into attack mode on you."

"I know," Monica said. "But it's not like I didn't goad you into it. I'm sorry, too. So now that we're back on speaking terms again, just where in the heck were you when I came by there last night? Don't tell me your invisible man finally materialized and whisked you off for some hot, romantic evening and threw in a couple of hours' worth of make-up sex to make it all worth your while?"

"If only," Aliesha said.

"You had me more than a little worried, you know. I don't think I've ever seen you lose your composure to that extent. So what happened? You weren't holed up in there hitting the bottle so hard you couldn't come to the door, were you?"

"No, actually I-I spent the night at Javiel's."

"Aliesha, tell me you didn't."

"I didn't mean to, but yeah, I did."

"You know, I'd hate to think what kind of craziness your little, fast behind would be pulling if you weren't running up to that church every Sunday."

"You mind sparing me the lecture? I feel bad enough as it is."

"Fine. I'm about five minutes away from your place anyway. You can finish filling me in when I get there."

Hell, Aliesha thought. *That's exactly what I'd been hoping to avoid.* She rose, unlocked the door, and started tidying. A few minutes later she heard Monica pull up and park.

"It's open," she called out when she heard the doorbell chime. "What?" she asked when her friend stepped inside with an odd look on her face. "Please don't start harping on what a horrible wretch you think I am."

Monica shook her head. "No, I was just wondering about

the mess on your porch. You have a hissy fit and decide to work out your frustrations by tearing up some stuff?"

Aliesha frowned, walked over, and stepped outside the door. A pile of debris decorated a wide area of her porch near the bushes. She peered down at it for a moment, then started poking through and turning over the material, only to find herself springing upright as if suddenly bitten by an unseen predator. She put a hand to her mouth and took a couple of steps back.

Monica rushed to her side. "What's wrong?! What is it?"

"Javiel's portrait of me," Aliesha said. "At least that's what it was before it got sliced and hacked to pieces."

CHAPTER 31

"What's his number?" Monica said after they'd cleaned up the mess and gone back inside.

"Why?" Aliesha asked.

"Why the hell you think? So I can call and ask if he's lost his damn mind."

"I don't know if that's such a good idea. Why not just let me handle it?"

"Oh, no! I've seen your way of handling things. And let me tell you, it's obviously NOT working!" Monica punched a couple of buttons on her cell phone and shouted into the receiver. "Hey, what's Javiel's number? I just need to speak with him, is all. Yeah, thanks. I'll call you back later."

With a look of complete outrage, Monica punched in another series of numbers, then with the phone to her ear she walked out of the room, into another, and slammed the door behind her. Even so, Aliesha could still hear some of the more colorful and heated sentiments Monica had taken upon herself to share with Javiel. After a few minutes, she reappeared, looking drained and somewhat perplexed. She held the phone out to Aliesha and said, "I think you want to hear this."

Aliesha waved her hands and shook her head. "You know what? I really don't."

Monica thrust the phone toward her again. "He's insisting it wasn't him. And it sounds to me like he's telling the truth."

Aliesha snatched the phone from Monica, and while leaving the room to chew out Javiel in private, she heard the doorbell chime. Before she finished vacating the area, she paused and motioned for her friend to see to the visitor. "Listen, Javiel," she said upon entering her junk room and bracing herself against a wall. "I'm sorry about last night. What I did was inexcusable and incredibly selfish, but in all honesty, I didn't come out there looking to hurt you."

"I know," he said. "I owe you an apology, too, Aliesha, especially about the way I acted and some of the things I said before you left. Are you all right?"

"No, if you want to know the truth. I'm pissed and more than just a little shaken after having seen what you did to the painting. What would ever possess you to do something so awful?"

"That wasn't me, Aliesha. I mean, I did bring it by and drop it off at your front door, right after you left this morning. But I didn't destroy it. The painting was in perfect condition when I saw it last."

"Yeah, right, Javiel. Who else would feel compelled to do something like rip the entire face and head off the painting?"

"How about this Dante guy you've been seeing? Could be you don't know him as well as you think you do."

"What?!" she said. "Do you seriously think—"

Before she could finish, Monica burst into the room and said, "Hang up, you've got company."

Aliesha glared and spit a terse "Do you mind?! Tell who ever it is I'll be out as soon as I'm finished here."

Monica walked over, seized the phone, and clicked it off. "You're finished."

Stunned, Aliesha said, "Okay, now it's my turn to ask, have you lost your ever-loving mind?!"

"Not yet," Monica said. "But if I keep fooling with your ass, I'm sure it's only a matter of time."

"This sure as hell better be important," Aliesha said as she followed Monica from the room.

"Well, I'll let you be the final judge of that," Monica said. "But you'd best prepare yourself. Your visitors have come bearing some not-so-great news about your former flame . . . Kenneth."

On reentering her living room, Aliesha was shocked to see Kenneth's daughter, Rihanna, and Barbara Phillips, neither of whom she'd ever expect to turn up unannounced on her doorstep at such an hour, unless . . . unless something unthinkably horrible had occurred. "What's going on?" she said in a voice drifting toward hysteria. "Oh, dear God, no! Please don't tell me something's happened to—"

Mrs. Phillips rushed to Aliesha's side and said, "Calm yourself, child. Everything is going to be just fine." With Monica's assistance, the older woman steadied a shaking and visibly distraught Aliesha and guided her to the couch. "Give Rihanna a chance to explain before you go getting yourself all worked up," Mrs. Phillips said on seating herself beside Aliesha and clutching one of her hands.

Rihanna, whose bloodshot eyes and puffy face did little to appease Aliesha's alarm, said, "Forgive me for upsetting you like this, Professor Eaton. I wouldn't have disturbed you at all tonight had my father not insisted I give you this along with his sincerest apologies."

Aliesha immediately recognized the article in Rihanna's outstretched hands as canvas, the kind commonly used by artists. Upon taking the ragged and torn material and carefully unfolding it, Aliesha once again found herself gazing upon Javiel's masterful depiction of her lovely face and her God-given crown. She looked from Rihanna to Barbara Phillips and back to Rihanna again. "Are you trying to tell me Kenneth did this?"

Rihanna nodded and dabbed tissue to her runny nose and eyes. Mrs. Phillips placed a reassuring hand on Aliesha's back and said, "It seems as if our dear Kenneth was picked up and charged with a DUI earlier today. From what I understand, last night, there was some sort of big falling out between him and his new lady-friend. During the course of trying to drink his sorrows away, he got the not-so-bright idea to come by your place."

"In case you didn't know," Rihanna said, somewhat regaining her composure, "my father is still very much in love with you, Professor Eaton. He told me that the argument he got into with Donna was about you."

"Is he okay?" Aliesha asked, suddenly feeling both guilty and partially responsible. "Are the authorities still holding him?"

"He was released a little while ago on his own recognizance. And given the circumstances, he's as well as can be expected. Just a little embarrassed and incredibly remorseful for all of the pain and aggravation he's caused everyone."

An angry Monica, who'd been seated on an arm of the sofa steaming and growing redder with each passing second, said, "So what the hell was the point of all of this?!" She leaned over and seized the sliced and torn piece of canvas from Aliesha's possession. "He didn't just destroy the painting—from the looks of things, he took a freaking knife and ripped her whole damn face off. What kind of love is that?"

"Would you calm down," Aliesha said.

Monica's face grew even redder. "No, I will not! And where the hell were you that you didn't hear or notice any of this foolishness happening on your front porch? You've got one nut dumping paintings at your front door and another stopping by to hack and slash 'em up!"

Aliesha closed her eyes and shook her head. "I don't know. I was probably asleep. After I got in this morning, I showered, took some sleep medication, and spent most of the day pretty much under the covers and out of it."

"I hope you won't hold this against him," Rihanna said,

sounding defensive. "I've never known my father to behave like this. He said all he wanted was to see you, but when he noticed the painting something came over him."

"Yeah," Monica mumbled. "Something commonly known as a jealous rage."

Rihanna, who appeared on the verge of a fresh round of tears, said, "He was jealous, yes, and most definitely intoxicated. But I know my dad and I'm pretty sure his intent wasn't to hurt or scare you, Professor Eaton. According to him, all he wanted was to keep a little piece of you for himself."

"Hah!" Monica interjected again. "If I'm not mistaken Ted Bundy held the exact same sentiments about his victims."

"Monica, please," Aliesha said, issuing her friend a heated glare before turning back to Rihanna. "Is there anything I can do?"

Before Kenneth's daughter could reply, Barbara Phillips stood up and said, "You mean, besides pray for him?"

***

Before Rihanna and Barbara Phillips left the house that night, the older woman pulled Aliesha aside and enveloped her in a long, tight embrace. Upon releasing her, Barbara looked Aliesha in the eyes and in a soft but stern voice said, "You can't save him. I know a part of you wants to try. But getting himself together is something Kenneth has to do on his own. You hear me? By himself."

Aliesha nodded. "I know, you're right. I just can't help but feel like I contributed in some way to the less-than-admirable behavior he's demonstrated here of late."

"Well, don't! I've known Kenneth every since he joined the church as a young man, back in the 70s. Even though there was more than a ten-year age difference between us, I was close to his wife, Annie, too. This may surprise you, but I think a lot of the drinking and carrying on Kenneth's been doing is more about Annie than it is about you. I suspect he's still grieving her passing, yes, even after all these years. That's not to say what the two of you had wasn't real, it just wasn't as solid as it could have been."

A sad smile creased Aliesha's lips. "Not exactly the truth I wanted to hear, but I appreciate it, nonetheless."

While she managed to read a couple of chapters from a textbook she'd assigned one of her classes, and jot a few notes for an upcoming lecture, she spent most of Sunday like she had Saturday—dozing, piddling around, and fielding phone calls. Monica made it her business to check in every couple of hours, just to make sure Aliesha was all right, and later in the day she and her cousin Gabe insisted on bringing Aliesha dinner and keeping her company well into the evening. Even Jesus called to let her know that he wasn't choosing sides and if she needed him, she could call.

Grateful for her friends' loving support, Aliesha still hated the thought of so many people worrying on her behalf. When Pat and Mrs. Phillips placed separate calls to express their concerns about her well-being, Aliesha elected to gloss over the depth of her malaise and spare them the raw and gritty details of the mess she'd inadvertently created for herself over the past couple of days. Try as she might, she couldn't quite shake the guilt of her own bad behavior, which trailed behind her like a metal ball and chain fastened around her ankle.

When Tamara called around the time Garden View's Sunday school generally wrapped up, Aliesha summoned up the wherewithal to sound halfway chipper. "No, there's no need for you to come by here," she said. "I'm fine and I fully expect to see you at school tomorrow. So don't even think about cutting my class."

"Well, that's good to hear," Tamara said. "Because after we learned you weren't feeling well, I overhead Mr. Phillips insinuating that you just might be in the family way."

After muffling a curse and a groan, Aliesha laughed. "Yes, ole brother Phillips is quite the kidder."

"Hey, guess what? I brought another guest to your class today. I'd hoped to surprise you like I did last Sunday."

"Really," Aliesha said with her face encased in a genuine smile. "Umm, let me guess. One of your other favorite professors? Dr. Beale or Dr. Wilbun, perhaps?"

"Oh yeah, real funny," Tamara said. "Hold on."

"Hey there, Miz Babygirl," Peaches said. "Something's wrong, isn't it."

"No. No, I'm fine," Aliesha said, hoping she sounded convincing.

After a pause, Peaches said softly, "You know, Aliesha, when Mama made us promise to look out after one another—that was something she expected to work both ways. Not just you looking after me. If you want to call me or come by later, you can."

Somewhat rattled and taken aback, Aliesha nonetheless stuck to her story. "I appreciate the offer, Peaches. But really, it's not necessary. I'm good."

Peaches responded with a hard-hitting *"Umpf,"* before passing the phone back to Tamara.

The Saturday morning Dante left Aliesha's house, he'd driven to work, still savoring the feel of her head against his shoulder and the sweet scent of her hair, while ruminating as well on the various highlights of the evening they'd spent together—the dinner, the conversation, the music, and the lovemaking.

Yes, the lovemaking. His heart had thumped hard, loud, and fast like an improvised African drum solo each time he'd recalled how both the opening in his side and the tear in the fabric of his soul had closed in the instant their bodies had become one. In that moment, an all-encompassing warmth and a sense of peace had washed over him like the cleansing waters of a creekside baptism. The intense oneness of the moment had gratified him even more than the satisfaction he'd drawn from being the source of her physical release or the pleasure he'd derived from his own.

Enthused about the possibility of a future with Aliesha, he'd strutted into the barbershop that Saturday morning, only to have his bubble summarily burst when, upon returning his cheerful "Good morning!" Wally said, "Laylah called here a couple of times last night."

Dante knew he should have figured as much. She'd called him on his cell, but he hadn't bothered picking up or calling back. He'd known of her plans to be in town that weekend. She'd been flying in from L.A. a lot over the past several months. He still wasn't certain of her motives. Had she finally sensed that he was slowly but surely slipping from her grasp? Or had she finally grown serious about coming back to Roads Cross—something she'd been half-heartedly promising for years.

Dante couldn't imagine Laylah finding contentment in a place like Roads Cross or even neighboring Riverton. She'd been away too long and had developed an appetite for comforts and luxuries that were more readily available in larger, more cosmopolitan areas. And then there were the needs of her two young children to consider, Ozzie and Zachary, the latter of whom she'd conceived with her husband, Stewart. But as far as Dante was concerned, Stewart's needs had never really counted for much. After all, he'd married Laylah, with the knowledge and understanding that at least one other man would always occupy her bed.

Determined not to let Laylah distract him or steal his joy, Dante had decided putting off speaking with her until the end of his work shift. But as always, Laylah's plans had found a way to upstage his. He'd been working on his last customer of the day when the barbershop's phone rang. A few minutes later, Wally, wearing a perplexed expression, had appeared at Dante's station. "It's Laylah. I think you'd best talk to her."

Wally was one of the few in whom Dante had ever confided about Laylah. He knew some of the intimate details of their long and sordid history together.

It had been Dante's experience that most guys fell into one of two categories when it came to how they viewed relationships like the one he had with Laylah, where the woman's wealth and financial clout exceeded his, and the money she made, more often than not, paid his way and hers. Most brothers either lauded the male in the equation for what they perceived as his superior skills as a pimp or a player in having drawn such a gullible and willing mark or else castigated him for allowing some ball-busting female to treat him like a puppet or play him for a chump.

But Wally was different. Even though he'd let Dante know that he didn't fancy the relationship and warned that nothing good was bound to come from it, he never preached or made attempts to butt in. He typically offered advice only when asked and merely listened on those rare occasions when Dante felt a need to vent.

Angered and frustrated by her persistence, Dante had picked up the phone and said, "Look, Laylah, this has to stop. Obviously, if I'm not answering or returning your calls, I must be busy, right?"

He'd waited for Laylah's heated response. Instead in a cool, soft voice, she'd said, "Dante . . . I'm calling about your Big Mama. She's in the hospital, the Mercy Medical Center in Harvestville. Knowing how upset you were liable to get on hearing the news, I went ahead and sent a car. The driver is waiting outside for you."

CHAPTER 32

Dante knew that had he been behind the wheel that night and on his way to Mercy Med, he no doubt would have been pulled over and ticketed for speeding. He might have ended up spending the night in jail and possibly even found himself being knocked around a bit for copping an attitude with the arresting officer. Be they Black or White, or be your Big Mama sick, hurt, or damn near dead, most of the boys in blue didn't play that in these parts—particularly when it came to men who fit Dante's profile.

The driver Laylah sent turned out to be someone Dante knew—Miz Irma Bell's son Ace, and accompanying Ace, his older brother Timothy. The presence of the two men Dante had known since they were all rusty-kneed boys throwing dirt clods and shooting marbles in Roads Cross lent him a bit of comfort. From them he learned that his Big Mama had collapsed in her yard earlier that day while tending one of her gardens. On hearing the details, Dante immediately felt guilty. He'd neglected to call the old woman on Friday night or Saturday morning on account of his date with Aliesha.

He climbed in the Lincoln Town Car with Ace, while Timothy trailed behind in Dante's vehicle. After making sure he didn't want to stop by his condo for anything, the brothers hit the highway and headed for Harvestville. After they arrived at the hospital almost two hours later, Timothy showed him the way to Vivian Lee's room.

Two others were already at her bedside when the two men walked in. As Dante's eyes filled with tears at the sight of his Big Mama's prone and listless figure, Doris Ferguson, a friend and church member, hurried to his side. After a reassuring hug, she informed him that the cause of his Big Mama's collapse had yet to be determined. The doctors were still running tests, but he needn't worry because whatever the outcome, Miz Vivian's faith would see her through.

The other individual's presence in the room—a dark, somber, wheelchair-bound man everyone knew as Mr. Jessie—was anything but comforting. Mr. Jessie was a businessman who'd long made a good living from embalming and burying Roads Cross's dead. He was also Laylah's father. Always one of few words, "Young man" and a firm handshake was all he offered Dante by way of greeting and consolation.

The silence between the two grew even more pronounced when Timothy volunteered to escort Sister Ferguson to her car. A solid five minutes passed before Mr. Jessie said, "I take it my daughter was able to get in touch with you?"

"Yes, sir," Dante replied.

Mr. Jessie pulled a business card from his vest pocket and handed it to Dante. "Should you need anything, don't hesitate to give me or my people a call."

"Yes, sir," Dante said again.

When Mr. Jessie wheeled toward the door, Dante walked over and opened it for him. His eyes cold and bearing a yellowish tint, Mr. Jessie looked up and stared at Dante a moment before he said, "After Miz Vivian's situation gets squared away, I've got a business proposition I'd like to discuss with you."

Dante nodded and offered yet another subdued, "Yes,

sir." But as soon as the door closed shut behind Mr. Jessie's wheelchair, Dante ripped the old man's business card into pieces and tossed them into a nearby trash can.

When he shifted his gaze to his Big Mama, her smile and opened eyes took him by surprise. "That ole vulture gone?" she asked. "I must really be bad off if the likes of Jessie Thomas is 'round here hovering."

A rush of relief flooded Dante's body until he saw his Big Mama struggling to sit up. "Settle down and relax, why don't you," he said on approaching her bedside and with his face twisted into a frown. "Where's the buzzer for me to call the nurse?"

"You bet not call none of them ole mean nurses," his Big Mama scolded. "They done poked and prodded me enough as it is." She pushed a button that raised the bed behind her head. "Now, that's better." She pointed to the chair beside her bed, but before he could take a seat, a nurse entered.

Vivian Lee groaned and muttered in protest, but Dante felt much better after the nurse's quick examination of both his Big Mama and the array of machines, tubing, and drips around her bed. In a calm and reassuring voice, the woman fielded Dante's questions and showed him how to contact the nurse's station.

He thanked her and waited until she'd exited the room before collapsing into the chair next to his Big Mama's bed. Before he could say anything, she threw a question at him. "You done made a choice between them two women yet?"

He blinked a couple of times and said, "Why in the world would you be thinking about something like that at a time like this?"

She closed her eyes and smiled. "I would think you'd want your Big Mama to have some peace of mind before she goes to meet her Maker."

He sat upright in the chair. "What have I told you about

talking like that? What you need to do is hurry up and get up from there so we can take our trip to Egypt and see those pyramids."

She chuckled and looked at him. "I bet that nice professor you so sweet on would love to go with you to see them pyramids."

"I'm sure she would," he said, unable to keep from smiling at his Big Mama's teasing. "Maybe I'll take her one day."

She sighed and closed her eyes again. "Don't mind me meddling, son," she said, in a voice turned serious. "You do whatever's gonna make you happy. If staying with Laylah does that for you, so be it. But if you choose her, son, you really oughta find it somewhere in your heart to forgive her for that baby."

Dante shook his head. "Why you think I'm holding on to that? I put that behind me a long time ago."

"I ain't talking 'bout Ozzie, nor that young'n she done had since she been married. I'm talking 'bout that other child. The one she was supposed to have with you."

Dante's mind raced backward in time. In the weeks prior to his high school football injury is when Laylah had informed him of her pregnancy. He'd been shocked and scared, but foolish enough to believe it could all work out. He'd told her he wanted to get married, if not before the baby's arrival, then sometime shortly thereafter. He'd get a part-time job or possibly something full-time over the summer and until he finished high school. Laylah and the baby could join him when he went off to college to play ball. He'd even gone out and bought her an engagement ring.

She'd never said yes. But she'd never said no, either. What she had done, in the weeks after his injury and without his knowledge or consent, was visit a doctor in Riverton and pay him to perform an abortion.

His Big Mama looked at him. "What? You thought I didn't know?"

He stared at the floor. "How come you never said anything?"

"Wasn't nothing for me to say—not that would have made much difference anyway. But it's time you stopped holding what happened against her. I could be wrong, but I suspect it was more her daddy's doing than her own. Wasn't like he ever hid the fact that he always favored Reuben over you."

As a star high school football player with his sights set on college and the potential for a pro career, Dante had been tolerated but never fully endorsed by Laylah's daddy. In the aftermath of Dante's sidelining leg injury, any semblance of pretense between the two had come to an abrupt end.

The door to the room eased open and Ace's smiling face appeared. "Hey, guess who I found?" he said softly. His mother, Irma Bell, tiptoed in behind him.

"Vivian Lee, chile!" she said in a loud whisper. "What is you doing in this bed?"

Vivian grinned. "Your guess is 'bout as good as mine or any of these know-it-all nurses and doctors, I imagine. Anyhow, I thought you was on your way to Birmingham to see that new grandbaby of your'n."

Miz Irma joked about making the Greyhound bus driver make a U-turn when she got word about Vivian's mishap. The two old friends traded a few more barbs before Miz Irma turned to Dante. "You go on and get yourself some rest. I'll stay with her through the night. Just make sure you leave one of my boys a number where we can reach you."

Dante realized the futility of trying to argue. He kissed his Big Mama on the cheek before he said, "All right, ole girl, I'll be back. In the meantime, behave yourself. Don't let me hear tell of you giving these doctors and nurses up here a lot of grief."

On his way down to Mercy Med's lobby, and while leaning against the wall in the hospital's elevator, Dante started
thinking about Aliesha and how nice it might be to hear
her voice. It was late and he knew she'd probably been
asleep for hours. One easy way of getting around disturbing her while still satisfying his need would have been to
call her office number and listen to her voice mail. But
given the particulars of the situation with his Big Mama,
he wondered if she wouldn't mind being awakened. Moreover, before he'd left her that Saturday morning, he remembered having promised to call.

When Dante and Ace finally stepped out into the still of
the night, they spotted Timothy on the far right side of
Mercy Med's main entrance. He sat on the stairs with a
plume of smoke dancing around his head and a cigarette
bobbing on his lips. "Yo, D. man, you straight?" he asked.
"You wanna go back to Riverton? Or are you staying out
at your Big Mama's house tonight?"

Dante sighed. "I don't know, man. I should probably
stay in Roads Cross tonight. But at the moment, all I really
want to do is check in with my girl. Give me a minute, all
right?" He whipped out his cell phone and pulled up the
numbers he had for Aliesha, the set at her office and the ones
she'd given him after inviting him to her place for dinner.

But before he could make his choice, he heard Timothy
say, "Hey, man, if I'm not mistaken, here comes your girl
now."

Dante looked up just as Laylah emerged from the passenger side of the taxi that had rolled up and parked at the
hospital's entrance. After untangling his gaze from the head
full of perfectly coifed locs, he took in the taut and un-
blemished face that had first seized him as a preadolescent
boy and whose sweet milk chocolate and caramel mix still
refused to let him go without a struggle.

Under the moonlit sky, Laylah's larger-than-life aura

seemed to loom even bigger and brighter. Even after the countless years of heartache he'd suffered in her hands, Dante knew there was no denying the catch that still arose in his throat in those first few seconds she assumed command of his line of vision.

While Ace hurried over and retrieved her bags, Laylah walked over to Dante, cupped his face, and kissed him on the lips. The public display of affection left him stunned. Even though nearly everyone in Roads Cross knew or suspected there was still something going on between them, Laylah had always insisted on discretion and cloaking the illicit nature of their relationship. As far as Dante had been able to determine, her deference had little to do with any warped sense of allegiance to her husband but rather the respect she felt due her father. Mr. Jessie's reputation and standing in the community, she valued more than her own, Stewart's, and Dante's put together.

"How is she?" Laylah asked while peering into his eyes and proceeding to deepen her spell.

"Good," he said. "They're gonna run a few more tests and, if all goes well, they may let her out tomorrow. Miz Irma is staying with her tonight."

Laylah glanced at her watch and looked toward the building. "I'd like to see her, unless you think it would be better to wait."

Dante stared at the numbers glowing in his cell phone's display window before finally pressing the button that would banish them to black. On pocketing the phone, he took the hand Laylah offered him and escorted her to his Big Mama's room.

When Dante and Laylah entered the hospital room, they found a now house-shoe-clad Miz Irma seated in the chair next to Vivian Lee's bed and reading aloud from the Bible in her lap: "*I opened to my beloved; but my beloved had withdrawn himself, and was gone: my soul failed when he spake: I sought him, but I could not find him; I called him, but he gave me no answer.*" At the end of the verse, Miz Irma closed the book and Dante's Big Mama opened her eyes.

"I'm sorry, I know it's late," Laylah said, while smiling at the two old women, neither of whom smiled back at her. "But I was worried and I wanted to see for myself how you were doing."

Miz Irma grunted and crossed her feet at the ankles. Undeterred, Laylah left Dante's side and, on reaching the bed, took one of his Big Mama's hands. "Miz Vivian, please, if there's anything at all I can do to help . . ."

Vivian Lee adjusted the angle of her bed and, wearing a more pleasant expression, leaned forward and patted Laylah's hand. "You really wanna do something for me, chile? Well, there is this one thing. You see that little boy in that grown man's body you come in here with? The one who's standing over there with the sad look on his face?"

Laylah turned toward Dante and smiled. "Yes, ma'am."

"Well, that boy there owns a big chunk of my heart, always has. And I ain't never liked seeing him in no pain. So if you love him anywhere near as much as you claim you do, you'll stop hurting him. If you're really serious about doing something for me, make it that. All right?"

Laylah bowed her head, like a scolded child and nodded. "Yes, ma'am."

⸙

On leaving the hospital Dante followed Laylah's lead and climbed into the backseat of Ace's waiting vehicle. "Where to?" Ace asked.

"Roads Cross," Laylah murmured, a response that struck Dante as unusual given his knowledge that the upscale-area hotels she typically preferred were either in Riverton or only minutes away right there in Harvestville.

He knew the exchange she'd had with his Big Mama upset her. She sat beside him, cloaked in an uncharacteristic silence, her head turned toward the window next to her and exhibiting none of the over-the-top gregariousness that made her such a hit among the B- and C-list entertainers whose legal interests she represented and served.

Several minutes passed before she turned and looked at him. "She hates me, doesn't she?"

He couldn't see her eyes but knew better than to think there'd be tears. Sadness and defeat, perhaps, but not tears. The last and only time he'd ever seen Laylah crumble beneath the weight of her emotions had been at Reuben's funeral. He often wondered if having grown up in a family that worked among the dead had somehow made her tougher than most.

"She doesn't hate you," he said. "I think it would be more accurate to say she's not terribly happy about some of the things you and I have done."

When Laylah resumed her gaze out the window, Dante's natural instinct led him to reach across the backseat and begin massaging her neck and shoulders. He couldn't help himself. Coming to Laylah's comfort and aid had been the role in which he'd found himself assigned, ever since that day back in grade school when he'd stood up with her against the group of fourth-grade girls determined to bring her down a notch.

Every now and then, the loud taunts of Willa Mae Rodgers, the biggest and baddest girl in the group, still rang in Dante's ears: *"Ain't no wonder she won the spelling bee. Her glasses so damn thick she oughta be able to read through walls. Who she think she is with her ole black, four-eyed, proper-talking, stuck-up self?!"*

Dante remembered, too, the whipping his uncle Mack had administered upon hearing tell that his nephew had been somewhere duking it out with a girl, even though Reuben, in a rare moment of solidarity, had offered that at five foot six, 180 pounds, and possessing one heck of a mean left hook, Willa Mae Rodgers was no ordinary fourth-grade girl.

With Ace stealing an occasional puzzled glance at them through his rearview mirror, Dante figured at some point Laylah would remember that they were the couple who'd been relegated to a lifetime of creeping. The pair who snuck around and did their dirt behind closed doors until somebody died or else packed up and left town for good.

But rather than shrug him off, Laylah unbuckled her seat belt and moved toward him. She leaned her head against his shoulder and whispered, "If it's not too much to ask, I'd like to stay with you tonight."

A storm full of brilliant flashes and deafening claps greeted their arrival at Dante's Big Mama's house. After Ace brought Laylah's luggage inside and Timothy parked Dante's Jeep in the drive, they each extended Dante a hand clasp, a brother man hug, and a sly grin before wishing him and Laylah a "good night."

With his back pressed against the closed front door, Dante looked at her and said, "You do realize by noon tomorrow everyone in Roads Cross, Harvestville, and the surrounding area, your daddy included, is gonna know . . ."

"Know what?" Laylah said with a weary smile. "You mean what most of them have already known for years now?"

Dante seized her bags and with her trailing behind him led the way to his old room. On depositing her luggage in a corner, he hurriedly turned down the bed and retrieved a clean set of towels for her from the linen closet. After placing the towels on the room's dresser, he said, "The bathroom is across the hall. If you want something to eat or drink, you're welcome to help yourself to whatever's in the kitchen."

When he turned toward the door, she said, "I take that to mean you won't be staying in here with me tonight?"

He scratched his head and, in keeping with their age-old habit of sparing each other the full truth without telling a complete lie, he said, "I'm feeling a little antsy. I'm gonna stay up and read for a while. I'll be in the den if you need anything."

She looked hurt but didn't protest. Things hadn't been right between them for some time and had only grown progressively worse since Reuben's death. The day of his funeral had, in fact, been the last time they'd submitted to their inexplicable need for one another.

After the burial and the repast, Laylah had tried to convince him to do what they'd done on countless occasions in the past—meet up at the Westin in Riverton or the Hilton in Harvestville. She'd check in one room at one time, and he'd do likewise in another at another time, with the credit card she'd given him years ago for that specific purpose. And there he'd wait, until she called. There he'd wait until she could complete her getaway. But on that occasion he'd refused, something he rarely did. If she wanted him, he'd told her, it would be on his terms, which on that particular evening turned out to be while the kids, Ozzie and Zach, were away visiting with her relatives and Stewart, her husband, was off drinking and gambling with friends at a nearby casino.

Defying her protests, he'd met her in the same hotel and suite she'd checked into with her family. And the love he'd subsequently made to her in the bed in which only hours before she'd lain with her husband had been so fraught with fervor and intensity it had bordered on anger and, in truth, had frightened him, though Laylah, as always, had seemed remarkably unfazed. Afterward, instead of triumph and vindication, Dante had been filled with a sense of shame, remorse, and disappointment on a level he'd never experienced in all of the years he and Laylah had been sleeping together. Ever since then, he'd gone out of his way to avoid being alone with her. But he knew at some point she would insist they address the reasons behind their sudden disconnect and, as well, those underscoring his growing and obvious discontent.

While the house his uncle Mack built creaked and groaned beneath the wind's fury, an exhausted and emotionally drained Dante fell onto the couch in the den and briefly closed his eyes. He thought about Aliesha and, even though he knew it was way too late to call, he flipped open his cell, pulled up her numbers, and ran his fingers over the warmth emanating from the phone's brightly lit screen. He longed for the peace, comfort, and joy being with her lent him and wished he possessed the power to magically transport the woman currently occupying his bed out for good, while transporting the one on his mind into it forever.

After a moment, he rose and unfolded the couch's sofa bed, and from the cedar chest that doubled as a coffee table, he collected the sheets, pillows, and blankets he'd need to make himself comfortable. Had the storm outside not been so intense, he might have ventured outdoors and retrieved the book Aliesha had given him. On stripping down to his boxer briefs, he did the next best thing and reached for the Kafka that was never too far from his side.

He'd barely settled beneath the covers and opened the paperback when Laylah appeared at the room's entrance. "Did you have the television on?" she asked, her eyes big and her face drawn. She was barefoot and clad in one of his old high school football jerseys. "I could have sworn I heard a baby crying."

Dante shook his head. "It was probably the wind or one

of the neighbors' cats." He grinned. "Then again, it might have been my uncle Mack. He's been known to prowl around here at night sometimes."

Laylah opened her mouth, but before she could say anything, a sonic boom of thunder shook the house and made the lights flicker and dance. She darted over and curled up in the closest easy chair. "I'm not sleeping back there by myself," she said.

Her cowering figure and the fright he saw on her face and heard in her voice stirred within him a soft blend of sympathy and amusement. Again, he couldn't help but think of the precocious nine-year-old he'd rescued from the wrath of the big and less-than-bright schoolyard bullies. Laylah, the scrawny little brown-skinned girl with the thick glasses and the noticeable overbite who, with the help of her daddy's money and her own smarts and determination, had gone from being an awkward, timid duckling to a confident and powerful head-turning swan.

Dante eased one of the pillows from beneath his elbow, placed it beside him, and tossed back the covers. Without a word, she came over and slid in next to him. His fear, that she'd take the invitation as one that included a desire for intimacy, quickly fell by the wayside when she turned her back to him and rubbed her cold feet against his calves as was her habit before she drifted off to sleep.

As her breathing grew deeper and more regulated, he rolled over and stared into the sister locs she'd only begun wearing within the last several months. He longed to caress the curve and intricate wind of the neatly arranged strands, but knew she'd probably awaken with the wrong impression.

His gaze fell to the blue and white jersey bearing his last name and old position number, 87. The familiar colors and the big, bold letters and numerals always made him ponder the "what if"s. Like, what if he'd never broken his leg? What if a pro football career had actually panned out for him? What if Laylah had never slept with Reuben? What if he and Laylah had gotten married? Would they have stayed together? If so, would they be living in L.A. and in the spectacular home she currently resided in with Stewart and her two sons? Would the two of them now have two sons? Two daughters? Or just the one child ... the one and only child Laylah had opted not to carry to term?

While his uncle wandered through the rooms, haphazardly bumping into walls and rattling windows from the inside, Dante squeezed his eyes shut and fell asleep pondering which factor or its absence might have possibly altered his fate.

CHAPTER 33

He awakened to an empty bed and the sound of Laylah's laughter coming from another room. He glanced at his watch and on noting the time—7 AM—he reached for his phone, thinking maybe he could slip in a quick call to Aliesha. But an incoming call from Timothy derailed his plans and shifted his focus.

According to the report Timothy had received from his mother, their cranky patient had rested comfortably last night and was anxious to get back home. She wanted Dante to bring her pocketbook and a clean change of her clothing on his return to the hospital. After Dante got off the phone, he jotted a mental note of the requests before heading off to the bathroom. If his Big Mama was feeling better, she no doubt would soon be giving the hospital staff and even Miz Irma holy hell. He figured he'd best waste little time in going to their rescue.

As he closed the bathroom door behind him, he once again heard Laylah's cheerful voice and merry laughter. He briefly wondered with whom she was speaking. Certainly not her sons or Maria, their live-in nanny. Timewise, Los Angeles was three hours behind Roads Cross, so it would only be a little past four in the morning there. Her husband? Hardly. Stewart would be either resting up for his next flight or already navigating one of the commercial jets he piloted for a living. Besides, Stewart and Laylah conversed more like bored business partners than a happily married couple. With the exception of Mr. Jessie, she wasn't really on the best of terms with any of her kin. A girlfriend, perhaps? But more than likely it was a client. She had plenty of those; the bulk of them washed up celebrity has-beens or long-suffering wannabes who didn't keep normal hours or accord much respect to those who did.

When Dante stepped into the shower, his thoughts of Laylah faded and were soon replaced by slow-motion clips from his night with Aliesha. The steady pelt and stroke of the hot water soothed the tension from his muscles and reminded him of the repetitive press of her lips and the gentle glide and knead of her fingers. His body responded in the affirmative. But before he could derive any additional pleasure from his memories, the shower curtain parted and a naked and smiling Laylah joined him beneath the falling water and rising steam.

On appraising his state of arousal, she said, "Well, looks to me like you could use some help with that."

Caught off guard and at a loss for how best to respond, when she eased her body against his, he tried to play along. He returned the hungry nips and pecks she planted on his mouth and chin. He ran his hands down the length of her back and over the curve of her behind. Having years ago committed both the route and the terrain to memory, he needed no instructions on what to do where. But the feelings, the ones he harbored deep inside, he couldn't fake, and in a matter of seconds he'd gone soft where he'd once been hard.

When she pulled away, he saw what he knew to be frustration and resentment smoldering in her eyes. "I'm sorry," he said. "It's the stress."

"Sure," she replied, before leaving him in the shower alone.

He finished bathing, dreading all the while the showdown he knew would surely come next. He dried off, wrapped a towel around his waist, and paused to shave before leaving the bathroom and the sweetness of his memories behind. A detour by his Big Mama's bedroom, so he could collect and assemble the items she'd requested, lent him yet another reason to delay the inevitable.

When he finally entered his bedroom, he found Laylah dressed in a robe and seated on the side of his bed with her legs crossed and a good portion of her bare thighs and shapely calves exposed. One of her bags stretched open in front of her, but rather than packing, she appeared to be taking things out.

Neither of them said anything as he dropped the towel and began to dress. He managed to slip into clean underwear and a fresh pair of slacks without a hitch. She waited until he was seated on the bed and rolling up his socks before she said, "So, how long have you known her?"

"Known who?" he said, stalling for one last second or two.

"The woman who's obviously got her hooks sunk so deep in you you're no longer interested in making love to me."

He squared his shoulders and looked at Laylah, knowing, like did she, it would be foolish to keep dancing around the truth. "Not long . . . at least not in the physical sense. In the spiritual, I'm not sure, but quite possibly all of my life."

She leaned toward him with her eyes ablaze. "The spiritual?! What the hell is that, Dante? Your way of telling me you think this woman is your soul mate or something? All of these years, I thought that's what you and I were, soul mates."

He looked away from her. "Right! Now, that's funny, 'cause I'm not sure I've ever known exactly what you and I were, Laylah."

She reached over and touched the back of his hand. "I

know how difficult coping with Reuben's death has been for you—"

He jerked away from her and, in a voice one breath away from a shout, said, "Why do you always have to go and bring him up? What I'm feeling doesn't have a damn thing to do with Reuben or his death."

"Then what? What, Dante?! Now that I'm free, all of a sudden you don't want to do this anymore?"

"Free?" He shook his head and locked his steely gaze against hers. "What do you mean, free?"

She pried a large manila envelope from her bag and tossed it in the space between them on the bed. "Free, Dante. My divorce is final and I'm here in Roads Cross to stay. Isn't that what you've always wanted?"

He stared at the envelope. "What I wanted, once upon a long time ago, Laylah, was a life and a family with you." He shook his head. "It's too late for any of that now."

"No, baby," she said, while scooting closer to him. "It's not too late. We can still have those things. A life together. A family. Even children of our own, if that's what you want. I've done everything necessary to make it happen."

"At this point, Laylah, it's not even about what you've done," he said, with emotion strumming his vocal cords like fingers on an upright bass. "Don't you see? There's so much you can't undo . . ." He brushed off the hand she'd placed against his shoulder before abandoning the spot on the bed he'd occupied beside her.

⁂

He sought refuge in the bathroom, cursing himself for having tolerated and forgiven her selfishness, her bullshit, and her constant betrayals for all of these years and yet having wanted her in spite of it all. Why? Had it been a need predicated on the improbable chance that one day things would go back to the way they'd been before he'd broken his leg? Before she'd aborted his child? Before she'd allowed Reuben to con his way into her bed?

Dante balled his fists but suppressed his urge to punch the walls. Destroying something his uncle Mack had crafted from love wouldn't make him feel any better and having to explain his actions to his Big Mama would only make him feel worse.

On regaining some sense of calm and composure, he exited the bathroom and reentered the bedroom. Rather than Laylah's accusing eyes and pleading tone, his presence was greeted by the echoing sound of silence. The open bag had been removed from the bed, but the manila envelope still sat where he'd seen it last. The room's curtains had been pulled back and with a glint and a glare, a beam from the morning sun shimmied across an object that sat atop the envelope.

Dante walked over and picked up the object, which turned out to be jewelry. A ring attached to a chain. A ring, it slowly dawned on him, that was the same one he'd given Laylah back in high school when he'd proposed. He sat on the bed and turned the ring so its tiny stone could catch the rays from the sun's light.

In that moment, it crystallized for him that hope, plain and simple, is what had kept him there. The same kind of hope his Big Mama and his uncle Mack had sought to implant within him when they realized his stay with them was apt to be permanent. Along with the big helpings of grits and bacon, cornbread and greens, candied yams and pork shoulder, they'd fed him the hope that his birth mother, Helen, would one day get herself together and come back to show him the love and affection he rightfully deserved.

Perhaps even his compulsion to save Laylah from the wrath of the bullies who'd assailed her so unmercifully that day was born of his inability to spare his mother the pain of the taunts hurled at her—"thief, junkie, low-down skank, drunk-ass whore . . ." He'd heard it all and even knew some of it to be true. But still, he'd seen both the good and the potential for better . . . just like he'd seen in Laylah.

He looked around the room and noticed her luggage was missing. He jumped up in a panic and called her name. "Laylah! Laylah!" On hurriedly grabbing a shirt from his closet, he went through the house in search of her. He spotted her bags in the living room next to the front door. But the door's chain lock was still intact, and when he peeked out the living room's windows, he saw no sign of her. He slipped into the den and snatched his cell phone off the coffee table before he bolted down the home's center hallway and into the kitchen. "Laylah?" he called out in a voice seeped in equals portions of exasperation and longing. On noticing the opened back door, he peered out and spotted her in the yard. Dressed in a pair of jeans and the football jersey she'd worn the night before, she appeared to be appraising his Big Mama's raised flower beds.

He stepped outside and winched as the coolness and moisture residing atop the back porch's wooden planks grabbed the bottoms of his socked feet. In his haste, he'd neglected to don shoes, but having walked, run, and tumbled barefoot across the same porch and yard so often in his youth, the thought of retreat never occurred to him. By the time he reached Laylah she'd wandered away from the colorful spread of daylilies, petunias, and impatiens and found herself a seat on the ground beneath the yard's towering weeping willow.

She had a tissue pressed against her nose and was clearing her sinuses when he dropped on the ground next to her. "Allergies," she said, on lowering the tissue and averting her runny eyes.

He sighed and held up the ring. "Why'd you keep it all of these years?"

She leaned back and allowed her head to roll against

the tree's trunk. "Because you never asked me to give it back," she said softly. "But if it's over between us, it kind of loses its meaning, don't you think?"

"I loved you, Laylah. I loved you even before I really knew what the word meant. Once upon a time I would have done anything for you."

She sniffled and dabbed her nose. "I know. I guess our timing is a wee bit off, huh? The way you *felt* about me then is the way I *feel* about you now. Unfortunately, it just took me a little longer to get there." She turned and looked at him. "But I do love you, Dante. And I'd do anything for you. I would and I have. I know I've given you plenty of reasons to hate me over the years. And I'm sorry about all of— Reuben, Stewart, the babies . . . any- and everything I ever did to hurt you. If I could take it all back, I would. But I can't." She moved her gaze to Vivian Lee's flowers. "All I can do going forward is try to prove myself worthy of the love you once felt for me. But if you really want me out of your life, for good, I mean, then I'll go. Just tell me what you want."

Dante twirled the ring between his fingers and didn't say anything for several long seconds. Finally he said, "I don't know what I want anymore. Okay? Between your divorce, your moving back, my Big Mama, and the feelings I've got for the woman I've been seeing in Riverton— that's a lot for me to deal with all at once. I need some time to think and sort things out."

"Sure, I understand," she said.

He held the chain with the engagement ring out to her. "Like you said, I never asked for this back."

She paused before rising to her knees, taking the jewelry, and draping it around his neck. "I suggest you keep it until you've decided what it is you want to do."

Dante stayed outside under the tree, while Laylah went back inside to get cleaned up so she could accompany him to the hospital. He fingered the ring around his neck and wondered what if anything he should tell Aliesha about the unexpected situation he'd found himself in with Laylah. Maybe he really didn't need to tell her anything. He hadn't exactly made a decision one way or the other. Maybe he could just tell her about his Big Mama and let the other things work themselves out. But when he pulled out his cell phone and flipped it open, instead of lighting up, the screen stayed black.

On arriving at the hospital and learning that Vivian Lee wouldn't be released until Monday, Laylah volunteered to take Miz Irma home, a favor that permitted Dante a resumption of his post at his aunt's bedside. While Laylah spent most of the day out and about in his Jeep, running errands and visiting with her folks, Dante did what he could to make his restless and headstrong Big Mama comfortable. He made a point of speaking at length with the nurses and her doctor about the series of tests they'd been conducting and he made sure Vivian Lee's steady stream of well-wishers didn't inadvertently wear her out or exacerbate her condition.

When she wasn't napping, visiting, watching TV, or grumbling about some aspect of the hospital's care, Vivian Lee was giving Dante instructions for what she wanted done in the event that her health concerns worsened or, more tragically, led to her death. It grieved Dante to hear her speak so bluntly of the fate that one day awaited them all, but he understood how important every detail, big and small, was to her. In truth, he'd heard a lot of it before. So he mostly played the role of the good nephew who listened and nodded without comment. It was only when his Big Mama started talking about his birth mother that he found himself listening more intently and growing more anxious.

"Should Helen show up, see that she's well taken care

of, hear? Let her know she's welcome to stay out at the home-house for as long as she likes. And if you ever take a notion to sale off any of your uncle's land or the timber on it, I hope you'll be generous enough to share some of the proceeds with her. 'Course you know she's got a plot of her own in the family's cemetery and I suspect it'll be left to you to handle that, too, when her time come. She's been clean for a while now. Got her a little piece of a job and done even joined a church, so I hear. I'm thinking it might be time y'all reconciled and started acting like family again."

Stunned by what carried the sting of a pointed accusation, Dante said, "You said that like I'm the one who's been keeping it from happening all of these years. She left me, I didn't leave her. I was a child, remember?"

His Big Mama smiled, closed her eyes, and in a voice thick with sleep said, "Yes, and how long you been a man now?" She chuckled. "Both of y'all just alike. So scared of being rejected you too afraid to be the one to make the first move. All I'm saying is give her a chance and see what happens."

Of all the subjects he and his Big Mama discussed that Sunday, the one about his mother troubled Dante the most. In recent years, the only time he'd seen Helen had been at funerals, the last being his cousin Reuben's and the one before that, years ago, when his uncle Mack had passed. Still, he wasn't ready to admit how much he resented the fact that upon learning of a family member's death, Helen always found a way to show up, something she'd apparently never found a compelling reason to do for him.

———⊂∞⊃———

The remainder of the week passed by Dante in a blur. After his cell phone died, his efforts to call Aliesha fell aside in lieu of other pressing concerns. From the rotary phone at his Big Mama's house, he called Wally about his desire for some time off in the coming days. Wally encouraged him to take as much as he needed. His chair would be waiting on him when he returned. In the interim, they agreed to call in a temp to take up the slack.

Rather than check into a hotel or temporarily move in with her father and stepmother, who was a woman Laylah had long despised, Laylah asked Dante if she might continue staying with him, at least until his ailing Big Mama's situation stabilized. Even though he harbored a few reservations about the peaceful coexistence of the four, his uncle Mack's ghost included in that number, in the end Dante gave his nod to the plan. While his Big Mama's nonchalant acceptance of the arrangement surprised him, Miz Irma's disapproval hadn't. "All right, just 'cause that ole fast-tail girl claim she done got a divorce don't give y'all license to be up in your uncle Mack's house, fornicating and carrying on in, especially with your Big Mama laid up sick in the next room and all."

But to both Miz Irma's and Dante's relief, Laylah kept a respectable distance. She made no surprise appearances while he was showering, and at night she retired to his room alone and stayed there, even when Mack's ghost got riled and took to stumbling through the house. She appeared earnest about wanting to start anew with Dante, if not make amends for some of the heartless errors she'd made in their past.

A couple of days after Vivian Lee returned home, Mr. Jessie called and asked when he and Dante might discuss that business proposition. Laylah pleaded ignorance, but given her repeated request that Dante at least go and speak with the man, he suspected she'd had a hand in her father's presenting him with what turned out to be a job offer. Over an expensive steak dinner and a bottle of wine, Mr. Jessie informed Dante of his need for an apprentice, someone he would personally feel comfortable handling his business should he become fully incapacitated, someone he'd be open to making a full partner were he interested and able to prove himself worthy.

Dante politely refrained from inquiring about Mr. Jessie's two sons, the younger a local pastor, currently on his way to prison for dipping once too often and way too deep into his church's coffers, and the elder, Mr. Jessie's namesake, already there for having shot and killed the husband of the woman with whom he'd been having an affair. "What about Laylah?" he asked. "I'd assumed one of the primary reasons she decided to move back to Roads Cross was to help you with the funeral home."

"Young man, not that I'm discounting my daughter's help or her affection for me, but you and I both know Laylah Louise ain't never gave a rat's ass about that funeral home. Her showing up and helping me get my affairs in order is truly a wonderful thing, but it also gives her something productive to do while she's here keeping company with you. Only way she don't sell the damn thing after I'm dead and gone is if one of them boys of hers happen to take an interest in it. I'd love to see that happen. But like your Big Mama, son, I'm slowly coming to grips with the fact that my days are numbered. Ain't no telling if I'll even live to see them boys come of age, but you will, unless Laylah's ex suddenly grows a pair and takes a notion to come gunning for you. What I'm saying, son, is I'd like to put whatever past animosities we've held toward one another behind us and make you an integral part of the family, so to speak."

Dante could hardly believe this was the same man he'd once overheard chastise his young, starry-eyed daughter upon listening to her claim that Dante would one day be her husband: "Young lady, allow me to issue you a fair warning—if you marry that boy, not only will you end up living in a squalid shack or a broke-down trailer somewhere, but all of your children are liable to be nappy-headed and black as tar."

Mr. Jessie, who himself was nappy-headed and black as tar, had proudly married the whitest-looking colored woman in all of Roads Cross, only to have all three of their off-spring emerge from the womb bearing a head full of un-ruly kinks and skin a similar caramel chocolate mix. To Laylah, his youngest and only daughter, had gone the special blessing of being the darkest and the most kinky-headed of the bunch. All were facts that tickled Dante's Big Mama to no end and on more than one occasion prompted her to say, "The Good Lord's sense of humor is something else, sho nuff, ain't it?!"

"He's changed. Really, he's not like that anymore," Laylah insisted. But Dante wasn't so sure. He wondered if the love and pride Mr. Jessie felt toward Laylah's sons had anything, if not everything, to do with their fair skin and the lack of kink in their hair.

It was a Friday night, a full week to the day after his date with Aliesha, when Dante finally drove back to Riverton to check on his condo and gather the additional items he'd need for an extended stay in Roads Cross. While packing his bags, he called Wally and shared with him the details of Mr. Jessie's pitch. Wally's suggestion that Dante give it some serious thought was in part what he'd expected.

"It's not every day a man can just turn his back on a le-gitimate hustle at double the money he's been making and with a guarantee to make even more over time," Wally said. "If nothing else, working there, at least a couple of years, would put you that much closer to the shop you said you wanted to open one day, or you could even take that money and go back to school with it." He laughed. "Only real drawback I can see is your having to find a way to keep this particular mix of business and pleasure from straight blowing up in your face one day. Speaking of which, your lady-friend, the professor, has been 'round here look-ing for you. So what's up? You not feeling her no more?"

"It's not that," Dante said, wincing at the jagged stab of guilt in the center of his chest. "It's just—between the situ-ation with my Big Mama and the one with Laylah and now this thing with Mr. Jessie, I'm not in the right frame of mind to deal with the professor on the level she deserves to be dealt with. You know what I'm saying?"

"What you want me to tell her the next time she calls or comes in asking for you?"

Dante faked a laugh and said, "Hey, like Yazz says, Brother Man rules in full effect."

A few quiet seconds ticked by before Wally said, "Let me drop some knowledge on you, son, all right? You can't keep a woman—not a real woman, anyway—playing some little boy's game. And that ain't something I heard. That's something I know from experience. Now, if you looking to run her off, you just keep doing what you doing."

Dante scratched the growth on his cheeks and said, "All right, man. I hear you."

He hung up the phone still smarting from Wally's blunt-edged scold. He couldn't dismiss the advice as readily as he might have had the person dispensing it been someone like Ace or even his cousin Reuben, who would have likely told him, "Shit, man, if it was me, I'd be doing my damnedest to juggle both them bitches." Dante knew better. While Laylah, as long as she felt like the queen bee, might have cer-tainly been accepting of such, Aliesha had already made clear her lack of interest in embarking upon any sort of time share arrangement with him.

While locking up his condo and tossing his packed bags into the backseat of his Jeep, he weighed the pros and cons of contacting Aliesha before he headed back to Roads Cross. So many days had passed since his promise to call, he knew her reaction to the sound of his voice wasn't likely to be a pleasant one. No, she'd be upset and rightfully so. But what could he possibly say that might make her feel any better? Surely not, I'm gonna be in Roads Cross for a minute, caring for my sick Big Mama and trying to see if there's anything worth salvaging in the torrid, lopsided relationship I've been in with this woman named Laylah for the past twenty-plus years.

He climbed into the driver's seat and sat for a moment tugging and toying with the ring still dangling from the chain around his neck. He had to give Laylah credit for trying. After years of promising to do so, she'd finally divorced and moved back to Roads Cross, even though it meant a huge disruption in her and her children's lives. His sense of guilt had lessened about the latter upon learning that the boys would be joining their mother at the end of the school year and would spend most of the summer with her in Roads Cross.

Sacrifices like those and made on his behalf, no less, weren't the kind Dante could readily dismiss. He felt like he owed Laylah something . . . an opportunity to make things whole between them . . . his cooperation, however begrudgingly . . . something.

But what, if anything, did he owe Aliesha? As Dante backed his vehicle out of the driveway and drove off into the night, he found himself regretting the unfinished and abrupt way he'd left things. He hated that for her what had happened between them would likely be relegated to either a memorable one-night stand or a painful mistake.

In attempt to keep a tight lid on the misery he sensed churning to a boil somewhere inside of him, he turned up the song "Closer," the first cut from Ne-Yo's *Year of the Gentleman* that was already bumping and pounding from his Jeep's stereo speakers. But before he could steer toward the highway, something his uncle Mack said after disciplining him for fighting with Willa Mae Rodgers came back to him: "One day you'll learn a honorable man always tries to do what's right."

While reflecting on the statement he'd heard his uncle

repeat on a number different occasions, Dante turned the vehicle down a street and in a direction that would take him by Aliesha's house. As a child he'd lack both the words and the maturity to tell his uncle Mack that while tussling and trading blows with the overgrown fourth-grade girl who'd been Laylah's tormentor might not have been the right thing to do, given both the circumstances and his way of looking at things, it had surely been the most honorable.

Dante wondered if his uncle Mack had ever considered that being honorable and doing what was right weren't, necessarily, always one and the same. He wondered, too, if there wasn't some way to alter the fact that currently his behavior toward Laylah felt like one and his feelings for Aliesha like the other.

He noted the time on shifting his car into park across the street from Aliesha's residence. 8:30 PM. A dim light cast odd shadows across the front porch, but as far as he could tell, no lights glowed anywhere inside of her house. He pulled out the phone he'd recently charged and almost called just to see if she were home. Then he remembered and realized wherever she was, she'd probably written him off as a liar and a pretender. Alas, her awful, drunken assessment of him on her porch that tension-filled night he'd brought her home had been correct after all.

He dropped the phone and slammed his hands against the steering wheel. What he hated most of all was that Aliesha would never know that his intentions had been honorable and how disappointed he'd been at not being able to live up to his own expectations. How for him, being with her had filled him up in a way no preacher's sermon, no home-cooked meal, no single moment of physical pleasure, sexual or otherwise, ever had. And how he'd wanted, truly wanted so much more . . . What Dante would never know was that at that very moment, on another side of town, Aliesha sat in a parked car, wanting him just as intensely as he wanted her.

CHAPTER 34

While walking across campus on the Monday after her harrowing weekend, Aliesha had all but arrived at her destination—the administration building—when she spotted a lone figure on the student plaza near the fountain. The well-dressed woman's slow, circular movements suggested she just might be lost or in need of assistance. As Aliesha detoured in her direction, she made note of the small campus map the woman kept turning over in her hands and peering at through the large sunglasses covering her face. But on drawer closer yet, Aliesha made an even more startling observation—the lost woman was no stranger.

"Julia?" she called out.

Javiel's mother looked up from map and, on removing her shades, smiled and said, "Why, Aliesha! How are you, dear?"

The cheerful greeting and warm embrace took Aliesha by surprise. While keeping an eye out for signs of a hidden dagger, she said, "I'm fine, though admittedly more than a little shocked to run into you. What brings you here, if you don't mind my asking? Are you looking for something?"

"Yes," Julia said, adjusting the beautiful and expensive-looking scarf around her neck, while telling Aliesha about a lecture and discussion on the federal government's inept response to Hurricane Katrina, which had lured her onto Wells's campus.

On informing Julia that the lecture for that particular event was being held in a building near the library, Aliesha volunteered to show her the way. During the course of their brief walk over, the two women exchanged a few of the usual pleasantries before Julia took it upon herself to address the pink elephant marching in step alongside them. "I'm sorry to hear things didn't work out between you and Javiel."

Aliesha wondered just how much Julia knew, particularly with regards to the ugliness that had transpired over the weekend. She swallowed the knot of embarrassment growing in her throat and said, "As much as I appreciate the sentiment, something tells me you're not terribly disappointed."

Julia slowed her pace and removed her sunglasses again. "Seeing either of you hurt is the last thing I'd ever want. But in all honesty, I do think it's better it happened now than before the two of you made the horrible mistake of getting married and bringing children into the picture. It never was anything personal against you, Aliesha, in spite of what you might think. Perhaps one day when you're older, you'll understand."

Neither of them said anything else until a few minutes later when they arrived in front of the building Julia had been in search of. "Okay, let's say I accept your insistence that it wasn't personal," Aliesha said, abruptly picking up where they'd left off. "What about the business with Evelyn? Did you ever truly believe Javiel had something to do with her death? I'm saying, you do realize you had me wondering if my life was in danger, don't you?"

"And it was, dear." Julia smiled and placed the bejeweled and perfectly manicured fingers of one hand on Aliesha's shoulder. "Take it from someone who knows. It's possible to take a person's life without actually putting a gun to their heads and pulling the trigger. Eventually, it would have happened. It might not have been as bloody. But a slow death is a death, nonetheless. Don't you think?"

She knew he wouldn't be there, but she showed up at Wally's Cool Cuts on the day of her regularly scheduled appointment anyway. She needed some answers and was determined to find someone who'd give them to her.

Just as she pulled up to the shop, she spied Wally coming out of the front door. He was just the person she'd hope to see. But rather than acknowledge her presence, he'd quickened his pace toward his SUV. By the time she'd exited her vehicle, he'd started his own and was already halfway out of the parking lot.

She shook her head, muttered a few choice profanities, and headed into the shop. She peered up with a frown as the bell above her head clattered and clanked, rather than sounded off with its usual pleasant ding. *"I want revenge!"* the classic line from James Brown's "The Payback," ripped and pulsated through the air.

When she lowered her frown, it landed on Gerald, who appeared to be losing in his battle to keep one of Sam Junior's squirming, kicking, snot-nose twins seated still long enough to get his hair cut.

Gerald greeted her with a scowl and barked, "Before you ask, naw! He ain't here. If you still wanting a haircut, check with Boyd, the new fella in the back. I'm sure he'll be happy to take care of it for you."

Aliesha walked toward the man who was occupying Dante's old workstation and who was hard at work on the head of the customer seated in Dante's barber's chair. But what seized her attention and held it for several seconds was the coatrack in Dante's station. Hanging from it was the now-familiar smock with the ever-present paperback jutting from its pocket.

"Something I can help you with, ma'am?"

She blinked and looked at the man. "Yes, I'm one of

Dante's customers, well, used to be, anyway. You're filling his spot now?"

"Yes, ma'am. I'm Preston Boyd. And you are?"

"Aliesha Eaton," she said on shaking the hand he held out to her. "Pardon me for asking, Mr. Boyd, but is your presence here temporary or permanent? I mean, I noticed some of Dante's things are still here."

"Yes, ma'am, I was filling in temporarily, but as of this week, I am officially the new hire. I haven't quite had time to move all of my things in just yet."

"So, I take that to mean Dante's not coming back?"

"From what I understand, no. He quit."

"He quit! Wow, what about Yazz? Do you have any idea when he might be in?"

"You mean that young knucklehead that used to run his mouth all the time? He went and got his self fired."

"What?! Okay, then, I guess that takes care of that."

Mr. Boyd shut off his clippers. "You sure you don't want me to cut your hair? I should be finished with this gentleman in another ten minutes or so."

"No, not today. Thank you, though. Maybe some other time."

On her way out, she noticed Gerald yelling into the phone mashed against his ear, while Sam Junior, now seated in Gerald's chair, sat thumbing through a sports magazine and ignoring the twins, who were trading slaps and insults. She walked out and was about to open her car door when she heard someone call out behind her, "Hey, hey, hold up!"

When she turned, her eyes widened at the sight of Gerald lumbering toward her, cell phone still glued to the side of his head. She couldn't help but wonder why he just didn't get a phone with an ear attachment.

On reaching her, he snapped the phone shut and dropped it into his pocket. "Look here, Miz Professor, if it make any difference to you, I honestly don't know where Dante is. I, for one, would have been happy to see him around here today. He's 'bout the only somebody with patience enough to handle them badass twins. I can't count the number of times he's settled one of Sam Junior's lil monsters down with a handful of comic books or by taking them over to his station and reading to 'em."

"Well, guess I should take some consolation in the fact that I'm not the only one he's left hanging."

Rather than react to her sarcasm, Gerald said, "Some of these young boys pull that kind of shit . . . I mean mess, on the regular. You know, run off and be gone three, four days? Have folks wondering if they dead or alive. Long as I've known D., I ain't never known him to be that type."

"So, what are you trying to say? Because according to Mr. Boyd, Dante quit."

Gerald scratched the scraggly bush growing atop his head. "Yeah, that's the story Wally's sticking to, anyway."

"You don't believe that?"

"I'ma tell you what I believe, Miz Professor, or rather what I know. Sometimes when a man up and disappear like that, he ain't trying to be found."

She pursed her lips, nodded, then said, "Yeah, I guess you've got a point. Thanks."

"Hey, wait a sec." Gerald reached into the pocket of his smock and pulled out an iPod. "I found this over in D.'s spot the other day. Why don't you take it?"

She reached for it, then shook her head. "No, I probably shouldn't. If he does come back for his things, I'm sure he'll wonder where it is."

"Yeah, all the more reason," Gerald said. "'Bout a week before Dante disappeared, I ran up on him back there in the laundry room on his break. He had this here thing hooked up to his laptop some kind of way, and our former resident know-it-all, Yazz, was standing there overseeing, you know, trying to tell him how he was doing it all wrong." Gerald laughed. "Anyway, I said, 'Man, what is it exactly you call yourself trying to do?'"

"D. looked at me real funny-like and said, 'Man, I'm just putting together a little something for Aliesha.'"

"I was like, who? He said, 'You know Aliesha, Dr. Eaton, you know, man, Miz Professor!' And I could tell by the look on his face and the way your name come outta his mouth, something between y'all had changed. To him, you were somebody special, not just any other customer . . . or any other woman."

Aliesha gave in to a little smile. "I'd like to think that. Of course, with him having gone and pulled this little stunt, I'm not so sure."

"Go on and take it," Gerald said, shoving the iPod at her. "I know for a fact he got a couple others. And if he does show up around here again and he starts asking 'bout this one, I'll be sure to let him know where he can find it."

Aliesha waited until later in the evening before giving the iPod a listen. She plugged in the earbuds, stretched across her bed, and closed her eyes. "The Chosen," the song Dante had insisted she listen to the night before his disappearance, gently flooded her ears and spread downward until it, like a blanket, covered her entire body.

Upon realizing that it was the only song on the iPod, Aliesha found herself playing it over and over again and wondering why. Why would Dante record such a beautiful song for her? Is that how he felt? Was she his "chosen"? If so, why had he taken to treating her as what could only be described as less than special? Where the hell had he gone that he couldn't call? And what did any of it mean? Her gut told her something wasn't right. Something had happened to Dante. But what?

She took the iPod to work and listened to the song every free moment throughout the day. Around about the thirtieth time, it finally struck her—she knew someone who just might be able to give her a few definitive answers. At that point, her attention turned to the most important question she had yet to ask herself: Was she honestly prepared to hear and accept the truth?

Aliesha had packed a lunch, and her original plan had been to eat alone in her office where she could continue to listen to the song Dante had recorded for her. But Monica had insisted they visit a new deli and sandwich shop not far from campus.

Monica tapped a fork against her glass of ice water and cleared her throat. "Hey, Ms. Thing, you made plans for this evening?"

Aliesha looked up from the salad she'd been picking over. In no hurry to revisit any of the biting nastiness of their previous falling-out, Aliesha had become more guarded about what she told Monica with regards to Dante. She'd said nothing to her about the last visit she'd made to Wally's or the iPod Gerald had given her or the song that kept playing in her head even when she wasn't listening to it. "Yeah, sorta," she said.

Monica grinned. "Hopefully they don't involve you driving aimlessly around town again, looking to accidentally run into you know who in order to tell him Lord knows what."

Aliesha forced herself to smile. "They don't. If you must know, I'm going to see Peaches. I'm letting her twist my hair."

"Wow, can't exactly say I saw that one coming. I guess that's one way of moving on and literally getting dude out of your hair. Want me to go with you?"

Aliesha's eyebrows rose in surprise and a genuine smile replaced her fake one. "What? You're not scared of Peaches anymore?"

Monica frowned. "Let's get this straight—I didn't say a

word about letting her come anywhere near my head. To be frank, yes, she still gives me all kind of heebee-jeebies. But given the little stunt you pulled last Friday night, I'm even more afraid of letting you roam the streets alone again. Pardon me for being so blunt, but you ending up in the wrong bed again with your damn legs spread is still very much a distinct possibility."

Aliesha used her napkin to take a playful swat across the table at her laughing friend. "Why do you always have to be such a mean ole heifer?" she asked before joining in with a chuckle of her own.

When Aliesha called Peaches on Thursday night, she'd learned that only hours before, "King," the last stray mutt Miss Margie had made a part of her small family, had died. Mixed in with the sadness, Aliesha detected a note or two of both excitement and relief in Peaches's voice. "I'm canceling most of my appointments tomorrow. I'm taking King to the vet, so I can make arrangements to have him cremated. Then I'm going by the pet cemetery and see about getting him a plot."

Aliesha found the last tidbit of information the most in-teresting, given her knowledge that all of Miss Margie's other dogs had simply been buried in the backyard.

"But I can still do your hair at the house, sometime to-morrow evening, if you want," Peaches said.

"What time were you planning on leaving for the vet?" Aliesha asked. "I can stop by early in the morning or else sometime after three, tomorrow afternoon, if you need a hand."

"Oh, thanks, but that won't be necessary. Tamara and LeRoy have already volunteered to do the honors."

"LeRoy?" Aliesha asked.

"Yes, he's a guy I've been talking to. He goes to my

church and picks me up from work sometimes. Remember Mr. Hardy who owns the cab company me and Mama have been using every since I started working at Beulah's? Well, Leroy is his son. He moved down here from Detroit and started working for Mr. Hardy a couple of months ago."

Aliesha wasn't sure what to make of the revelation. A part of her was tickled by the knowledge that Peaches had landed herself a boyfriend or else was well on her way to doing so. On the other hand, she couldn't help but feel somewhat concerned. Who was this guy? Some Detroit slick looking to get over on some blind, sheltered church girl? One thing she knew for sure, who ever he was, Miss Margie would not have approved. Over the years, Aliesha had come to suspect that beyond simple protection, one of the primary reasons Miss Margie kept some surly, mean-ass dog around was to serve as a deterrent to any man who might be harboring thoughts about getting too close to Peaches.

A flood of memories descended upon Aliesha as soon as she opened the gate and placed her foot on one of the circular concrete pavers that led to Miss Margie's house. She still thought of the simple but sturdy brick structure at 6622 Alameda Drive as Miss Margie's. She had never imagined herself thinking otherwise until she walked through the wrought iron door that day. A number of cosmetic changes had been made since Aliesha's last visit. The old plastic-covered furniture in the living room had been replaced with a more contemporary leather sofa and a pair of comfortable-looking, overstuffed leather chairs. In place of the dark, heavy drapes were bamboo drawstring blinds. The old, shag carpeting, dingy and worn from age and years of repeated steam cleanings, had been ripped out, revealing unmarred and barely walked upon hardwood floors.

"My goodness, Peaches," Aliesha said, with her gaze still navigating the room. "You didn't tell me you'd been redecorating."

"I'm just getting started, really," Peaches said, beaming with pride. "Next on my list is to put a little paint on the walls and have the floors buffed and polyurethaned."

"Do you have a contractor? If not, I have a friend from church, Archie Phillips, who does a lot of my handiwork. I'm sure he'd be glad to come out and give you an estimate or else recommend someone."

"Well, I've been thinking about letting my friend LeRoy take on a few of the jobs over the summer."

Aliesha followed Peaches into the kitchen. "You and this guy LeRoy are pretty serious, huh?"

Peaches sat down at the kitchen table and broke into a sheepish grin. "I like him a lot, Miz Babygirl. He's a few years younger than me, but we've got a lot in common and so far he's been a real gentleman. Last night, when he came over and helped me with King was the first time we ever even . . . you know, kissed."

Aliesha remembered Peaches asking her, not all that long ago, what it was like to have a boyfriend. She couldn't imagine being in her midthirties and trying to navigate an intimate relationship for the first time. As she settled into a chair across the table from Peaches, she said, "So, you think maybe I could meet Mr. LeRoy sometime?"

A stern expression replaced the happy look of contentment that had been on Peaches's face. "Only if you promise not to try and pick up where Mama left off."

Aliesha laughed. "Okay, but in return, I want you to promise if you ever need any relationship advice or if LeRoy should start acting up and giving you problems, you won't hesitate to call me."

Peaches's grin returned and she reached out to shake Aliesha's hand. "All right, it's a deal." On resettling her hands in her lap, she said, "Aliesha, I know you ain't never been all that comfortable around me. So I appreciate you checking on me like you been doing here lately. Have to say, I'm surprised though. Even with you promising Mama like you did, I never thought you'd actually be able to go through with it."

"Surprised? You?" Aliesha said. "I thought you had the gift of discernment. Aren't you suppose to be able to read what's on a person's heart?"

Peaches chuckled. "I only wished it worked like that."

In truth, Aliesha was glad it didn't. As of late, when it came to interacting with Peaches, her motives had become increasingly selfish. "How does it work?" she asked. "Seriously . . . your gift, I mean?"

Peaches shrugged. "Tell you the truth, Miz Babygirl, I'm really not sure."

"So, is it sorta like mind reading? Do you get a vision— well, obviously, being blind, you don't get a vision, or do you?"

"No, I wouldn't say a vision, or a voice, even," Peaches said. She titled her face toward the ceiling. "It's more like a feeling. Whenever I touch someone's hair, I get a feeling for who they are and what they're going through in that particular moment. The more natural the hair, the more intense the feeling. If someone in your life is touching your hair on a regular basis, I can also get a feel for what's going on between the two of you."

She stood and circled behind Aliesha's chair. "Remember that time a while back when you came by the house? And after I touched your hair, I asked if you were okay?"

Aliesha nodded. "Sure, I remember."

Peaches brushed her palm over the unruly curls atop Aliesha's head. "I didn't feel anything," Peaches said. "That's why I asked. The man you were seeing at the time, what was his name?"

"Javiel," Aliesha said.

"Yes, Javiel," Peaches repeated. "Javiel must not have touched your hair much."

"No, I guess he didn't," Aliesha said.

"You've seen him recently though, haven't you?"

"Yes," Aliesha cringing through the guilt that accompanied her admission.

"But this new man in your life, he's different, just the opposite actually."

Aliesha swiveled around and stared at Peaches. "How did you know? I mean, yeah, you're right. Dante, my new . . . friend, he's a barber. He's the person who has been doing my hair for the past couple of months."

"So how come he stopped?" Peaches asked. "What happened to him?"

Aliesha dropped her head. "I was kind of hoping you'd know," she said, struggling to keep her emotions in check.

Peaches plunged her hands into Aliesha's hair and began searching with her fingers. "Umm, there so much . . . so much energy, it's hard to say. I can tell there's been a death. I get a sense of water. So much water . . . It's too much for him, Miz Babygirl."

Aliesha sprang to her feet, her face twisted in horror. "Is he dead? Is that what you're telling me? He drowned?"

Peaches shook her head and scrunched her face, which only made her sunken eye sockets close up even tighter. "Dead? A part of him, yes. Drowned? I'm not sure."

The two women collapsed into their respective seats at the kitchen table, as if they'd each just crossed the finish line of a long and arduous race.

"You wanna know the worse thing about this gift?" Peaches said softly after a moment of silence. "I can tell what's going on in everybody's life 'cept my own."

❦

Aliesha left Peaches's house with a new hairdo and filled with even more confusion and angst over Dante's disappearance than when she'd arrived. *A part of him was dead? What in the hell did that mean?*

Peaches's reference to water instantly brought to mind the river and Dante's mention of his cousin, who'd elected to wade into its murky, churning depths as a final cure for whatever had been ailing him. Try as she might, Aliesha couldn't keep herself from wondering if in his own unresolved grief, Dante had followed suit. Rather than follow her urge to race down to the river and launch an immediate investigation into the matter, she took a more sensible and practical approach. She waited until the next morning before she called the local newspaper, the *Riverton Appeal*, and asked if there had been any reports of a drowning in recent weeks. They informed her the only person they had any knowledge of was a one "Reuben Reese" and that his drowning had been more than three months ago. Aliesha immediately recognized the name as that belonging to Dante's cousin and recalled how she'd first spotted it on the inside flap of Dante's worn copy of *The Metamorphosis*.

Reese? Being cousins, wasn't it possible that Reuben and Dante shared a last name? Aliesha searched through the library's newspaper archives for Reuben's obituary, thinking it might offer her some additional clues. But on finding it, she again encountered more disappointment. The five-line obituary included no more than the basics— name, age, date of death, and the time and place of Reuben's funeral. No mention of Dante or any next of kin.

A quick call to information turned up more of the same, and that being nothing. They couldn't locate a telephone listing for a Dante Reese.

Weary of repeatedly coming up empty-handed and knowing she was straddling the borderline of obsession, Aliesha decided that maybe Gerald had been right. In spite of the intensity of the night they'd spent together, the sweet and tender words he'd whispered and moaned in her ear, or even the music he'd left behind, maybe Dante didn't want to be found, at least not by her.

She abandoned her search and threw herself into her work in hopes that in time the longing would go away. She contemplated tossing out his iPod and even Miz Babygirl, the adorable, dark-skinned, natural-haired doll Dante had given her. She even considered relegating them to the junk room where they could keep company with the suitcase containing Kenneth's belongings.

But in the end, she'd cleared a spot on one of the crowded bookshelves in her den and placed both items there, side by side. Occasionally, she'd pull them down and allow herself a moment to reminisce. But not often. She didn't want to put herself at risk for turning into that kind of woman—the kind, like her aunt Mildred, whose thirst for life got swallowed up and turned into bile by her own desperate and obviously, insatiable want of a man—a man who seemed intent only on bringing her heartache.

Oddly enough, unlike her relationship with Javiel, Aliesha harbored no regrets over her involvement with Dante. Even knowing how things turned out, had she to do it all again, she probably wouldn't have changed much. Beyond wanting to know why he'd vanished, she only wished their time together hadn't been so brief.

CHAPTER 35

He spent all of twenty-one days with his Big Mama before she seized his uncle Mack's hand and went off to be with the Lord. In the days prior, she'd rested in comfort and contentment between the sturdy walls her beloved had sawed, hammered, nailed, and erected on her behalf. Having given up on trying to talk her into the surgery her doctor recommended, Dante and Laylah took turns indulging the old woman's whims and catering to her every need.

Dante grew to appreciate Laylah's presence during that period, if only because, in her, he had someone with whom he felt comfortable sharing his burden and some of his concerns. Laylah, in turn, acted like she was only too happy to assist with the preparation of meals, administering of medication, escorting of Vivian Lee to and from the bathroom, and keeping her and Dante company. When Dante wasn't with Laylah and his Big Mama, he was somewhere in Mr. Jessie's funeral home, listening, taking note, or observing some aspect of the business and trying to decide if he owned the heart and the desire to work among the dead, even for a little while.

Oddly enough, Laylah didn't press him one way or the other. She even told him if he wanted to take another shot at school, she'd be willing to help with the financing. But having ventured down that hazardous route with her before, Dante wasn't eager to go there again. Once, some years ago, he'd allowed her to foot his college expenses, only to have her and Reuben pronounce his interest in history and African American studies a colossal waste of time. At their urging, he'd declared himself a business major and had even completed a couple of semesters' worth of courses when his uncle Mack had suffered a second stroke, after which Dante had again abandoned furthering his education altogether.

Even with Laylah doing all that she could in support of his efforts to see after his Big Mama, school wasn't a pursuit Dante felt in a position to commit to just yet. When he did go back, he wanted to do so without feeling in any way indebted to Laylah or worrying about a loved one's well-being.

He'd convinced himself that his Big Mama would, in fact, experience a full recovery and they'd take that trip to Africa, the Caribbean, the Middle East, and Europe together. In the days prior to the end, she'd appeared to be recuperating well and regaining her strength. On her last Wednesday night, she'd practically been giddy during the midweek Bible study, which thanks to Miz Irma and Doris Ferguson's expert handling and orchestration had taken place in Vivian Lee's living room.

On the very next day, she'd arisen early and after a hearty breakfast had insisted that Dante and Laylah help her inspect each one of her flower beds. Ignoring their protests, she'd donned her favorite floppy hat and from a motorized wheelchair seat she'd passed a couple of hours fussing over the gardens she'd spent half a lifetime cultivating, while giving her caretakers specific instructions on where to weed, clip, dig, and prune.

On Friday, she'd spent some time lounging on the front porch with Dante before later in the evening having him drive her to the family's cemetery, which took up a small plot of land, not more than a mile from the house. She sat on a nearby stone bench and watched as Dante placed the bright bunches of zinnias, carnations, lilacs, tulips, and roses she'd culled from her gardens and carefully arranged for each individual grave.

On completing the task, Dante went over and joined her on the bench. She patted his knee and said, "I've already talked to Laylah about having some of her daddy's folks come out every once in a while and see about these plots, you know, after I'm gone."

Dante looked at her but didn't say anything.

His Big Mama continued. "I guess you oughta know as well, the last time Laylah was here, I got her to draw me up a will. Most everything, the house, the land, will go to you, of course. But I did put a little something aside for Blessed Rock's Women's Guild and Irma, who really has been like a sister to me. And then, there's your mama, Helen—"

Dante rose and walked back over to the graves. He swallowed back the grief he felt threatening to erupt in one consuming wave after another.

"I don't guess you feel like talking about none of this, huh?" his Big Mama said.

"No, ma'am," he said, kicking at the dirt beneath his feet.

"So what do you want to talk about?" she said. "Maybe that woman in Riverton you still so sweet on?"

He cocked his head and took in her slow-moving grin. She touched the spot he'd vacated next to her on the bench. After he trudged back over and dropped down beside her, she rubbed his back and said, "Far as I can tell, son, Laylah really does love you. But if you no longer feel the same way about her, ain't no good liable to come from you pretending. Life is too short and seems to me you done wasted enough of it as it is."

"Yeah, I know," he said. "I know."

"So why don't you tell me a little something about her, this other woman, I mean, the professor who's got your world so shook up."

He smiled and shook his bowed head. "Why you wanna know about her?"

His Big Mama chuckled. "Well, for one, so as I can know who it is I need to be on the lookout for after I've crossed over to the other side."

The end came quietly, like the soft unclicking of the tumblers on a brand new lock, like a breeze, which only stirs the very tops of the trees, the type most will miss, unless, by chance, they're looking up when it happens.

On returning home from the family's cemetery that evening, Vivian Lee asked Laylah to help her with a bath, after which she retired to her bedroom. She said her prayers, called for Dante in order to give him his good night kiss, and in the morning she was gone.

While the ever-stoic Laylah made all of the necessary phone calls, Dante sat next to his Big Mama's bedside and wept until Mr. Jessie's people showed up for the body. For the remainder of the day, he ambled about as if in a stupor, his limbs stiff and his eyes vacant. Upon the fall of night and as soon as the last consoling visitor stepped off the front porch, he stumbled into his Big Mama's empty room and sought the comfort of the pillow where she'd last laid her head. Laylah joined him atop the bed's patchwork-quilt-covered mattress. She gently stroked his shoulder, his arm, and the back of his head, while he buried his face and cried into what he knew to be Vivian Lee's scent—a volatile blend of baby powder, coconut oil, black licorice, and butterscotch.

Laylah's sons flew in for the funeral, and their presence, Ozzie's in particular, helped soothe Dante's grief and lift his sagging spirits. When the smart and playful thirteen-year-old, with whom he'd long been close, asked him one day, "So, does Mama's moving back here mean you fixing to be my new stepdaddy?" Dante had been surprised at the ease at which he'd responded, "I don't know about stepdaddy, but I'm always gonna be your uncle D."

He'd been stunned as well by the ease at which he'd extended the olive branch to his birth mother. Somehow, like she had so many other times in the past, after receiving word of Vivian Lee's passing she'd showed up on the very day of the funeral. Dante had been leading the procession of friends and family members down Blessed Rock's center aisle and toward the opened casket when he'd spied Helen's slight and forlorn figure standing among the other mourners who'd come to pay their respects. The sadness he'd seen in her eyes told the tragic story of a loss that had little to do with the death of his Big Mama. He'd stopped in midstep and motioned for her to join him. After a tearful embrace, he'd escorted her to a seat on the front-row pew next to him.

Later, he'd insisted that Helen check out of the cheap motel she'd booked for the week and come stay with him. Her acceptance paved the way for the reopening of the doors between them that had for too long been barricaded and sealed. Before she left, they'd even begun discussing the possibility of her moving back to Roads Cross and taking up residence in the old but solidly constructed home that Dante couldn't bear the thought of renting out, much less selling to some stranger.

During the week of Dante's reconnection with his birth mother, Laylah took her boys back to L.A. to help them pack and prepare for their summer stay in Roads Cross. Upon the trio's return, she sent the children to stay with their dour but doting grandfather, Mr. Jessie, while she rejoined Dante at his Big Mama's house.

In Laylah's absence, Dante had begun sleeping in his old room again. Though still uncertain of how to go about repairing all that had been damaged and broken between them, he couldn't shake the obligation he felt to at least try. So when she crawled in next to him that night, naked and ravenous for the love they hadn't made in months, he did his best to oblige her. He kissed, fondled, and stroked all of the places he'd known since the spring he'd turned sixteen, only to discover that none of them felt right. Rather than stir and harden in eager anticipation, he'd remained soft and pliable, like an unfilled sock with its match nowhere to be found.

Unwilling to concede defeat or admit the obvious, Dante had used his hands and fingers, his mouth and his tongue, to take Laylah where she wanted to go. And afterward, when he'd experienced the tender shock of her tears as they'd rolled down his chest, tears that he knew weren't full of sweetness and joy, he'd caressed her tightly coiled locs and acknowledged her sorrow with a softly whispered, "I'm sorry, baby. I'm so sorry."

The following morning, Dante found himself staring at the ceiling and thinking about how he'd been awakened in the middle of the night by the sound of a crying baby; about how since Vivian Lee's death, instead of bumps and creaks at night, he heard the soft buzz of whispering, which made him wonder if his Big Mama wasn't somewhere shushing his uncle Mack. He found himself thinking about the possible reasons behind Reuben's decision to leave him all of those damn copies of Kafka's *Metamorphosis* and what his uncle Mack had once told him when Dante had gone to him upset about some mean-spirited prank Reuben had pulled: *"That's a boy that's got a hurt that can't be fixed, way down deep on the inside. But he blood and you gonna have to find a way to love him, in spite of it."* Dante thought about Reuben's hurt and wondered if, like his, it had somehow been tied to the mother who'd abandoned him, Miriam, who'd died in prison before Reuben turned three or perhaps to Reuben, Sr., the father who'd beaten him yet again before depositing his bloodied and broken body on Mack and Vivian Lee's doorstep and vanishing into the night, never to be seen or heard from again.

Dante was still staring at the ceiling and thinking about Reuben when he noticed the spider. He followed its jerky movements, praying all the while it wouldn't fall into the tangle of sheets covering him and Laylah. As the spider inched its way across the plaster, Dante noticed it pass over the long-forgotten words Reuben had carved above Dante's bed when they were kids: *No way, you f-ing nitwit!*

He smiled and thought about the "That's my car!" game he and Reuben had played as boys. Whenever Dante managed to call dibs on a really nice car before Reuben, he'd get mad and tell Dante, "No way, you f-ing nitwit!" One day he'd taken a Swiss Army Knife and etched the words into the ceiling above Dante's bed.

He felt Laylah stir beside him and stretch her limbs. "Reuben could really be a jerk sometimes, couldn't he? I'm surprised you never spackled over that."

His smile sank into a frown as Laylah abandoned the bed for the bathroom. He couldn't recall having told her about the words carved above his bed. How did she know Reuben was responsible? And what made her so sure he, Dante, was the statement's target? Might Reuben have told her? Possibly. Had she, perhaps, overhead Reuben hurl the verbal taunt at him? Maybe. Dante had certainly never invited her into his bedroom prior to his Big Mama's hospitalization. Neither she nor his uncle Mack would have ever permitted such a thing. And even back when he and Laylah first started fooling around, the thought of sneaking her past his uncle and aunt would have never occurred to him. But it certainly would have to. . . .

Dante threw back the sheet and sat up on the side of the bed. How else would Laylah have known about the meaning behind the message carved into the ceiling above his bed unless she'd asked Reuben about it, after having lain there on her back staring up at it? He rubbed his hands over his head and up and down his face while reflecting on that period during his teens when he'd believed in earnest that the puppy love between him and Laylah was the real thing and might actually last.

He remembered how whenever he'd return from a date with her, Reuben would either whisper across their darkened bedroom or else come over and snarl into his ear, "Nigga, please. You really think you're the first somebody to tap that?" Dante had always written it off as just vicious teasing or even jealously on Reuben's part. Now, he wondered. He glanced up at the words hovering over his head. When had it really started between Reuben and Laylah? And more important, when had it actually ended?

He waited until after they'd both showered, dressed, and downed half a pot of coffee and she'd spoken on the phone with her boys before he cleared his throat and said, "Just for the record, when was the last time you were with Reuben?"

Laylah, who'd been standing at the kitchen sink, swiveled toward him and said, "What?"

Dante leaned back in one of the old kitchen chairs until its front legs were inches off the floor. "I'm saying, when was the last time you slept with him?"

Laylah finished rinsing out their coffee mugs before she said, "Reuben's dead, Dante. Don't you think it would be best to let him rest in peace?"

The front legs of Dante's chair hit the wooden floorboards with a sickening thud. "Do you really think I give a damn how Reuben rests?" he asked. "Right now, it's my own peace of mind that most concerns me."

Laylah crossed her arms and glared at him. "It might not be wise to ask questions you really don't want to know the answers to."

Dante stood and returned her angry pose. "When, Laylah?" he asked in a quiet voice. "When was the last time you screwed him, fucked him, whatever you want to call it? When and where?"

She looked away. "A month before he died, okay? In Montreal."

He thought about all of the places to which he'd traveled at Laylah's request and on her dime, Montreal among them. He threw back his head and laughed. "Wow! And all of these years you had me believing I was the only one. That Reuben was a mistake and you and I were really gonna be together one day. Tell the truth, Laylah, it was never me, was it? It was always Reuben, wasn't it?"

Her folded arms fell to her sides and her eyes pleaded with him. "You don't understand, Dante. It wasn't like that at all."

He slapped an opened hand against the tabletop. "The hell it wasn't!"

She reached out and grabbed his arm. "Let's talk about it."

He shrugged her off. "No, I'm through talking, Laylah." He reached around her and snatched open the cabinet beneath the sink. On pulling out his Big Mama's gardening trowel and pruning shears, he jabbed them in the uneasy space between him and Laylah. "And I'm more than done waiting for you to get your shit together and do right by me."

On noticing her eyes widen and her gaze latch onto the shear's razor sharpened blades and the trowel's flat and pointed metal face, he lowered the tools and said, "I'm going for a walk. And while I'm gone, I suggest you call your father, Ace, or one of your other admiring fans or flunkies and have them come and get you."

⸻ ∞ ⸻

He ended up in the family cemetery. He stared at the graves for a moment, paying particular attention to the ones he knew best—his Big Mama, his uncle Mack, his cousin Reuben, his aunt Miriam, they were all there. He knew that one day he and his mother, Helen, would be, too. He turned and walked to a spot situated between the stone bench, where he'd last sat and conversed with the woman whose love he'd never doubted, and a majestic-looking weeping willow, a tree almost identical to the one in the backyard of the house that now claimed him as owner.

He put down the bucket he'd brought along to make carrying his items eaiser and dropped onto his knees beside it. He pulled out the trowel and shoved it into the ground. He dug until he found the large polyethylene jar with the screw-top lid he'd buried there one bright spring day in the twilight of his youth. He used the gardening shears to break the jar's seal and dumped the contents on the grass beside him. Beneath the crumpled wads of archival paper he found the deflated football and the two tiny sets of knitted baby booties, one pair pink and the other blue. He picked up the delicate items and gently placed them in the bottom of the deep dirt hole. He reached into the bucket for the copy of *The Metamorphosis* he'd grabbed before leaving the house and placed it into the hole with the other items. A light breeze descended and swept across his glistening brow as he removed the chain bearing the ring from around his neck. On placing the jewelry atop the book, he carefully refilled the pit with the rock and earth he'd removed.

He'd brushed off his hands over the dark patch and had nearly risen to his feet when he remembered the baby's breath he'd pulled from one of his Big Mama's gardens. He eased the collection of tiny white flowers and greenery from the bucket. He paused, lowered his face, and inhaled a bit of the scent before arranging it atop what was now, for all practical purposes, a grave.

On his return to the house, Dante spied Ace's town car in the drive and Laylah seated in one of the rockers on the front porch with an opened book in her lap. As Dante walked up the path that led to the porch steps, he barely noticed Ace or heard the greeting he muttered as he scurried past him with Laylah's bags. When Dante reached the landing, Laylah closed the book and rose from the chair.

He'd expected hostility or hurt, but her eyes glowed with warmth and tenderness. She pressed the book to her chest and said, "It was his way of warning you. He didn't want you to end up like him. You know, one morning you wake up only to discover you've turned into something monstrously grotesque? That's why he left you the books. He feared one day it would happen to you too."

She tossed the paperback into the rocking chair and before stepping off the porch, she kissed Dante on the cheek and whispered, "It was never our intent to hurt you. Forgive us for all of the times we did."

CHAPTER 36

Nearly a month and a half had passed since Dante's disappearance. At school, the spring semester had ended and, after a brief break, the summer semester had begun. For Aliesha, the days and weeks had rolled one into another, monotonous and indistinguishable, until one Sunday, near the end of service when she'd looked up and spotted Kenneth in one of Garden View's back-row pews.

She'd heard from Mrs. Phillips that he'd been going to grief counseling and regularly attending AA meetings. After the slashed painting incident, she'd fully expected to hear from him at some point, if only to have him personally offer an apology. But he hadn't called, not even to let her know he would be at church that day. She hesitated when she saw him, but her palms stayed dry and her heart didn't begin to flutter. She acknowledged him with a nod. No smile. No "How are you doing?" Just a nod. Kenneth returned the gesture and added a wave, before he turned and left the building.

The following Monday night, in need of a little something to spice up her mood, Aliesha stopped by Nelson's. She'd just finished placing a take-out order at the counter—barbecued smoke sausage, baked beans, coleslaw, and a thick slice of lemon pound cake—when she heard, "Say yo, Miz Professor!"

She recognized the voice in an instant and, while familiar, it unfortunately wasn't Dante's. She turned and took in the long-legged figure bounding toward her. He flashed his trademark grin and spread his arms. Her own face lit up in a grin, and she willingly granted the affection he sought.

"What's up, Doc?!" he said, on releasing her. "Good seeing you again."

"Same here," Aliesha said. "So where have you been and what have you been up to? I mean, besides using that mouth of yours to create all kinds of agitation?"

"Just hanging," he said. "You know I don't work at Wally's anymore, right?"

"Yes, I heard. Actually, I heard you went and got yourself fired. You must have really showed out to make Wally mad enough to hand you your walking papers."

"Naw, see that was all D.'s doing. He told Wally if he didn't give me the boot, I'd probably keep goofing off around there instead of trying to get my butt into somebody's college. And he was right. But don't worry, it's not like I'm hurting for money or anything. I'm still clocking some part-time hours over at my unc's detailing business. And if all goes well, this fall, you just might see me over there at Wells."

"Really?!" Aliesha said.

"Yeah, I'm taking a couple of classes at the community college this summer and I'm working on transferring to a four-year institution either this fall or next spring."

"Good for you!" Aliesha said, genuinely pleased and happy for him. "Make sure you let me know when you plan to be on campus." She reached into her bag and pulled out a business card. "I'd be happy to give you a tour or treat you to lunch even."

"Oh, you know it!" Yazz said. On pocketing the card, his face fell somber. "I guess you heard about D. quitting and everything."

"Yes," Aliesha said, suddenly feeling awkward about

acknowledging the man who'd exited her life without saying so much as "I'm gone." She shifted her handbag from one arm to the other and finally said, "So, where's Dante working these days?"

"Well, when I saw him at his auntie's funeral, he was talking about taking a break from it all."

His auntie's funeral?! Her purse slid down her arm. "Wait, his aunt passed? You don't mean the one who raised him, his Big Mama, do you?"

"Yeah, that's the one. Dude took it pretty hard. What? You didn't know?"

Aliesha shook her head. "I haven't seen or spoken with Dante in quite some time. Next time you see him, be sure to give him my condolences and tell him . . . tell him I said, 'Hello.'"

Yazz scratched his head and looked puzzled. "Okay, sure. I'll do that."

"Pick up for Eaton!" the man behind the counter barked.

"Well, that's my order," Aliesha said. "It was great catching up with you, Yazz. You take care." She gave him another hug. "And don't forget to give me a call in advance when you decide to stop by the campus."

She turned and paid for her order. On removing the plastic sack full of food from the counter and swiveling around with it, she nearly collided with the tall, gangly youth who hadn't moved from his spot behind her.

He looked up from the cell phone he'd been tinkering with and caught her before either her bags or her body landed on the floor. "I'm sorry," he said. "You wouldn't happen to have a pen or a pencil, would you?"

She gave him a pen from her purse and watched as he took what she recognized as a Wally's Cool Cuts business card from his wallet. He glanced at his phone and scribbled something on the card before passing it to her.

"What's this?" she asked.

"A number where you can reach Dante."

She smiled. "You sure that's wise? Isn't this in direct violation of one of your 'Brother Man rules'?"

Yazz laughed and said, "Possibly. But since D. did me the favor of getting me fired, I figured this is the least I could do for him."

Once she moved beyond the initial shock, the news of Dante's Big Mama's death saddened her. She remembered the image she'd seen of the small, proud woman seated between the two young boys. She recalled as well the affection she'd always heard in Dante's voice whenever he'd spoken of her. No doubt he had taken it hard, especially having just buried his cousin.

She spent minutes on end staring at the seven digits on the card Yazz had given her. As much as she longed to talk to Dante, as much as she ached to hear his voice again, as diligent and persistent as she'd been in her search for him, now that she had his number, she couldn't bring herself to dial it.

Late on the following Tuesday afternoon, Aliesha cut short her lecture and dismissed her Intro class early. She watched as the six or so students who'd been nodding and dozing in her class of twenty suddenly perked up and beat most of the more alert students to the door. She could hardly blame them. Who wanted to be cooped up in some artificially lit and air-conditioned room, reviewing the definitions of words like *ethnography* or taking notes on the lives of long-dead thinkers and scholars, like Boaz and Herskovits, when they could be outside breathing in the fresh air and soaking up the sun?

Uppermost in her own mind was getting home so she

could change into a pair of shorts, hop on her bike, and embark upon a leisurely ride around the neighborhood. She could already feel the early summer breeze caressing her face and bare legs. But she found her plans temporarily thwarted upon arriving at her office and discovering Tamara and Kristen loitering outside of her closed door.

Aliesha couldn't help but break into a smile whenever she spotted the two of them together. They'd become quite the odd couple, if not the best of buddies in the days since their first awkward meeting at the mall. Aliesha also drew a considerable amount of pleasure in knowing how much grief the unlikely pairing was undoubtedly causing Shelton. It was better payback than any she could have ever orchestrated on her own, and it wasn't like it didn't serve his arrogant, monkey butt right.

She opened her office door and listened as the two young women trailing behind her continued their ongoing debate about the various ways in which Tamara's research at the Black-owned and primarily Black-patronized strip club might have differed had Kristen been conducting the interviews with the dancers and their customers. In truth, Aliesha was as eager as Tamara for Kristen to officially join the graduate program. She already had a project in mind that the two of them could easily work on together. She'd intended to break into their conversation and share a bit of her own thoughts and plans when her phone rang.

While the two headstrong friends sat and loudly debated some obscure point, Aliesha reached across her desk and hoped whoever was calling wouldn't keep her on the line too long. "Yes, this is Dr. Eaton speaking. How may I help you?"

"Well, that depends on how long it's been since your last decent haircut."

She fumbled and nearly dropped the receiver at the sound of the familiar baritone and tease-filled voice. She sat up straight, then leaned back in her chair before she summoned up a soft, "It's been a while. Too long, actually."

He chuckled. "I'm at a new shop now. Why don't you come on down sometime this week and let me take care of you?"

She felt her jaws stiffen. A wave of heat crept up her neck and over her face. *Just like that! No, I'm sorry I vanished into thin air on you. No, I meant to call you, baby, but . . .* Still, she tried to be patient and give him the benefit of the doubt. She said, "I guess Yazz told you he ran into me at Nelson's?"

"No, I haven't seen Yazz in a while."

She jerked forward against her desk, dropped her head, and in the most fierce whisper she could muster let him have it. "Seriously, after forty days of me not hearing a word from you, the day after I see Yazz, you decide to call, just out of the blue? Exactly what kind of fool do you take me for? And why in the hell do you insist on playing these games with me?"

Her torrent of angry words drew the attention of both Tamara and Kristen, the latter of whom hurriedly rose and mouthed a quiet, "We'll check back with you later."

A scowling and hot-faced Aliesha watched as Kristen verbally prodded and physically pushed a slow-moving and slightly amused-looking Tamara out of the office.

Dante said, "Aliesha, I know I've got a lot of work to do in order to regain your trust."

She left her desk and went over and locked the door. "Yeah, right. You know what? I really don't have time for this."

"Okay, but hold up a sec! I mean, you wanna call me back later or what?"

"Call you back?!" she said, abandoning her whisper in exchange for her normal speaking voice. She started pacing in the cramped, cluttered space. "Oh, so now I'm suppose to call you? With what, Dante? The number Yazz gave me from the meeting that you claim you don't know anything about? What am I suppose to think, Dante, after you disappear and stay gone for days on end without leaving me the slightest clue as to your whereabouts or how to get in touch with you? Do you have any idea how worried sick I was?"

"I get that. I do and I'm sorry. I didn't mean to stay away this long and I know I should have called, but . . . it's a long story, babe. But really and truly, I am sorry."

She stood still and squeezed her eyes shut. "I am, too. About us. About your Big Mama. About everything."

After a moment of silence, Dante said, "Does that mean you don't want to see me again? Can't you at least give me a chance to try to make it up to you?"

"I don't know," she said. "But right now, I'd really prefer not to talk about it."

She slammed down the phone but rather than give in to the scream she felt building inside of her, she forced herself to breathe and count to ten. How dare he attempt to casually stroll back into her life as if he'd only been gone an hour. Did he really think she was going to put up with being treated in such a cavalier fashion?

She reached for the phone again, intending to call Monica and fill her in on the latest, but thought better of it. Nine times out of ten, Monica's response would be one reeking in biting sarcasm and unwarranted criticism, none of which would likely make Aliesha feel the least bit better. Besides, lately Monica had been keeping busy with other things—chiefly beefing up her knowledge of the American Cherokee and hanging out with the newly hired curator of Riverton's Native American Museum. Aliesha knew Monica's actions stemmed in large part from Jesus's recent acceptance of a position in another state and were in full keeping with her dating preference of men whose racial identities couldn't readily be checked off in a box labeled Black or White.

No longer in the mood for a bike ride or anything of a fun and lighthearted nature, Aliesha sat at her desk and brooded. Just when she'd thought herself cured of the pain of Dante's sudden, unexplained absence, he decides to pop back up again without even attempting to adequately justify or explain his actions. Well, forget his ass. She'd happily add his name to the growing list of men who'd recently proved themselves undeserving of her affection, men who obviously who didn't know who she was, none other than Will Eaton's daughter—a smart, beautiful, and talented child of God who knew her worth in the world.

CHAPTER 37

She didn't notice the flowers when she drove up to the house. Like usual, she parked the car in the garage, collected her things, and went inside. After checking her landline for messages, she made a quick detour by the bathroom before heading out to her front porch to see if she'd received any mail.

She opened the black mailbox attached to the wall, pulled out its contents, and was busy rifling through the junk mail in search of bills when the four large, gray, flower-filled containers on her porch suddenly seized her attention. She frowned, then stepped closer and peered down at the bright yellow and orange daylilies and the purple and pink assortment of petunias.

She noticed a index card jutting from beneath one of the pots. She knelt and picked up the item. Printed on one side of the card in large letters was the name Dante Douglass along with two phone numbers and two addresses—one e-mail and the other to an actual residence. On the card's opposite side Aliesha discovered a partial quote from 1 Corinthians 13:4–7. *"Love is patient, love is kind . . . it always protects, always trusts, always hopes, always perseveres."*

Without pausing to deliberate or second-guess or talk herself out of it, she went inside and called him. He picked up on the first ring. In response to his "Hello," she said, "So I guess now your plan is to use Scripture to try and make me feel guilty?"

"No, that was one of my Big Mama's favorite quotes and the only halfway profound thing I could think of in that particular moment. . . . You like them? The flowers, I mean?"

"Of course I do," she said. "They're my favorites. At least you remembered that much."

"I got them out of my Big Mama's gardens. I was sitting on your porch with them when I called," he said. "After you chewed me out, I figured I'd better leave a note. I know what it looks like, Aliesha, but I promise you, I didn't deliberately set out to leave you hanging for so long. It all happened so fast, with my Big Mama and everything, I mean. Soon as I heard she'd taken ill, I went to see about her. And while I was there, I just got incredibly overwhelmed by everything. And things got complicated."

"I understand all of that, Dante. It still doesn't keep me from being angry with you for not finding a way to let me know what was going on. A thirty-second phone call is all it would have taken."

"Okay, I made a mistake. I should have called sooner. But I'm calling now, Aliesha. So, where do you want to go from here?" he asked with more than a bit of plead in his voice.

The seconds ticked by as she contemplated the pros and cons of ending her association with him and forgoing answers to any of the questions she'd been asking herself over the past month and a half.

"Come on, Aliesha, please. I'll explain everything when I see you. It'll never happen again, I promise."

Finally she said, "Look, where's this new shop? And what's the name of it?"

"It's under new management and doesn't officially have a name yet," he said prior to giving her the address, the phone number, and directions. "I don't want to rush you," he said after he'd finished. "But it would be nice if you could come tomorrow around lunchtime, like you used to."

Later that evening Aliesha got a phone call from Peaches. Rather than resume her search for another barber or beautician, Aliesha had finally consented to what she'd once considered unimaginable—allowing Peaches to regularly twist, style, and handle her hair. The time they'd spent together had drawn them closer and had all but eradicated the heightened sense of discomfort Aliesha had once felt in her bald and blind counterpart's presence. Like old girlfriends, they'd fallen into the habit of calling one another several times a week and talking for twenty to thirty minutes at a time. Every time they spoke, Aliesha could almost feel Miss Margie and her Big Mama smiling down on them.

She sometimes still wondered though if Miss Margie would have ever grown to accept Peaches's relationship with LeRoy. In her own first meeting with the man, Aliesha had admittedly been taken aback upon her discovery of the one thing Peaches had neglected to tell her—her new beau, LeRoy, was an albino. But it hadn't taken Aliesha long to decide that the laid-back and easygoing LeRoy was more than a suitable match for her mild-mannered friend.

"You know, LeRoy is still raving over the jambalaya you served the other night," Peaches said. "I figured I'd better make sure I remembered the recipe correctly before I tried to make him some."

After Aliesha repeated the recipe for Peaches, they chatted for a couple of minutes. She didn't really feel like talking, a fact Peaches had been quick to note. "Something bothering you, Miz Babygirl? You don't sound like yourself this evening."

Aliesha hesitated, then blurted, "Dante called. You know, the guy who used to do my hair?"

"Really?" Peaches said. "Well, that's a good thing, isn't it? At least now you know for sure he's all right."

"He's working at some new shop and wants me to come see him tomorrow. I've got half a mind to give him a taste of his own medicine and not show up."

"No, don't do that," Peaches said. "Two wrongs don't ever make a right. Besides, I thought you wanted to see him."

Aliesha frowned. "At the moment, all I want is a plausible explanation for his disappearance, something he has yet to give. His Big Mama died and I can understand him grieving her death and everything. But still, forty days? Anyway, I think I might have rushed things between me and Dante. I should have spent a little more time getting to know him."

Peaches said, "Hmm, Dante, Javiel, and Kenneth, too."

Had Peaches's dryly rendered observation not cut so deep, Aliesha might have laughed. Instead she said, "Coming from someone else I'd be insulted, but coming from you—well—I'm pretty much resigned to accepting it for what I know it is, the truth."

"I'm sorry," Peaches said. "I hope I didn't come off sounding too harsh or judgmental. The last thing I'd want to do is hurt your feelings."

"No, it's fine, Peaches. Actually, I'm glad we finally feel comfortable enough with each other to openly say what's on our minds."

"I am, too," Peaches said, sounding relieved. "And I've gotta tell you, Miz Babygirl, in the many years that I've been listening to women talk about their love lives, I've noticed that what they think and the way they act and what's really going on in their lives are rarely the same. Even smart, confident, fully sighted women like yourself prefer to act as if you're blind when it comes to certain things. Take Kenneth, for instance, and those dirty movies he was into. Had you talked to him about it and shared your reservations and discomfort from the jump, rather than go along with it for as long as you did, things might have never ended the way they did."

On sucking up and filing away the accurate assessment, Aliesha said, "And Javiel?"

Peaches sighed. "Deep down, Miz Babygirl, you always knew Javiel wasn't the best match for you. But like a lot of women, you were lonely, feeling rejected, and willing to settle. Of course, based on what you told me, I'd say Javiel had a bit of a 'Black girl' fetish, which didn't exactly help matters between the two of you any."

Aliesha laughed. "You got that right. Lucky me, huh? I dump the guy who treats me like a party doll only to land another who insists on propping me up on a shaky pedestal. So what about Dante? Why not spare me the headache and the hassle and just tell what the deal is going to be with him?"

Sounding more serious than amused, Peaches said, "With all due respect, Miz Babygirl, there are a few things I don't even know. But since you appear to be going into this with your eyes wide open this time around, I'm sure you'll find out soon enough."

"Yeah? Well, you know if I do start seeing Dante again, I probably won't be seeing you as often—at least when it comes to my hair, anyway."

"That's okay," Peaches said. "It's not like I don't understand. Ain't nothin' like the feeling of a man's fingers in your hair and against your scalp."

Aliesha couldn't keep herself from wondering what, if anything, Peaches knew about that particular experience—especially with her being bald and all.

Peaches said, "You remember that time your daddy did our hair?"

Aliesha laughed and said, "Excuse me? Our hair?! Peaches, girl, what are you talking about?"

"When we were little. You remember—my mama and your grandma were both really sick. Something had been going around the church—flu, food poisoning, or something. Anyway, you and your daddy were in town visiting. You needed your hair washed and since neither Mama or sister Eaton felt up to doing it, your father volunteered."

"This was at my Big Mama's house?" Aliesha asked, trying to summon up a recollection of the memory.

"Uh-huh, you must have been around four or so, which meant I was six. So your daddy got all of the stuff together and hoisted you up on the counter in the kitchen and washed your hair in the sink. I remember standing there listening really hard and trying to take in his every move. After he was done, he asked if I wanted a turn. I can remember telling him, 'Mr. Will, you know I ain't got no hair.'"

Peaches and Aliesha both laughed.

"But your daddy was like, 'And what difference does that make, little girl? You want a turn or not?' He helped me up on the counter, leaned my head back into the sink, got it all good and wet, and worked up a real nice, thick lather. Girl, talk about a good feeling. I'd never felt anything like it. You know my mama wasn't the most patient or gentle somebody, so she'd certainly never spent that kind of time and energy washing my big bald head."

Sadness accompanied Aliesha's recollection of the gruff manner and tone in which Miss Margie had typically conversed with the shy, soft-spoken Peaches.

"When he finished," Peaches went on, "he ushered me and you both over to a mirror and told us to *look* at ourselves. And just like before, I was like, 'Mr. Will, you know I can't see!' And he said, 'Yes, you can. Use your inner eyes. We've all got them. They help us figure out who people really are beneath the outer packaging.' I said, 'I don't know, Mr. Will.'"

Aliesha closed her eyes and she let her mind re-create an animated picture of Peaches's words.

"He said, 'You wanna know what I see? I see two smart, beautiful, and remarkably gifted children of God who'd be wise to always know and recognize their worth in this world. That's what I see.'" Peaches took a breath, then said, "I'm surprised you don't remember any of that, Miz Baby-girl. I know I never will forget it."

Aliesha smiled. Apparently, she hadn't been the only little Black girl whose life had absorbed the power, beauty, and impact of Will Eaton's words.

CHAPTER 38

She steered into the empty lot and immediately wondered if she'd made a wrong turn. She slowed the car and reached for the slip of paper with the address and the directions Dante had given her over the phone. No, this was the right place, even though hers was the only car in the lot of what appeared to be an otherwise abandoned strip mall.

She parked in front of the address she'd written down but saw no signs indicating that it was a barbershop or a business of any kind. Okay, what the hell was going on? Was this his idea of a joke? She dug her phone from her purse and looked for the numbers she'd programmed into its memory. Then she told herself, *You know what? I'm not putting myself though this shit again. He can have himself a damn ball playing hide-and-seek all by his lonesome.* She'd restarted her engine and shifted the car into reverse when the door to the establishment swung open and Dante stepped out.

The sight of him after so many days of wondering and worrying sent a surge of relief through her. But it was quickly replaced by the return of her outrage and disappointment. Her negative thoughts wouldn't allow her to return the bright smile he broke into upon her exit from the vehicle. She moved toward him and met his "Hello" with little more than a nod.

He looked as if he wanted to reach out and caress her, if not take her into his arms, but seemed to know better than to attempt either. Locked in a loaded silence and staring into his dark, handsome face, she suddenly remembered the taste of his lips, the perfect blend of his fingers against her breasts, and the slow, steady rock of his pelvis against hers. She tried, but she couldn't keep her pain from being infused with a heavy dose of pleasure.

He shortened the distance between them with warmth of his eyes and said, "If it helps any, I thought about you every night."

She averted her gaze. "Yeah, just not enough to pick up the damn phone and call. But I guess I should have known better than to expect any more than that, huh? I mean, all we did was sleep together that one time. It's not like I was your girlfriend or anything."

"I know you're hurt, Aliesha. I know you're angry," he said, raising his voice and rushing his words. "And I hate that I made you feel as if what happened between us wasn't meaningful and significant. It was all of those things to me and more. I know it's going to take some time—"

"Time?!" she said, focusing squarely on him again. "Please, what assurance do I have that something like this won't happen again, Dante? You just up and disappearing again, I mean?"

He moved his fingers to her head and eased off the scarf she'd donned to cover her fraying twists. "And what could I possibly say that would ever reassure you, Aliesha?"

When she turned away from him, wearing a look of disgust, he said, "Okay, okay, you want reassurances? How about this—I used to wonder why whenever I was around you I'd get this awful pinch in my side. It's only been within the last week or two that I've come to realize that when I look at you, Aliesha, I feel the same way my uncle Mack felt about my Big Mama. Sometimes when he'd see her standing out in the garden he'd turn to me and say,

'You see that woman there, boy? There stands the woman the Good Lord made especially for me. Bone of my bone, flesh of my flesh.'" Dante drew her fingers to his rib cage and whispered, "And I swear, that's the same way I feel about you, Aliesha." But when he leaned forward to kiss her, she shook her head and backed away.

A month and a half had passed without her hearing so much as a peep from him. She simply didn't have it in her to let him off that easy. The pain of rejection she saw unfold on his face closely resembled some of what she'd battled for weeks. A part of her wanted to comfort him, but the inflexible nature of own pride kept her welded to her anger. "So you just want me to take this giant leap of faith? Is that what you want? Is that why you asked me come here today?"

He closed his eyes and briefly tilted his head to the heavens. When he looked at Aliesha again, the cracks in his ebony mask were readily visible. "Do you remember what you told me once, how you live for the here and now because tomorrow isn't promised? Well, call me crazy 'cause that's exactly what I want from you, Aliesha, the promise of tomorrow. Just like you made it clear that you weren't interested in joining the roster of women who rotate in and out of my bed, I don't want that, either. I want you to be my one and only and I want to be yours. Not your hump-buddy, not your standby guy, or your second-string pick. I want to be your chosen, Aliesha. I want the promise of all your tomorrows."

Something beneath the quiver of his lips and the sincerity of his words seized her attention. She reached up and touched his face. "It was a woman, wasn't it? Someone other than your Big Mama, I mean? But someone who obviously means to you just as much . . . That's why you stayed away? Isn't it?"

The truth hit him like a punch in the gut and all of his bottled up emotions came spewing out in waves. "I wasn't trying to hurt you, baby. I was trying to protect you. Don't you see? I had to stay away long enough to know. I didn't want to have any lingering doubts that might one day lure me back into her arms. I couldn't take a chance on calling you or seeing you again until I knew for sure."

His tears spilled over her fingers and touched her heart. "It's okay, Dante. I understand. I mean, if you're still in love with this woman, then maybe—"

"No! No!" he insisted. He pulled her hands against his chest. "It's been over for years. I just didn't know how to leave. I just didn't know how to let go."

Aliesha knew in light of her own recent past with Kenneth, as well as the regrettable manner in which she'd behaved with Javiel, she was in no position to scold or condemn Dante for whatever might have transpired between him and some other woman while he'd been away. If she wanted forgiveness for her transgressions, it was only fair and right that she be willing to extend an equal portion of such.

She eased her fingers down his chest and over his rib cage. "We need to talk, Dante. And not just about you and her. If there's any chance of us starting over and making a sincere go of this, we both need to know what we're signing up for."

"Are you saying it's not too late and you're still willing to try?"

She smiled and said, "What? You really think I came all the way down here for a haircut? Doesn't it go without saying that I wouldn't have shown up at all today if some part of me weren't still desperately longing to be with you?" She surveyed the building behind him. "But I must admit, I'm still somewhat leery of this place you're claiming is a legitimate business. How come it doesn't have a name? And why is my car the only one in the lot?"

"My car is parked around back," Dante said. "Why don't you come inside and let me show you the rest."

On moving past the door he held open for her, a whiff of fried fish flared Aliesha's nostrils and the sound of the soft, sultry piano and guitar duet that marked the song now burned into her brain's audio memory as "The Chosen" landed with a feathery swoop inside her ears.

Dante hurriedly moved from her path, a couple of large flower-filled containers, similar to the ones he'd left on her porch. "Sorry, I was going to put these outside," he explained.

She stood and quietly assessed the room's interior. She saw one lone barber's chair, several barren workstations, but no barbers. Nor did the strategically placed benches she noticed in the waiting areas hold any customers. Tall but neat stacks and piles of books lined the walls. But what really raised Aliesha's eye brows, before sending them into a deep furl, was the beautifully set and fully loaded banquet table that stretched down the middle of the room.

She turned to Dante. "Would you mind telling me what's going on?"

"This is my new shop. Or, at least, it will be soon. My plan is to bring in a few more barbers as well as a couple of beauticians who specialize in natural hair." With excitement ringing in his voice, he pointed to one of the numerous stacks of books. "All of these are going up on the shelves that I plan to have a carpenter attach to a good portion of the wall space. If it all works out, I'll have the majority of them in the reading corner I hope to set up with a few comfortable chairs and a table. And get this, I'm thinking of calling the shop 'Dante's Metamorphosis.'"

She met his broad, proud smile with one of her own. "Okay, I see. Basically, what you have in mind is a place where a transformation of what's inside your head and what's on it are both possible." She walked over and waved a hand over the bowls, plates, and platters of food. "But what is all of this?"

He came and stood next to her. "Well, this, my dear, is

my peace offering. From the tablecloth, china, silverware, and even the food, most of what you see here came out of my Big Mama's house and gardens. She was big on canning and freezing. She had so much, I had to give a lot of it away. But some of it's fresh, like the tomatoes. I've even got some fish in the back that I seasoned with some of the herbs she grew."

She turned toward Dante and circled her arms around his waist. "Let me guess. You caught the fish yourself and they came out of the creek? The same creek your Big Mama drew her water from and added to the other secret ingredients of her lavender-scented shampoo?"

"What's that?" he asked, while donning a mask of pretend agitation. "Your way of teasing me about being a mama's boy?"

Aliesha shook her head. "I'm sorry I didn't get a chance to meet her. I really wish I could have, if only to thank her for you."

Dante stroked her face. "Don't worry, I told her all about us. I'm sure she and my uncle Mack are somewhere nodding their approval as we speak. Hopefully, your own mother and father are right there with them."

When Aliesha eased her body against his and rested her chin against his shoulder, he embedded his fingers in the twists and twirls of her natural hair. She sighed and said, "That encore you promised me is long overdue, I want you to know."

He whispered, "Don't worry, I plan on giving you what I owe you and a whole lot more." While massaging her scalp, he added, "Can I let you in on a little secret? I knew from the moment my fingers got lost in your hair, I was destined to be your man. No lie, baby, somewhere deep inside, I knew from day one you were the 'Natural Woman' made and sent especially for me."

A NATURAL WOMAN

Lori Johnson

The following questions are intended
to enhance your group's
discussion of this book.

DISCUSSION QUESTIONS

1. Why do you think Wally might have been reluctant to cut Aliesha's hair?

2. Discuss some of the negative and positive assumptions you've heard and/or made about African American women who sport "natural" hairstyles.

3. Share your thoughts on the significance of the relationship many African American women have with their hairstylists.

4. Do you think Javiel was truly oblivious to the change in Aliesha's appearance? If so, why do you think he didn't notice? If not, why do you think he chose not to comment?

5. In spite of their many differences, why do you think Aliesha and Monica were such good friends?

6. Discuss some of the more unexpected ways the women in *A Natural Woman* supported one another. Which alliance(s) took you by surprise?

7. What impact did Aliesha's father have on her life? In what ways were Kenneth, Javiel, and Dante like her father? In what ways were Kenneth, Javiel, and Dante different from Aliesha's father?

8. Compare and contrast how Aliesha's and Monica's relationships with their fathers affected their relationships with men. In what ways might Laylah's relationship with her father have influenced her relationship with men?

9. Did you share any of Monica's concerns about Dante? About Kenneth?

10. Do you think Kenneth loved Aliesha? Had Dante not entered Aliesha's life, do you think she would have eventually given Kenneth another chance?

11. What did you make of Aliesha's involvement with her church? Did the depth of her involvement with her church surprise you? If so, why? If not, why not?

12. What did you make of the tension between Aliesha and Shelton? What do you think was behind his rude behavior?

13. Discuss the role of the deceased in *A Natural Woman*. What impact did Aliesha's dead loved ones have on her life? In what ways were Dante's actions influenced by his dead loved ones?

14. How did Aliesha's interactions with Pat and Kristen differ from her interactions with Monica and Tamara? What did you think about Aliesha's relationship with Peaches? Did you get the impression that any of these relationships might change over time? If so, which ones and in what ways?

15. Did you notice any parallels between Aliesha's relationship with Tamara and Dante's with Yazz?

16. Did you feel Aliesha should have exercised more caution or restraint before she invited Dante to spend the night?

17. By the end, Wally, Gerald, and Yazz had each demonstrated their support of Dante and Aliesha's relationship. Which man's support surprised you the most?

18. What do you think the future holds for Dante and Aliesha? What problems might they encounter as a couple?

Want more Lori Johnson?
Turn the page for a preview of

AFTER THE DANCE

Available now wherever books are sold

HER

I had never really paid that much attention to him before, even though he lived right next door. Usually when we ran into each other we'd nod, speak our hellos, and keep on 'bout our business.

Nora, my roommate, was the one who told me his name was Carl. She'd talked to him on several different occasions. She also told me he'd tried to hit on her—like I wouldn't have guessed it. Nora's got this, well, this sluttish quality about her. And I'm not trying to talk bad about the girl or anything, it's just that I don't know how else to describe it. She kind of puts you in mind of some of those girls you see dancing on *Soul Train*. You know, the ones who look like their titties are about to shake outta their clothes? Or, the ones who are always turning their asses up to the camera? And that's cool when you're twenty-three and under, and don't have the good sense to know any better.

Anyway, according to Nora, our tall, dark-skinned, bearded neighbor was sweet, but not her type. I kind of looked at her sideways when she said that, but I didn't say anything. Me and Nora go way back. I know all about her "type." It's dog. Straight up and down, dog. I'm telling you, she's not satisfied unless some guy's smacking her upside the head, taking her money, whoring all over town, or some combination of the three.

Problem with Nora is that she's still under the impression that there's actually something called love out there, and if she searches long and hard enough, she'll eventually find it. I don't have any such illusions. See, I know ain't nothing out there but game. And having played hardball with the best of them, I also know the secret to winning is knowing how not to get played—something Nora has yet to learn. That's why every other month, just like clockwork, you can find her sitting up in the living room of the condo we share trying her best to kill off a fifth of scotch, looking crazier than Bette Davis did in *Whatever Happened to Baby Jane?* and playing them same old sad-ass songs over and over and over again. And Lord knows I'd go to bat for my girl Phyllis Hyman (God rest her beautiful soul) any durn day of the week, but listening to "Living All Alone" fifty times straight on a Friday night, with no interruption, is enough to drive even the sanest sister out of her cotton-picking mind.

And that's how it happened that Carl and I had our first real conversation—if you want to call it that. I had just stepped outside for a break from the music and the madness and was settling comfortably into my patio chair with my pack of Kools, a chilled glass of wine, and a romance novel, when he opened up his back door, stepped outside, and noticed me sitting on the other side of the fence.

He said "Hey" and I said "Hey," and I thought that was gonna be the extent of it before he went on his merry little way. But no! He decided he was going to be sociable.

"Must be Nora in there jamming to Hyman."

I said, "Yes. If it's disturbing you, I'll ask her to turn it down."

He said, "No, I was just wondering 'cause you don't exactly look like the Hyman type to me. No, you look more like a—let's see—Millie Jackson. Yeah, you look like the kind of woman who could really get into some Millie Jackson. Am I right?"

I guess he was banking on me not knowing about Miss Millie, the late '70s and early '80s trash-talking forerunner to the likes of today's Lil' Kim and Foxy Brown.

No, you ain't right, smartass, and you must be blind is what I started to say but didn't. Instead I blew my smoke, swirled the wine in my glass, cut my eyes, and said in my coolest "don't mess with me, man" voice, "Is that supposed to be funny?"

HIM

I knew I was taking a risk when I opened my mouth. My Uncle Westbrook was the first to warn me, way back in the day. "Son," he told me, "you never know how a woman's gonna react to what you say. Sometimes you'll get a smile, sometimes you'll get an attitude."

But really, I should have known better 'cause every time I see this chick, she looks like she's got her jaws tight about something. I mean, we've been neighbors for nearly six months now, and she still acts like she don't hardly want to speak.

Some women are like that, man. If you didn't know any better you'd swear they were born with permanently poked lips. Have to say, though, I've noticed it more in fat women. Not that I have anything in particular against fat chicks. Matter of fact, I've gotten right close to one or two. But a fat chick with an attitude—hey, that's something else altogether.

Yeah, she's one of them feisty big-boned girls, man. She's got a pretty face, though. Actually, she'd probably be a stone-cold fox if she lost, say, thirty or forty pounds and smiled every once in a while. But I guess that'd be asking for too much, huh?

So I was standing there, right, trying to figure out how I was going to work my way out from under this Millie Jackson comment, when Nora came out and got me off the hook by informing the fat would-be-fox with the pretty but unsmiling face that she had a telephone call.

Now, me and Nora, we're cool. She kinda puts you in mind of a young Lola Falana with a double dose of spunk, you know? Though I'll be damned if she ain't always crying the blues over some dude. And this particular evening was no exception. Before I could even get out a proper hello, she'd launched into an all-too-vivid, blow-by-blow account of her latest hellacious affair. I don't know, man, I guess it's just something about me that brings out the worst in a woman. But being the polite fool that I am, I stood there nodding, grinning and grunting in all the right places, until both boredom and curiosity got the best of me and I walked over and picked up the book left by her roommate.

Call me a proper bourgeois if you want to, but I still say you can tell a lot about a person by what they read. And it wasn't like I was expecting the big sister with the bad attitude to be into something as heavy as Fanon's *Wretched of the Earth* or anything, 'cause I'd seen her sitting out on the patio enough times with her head propped up behind a Harlequin to know better. But yet and still, I wasn't at all prepared for anything on the level of a *Jungle Passions* either. I mean, the title alone was a bit much, but on the cover was this crazy Tarzan-looking character who's got this even crazier-looking, big-breasted blonde wrapped up in one of those back-breaking, humanly impossible embraces. And you know me, I wasn't about to let something like that pass without comment.

"Excuse me for interrupting, Nora," I said, "but might this be the type of relationship you're looking for?"

She glanced at the book and rolled her eyes. "Honey, don't even try it! I'm into real-life, flesh-and-blood romances, not paperback ones. But yeah, Faye, she's always reading that junk. And then got the nerve to tell me I live in a dream world. Ain't that a blip?"